THE BOOK OF JAMES

CHANGING DIRECTIONS: PART 1 OF 3

LEILA KLASSE

ISBN: 9798649137690

DEDICATION

A huge shout out to my story editor Bridgette Shade. Her unique style of motivating; genuinely wanting to know more about the story and the characters, opened my eyes to the joys, yes it can be joyous, of revising and editing. Thank you, dear muse.

I'd also like to thank my publishing consultant Lynne Hansen for her help.

PART 1
WALKING AFTER DARK

1 / GETTING OUT

Smoking a joint, listening to the Black-Eyed Peas while driving to work, James anguished over the argument he'd had with his mom the night before. He'd raged at her, his fist raised to hit her. But then, he was quite sure he'd never hit her. No. He was sure he wouldn't hit her, would he? He clenched his knuckles until they were white on the steering wheel. After the fight, seething in his basement room, he knew there was no going back: it was time to move out.

It wouldn't be easy. His mother had already started the psychological warfare to keep him home.

She in the kitchen, writing on their message blackboard, when he came up from the basement this morning. He bypassed her to walk to the fridge, grab the milk, and drink it out of the carton. Then he turned to see what she'd written.

"I love you James!" she'd written in her careful curlicue script. He hated the handwriting and the message and her standing there, smiling, with her hands locked behind her back. What's love got to do with it? But he turned and put the milk back into the fridge and walked out of the back door, without saying anything to her or slamming the door. Let her try to kill him with kindness—none of it was going to work. He was moving out.

HE'D MADE this quick drive to work a thousand times; he could do it with his eyes closed, but today a little white-haired lady swerved into his lane going a good ten miles less than the speed limit and caused him to put on his brakes. He was pissed! He rammed up behind her in his sudden anger, and they were nearly bumper to bumper. Her car wobbled, and he backed off. The suddenness of his fury scared him, and he backed off even more. He didn't want to be responsible for someone getting hurt or killed, did he?

His mother said last night she feared he'd changed, he hadn't, had he? He swung into the parking lot behind the store and glided into a diagonal space. Wiping his sweaty hands on his pants, his mood started to lift. It was a beautiful late summer day, why let old women ruin his day? Today he was quitting his job. Tomorrow he'd be looking for a place to live.

He turned up his ear buds and listened to the Black-Eyed Peas:

"Burn it till it's burned out,
Turn it till it's turned out
Get it started, get it started, get it..."

As per usual, James smiled while walking through the front doors of Sports Center West, putting on the persona of his near-brother and next-door neighbor, Chuck. Chuck was an extrovert; he had a warm greeting for everyone. James could imitate his bro perfectly. He gave the staff and Dylan, the young manager, toothy Hellos but walked right by them. This was the plan, his last day in this hell hole and he wasn't chatting with any of them.

Careful to avoid Dylan, he strolled through the aisles. Twice he climbed onto an empty loader and tooted around the dim surplus area at the back of the store. He grinned remembering the first time they'd let him use the loader. The first two years here when he was in high school had been fun.

Passing the bicycle 'tune and repair' shop, he looked in on old man Kennedy. He still sported suspenders and the frameless glasses that slid down his nose. James waved but didn't stop to talk. James had spent hours there listening to Kennedy's Vietnam stories and giving the old man a helping hand.

At one point, James stood in the shadows and watched Dylan nearly running to help a front cashier who'd put in a call for assistance. James had once been like Dylan. That was the old James, rushing to please everyone. What a pussy, all that time spent pleasing his mom, his managers, his teachers, his college professors. "Screw them," he said and turned to make sure no one had heard him.

At lunch break, James walked down the back street behind the store, smoking another joint, enjoying the buzz of a high on a blue sky, warm summer day.

"I'm alive," he said aloud in the empty gravel alleyway, throwing his arms to the sky and chuckling at his boldness, marveling at his newfound freedom to tell it like it was.

After a #10 at Jimmy John's, he returned to the store.

He'd planned what he was going to say to Dylan. Dylan was the same age as James, and they'd started work at the store the same summer day over four years ago. Then, after high school, Dylan started working full time at the store instead of going to college. Now, two years later, Dylan made more than twice James' salary. He had a new Audi Q3, his own apartment, and a steady girlfriend.

James was living with his mother who pinched pennies to send him to a private college. He drove her twenty-year old car and lived in the basement, no place to bring a girl. He knew well her expectations for him. Not only a four-year degree but graduate school as well.

It was time for James to step up, to live his own life.

DYLAN WAS SCOWLING when James finally walked up to him.

"Dylan, my man," James said, reaching out to shake hands.

Dylan thought James had been gaming all day, but now he hesitated, maybe something was wrong and James needed his help. He grabbed James' hand and asked, "What's wrong with you? You've been wandering around all day like a casual customer."

James laughed and pulled away from Dylan's grasp. "I'm saying goodbye Dylan, I'm letting go of this place. It's already in my rear-view mirror. I'm never wearing rubber soled shoes to work on a concrete floor again."

"What are you saying? You got to give two-weeks' notice, James."

"Or what, Dylan? I don't 'need' to do anything for this store. I need to start doing something for me. I'm getting my own place this weekend in St. Paul. I'm not giving the best years of my life to a concrete floor."

James turned and walked away. He was done with Dylan. They'd been good boys together, nudging at each other, high fiving and low fiving. Now, James left Dylan standing there with his jaw hanging.

2 / SHE'S TRYING TO MAKE ME GO TO REHAB

Later that day, after changing into his shorts and eating a couple of frozen burritos heated in the microwave, a stoned and satisfied James Holden ran full hilt along the crushed stone path at Keene Creek Preserve. He'd loved track in high school and still ran a good five miles nearly every day.

"What—" he said, falling hard to the crushed stone path. Searing pain from his scraped bare knees kept him down on his butt for a minute, looking about the path suspiciously. No roots, no rocks. He looked again, no invisible wire. He'd run the same Preserve path a hundred times; never had he dropped for no reason.

He checked his short's pockets, nothing to wipe the blood and gore from his knees. He limped, then jogged to a park porta potty and cleaned his ragged wounds as best he could with toilet paper and hand disinfectant. Running home, a mantra played in his head, matching his steps. "Get away from her. Get away from her."

All his mom appreciated in him was his good college grades. "Higher education is the key to the kingdom," she said. What did the 'key' give her? She'd wallowed in debt the best years of her life, paying for her PhD in psychology. Why? Just to work for a nonprofit and make about as much as a school teacher? Who was she trying to impress?

The days of James being his mama's boy were long over. When he was a boy, James loved going to their little cabin in Wisconsin. Sometimes James' friend Jerome and his dog, Sassy, went with them. Ellen read and took hikes by herself when Jerome came, but she also fished with the boys and played board games with them if they ever tired of playing video games. In the city, James and Ellen biked along the Mississippi or went to double features at the cheap movie houses or skied cross-country. But his Mom was a weekend mother; Sandra was the day to day Mom.

Now just having her in the house, her light footsteps above his room in the basement, felt suffocating. If they did spend time together, it was planted in front of the 54" TV, binging on cable. They hardly looked at each other.

Nearing the home stretch, James caught sight of their little grey bungalow. "Ho hum," he said.

After a hot shower and a cold rinse, he poured hydrogen peroxide on his knees and grimaced as it fizzed. Then he stretched out on his futon. Reaching for his roaches, he took a few drags, his bare feet jiggling to a tune in his head. He'd quit hiding his use from his mother and now blew the smoke out defiantly. He reached for his ear buds, keeping the sound low so he'd heard his mother coming home.

WHEN HE HEARD the familiar sound of the stubborn back door being forced open, he cleared his throat and shouted, "Hi Mom."

Ellen shouted back, "Your home?"

"Down here—didn't I just yell, 'Hi, Mom?'"

"Well, yes. Will you please come up and talk to me?"

After a pause, James mumbled, "Yeah."

When he reached the kitchen, Ellen had her head in the refrigerator, pouring herself a glass of boxed wine.

"How about pouring one of those for me, too?" James asked.

Ellen involuntarily jerked, turned to James and tried for a smile before grabbing another wine glass from underneath the upper cabinet.

They walked into the living room toward their usual positions: Ellen and her navy wing chair, James and the couch. "It's Friday. I'm beat," Ellen said, placing her glass on a coaster. "No cancellations all week. Mind if I do a few Sun Salutations to stretch my back out before we talk?"

"Whatever," James answered, setting his wine glass down untouched.

He wore shorts, waiting for her to notice his skinned knees, but she didn't. She was zoned out in her yoga mind set.

Ellen was thinking about their shouting match last night. She felt as ashamed of her own behavior, even though she was justifiably angry with James. The shouting match had escalated alarmingly. She hoped she hadn't wounded him as much as he'd wounded her. She tried to focus on her concerns for him. She was the professional, after all. She recognized a drug problem when she saw it.

James looked around the living room. The space disgusted him —the interior painted a consistent off-white except for the flat, light green in the kitchen. The trim on the windows was thin, the doors hollow, all cheap construction. The picture window had a broken seal and was fogged over on the right side, the thin Berber carpet was frayed, poor maintenance, he thought. We perch here like renters.

James turned back to his mother as she lowered herself into the wing chair and assumed her attentive 'therapy' pose. James slumped deeper into the couch.

Ellen inhaled deeply. "Can we have an adult, rational talk today? I promise not to get upset like I did last night."

"OK, but one thing, how is smoking a joint after finishing a day's work any different than having 'a few' glasses of wine, alone, like you do? Like you have for years. I'm smoking in my own room, not in your space, and I'm not sneaking behind your back."

"James, you spend too much time smoking marijuana alone."

"And you drink alone. I worry about you sometimes. Why don't you ever date? You live like a nun, and you expect me to watch TV with you. Think about your own life instead of focusing on me! I'm grown-up. I'll be twenty-one and absolutely legal in a few months."

Ellen was quiet, brushing imaginary lint off of her good work pants.

James regretted blurting that out. He'd hurt her again, but maybe cruelty was his way out. "I'm done arguing," he declared and sat back into the couch, his legs stretched out in front of him. "Look, I'm sorry. That was rude. I don't want to hurt your feelings, Mom, but I smoke; you drink. I admit I got crazy last night when you repeatedly told me I needed treatment. You threatened me."

Ellen cleared her throat. "Let's not escalate. I didn't 'threaten you,' and I can't force you to go to treatment. Let's move away from that. Let's move forward to registration for fall classes, to getting you back in the swing of things."

James jerked forward, arms on his jiggling knees and pressed on. "I've decided to move out. I'm ready to get my own place."

"Student housing is available—" she started, then looking startled, she finally noticed the raw scrapes on his knees. "What happened to your knees? Did you fall down running?"

"What do you think? I hit a root on a deer path, almost invisible."

"You put antiseptic on it, right?"

"Yeah. It hurt like hell."

"Sorry—"

James interrupted her and lowered his pitch. "I just want to move out, find my own place near campus. I'll get a part time job. I want what the other guys have, not just classes. There is more to life than classes, than degrees."

"It will cost too much to live alone," Ellen said, cautiously. "Rent, food, utilities, there'll be a lot of hidden costs. If you move to St. Paul, you'll probably need another job."

"I've got $10,000 from the fund you saved for me from Dad's child support. I haven't touched it, and it's in my bank account. I've also got money from working this summer. It's my money," he reminded her.

"We talked about you using that money for graduate school. Tell me—why leave home? I give you all the freedom you want. You come and go as you please. You have the whole lower level. I'll—" Her voice trailed off. "I'll stop complaining about your marijuana smoke."

James looked at her in disbelief. He shook his head no. He kept shaking his head and looking down at his jiggling knees.

"You've really caught me off guard," Ellen said, hoping to keep him talking. "Can I play devil's advocate?"

"No, I don't want your advice, Mom. 'Treatment' was your advice last night. I'll never go to treatment—got that? I have to do this. I have to get out of this sandbox and explore the world. I'm looking for a place in St. Paul tomorrow."

With that, they both turned toward the TV.

"Want to watch the local news?" he asked. She nodded yes and brushed away tears in her eyes.

James grabbed the clicker and turned to the news channel they preferred. "I'm going down to my room," he said and got up from the couch. He took another look at her, and when she didn't immediately respond, he headed out of the room, breathing a sigh of relief.

James took the steps two at a time. It's happening, he thought, pumping his fists. Safely in his room, he raised his arms and pushed against the ceiling, pretending to lift the house off of its foundation.

"Up goes the house," he said in a husky voice. "Crawl out now, boy," he demanded of himself. "Quick before the house settles back down."

James closed his door, collapsed on the futon, and fumbled underneath it for the open tin of roaches. He used his plastic red lighter, his lucky lighter, to light the best among them.

He turned his sounds up and nodded his head, singing softly along with a droll Amy Winehouse. "They tried to make me go to rehab, but I said no, no, no."

Amy was another of his enduring fantasies. He loved drawing her and her band. Amy, almost slipping off of a raised stool, stoned to the gills on heroin, nodding, starting the beat for her band. A scrawny, awkward woman with strands of bee-hived hair coming loose, she swayed and snapped her fingers, and her band began to blare.

Amy turned to look James in the eyes and gave him a wicked smile. She knew he was more than just another white boy.

3 / *WHAT TO DO ABOUT JAMES?*

Ellen looked vacantly at the six o'clock news, her eyes glassy. She held her stomach with one arm and rocked back and forth. I can't handle him, she thought. I need to talk to Sandra.

Sandra Dahlberg, their next-door neighbor, had been Ellen's best friend for more than thirty years. Sandra did more than help raise James; she thought of James as her fourth child. He'd spent most of his weekdays with her family.

Ellen finished her wine, opened her back door, and took a long peek at the deck next door. Sandra was sitting outside, feet up on the railing, drinking lemonade and watching her garden grow.

"Yoo-hoo," Ellen croaked out and waved to Sandra.

Sandra looked in Ellen's direction and waved her over, quickly putting her paper and pen under the cushion of the lounger next to her.

"Out of the blue, like you used to do, marching over here. I love it, Ellen. Wish you would do it more often. Do you want a glass of raspberry lemonade?"

"I'll have lemonade, if you'll add a shot of vodka."

Sandra raised her eyebrows. "I'll bring out the IDÔL. Do you have something to celebrate?"

Ellen brushed off a padded lounger and laid on her side. She turned her head away from Sandra and curled up in the lounger, near tears.

Sandra watched Ellen in disbelief. Her very composed friend did not roll into a fetal position and turn away from her. Sandra didn't dare touch her or speak. She walked into her kitchen, got the vodka and another glass, and waited until Ellen composed herself before bringing the drinks out to the patio.

Ellen and Sandra met at college decades earlier and had stayed roommates into their twenties when Sandra married Ralph Dahlberg. Years later, Ellen married Jay Holden and gave birth to James. Sandra, pregnant and raising two little girls, insisted on helping Ellen and Jay care for their colicky newborn.

Sandra kept infant James overnight several nights a week while she was hugely pregnant with her third baby, Chuck.

During those first months of James' life, Sandra and infant James bonded. When Ellen's marriage ended in divorce, Sandra rescued Ellen and James again. Ralph and Sandra helped Ellen buy the bungalow next door to their sprawling ranch house, and, being a stay at home Mom, Sandra volunteered to care for James while Ellen finished graduate school and started her career as a Behavioral Psychologist.

Sandra and Ralph's girls were eight and ten when Chuck and James started kindergarten. James got off the bus with Chuck, and they both went home to the Dahlberg house.

Chuck was a husky, bullish kid who played rough with the skinny, timid James. But while James lost the physical battles, he could play rough with words. When they were teenagers, James gave Chuck the nickname "Chunky," and it stuck all the way through high school.

Chuck often left James bruised and battered, but he was always eager to spend time at the Dahlberg's, and the boys remained contentious but faithful brothers throughout school.

Now, the tempo at the Dahlberg's was down beat. Sandra's brood was grown and out of the house. Chuck lived in a frat house at the main campus of the University of Minnesota, and the girls were already married with children.

Sandra's husband Ralph, like many doctors, was as married to his career as to his wife. When the kids were young, Sandra hardly noticed her diminished role in Ralph's life. Now, Sandra, rambling in her empty nest, missed both her kids and her husband.

Sandra came back carrying a tray loaded with lemonade and vodka, ice and a glass for Ellen, who sat stone faced, staring out into the garden. "Pour your own vodka, Ellen. This way you can decide if you want a single or a double." Sandra pulled up a chair next to Ellen, poured herself a double, and handed the vodka bottle to Ellen.

Ellen straightened up and poured a good splash of vodka into her glass and silently took a long draught.

Sandra began the conversation in her signature self-centered way. "Aren't *I* the gardener? See those ever-bearing raspberries? I picked two full quarts this afternoon. Fair starts next week; summer is almost over."

When Ellen didn't respond, Sandra continued. "You must have come straight from work. I don't know how you can wear linen pants and sit all day without your pant knees bulging. Do you pull your pants up a bit every time you sit down? I suppose it's easier because you're so thin. How I envy your body type. Have you read about Keto diets?"

Sandra realized she was starting to grind her teeth. She clamped her mouth shut, sat up straighter, and took a healthy swig of her laced drink, determined to outwait Ellen in a silence stand-off.

"For the umpteenth time," Ellen said, looking Sandra up and down, "Your body is fine just the way it is. You're the healthy, sexy, full-bodied woman you've always been."

"Once the garden is put to rest, I'll go back to the gym," Sandra said. "It's either that or fire the cleaning lady. Do you need help with fall window cleaning? Maybe I should start a cleaning business, good exercise"

Ellen sighed and broke into Sandra's singular conversation. "Sandra, can it be more obvious that I'm not in the mood for small talk? I'm here because James is in serious trouble!" Then the tears came again, and there was no stopping them.

Sandra passed the slightly soiled tissue she kept in her gardening vest and gave Ellen a minute to compose herself.

"I never know what to say to you, Ellen. You come over and then turn your head away from me. I get nervous; I chatter. What do you want from me?"

Ellen took a deep breath and nodded apologetically, caught in her own bullshit. She blew her nose loudly.

"So, tell me, what's up with James?" Sandra asked with feigned interest. She found it hard to listen to Ellen's over-reactions to James. James was mercurial, more like herself, an artistic soul. He could be difficult, but couldn't we all? Ellen certainly was no day at the beach.

"James is moving out," Ellen blurted, half rising from the lounge chair.

That got Sandra's full attention, "No way, what happened? James? He hardly has the gumption to come visit me, much less leave home."

"It was out of the blue, 'I want my own place', he announced today. He isn't talking about the dorm, of course, or living with friends. He wants to live alone. Do you know how expensive housing is getting? How lonely he'll be. He's only twenty."

Sandra nodded ambivalently. "He's lonely at home, too, isn't he? I mean with Chuck gone for the summer?"

Ellen ignored Sandra's jab. "He's been doing well in college. But his marijuana use keeps escalating. It's unhealthy. I try not to be critical—yes, I do listen to you—but last night I was so sick of his lying on the futon, smoking dope, I confronted him, and now he's running away from me."

Sandra sat straighter, mirroring Ellen's posture. "I know you're upset, but tell me again. Why do you think he has such a problem with marijuana?"

"Sandra, stop it! I hate it when you talk to me like you're a therapist. Don't do that!" Sandra moved back to her recliner and put her feet back up on the deck rail.

"We've been all over this before," Ellen said. "His room reeks of marijuana. Every time I go downstairs to wash clothes there is a cloud coming from his room. I think he smokes marijuana like a nicotine addict smokes packs of cigarettes. He's volatile, and, for a moment last night, I was afraid he was going to hit me."

"That's an exaggeration," Sandra said. "If he's anything it is non-violent. He wouldn't even play football. He works, he runs, he doesn't sit around and smoke upstairs when the two of you watch TV together. Don't forget our college days; we liked getting high; you liked it as much as I did."

"I never liked it as much as you did," Ellen said, staring daggers at Sandra. "I savored it on special occasions. I never bought it and never used it alone. Hasn't even Chuck stopped using it?"

"As far as I know he has, but Chuck doesn't live at home anymore. I asked him about marijuana this spring, and he said it wasn't conducive to the kind of studying he needed to do to get into medical school. He said it stayed in the system much longer than booze and made him sleepy. But that's Chuck. What worries you the most, beside the smells?"

"He's remote and irritable and isolates in his room. I can't say anything to him without him getting defensive. On top of that, he's become casual about registering for fall classes. He shrugs, 'Patience, Ma, it's going to happen.' I've choked down my concerns all summer, but classes are just around the corner, and last night I tried to talk to him about it. I suggested counseling, maybe a professional evaluation of his use. He reacted as if I was threatening to commit him to treatment."

"Then he escalated into, 'you never loved my dad. You kept me away from my dad' then he moved on to 'you never wanted me. You never wanted dad.' I'm not repeating all that was said, but he sure knows how to pick on my scabs. I'm the villain in his eyes, even though he knows his father left us to start another family. When I got home today, he blurted out this plan to move out. He is looking for a place tomorrow."

Sandra looked directly into her friend's eyes. "James is the same artistic, quirky kid he always has been. His comics show real talent and he excels in engineering classes. He is so bright. He's never had to study like Chuck does. You know I love him to death, but he's hard to read. You get what you see with Chuck, but James? My girls were very different too. Kimber has always been open, like Chuck, but Laurel is moody and has that secret side of her that drives me crazy. She thinks I'm probing whenever I'm just interested in knowing her."

"Enough about the other kids, Sandra. Focus, OK? We're talking about James here."

"Oh, sorry, Ellen." Sandra continued, "I think James will do fine. I think you and I did a great job raising him. Well, maybe we each spoiled him in our own ways. I admit I loved spoiling the kids, and you gave him all of your time when you were home." Sandra pounded a rhythm with her palms, "we did good by that boy!"

"It's been a hard summer for James. He will be in a better place when classes start. He wants to do something exciting like Chuck did when he moved into the frat house. Going out and renting an apartment is dramatic. We'll see if he follows through. I bet it doesn't happen. Doesn't marijuana make you lazy? This is James' bullshit; he's angry about your argument."

Ellen sat quietly, taking in all that Sandra said. She half believed her friend.

But before Ellen could reply, Sandra jumped in again. "Sorry to change the subject, and sorry I didn't call you earlier, but Ralph wants to have a family cookout Memorial Weekend, a week from Monday. I've got confirmation that all the other kids can come. Of course, Ralph expects you and James to be there to round out the family. I know a cookout won't be a good time for me to get personal with James, but I'll take him aside and ask him about his plans to move out and throw something out about the marijuana use, too. James isn't as sensitive to my probing as he is to yours."

"Probe all you want, Sandra. Maybe he'll listen to you. Try not to write off the marijuana. I think it is a problem. Take my side on this, please."

Sandra nodded and changed the subject. "Can you believe Ralph initiated the family cookout?"

Ellen finished her drink and acknowledged Sandra's beautiful, huge raspberries. Then she stood and looked over at her own house. "I'd better be going." The friends hugged deeply, rubbing their cheeks together as they always did.

ON THE SHORT trip back to her house, Ellen chided herself. Root out this negativity and start to believe in your boy.

Sandra watched her friend walk home. Ellen's hunched back started to straighten as she walked across the joint yards.

Sandra reached for her paper and pen and looked at her two columns, an assignment from the marriage counselor. The 'What Works' column and the 'Obstacles' column. She had written items in both columns. Now, she took her pen and boldly wrote SEX? on the bottom of the page, stared at it for a minute, and scratched it out before ripping up the whole sheet.

4 / JAMES' PLACE

Saturday morning James put on cargo pants, an old black loose T-shirt with a Mötley Crüe logo, and a Minnesota Twins baseball cap covering his top knot. He threw his camping gear in the trunk of the 2002 Corolla his mother gave him three years ago and drove the twenty-five miles on the freeway to St. Paul.

He drove by the three places he'd found on Craig's List but didn't like the concrete, heavy traffic setting of any of them. He wanted a bit of green and swung by a quieter residential neighborhood not far from Augsburg.

He drove down block after block of big square houses looking for a 'For Rent' sign. Most of the houses were two full stories with four bedrooms and a walk up to a third-floor attic.

James could tell which houses had been broken up into apartments by the number of black mail boxes on the front of the houses and by how the front yards were torn up for extra parking. 'College sprawl,' he thought.

He liked the charm of the early twentieth century houses. The builders were artisans, the first families actually gathered around the hearth.

James parked when he saw a sign in the window of a white stucco house with an open porch and green trim. The whole house had a clean look. He walked to the door and rang the bell. After a minute, a youngish guy walked out onto the porch.

"Do you want to see the apartment? I just put the sign up. It's small, an efficiency, with an extra alcove for a bed or study. You interested?"

James nodded and held out his hand. "My name is James Holden." The guy just looked at the hand James offered until he slowly lowered it to his side.

"Wait here," the guy said. "I'll get the keys. The place is around the back and has a private entrance."

"Do you mind if I walk around and wait for you in the back?"

The guy nodded and closed the door.

Lilies, irises, daisies, and oxeyes, some still blooming, bordered a concrete path five feet from the house. On the other side of the path, a narrow driveway led to an old garage. An extra parking space bordered the small garage. Sandra would be impressed by the flowers, he thought, as he stooped to inhale their fragrance.

He liked the raised, closed entry attached to the back of the house. On the far side of the entry, a large picture window replaced the original windows. James grinned. It's just like home.

When the guy came around back and let him in, James was amazed. Sunlight poured in from the big window. To the right was a kitchen defined by a bank of cupboards, a farmer's sink, and a small range and refrigerator. To the left was a larger living area. Behind a door to the rear of the living area was a small bathroom. Next to the bathroom was the alcove his futon could fit into and still leave some storage room. Yep, this place was the right size for him.

The whole apartment was probably the original house's kitchen and pantry. The floors were the original maple, nicely refinished.

The walls, high cupboards, and the wide beveled trim were painted white. The kitchen had a retro look. The whole place was sunny and clean.

He moved to the picture window. The backyard next to the garage was fenced in back and on the sides. The private little backyard with two tall trees was priceless.

James imagined his desk against the big window overlooking his yard. After years of living in the basement, it would be great to study and draw while watching the elm leaves turn yellow and orange and fall down like rain. He'd have orange carpets of leaves and naked black tree branches for his favorite time of year, Halloween.

The landlord interrupted his revelry. "You like the place, don't yah?"

"How much?" James asked.

"Twelve hundred per month plus another $100 for utilities. I want a month's deposit, last month's rent, and first month's rent. Thirty-nine hundred, if you want it. My name is Dan Peterson by the way."

James hid his sticker shock with a cough but didn't hesitate.

"Can I have it today? I've got a check or I could cash a check and come back. I'm an honor student at Augsburg. I have references." James pulled out his rental resume. He'd followed a template on his computer and written an exaggerated page the night before.

Dan took it, skimmed through it, and smiled with appreciation. He grabbed some folded papers from his back pocket and handed them to James. "Here's a pen," Dan said. He hated paperwork and believed he was good at reading people. James provided more information than he'd ever need and had a clean-cut look. When James was through with the forms, Dan folded them up and put the paperwork back into his pocket.

"Are you going to live here alone? Do you have a pet? Do you smoke?"

James thought quickly and decided that honesty is the best policy.

"I plan to live alone; although, I'm hoping I'll have a friend or two come by, no moving in or anything. I mean I don't have anyone now but…" a familiar blush raised up from his neck to his checks.

Dan laughed. "Hey, I can relate to that. Do you have friends or family coming around a lot? I'm only renting to you." James shook his head vehemently no.

"Do you smoke, then?"

"Not cigarettes. I'll be honest, though. I blow the herb now and then."

"That's honest. But I'll tell you now, no parties, no big noise, no trouble."

James wanted the place, but he didn't want some big brother, nosy landlord hovering over him.

"Well, it's your house, but is this going to be my place?"

Dan raised his eyebrows and laughed. "I'm not a snoop, but don't damage the apartment or cause noise, or your ass will be grass. Leave your rent check in my mailbox on the first of the month. You can smoke cannabis a little but don't smoke up the place, and no cigarettes. No hard drugs, of course, and no drunken binges either. But I don't think that's your style, is it?

James laughed, shook his head, and wrote the check. Now Dan offered his hand. He explained the garbage situation, parking to the side of the garage, and the deal was done. The keys exchanged hands.

James closed the door behind Dan and walked to the middle of his own place, jingling his new keys, tossing them in the air and catching them until he missed.

"I be the man," he said and rapped his chest with his knuckles. James was beyond satisfied and proud of the place he'd found.

He texted Ellen. "Found perfect digs u be impressed walk to campus private parking spending night here 1824 W. Currant Av. #3, St. Paul."

Ellen texted him back. "In one day? Unbelievable!" She held herself back from asking the cost and about the neighborhood.

After parking, bringing in his camping gear, and opening the side windows, James sat on the floor with his legs splayed out and smoked a joint, using a tin cup from the camping gear as an ashtray. He watched the light and shadow dance along the edges of the back wall. He laid on the smooth surface of the clean floor, facing one way and then the other, enjoying the smells of fresh paint and poly mixed with the outdoor breeze coming in through the windows.

Comfortable as it was, James was too excited to stay put. He was up in a flash, putting in his earbuds, locking his apartment, shoving his hands in his pockets, and walking. He walked along a number of residential streets before turning onto the major thoroughfare, University Ave. He ambled toward Augsburg, watching women on this perfect, warm summer day and thinking about his upcoming classes. He would register on Monday. He wanted an interesting class, literature or philosophy, something to round out the hard sciences. Caleb had told him about an interesting humanities professor. He'd try to get into this prof's Sci-fi class.

A woman in a hijab walked by, texting while she walked. Although she was covered head to toe, James watched her multi-colored fingernails flying over the keyboard of her cell phone. He kept watching her until a back and forth wag of her pointer finger expressed her disapproval of his staring.

Women of many colors, shapes, and ethnicities were enjoying the day, and James was attracted to them all. Two large black women in light-weight leather-trimmed jackets purred down the street like a couple of Cadillacs. He turned to watch the back sides of these lovely women and stumbled against a young woman pressing to pass him. He reached out to steady them both and came close to her face. There was a softness about her mouth and eyes that belied her urban style. Pulling himself a small distance from her, he gawked unintentionally at her crotch level sundress and quickly shifted his eyes down to her high, blocky sandals before, embarrassed, looked back up into her eyes.

Brown eyed contact! James blushed, the curse of the strawberry blond, blushing was his 'tell.' Her eyes, after a pause, slid by his, and she shook her head, ever so slightly. 'Helpless' she seemed to imply, and, yet, she smiled, a widening smile with strong teeth and soft, full lips.

She isn't wearing makeup, James thought. She is an amazing combination of foxy and fresh. Then she was past. He turned to watch her. She walked fast, comfortable in her saucy body.

"She smiled!" he said to the world. He felt a strong pull to keep watching her. Shiny black hair, kinky like his, her skin a satin caramel. He held her image, the backs of her arms, the angle of her elbows, the muscled backs of her thighs. Second base would be kissing the crook of those elbows and the backs of those knees. He watched until she faded into the busy crowd.

James was in the groove, belonging here. He watched everyone moving to their own music; he had his own music too, didn't he? Still, how was he going to talk to a woman like that? It would be a lot easier to talk to a woman he didn't find so attractive.

His thoughts turned to a time when he and Chuck were teens. Chuck was making fun of him for being too shy to walk up to girls and talk to them, and as usual, James struck back. "You can't recognize rejection. You think the girls like you, but I've seen them laughing, making faces behind your back."

Sandra overhead them and interrupted. "Hey, you two, you're hurting each other's feelings." She bullied her way between them and bluffed a thump on each of their heads. They'd grown tall and fast and easily evaded her. "The two of you remind me of your mother and me." James turned his attention to her. James always wanted to hear more about his mother.

"I could never understand why Ellen didn't just didn't walk up to people and start talking to them like I do." Sandra motioned to Chuck. "He is like me. We can go up to almost anyone and just start talking. Sometimes people walk away from us, but so what? We know if this one doesn't appreciate our company, somebody else will. But James, you're like your mother. She wouldn't approach a stranger. She wouldn't give anyone a chance to reject her."

"Later, with all of her degrees, your mother explained the psychology to me. She said that I'm an extrovert. I get energy from chance interactions with other people. Chatting with strangers cheers me up. But your mom, James, is introverted. Chatting exhausts introverts what replenishes them is time alone." Sandra looked closely at James. "Your Mother is reserved, but she enjoys outdoor activities, like she always has with you. She found your dad through the Sierra Club because they both loved biking. You are like your mom, James, not outgoing with strangers, but mind my words, you will find that special girl when you're ready, and she will love you."

"If Mom waited and then found the right guy, why did my folks get a divorce? What happened? Can't introverts stay in love?" James' voice broke.

"Extrovert, introvert," she answered James' questions, "I don't think that has anything to do with staying in love. Do you know how many marriages end in divorce? Your mother and dad both love you, James, and they both were incredibly sad when your dad had to leave Minnesota—and leave you—for his work."

She changed the subject and started a discourse on the skill of engaging others in conversation. "James, if you meet a girl you'd like to get to know, be smart. Start the conversation by asking her questions about herself; let her do the talking."

"What kind of questions are you talking about?" James asked.

"You need to ask questions that you genuinely want to hear answers to—for instance, 'Tell me about your brothers and sisters,' or 'What's the best movie you saw this year?' Don't ask questions that can easily be answered with a yes or a no. Follow-up with more questions."

"I have a question for a girl," James announced wickedly. "Do you want to have sex?"

"Oops," he said to Sandra. "That's a yes or no, isn't it?"

Then he let her thump him on the back of the head, and she did, hard.

James laughed thinking about being lippy with Sandra. He was comfortable with Sandra, but he wasn't comfortable with women his own age. This would change in his own place. He'd be in charge. He'd feel comfortable, and he'd make a woman feel comfortable, too.

James started running, taking a different route on emptier streets, back to his place, running on the sidewalk but moving to the street if someone was walking toward him. He passed his place once but kept running until he was sweaty and empty of feelings.

He stopped at a Taco Bell he'd seen earlier and bought a couple of loaded burritos and a giant Mountain Dew then he stopped at a convenience store to buy toilet paper and soap and a pumpkin pie for breakfast.

Walking into his own place, he had that excited feeling again, like when he first saw the house. He ate his first meal at his own home, enjoying every bite.

With a full belly, he reached into his backpack for a joint. Propping a sweatshirt from under his head, he lay on his back, smoking, watching the shadows deepen in the kitchen and thinking how glad he was to have distance from his mother's house. His eyes got heavy. He settled down and fell asleep.

5 / AFTER DARK

James woke from his nap. It was twilight, and it took a minute to reorient himself. The paint and poly smell were becoming familiar. Enough city light filtered in through the big window for James to get up and pee and drink water out of the bathroom faucet without turning on a light.

When he was fully awake, he turned on the bathroom light to search his back pack for the extra summer 'going out' clothes he'd carefully packed: a square cut madras shirt, light-weight pants, and leather sandals. He showered, brushed his teeth, and rubbed some product into his hair to tame down the natural frizz before tying it half up in a rubber band. He looked good—ready to explore the neighborhood again—to go out into the darkness of the city.

James walked to Spooner's, his favorite coffee house. He usually went there with Caleb, but sometimes he went alone to study. Spooner's had a stage and music on the weekends. He lit a joint and smoked as he walked the dark residential streets to the well-lit University Avenue. The night was warm and humid; the earthy sweet smells of boulevard gardens gave way to pavement and gas fumes as he neared Snelling and University Avenue.

At Spooner's, he paid his five dollars, got a coffee, and sat down alone at a small round table near a corner of the room. The pre-set house music played while the band set up—mellow jazz from mid-century—Ray Charles, Dave Brubeck, Sarah Vaughn, Ahmad Jamal, music that fit into his mood. James rubbed his nose and discretely looked around; mostly couples or small groups filled the tables and booths. They made a show of having a good time.

The local group was ready and the lights went down. He watched the female tenor sax player give a last lick to her reed with her red lipped mouth. She was a thin raw-boned woman wearing a 50's house dress and Doc Martens. He loved her big, beautiful mouth. Watching her, James wondered if he had the guts to talk to one of the prostitutes that hung out off of University Avenue, only a few blocks from here.

As the band played, he kept his shielded eyes on the sax player. She tucked her elbows in, too, like the woman he found so attractive on his walk this afternoon. She swayed with the sound, both the musician and the cobra.

He acknowledged his attraction to her, and a feeling of hunger settled in his groin. He leaned back and enjoyed the first set. When the lights went up for a break, he looked at his cell. It was almost eleven. Not much happened in St. Paul after midnight, if he was going to head to a bar or to talk to a prostitute, he'd better get moving.

He saw the two prostitutes before they saw him. One was blond with a few dark roots showing. She was nearly as tall as him. His eyes ran along her profile. She was quite a bit younger than he first thought. She didn't look dirty exactly, but her makeup was caked, her eye-shadow smudged. She staggered as she walked over to a car on her high wedges. She's high, he thought.

He walked a little closer when the car moved away. She turned and looked directly at him. She smiled eagerly, but her eyes were vacant. It turned him off. He abruptly crossed the street and walked the other direction, away from the girls.

He passed two or three Asian restaurants. They were open, but looking through the windows, he saw they were void of customers. He walked by a couple of bars without windows. He didn't want to walk alone into one of those lonely guys places he'd seen in movies.

He was almost ready to turn back toward home when he saw a well-lit Mexican place with a large plate glass window. A couple coming out of the place laughed at a private joke. Looking through the window, he saw a number of people eating at booths and tables. This was more his kind of place.

LATER HE WOULD FIND out her name was Willow. She was tired and a little pissed. Maggie had called in sick and her papa, Joe, called her on her way home from the dance studio to ask her to work a long shift on her day off. Joe said it would be a quiet Saturday night, and they would close about midnight.

"Right," she responded to Joe. "A quiet Saturday night? When it's almost time for the state fair, and the college kids are starting to stream back?"

Joe paused and said, "I'm sorry. I didn't know you had plans." They both laughed. As if she had any plans other than to go home. Gram would be in her own world writing her blog, and the house would feel empty on a Saturday night. She might as well work.

"I'm the only girl in St. Paul without a date on Saturday night," Willow said.

"And whose choice is that?" Joe asked.

"I'm waiting for classes to start, to start a whole new life."

"Sorry, honey, but as your Gram says, "Where ever you go, there you are."

"Pow, straight to the moon, Alice," she came back at him with his own favorite response.

Willow was still waiting tables when James peeked in the window.

"No," he said, to no one in particular. "Could it actually be her?"

Even in waitress clothes, James was quite sure Willow was the girl he'd nearly knocked over earlier in the day. He walked in and pointed Willow out to a nearby waitress. "I want to sit in that girl's section," he said.

Danielle looked over at Willow and laughed. "Good luck with that one," she said and pointed out a booth.

"Thanks," he said smiling, relieved he hadn't blushed.

Willow headed to his table carrying a damp white towel. "Excuse me, mind if I wipe your table?"

"No, of course, I mean, take all the time you need. I'm in no hurry." James smiled, fighting an urge to push himself against the back of the booth. Be cool, man, he cautioned himself.

Willow finally looked at him. "Do I know you?"

"We passed on the street this afternoon. This is me in Saturday night dress up; you saw the real me earlier."

"Oh, I remember, you. Cargo pants. You stared at me," she said putting her hands on her hips and leaning toward him.

"I couldn't help myself. I like the way you look." Now he felt himself blush down to his very roots. He thought about the rush that had gone through his body when he first saw her ('I like the way she walks, and I want to hold her body' he'd sung to himself.)

Willow laughed, enjoying his blush. She looked harder at him. She liked his looks, his square jaw. He was tall, quite thin. He didn't look right out of high school; he was probably from the suburbs or a smaller town, a scrubbed look to him.

She looked around, feeling conspicuous. The place was quiet. Joe and his crew were starting to clean up the kitchen. Danielle was cleaning a table, and the bell on the door rang. A couple walked in, unsure if they should wait or seat themselves.

"Well, then, I'll get you a menu," Willow said to James. "Do you want chips and salsa?"

He nodded.

"How hot?" she asked.

He looked at her with a crooked little grin. "I like mild salsa," he said, wishing he had the guts to tease her a little, but he didn't. She liked him; she didn't know why, but she did, and she smiled back at him.

After that, every time she came back to his table, she took the time to have a snippet of conversation with him. He was James Holden, a junior at Augsburg. She told him her name, Willow Gunderson-Reyes. He didn't think she looked like the Gunderson's he knew.

He was happy to say he had his own place in St. Paul rather than saying he lived with his mother in the suburbs. Willow lived off of Hamline Avenue, too, but on the other side of University Avenue, nearer ritzy Summit Avenue.

After he finished a good burrito plate (he could eat burritos at every meal) and two beers, he asked if he could walk her home. She said no. He looked around and realized he was the only customer and that the place was getting ready to close.

He paid his bill and when she came to collect the money, he reached out to shake her hand. She looked at him oddly and then took his hand. Both of their hands were warm and strong and pulsed with life. He wondered where that nervous gesture came from, twice in the same day, wanting to shake someone's hand. I am a social idiot, he thought.

He was pleased by how easy it had been to talk to Willow Gunderson-Reyes. What a coincidence, he thought. Sandra's mom and dad were Gunderson's. He'd been out to the family's farm a number of times.

Sometime he'd tell Willow he was partly raised by a Gunderson, too. They'd laugh over it. It wasn't a matter of if he would see her again; he knew he would see her again. It was a matter of when. He'd make sure it was soon.

AN HOUR LATER, on the quick drive home, Joe said, "Danielle watched you flirting with some guy. She said that he had specifically asked to sit at one of your booths. I'm not disapproving. I'm just curious."

"Well, don't be curious. He's just some guy I met a while back at a party at Hattie's." Willow didn't want Joe getting all bent out of shape by her admitting she'd met James on the street.

6 / WILLOW

Two days later, on a warm Monday morning, Willow walked the four blocks to the light rail, the line to the main campus of the U of M in Minneapolis, to register for her first college classes.

She wore a pink cotton sleeveless V-Neck under denim bibs. Her worn pant bottoms dragged along the pavement, half hiding her black toenails and worn huaraches. Her shiny, frizzy long hair was tied back at the nape of her neck. She was purposely wearing mismatched earrings. Once, when she was crying over a lost earring, Gram said, "Make a statement—wear mismatched earrings. See if anyone notices. It's hard to see both ears at one time." Now, mismatched earrings were some of Willow's good luck charms.

She liked the baggy, anonymous look on days when she would be around a lot of strangers. She preferred to watch, rather than to attract attention. Last Saturday when it was boiling hot, and James had run into her, she had been on the street wearing what Gram said looked like a bathing suit.

Willow wondered why she hadn't been offended by James' blatant stares. Nor was she offended that he'd somehow found Joe's and asked to walk her home. Willow was usually put off by the way men looked at her when she revealed too much. She especially hated it when they looked at her as if 'she could be had.' They were wrong, wrong. But James hadn't given off any predator vibes; she was certain he was attracted to her, but for once she wasn't put off by a man's blatant attraction to her.

She circuitously watched two girls transferring off the suburban line and waiting for the city line with her. They looked around at the people on the street in sort of a wide-eyed way. Willow bet they were just out of high school, too, and probably also going to the main campus to register for their first classes. They hadn't spent much time in her international corridor, she thought. Maybe she would see them in a class this fall. That would be a long shot with 10,000 freshmen signing up for classes at the main campus.

The two girls were wearing roughed up designer jeans and tight spandex tops. With such coordinated outfits, Willow surmised they were BFFs. Girls like these two abounded at her high school academy. Heavy makeup, trying to look casual, they were inauthentic.

Willow watched them take in the hustle and bustle of Midtown. They gawked and were oblivious to the subtle reactions of others toward them. One of them nodded her head for her friend to look at a small old man scraping along the sidewalk on a foot propelled scooter. He wore a leather pack on his back. The other girl looked at the old man and slanted her eyes with long lavender nails. They both laughed at the man who did look like he was straight off the boat from Asia. He caught the gesture and gave them both a withering glance. They missed it. Willow didn't.

She looked down, suddenly very interested in adjusting her sandals. If they knew how dangerous Lee Nag could be, they would be looking down, too. He packed a knife and wouldn't think twice about slicing a pretty girl in broad daylight. It would happen so fast, she wouldn't even feel it until he was long gone and smiling all the way to his lair, as if he had immunity from consequences in this neighborhood.

Across the street, two pimps greeted each other with sly hand to finger motions. They shimmered in the bright sunlight in bright nylon shirts. Willow knew of them. They turned their attention to the suburban girls. The girls squirmed, unconsciously acknowledging the pimps' reaction to them.

Willow was careful with pimps, politely ignoring them and walking into the street to avoid them after dark. It had gotten so bad that Joe wouldn't let her go home on her own after 9:00 p.m. when the traffic slowed down and pimps and prostitutes owned the streets near Joe's Cafe.

These pimps had working girls who occasionally came into Joe's Café, especially on frigid days when they froze on the cold streets dressed in their short skirts and cheap vinyl jackets that stiffened and cracked from the cold. At Joe's, the girls ordered coffee or coke and poured packets of sugar into their beverages.

Joe instituted a policy that the waitresses had to bring condiment trays back and forth to the tables to dissuade prostitutes and the destitute from filling up on freebies. The older waitresses hated the extra walk back and forth and were slow to serve anyone who looked like they couldn't afford food. Willow didn't blame the waitresses; they weren't lazy, just bone weary, raising children, taking care of men and running back and forth at the busy restaurant.

But Willow was compassionate toward the working girls. She served them promptly and often brought out chips and salsa, even though that was definitely against policy. She didn't care if Joe scowled from the kitchen. If he caught Willow's eye, she would lift her head and sashay past him.

In Willow's several years of waiting tables, she had witnessed working girls younger than herself coming into the café, some of them, at first, resembling the suburban girls in front of her now.

But within months, they aged. Some withered from AIDS. Drugs turned them into skeletons with broken fingernails, thinning wispy hair, loose teeth, and dead eyes. Crank use was especially hard on the face and teeth, but heroin did that, too.

She wouldn't judge them harshly. Her own mother had died of AIDS. As Gram said, "There but for the grace of God, go you and I."

Enough about street life, she thought. I'm heading for college. No one will know who I am; I'll be rubbing elbows with people from all over the state: suburbs, little towns, farms like Gram's. Plus, she'd meet people from out of state, from out of the country for that matter. She couldn't contain a little dance step as the bus arrived.

Willow waited for the crowd to get off and for the others to get on, hopping on last, smoothly reaching for a pole as the driver took off with a jerk. She stuttered down the bus aisle and took a moment to smile at the two young women who were sitting together near the front. They looked up simultaneously and smiled back at her. Still grinning for being bold, Willow continued to the back and slid into an empty seat, leaned against the window and put her legs up along the other seat to keep anyone in the half empty bus from sitting next to her. She imagined she would love it at the U.

James was back at Joe's later that morning. Willow wasn't there, but he got her schedule from the same waitress who had seated him before.

"I'm hoping we see more of you, honey," Danielle said as he moved toward the door.

"I'm hoping I'll be eating a lot of Mexican here," he said and quickly turned away from her with a blush. He hadn't meant a double entendre, and he hoped she wouldn't take his innocent response the wrong way, but she had turned away and didn't seem to be listening to him.

Danielle went back to the kitchen, "Hey Joe, remember I told you about that boy who was so interested in Willow last Saturday?"

"Yeah, I remember him. Is he back?"

"Yes. He said, 'I'm hoping I'll be eating a lot more Mexican here.' He asked for Willow's schedule and left."

Joe looked over at Danielle; he could never tell when she was teasing him. She was as deadpan as ever.

AFTER THE CAFÉ'S lunch rush, Joe came home as usual for his afternoon break.

"Where's Willow," he said, sounding as if something important was happening. Char was seated on a kitchen stool, completely absorbed in writing her blog. Hearing this concern in his voice, she hopped off her stool and gaped at him as if she didn't recognize him.

"Earth to Char; it's your husband home from the café. Where is Willow?"

"Don't you remember? She's registering for classes today. Is there a problem?" Char asked, setting her iPad on the counter.

He slowed down, walked jauntily over to his wife, and kissed her on the lips. "Remember the guy I told you about? The guy Willow knew who came in to eat late on Saturday night? He was back today, asking for her work schedule."

"Are you hoping she will show some interest in him, or are you afraid she will show some interest in him?" Char asked. "I can't quite read you on this."

Joe took Char's hand, "All I want is for Willow to live a full and happy life. You know that."

"Oh, I know," Char answered. "I feel the same. I know I should want her to date—a beautiful girl like her, not dating at eighteen—that's a worry, too. But truth be told, I want her to stay our little girl." Char's voice broke. "I'll never forgive myself for what happened to her mother."

"Stop it now," Joe said, a spark of anger showing in his eyes. "You beat yourself up better than Laila Ali could beat you." He watched her stifle a small grin. "Don't go there, Char," he said in a gentle tone. "Neither of us can change the past." He put his arms around her, and she nestled into the crook of his shoulder, reaching to kiss him on the cheek.

"Thank you, dear, for the hug," Char said. "I was just reading a response to my blog from a woman whose daughter died from an overdose, and, of course, I started thinking about Rainey. It takes me a few minutes to come back to reality after connecting to another person's pain. But, enough about me. Willow isn't home yet. I expect her home within the hour. Have you had lunch?" Char asked.

"I ate at work, and I'm not going back until dinner rush. Mind if I run up and take another shower? I worked hard this morning."

"Of course not. I'll be right here, writing back to this woman who lost her daughter."

Char sat back down at the counter, but instead of picking up her iPad, she thought about her daughter Rainey. Char had raised Rainey in this very kitchen. The counters had been replaced, the windows had been replaced, the floor stripped back to its original wood, but the lovely old wooden door with its beveled glass still rattled shut when Willow came home, just as it had when Rainey did.

Rainey, who at seventeen, left home with a drug dealer.

Years after Rainey's death, Char still wracked her brain, trying to understand how she'd failed her daughter. She'd loved her, but had she loved her in the way Rainey wanted and needed to be loved? Char should have slowed down and listened better, probed deeper. Instead, she trusted Rainey to find her own answers, to ask Char if she needed advice. Char thought Rainey knew she was there for her unconditionally. She should have made sure of that every day.

When she finally came back to Char, Rainey had AIDS and was pregnant with Willow. Char promised Rainey, dying from meningitis when Willow was six weeks old, that she would not fail their Willow.

Char remembered the words she spoke. "I will be there for Willow. I will take the time to listen to her, to ask her questions every day of my life. I promise you Rainey, on my love for you, I will not fail our baby."

Rainey sat on the spindle rocking chair, exhausted, propped up with pillows, holding her baby in her weakened arms. She grabbed Char's hand, raised it to her cheek, and kissed it. "I love you, Mom. Thank you."

When Rainey died, Char held her daughter's baby, cooing and singing to her, and Willow smiled, a smile much like her mother's.

By the time Willow started school, Char thought the darkest days were over. Willow was a healthy, beautiful, lively child. But she didn't like school; she often came home sad, not wanting to go back the next day.

Thank God for that honest call from the PTA president of Willow's elementary school. Word had gotten out amongst the elementary school mothers that Willow's mother died of complications from AIDS. A number of mothers, members of the PTA, worried that Willow was HIV positive. They didn't want their children to play with her.

Willow's doctor, Dr. Amy, came to the PTA to explain how HIV is contracted and specifically how Willow had been repeatedly tested and was HIV negative. But rumors persisted. Schoolmates' rejections persisted.

Char listened to Joe humming in the shower upstairs. What a blessing Joe had been, coming into the family when Char and Willow needed support. Char got the help she needed to raise her beautiful granddaughter, and Willow got a Papa who loved her.

Joe and dance were the two salvations in young Willow's life. Char remembered the day she took Willow to her first dance studio in Minneapolis. All the kids were new to dance and excited to try, but Willow hid behind Char. The skilled teacher winked at Char and encouraged her to stand nearby while Willow danced, unnoticed in the back row. That didn't last more than a class or two. Willow's irrepressible talent forced her naturally to the center stage. Char breathed deeply, thinking of the thrill of watching Willow dance.

WILLOW BANGED the side door open, rattling the glass, "I'm registered!" she announced loudly.

Joe heard the door and limped down the stairs with one shoe in his hand.

"Are you getting the classes you wanted?" Joe asked.

"I got into the honors program. It doesn't mean a lot. I'm taking the prerequisites everyone takes the first couple of years, but I got a good schedule. Classes three days a week and I can try out for the dance line. The counselor looked at my transcripts and said I shouldn't have any problem getting into the dance line. He scheduled me for an upper division dance class, too."

"You're already special at that huge university," Joe said, impressed. "By the way, the guy you were talking to the other night came by and asked for your work schedule."

"Oh, I tell you about my new classes and all you're interested in is some guy who came by?" Willow said.

It took a second for Joe to recognize the tease, but then he saw the smart grin on her face, and they both snickered.

Char said, "Let me in on the fun, you two. Is this the same boy who had the two of you giggling on Saturday night?"

Now the two of them were really laughing. "Gram, give us a break," Willow answered, laughing at both of her folks. "Nothing has happened between him and me but a little talk. Don't get your hopes up, Papa and Gram," she said and smiled at both of them in turn.

Joe smiled broadly. He loved it when she called him Papa, and she did it when she was pleased.

7 / FIRST DATE

Willow worked again on Tuesday. After the lunch rush, James walked in, and Willow saw him at about the same time. They swaggered up to each other, James smiling and fidgeting with the keys in his pocket, Willow smiling with a cleaning cloth in her hand. He was as tall and thin as she remembered, and he had a broad, genuine smile. They stood nearly eye to eye.

"Do you know why I'm here?" he asked, looking around to see if anyone was looking at them.

"Well, I bet you are…" she said, dragging the words out then finishing quickly, "here to eat."

"You're wrong. I'm here to find a time for us to go to the State Fair."

"You've got to be kidding," she said with delight and led him to a booth close to the door.

He swung into the booth, and she zipped in across from him.

"I should drag this out a little, like they say you're supposed to do when you meet someone you like," he said. "But I want to go to the State Fair with you! I want it to be our first date."

Willow looked around, not wanting anyone to be staring at them. The coast was clear.

"I love the State Fair; I've gone nearly every year of my life. I think I remember going in a stroller."

"Me too, not the stroller, but us kids went every year come hell or high water. My second Mom, Sandra, always enters something from her garden, and we have to go see if they award her a purple or a blue ribbon this year. When I was young it was the Midway, the dairy barn, and the animal exhibits. But I like all the exhibits now, the Education and Industry Building and Art Center."

"Those are my favorite buildings now, too," Willow agreed. "What about the Crop art? Oh, god, did you see that sneaky one of President Trump done in corn last year?"

"I hooted," James answered. "You like the Postcard collections?"

Willow nodded. "I've seen it all and the postcard collections? I thought maybe I was the only young person who liked those."

"No—I really like them, especially the ones that show Minnesota towns changing over the decades. They are a precursor to comics. I draw anime now, working a book about an illegal girl with superpowers."

"Wow," Willow said, looking at James in amazement. "I'm impressed."

"Oh, it's nothing," James said, embarrassed. "We'll ride the Ferris wheel, and maybe we can bungee cord dive. I puke when I do it, but I'll do it anyway."

"You have bungee before you start eating!" Willow said, laughing at him.

"I hope you can make it a whole day, because, you know, we're going to eat everything," he said.

"No bungee diving, no walleye on a stick, OK? And we get to stop and listen to some music every time we get something to eat, right?" Willow added.

"No walleye on a stick? What kind of a Minnesotan are you? My mom would be ashamed of you. But no polka dancing, OK?"

"You can't polka?" She rolled her eyes again, and they both laughed.

"When are you free? There are only five days of Fair left."

They agreed to go in two days, on Friday. He would pick her up at the restaurant at 11AM.

"You don't want me to meet your family?" he asked.

"No, not yet, James."

He loved the way she said his name, elongating the M.

After James left, Willow thanked her lucky stars that Joe wasn't at work. She imagined him coming out in his apron, wiping his hands to shake James' hand. She laughed at herself for feeling giddy. The tune from *West Side Story* went through her mind: 'I just met a guy named James, and suddenly that name will never be the same.' She'd played Maria in the high school production. She cautioned herself. It was too pathetic to let a little attention from a man make her feel so good.

FRIDAY ARRIVED, and with it, a beautiful day for the Fair—hot—but that was the way it was supposed to feel in late August. They both dressed in light-weight cottons and walking shoes. James brought a blue Minnesota Twins cap for himself and a green John Deere for her, but Willow had her own wide brimmed hat.

They spent time touring the Education and Arts buildings, saying all the witty little things that came to mind, the preponderance of pigs this year at the Peoples' art. They laughed at old couples looking so much alike, and James hobbled like an old man for a while. They took the air trolley for a good overhead view, and James caught a glimpse of his favorite foot long hotdog stand. They both liked foot longs with sauerkraut, onions, mustard and catsup. A Minneapolis grunge group was playing just down from the hotdog stand. They shared a big lemonade with their dogs and listened to grunge. James asked Willow what she thought he would cook for her when he had her over for dinner.

"Foot longs and smores?" she guessed.

"No—frozen burritos," he teased.

On the way to the Midway, they went through the Pig barn, and James pretended to love the smell. He said he could "call" pigs and got the attention of a big boar that put his dirty nose between the bars of his pen, and they just had to pet him, dirt and all. They called him Big Babe, and James said in a stern voice, "That'll do, pig."

Right before the Midway, they toured the Dairy barn and watched the state Dairy Princess sitting pertly in a freezing locker with her cape over her shoulders, posing while her image was sculpted into a huge block of butter. They ate deep fried cheese curds and mini donuts, pork chops on a stick with a chocolate milkshake chaser.

At the Midway, James tried knocking down bowling pins to win Willow a Teddy bear. His throws were wild and funny and in vain. They bounced all over the tent and nearly hitting the Carnie. James was a good sport, and Willow didn't laugh quite as much as she wanted to.

At the next stand, Willow won herself a Teddy bear sharp shooting, and James called her Annie Oakley for the rest of the evening. After dark, they rode the high Ferris wheel, with all the lights of the Midway way below them. When the ride stopped at the very top, James, who already had his arm around Willow's shoulder, pulled her over and kissed her on the lips. They backed away and looked at each other in amazement.

Later, James dropped Willow off at her house and waited for her to get in safely, to turn off the outdoor light before he drove off. He hadn't tried to kiss her again. He just said, "Good night Annie. I had a great day at the Fair." Willow slipped out of the car without saying another word, holding her teddy bear like a baby.

JAMES DROVE to his spot behind a co-op grocery store, high on the bluffs of the Mississippi River. The water was an inky liquid tonight, shimmering languidly in the full moon light. I'm going to use pen and ink to put that inky river on paper, he thought. Then he chuckled again, thinking about the day at the Fair. He'd been comfortable with Willow and awed by her extraordinary beauty. She seemed so unconscious of it. He reached into his glove compartment for the joint he'd found in a forgotten stash inside his camping kit.

She wasn't the kind of girl he had envisioned meeting. When he thought about girls, he thought about someone more like Sandra's daughter, Laurel. A Scandinavian blond with a suburban edge to her. He'd been in love with Laurel forever. She was his older, unavailable, sister/neighbor, but for a while she had paid attention to him and that time was unforgettable. He still fantasized about playing a little rough with her, overcoming her resistance to him.

He didn't go to that wild place when he fantasized about Willow. Willow was a gentle soul, a warm, gorgeous woman. He wanted her to make his balls melt with desire instead of pound with desire like the nasty hot pistols he so often fantasized about. He lit a joint and inhaled the sweet taste; Willow was as sweet as this joint.

8 / THE FAMILY COOKOUT

James strolled around the corner of the garage, taking in the action unobserved. James, the outsider. He'd always felt a disconnect from this idyllic family scene. He was the one who went home crying as a child, resentful, when Sandra tuned him out and told him he couldn't stay for dinner.

"Go home, honey," she'd say. "Your mother needs you."

He hoped the big group wouldn't make a fuss over his arrival. Sometimes they did, and that was awful. He felt on the outside and thought he always would be a little 'outside'.

Ralph stood at the grill, always on task; Laurel and Sandra were arguing. Kimber's little girls ran in circles around their dad, blowing soap bubbles at him. James enjoyed the feisty little girls; their long blond hair was in pigtails today. He loved getting glimpses of Laurel's little boy, Roy, too. Roy could locomote anywhere now. His gait wasn't pretty, but it got him where he wanted to go.

James watched his mother, Ellen, walking from their house. He slid back into the shadows of the garage, waiting to join the party until after she made her entrance.

Walking across the lawn between their homes, Ellen was shocked by Ralph's appearance. He wasn't the substantial Teddy

Bear he'd been for most of the years of his marriage to Sandra. She wondered if Sandra had quit cooking for him. He was manning the grill below the deck and wearing the silly apron his girls had given him, a life size image of him in baggy swimming trunks. Now the image of his bulging stomach was nearly wrapped around his trimmed down body.

Ellen walked to an ice chest and pulled out a Heineken, popped the top off and strode over to acknowledge Ralph.

"I'm doing great," Ralph said in response to Ellen's inquiry. "I got a couple of vegetarian burgers for you and me. The recipe was online. Sandra caramelized a bunch of chopped veggies, squeezed out the extra moisture, added cooked black beans then pulverized the lot. I put Worchester sauce on them as they cook. I'm becoming a vegetarian like you."

Ellen looked at him skeptically. Ralph, the dyed in the wool meat eater, favoring vegetables? She shrugged her shoulders. There was a pause in their conversation.

They did not have much to say to each other anymore. Two years ago, when Ralph was spending an inordinate amount of time at work and Sandra complained about it to Ellen, Ellen rather flippantly asked Sandra if Ralph might be having an affair.

"Ellen thinks you are having an affair," is how Sandra had phrased it to Ralph. Ralph denied it, but Sandra had seen through the denial. She persisted in her questioning, and he finally admitted that yes, he had made a terrible mistake with a young nurse and had already extracted himself from the relationship. Sandra was heartbroken, angry at Ralph and inexplicably angry with Ellen, too.

Ralph continued, "What's new with you, Ellen? Here '*Where all the women are strong all the men are good looking and all the children are above?*'"

Not one for small talk, Ellen blurted out, "I'm sure you heard that James moved out, literally overnight. He told me he was going to look for a place on Friday night, and by Saturday he was gone. He's been staying at his new place for a week."

"Sorry, Ellen. I didn't know it had happened that quickly." Ralph looked up to where Sandra sat and said, "Uh, oh, Sandra's looking this way. I'd better concentrate on getting the corn off the flame and getting the brats and burgers done." He picked up his tongs and started moving the sweet corn off of the flame. When Ellen's offer to help was rejected, she excused herself.

Ellen headed for the deck. The large deck held room for an expansive adult table and a children's table as well as an additional lounging area. At the far end of the deck, Sandra sat catty-corner to her younger daughter Laurel on deck benches. Both were good sized blonds, classic Scandinavian beauties with handsome noses and strong hair. Their postures mirrored each other. Each had one arm along the bench railing, the other arm raised and pointed at the other. Laurel was obviously cross.

Today's argument had started off innocently enough with Laurel asking her mother if she had any news. Sandra shared that James had found a small apartment and was going to live alone.

"James is moving into his own place? Does he even know how to boil water?" Laurel asked.

"He knows how to cook. I taught him how to make all his favorite quick foods. The last few years he's spent a lot of time alone while Ellen worked and hobnobbed at workshops with the professional set."

Sandra continued. "I've decided to give James the oak table from Grandma's porch. It can fit in almost anywhere, and he can fold down the sides for work space or expand it to a round dining table."

"Oh, he won't be cooking. He doesn't need our table. More to the point, Mom, you've always said 'that table is staying in our family.' I've been eyeing it myself, but I thought you still wanted it in the corner of the family room. If you haven't said anything to him, can I have it instead?"

"Where would you put it? You've never shown the slightest interest in anything I've offered you. You always want everything new. I can't believe you want to deny James an old table. Ellen worries that James will spend all his graduate school money, and I wanted to help them out."

"Take note Mother because I've told you this twice now. I'm becoming less interested in buying 'new things.' I think materialism sucks. But give the table to whomever you please." Laurel got up and turned away with a quiet, "You'd do anything for those two."

Sandra sat still for a minute. She wasn't as upset by the exchange with her daughter as she was again puzzled by Laurel's over-reaction towards James. Laurel had doted on James when they were teenagers, but something had happened between them. She wasn't sure what, then she thought to herself that she probably didn't want to know.

Ralph had the corn and brats and burgers on platters. It was time for Sandra to set the table and bring out the salads. Laurel walked over to her husband, Brian, who reclined on a lawn chair with his hand dragging in the kids' wading pool. She roughed up his hair. He looked up at her in a surprised way, she smiled pleasantly.

Kimber, Sandra and Ralph's older daughter, was the only one not wearing shorts. She was showing her third pregnancy and was dressed in a Hawaiian cotton dress with spaghetti straps. She was helping Laurel's toddler, Roy, pick raspberries. He waddled around, short-legged in bulky diapers, trying to pick the thorny fruit without getting pricked.

Kimber's daughters, Kenzie and Tally, had refilled their soap bubble guns and again chased and sprayed their dad, Paul.

James walked up to Ralph, the closest person to the garage. "Can I help you, Ralph?" he asked.

"James," Ralph addressed him quietly. "Glad you made it. Your mother just told me that you've split for the city."

"James," Sandra yelled from the porch. Everyone turned to stare at him like he was an alien. Exactly what he feared would happen. "James," she yelled again. "Come, help me carry out the salads."

James marched up the patio steps to Sandra, and she grabbed him, hugging his limp body. He turned to nod at his mother who just gaped at him like the rest.

"Are you still running five miles a day, come hell or high water?" Sandra asked, finally releasing him.

"I guess. I'm trying not to be so compulsive about it, but most summer days I do."

"Healthy compulsions are fine; unhealthy ones are not so good," Sandra said. They moved through the patio into the house. She closed the patio door behind them.

James frowned and looked at her sideways. "Has my mother been sharing her 'concerns' with you?"

"She shared you were planning to move out and then you did, immediately. She is worried. She worries you might be over your head financially, and, I'll just spit it out, she worries that you keep smoking that dope as if it were cigarettes."

"Good God, Sandra, you know that's an exaggeration. I know you and mom smoked dope when you were young; you told me that. I've had a lot of time on my hands this summer. I don't smoke much when I'm busy. That pisses me off. See why I don't like living with her?"

"That's quite a reaction, James. Remember, if she didn't care, she wouldn't say anything—neither would I." Sandra swung around and gave him another hug and rubbed her hand against his roughening facial hair. "Back when we smoked dope, we did it with others, in companionship. I just don't understand why you do it alone in your room. Explain that to me. Are you depressed?"

"Trust me—it isn't that bad. A few tokes after running. A smoke after dinner. It clears my mind."

"I'd call it clouding your mind," she jested, feeling a little relieved. She thought probably both of them were to blame, Ellen overreacting as well as James smoking too much. She found it hard to believe marijuana was that addictive. They had puffed on it quite a bit during the college days, and James was a very good student. College was important to him.

"I've got something for your new place," she said. "Come quick." Sandra gestured him into the family room.

James didn't know if he really wanted the oak table that she planned to give him. He remembered playing games on it and putting big puzzles together on it during winters. He liked that it came from the farm. He remembered seeing it on the farmhouse porch off of the kitchen. It had been an extra table for Grandma Gunderson to load up with desserts when all of the family came for Grandma's baked chicken Sunday dinners. Her savory chicken fell off of the bone. She and Grandpa Gunderson had treated him like another grandkid. Grandma even remembered his birthdays.

"Thanks, Sandra," he said, swallowing hard. "What about your kids? Won't one of them want it?"

"You are one of my children, James." Sandra put an arm around him. James was ready for her affection now and accepted the table gratefully.

Just then, Chuck popped in looking for them.

"I was just asking James if he wanted this table for his new apartment."

"What new apartment?" Chuck asked pushing through James to sweep his mother into a warm embrace. "Mom," he said, rubbing her cheek and looking her in the eyes.

When she had been hugged, Chuck and James addressed each other. They stepped back and opened their arms wide, pantomiming the start of a bear hug. Getting inches apart, they abruptly swung their arms down in unison, and grasping each other's hands in an exaggerated hand shake, they nodded their heads at each other and grinned as if they were long lost friends from a far earlier generation. They loved to spoof on how demonstrative both Sandra and Ralph were.

"I have my own place," James said, the big grin still on his face.

"You're going to be on your own, living alone?"

"Yeah, I am more than ready."

Chuck wiggled his eyebrows in response. "See how buff I am?" Chuck showed off his muscles. He had been working construction all summer and was deeply tanned from days in the sun. He looked good, James thought. James was taller, but Chuck was heavier. Chuck had his father's rather owlish features and heavy frame. He wasn't exceptionally good looking, but he had a healthy glow of youth and self-confidence.

Although the young men were seeing less of each other, they were still thick as thieves when they were together. They were brothers.

They helped Sandra carry out containers of food and trays of plates and silverware and napkins and plastic cups. Chuck and James set the table with the forks to the left on colorful napkins, next to a matching paper plate on a thatched holder, knives and spoons to the right. Everyone was responsible for grabbing their own beverage out of the cooler.

Chuck and James, done with their chores, got their heads together for a plan of action, and before Laurel's little Kenzie and Tally could take their places at the kids' table, Chuck and James were sitting on the girls' little chairs, their long knees jutting up over the little table. The little girls rushed over, and James and Chuck let the girls pull them down, then they got onto their hands and knees and motioned for the little girls to climb onto their backs.

The girls rode the backs of the boys, holding onto the necks of their t-shirts, pulling their hair. The boys grappled at each other, whinnying like horses and gently tried to unbalance the girls. Sandra yelled, "Get away from the table! Watch out for the food!" Roy squirmed off of his dad's lap and threw himself into the fracas, grabbing and pulling out the band holding James' hair in place. James shook his hair free and pretended to butt Roy in the belly. Laurel grabbed Roy and told James to 'lighten up'.

Finally, the boys plopped down on their bellies, and the little girls pounded on them to get up for another ride.

Sandra and Ellen and Ralph laughed with tears in their eyes. How wonderful it was to have the whole family together.

After dinner, before the dusk raised the blood sucking mosquito hordes, James put his arm over Chuck's shoulder, and they walked away from the group.

"How is your mom handling you moving out? I'm so glad you are doing it. I couldn't imagine living alone with Ellen."

"Watch what you say about my mom," James said with a fake frown.

"Just saying," Chuck said, giving him a friendly punch.

"No, you're right, its time for me to leave home."

Then James pulled Chuck closer. "You got to help me, Bro. Can you get me a couple of ounces, a quarter pound of the good stuff from the frat house? I'm getting low on smoke, and Caleb's coming back from New York."

"For God's sake, do you still have to supply him too?" Chuck asked. James shrugged his shoulders.

Chuck shook his head. "No can do. You know I'm staying away from that shit. It doesn't mix with a sharp mind, at least not for me. It ruins my concentration."

"But I don't know where to buy dope. You and the frat bros are my source. I'm too lazy to find my own contacts."

"See, what did I just say? Grass makes you dopey and lazy."

"That's you, Chuck. I concentrate better when I smoke. It's no problem for me."

"Well," Chuck said with his fist on his chin like he had to put some thought into it. "This might be a long shot, but remember Randall Sagan from when we were in junior high?"

"Yeah, I remember him. Catering to us junior high chumps while he was already in high school. We called him 'Egg for ego.' He gave us our very first smoke, our first high. We massaged that Egg's ego a few times, right? Finally, we had to start paying him."

"I ran into him at the frat house," Chuck said. "He remembered me, of course, and said he was there 'making sure everyone got what they needed, if I knew what he meant.' I played dumb, 'Drugs?' Randall said Steve was his man now. He's a sophomore, this Steven Buhl, and I guess he took over the frat house dealing when Bill Fisher graduated. Egg isn't selling; he's the supplier for the dealers. I always bought from Bill and didn't even think about where he got the stuff. I didn't know he bought it from the Egg."

"Unbelievable," James responded. "I never thought about the line of management in drug sales. Do you know where I could find the Egg?"

"I'm not going out of my way to help you, Bro. I don't like this kid Steve, and I'm done with that scene. But when Egg and I reminisced a little, he asked about 'the frizzy redhead,' and when I said you went to Augsburg, he said he had gone there for a while, too, and that he still hangs out at Spooner's. Your favorite coffee house, right? That's all the help you get from me."

9 / JAMES' NEW BEST FRIEND

In junior high, James and Chuck took different directions. Chuck focused on contact sports. He welcomed a little pain, throwing his body against his opponents ruthlessly and sincerely shaking hands with them afterwards. James didn't relish contact sports. He preferred cross country running, cross-country skiing, and photography.

Chuck, the epitome of a team player, valued everyone on the team and showed loyalty to all his team brothers. He remained loyal to James, too. Without making it obvious, Chuck made sure James was included in his crowd's activities on the weekends. Chuck's friends thought James was nerdy, but because Chuck said he was OK, the other guys tolerated him.

When it was time for college, Chuck went to the main campus of the University of Minnesota. Ralph, his dad, was a graduate of the U of M Medical School, and Chuck wanted to be a doctor, too.

James chose Augsburg, a small private university with a good academic reputation. He planned to major in Engineering. The private university was expensive, but Ellen had gone to a private college and was willing to pay for James to have the same experience. Living at home defrayed some of his mother's costs.

As a freshman, James discovered he'd have to extend himself academically, and he studied hard. His effort paid off, and his grades were good. His second year, he knew the ropes and did as well. Now, facing his third year, James was becoming bored with academia.

Last winter, James met a guy from New York City named Caleb. Caleb was two years older than James but only a freshman, while James was a sophomore. They met in an elective Ethics class, and James guessed Caleb 'wasn't from here' during the first class. Caleb was relaxed for a freshman, slouching in the classroom chair, his long strong legs crossed at the ankles and dangling in the aisle. He was disdainful of the young enthusiastic professor. After a simplistic run down of the class objectives, Caleb wrinkled his nose and asked the professor, "Is this your first year of teaching?" The young professor stammered sheepishly and tried to defend himself against Caleb's onslaught of questions.

From that first day, the other students glanced over at Caleb if they made an in-class comment, hoping he'd give his trademark nod if he approved of their comments. He intrigued James. James couldn't tell if Caleb was being sarcastic or honestly inquisitive when he asked the professor if studying classics was passé in our apocalyptic epoch.

Caleb had dark thick hair, razor cut short on the sides and au naturel on top. He had black thick stubble on his cheeks and down his neck. He had his own style, faded shirts buttoned at the neck without a tie. Local guys couldn't pull this off. They just weren't urbane.

James watched Caleb, sliding a glance in his direction for approval once or twice then chuckling at himself for doing it. One day after class, Caleb walked up to James, moved right into his personal space, and asked him if he had a joint to share. James always had a joint, so they smoked as they walked over to Spooner's.

"Thanks, man, I guessed right about you," Caleb said holding the smoke in his lungs. "I don't have the money for smoke right now."

"Yeah, Augsburg is expensive. It's full of the rich drips I hoped I had left behind in the suburbs," James said before his turn at the joint.

"What do you do, besides going to classes?" Caleb asked.

James was taken aback by Caleb's direct personal question. That definitely wasn't Minnesotan. He pondered how to answer it. Live with his mother? Work at 'Sports Center West'? Run almost every day? Then he thought about his Anime comics. He had a chance to think about his answer while they bought coffees and found a back table. After they sat down, James leaned forward a little, readying himself to share something he didn't usually share with guys.

"Drawing, I do Anime these days. I admired Picasso and Matisse way back in junior high." James looked sideways to see if he still had Caleb's attention. Caleb nodded to go on.

"Matisse interested me the most, especially his work with women's bodies. They were still drawings, but if you look at them carefully, you can see the figures twisting and turning. That's what comics do, Anime does, puts action into still life."

James looked at Caleb again; he still seemed to have his attention.

"I strive for that stark, linear splash of color action. You have to write a story, too. One of my characters, Karan, she's a changeling being chased by ICE. Men in suits and red ties, women looking kindly in dresses and stilettos trying to capture and cage her, but Karan sees behind her head. It's fun."

Caleb nodded at this, "I'd like to see some of your drawings. That's a forward concept, animating images seeing backward." They both chuckled.

Then Caleb leaned in. "I've got a hobby. I buy dollar plants at the grocery store. It started when I heard the ragged little plants calling to me at Target; sometimes they reached toward me. What could I do? I bought them." He narrowed his eyes, waiting for James' response.

James shrugged his shoulders. He liked strange and nodded for Caleb to continue.

"I got about a dozen little plants, and I can't leave them in those tiny green plastic containers forever. So, I'm out dumpster diving for unique planters for them. You know—a glass, a tin—I once found a ceramic dragon. It's amazing what you can find in the garbage. I walk around St. Paul, exploring the neighborhoods. I find the best dumpster diving is in the alleys behind the big mansions on Summit Avenue and the whole Macalester-Groveland neighborhood." Caleb smiled smugly. "I'm building the plants up, nutritionally, and then I'll transplant them and find homes for them. Maybe ring doorbells, knock on doors, run away—leave them like orphans on the steps. I've bought some paint to enhance their containers. It's a process, and I'm into it."

Caleb slid another glance over at James to see his reaction. James had settled down in repose, similar to Caleb, sliding down his chair, legs crossed at the ankles. He nodded as if he were giving it some thought.

"You give off this vibe in class, you know?" James said. "You're sagacious. Do you even notice that half the kids look to you for reassurance after they say something in class? And now I find out you're a little plant lover? I bet you could start a fad."

Caleb opened his mouth and whooped with laughter. He half rolled out of his chair. "Sagacious. What a word. No—I'm not sagacious; how about dopacious?"

They both laughed. James was laughing because he got Caleb laughing, Caleb was laughing because he got James laughing, and then both of them were laughing because they were stoned and happy.

"Potato, po'ta'to," James said stupidly and they both laughed over that.

"Tomato, to'ma'to," Caleb answered when he caught his breath.

James asked Caleb why he chose to move to Minnesota. Caleb said he just twirled a big globe at a library one day and closed his eyes. When it stopped, where his finger touched, he went. James laughed. "Man, that took balls."

They talked for hours. Time flew.

LATER, James stopped by the frat house to get some weed and told Chuck about meeting Caleb.

Chuck said, "Sounds like a bro-crush."

James looked hard at Chuck. "What do you mean?"

"Come on, you've heard guys use that term. It's the thing now, for guys to admit that they met a guy they want to spend time getting to know, you know, like the chicks do." Chuck added, "I didn't mean anything else by it. I'm glad you met a new friend, but I don't like that he sounds smarter than me."

A FEW WEEKS LATER, at Spooner's, Caleb asked James if he liked jazz. James had listened to Louis Armstrong and Ella Fitzgerald and a few others, but he admitted he didn't know much about jazz.

Caleb said Ernestine Anderson, who he'd heard in New York, was coming to the Dakota in downtown Minneapolis. James hadn't heard of her or of the Dakota. Caleb said, "Trust me, she's good. She can do soul, blues, jazz—this is going to be a trio, real jazz. You get us some good smoke, and we'll go hear her."

James returned to the frat and asked Chuck if they had any 'really good' smoke, explaining that he wanted to impress Caleb.

"For the bro-crush? Anything, my man," Chuck said, and he

found James something special, all right: marijuana laced with opium.

James and Caleb got stoned in James' car, parked outside of the Dakota. It was such good smoke. They sat in the car for a while, looking straight ahead, enjoying their high, until James said, "My God, that's a long walk," and they headed into the club.

The atmosphere was dark and intimate. People sat at small tables talking quietly. James was surprised to see an older black woman in a satiny dress come onto the small stage and acknowledge the crowds' enthusiastic clapping and whistling. She scornfully asked the crowd "Is this spring in Minnesota? Is this all there is here?" It was a wicked cold day, and she got a chuckle. She turned to her guys and set a beat by nodding her head, and they began—first the bass, then the sax, and then the voice. "Is That All There Is?" she sang.

Ernestine Anderson's voice, exact and harmonious, liquid smoke, was as versatile a musical instrument as the sax and bass. James listened to the vaguely familiar jazz standard and watched people at the other tables enraptured by the music. Someone acknowledged a particularly sweet riff with a groan of encouragement; others nodded to the beat.

James let go and just listened. His senses, his mind, elongated with the sweet sounds. He wasn't just listening to the sound; he was accessing the ingresses of the silence between the sounds. Something quieted within him, and he felt moved beyond the boundaries of his former self.

James marked the night at the Dakota as the night he understood what being high was all about. He credited this dope and jazz with "an access to his soul." He'd drifted into a new plane of consciousness. He paradoxically felt more in control and less in control.

None of the later highs were as mind blowing as 'the wakeup call' at the Dakota, but James had come to believe that getting high enhanced his experience of life. Although he enjoyed smoking with Caleb, his best highs were often alone. Sounds, visions, and compelling ideas flowed.

He believed he'd outgrow drugs sometime, probably by the time he was 25 or 27. He reckoned by then he would be moved on to another life stage, something less stupid than being a college student.

After the Dakota, James started listening to jazz on public radio, late at night, in his darkened room, stoned. He downloaded what he liked and listened to it when he was stoned again and again. He loved the jazz genre—the voice, the progressive instrumentation—fusion, fugue, and crossovers to other musical styles like blues and soul and even some classical.

James bought more of the expensive, opium laced herb to impress Caleb. They also tried grass laced with crank, but neither of them liked the jagged high it gave them. Sometimes they'd get high in Caleb's room in an old brick boarding house. Caleb sat on the floor leaning against his bed, and James slouched on the armchair. They'd listen to music and talk about classes or about the future of the world or chance encounters with women. Caleb's world view was extremely dark, James' less so. Caleb planned to observe and write on the apocalyptic fall of humanity. James wanted to help build a startling new future with recycled materials, garbage from the oceans, alternative energies, fewer people.

James talked about his mom and his second family, the Dahlberg's, and waited for Caleb to reciprocate with stories about his family, too. Caleb peppered James with questions but didn't offer his own family history.

After weeks of one-way sharing about family, James sitting on the floor and Caleb on the chair, James said, "Come on, tell me about your family."

"You want to know about my family? It's like I wasn't really there, but they were the typical, mom, dad, older sister."

"If you weren't with them, were you sent away or something?"

"Not that dramatic. Nobody cared much about me. My pussy dad had his whiny girlfriend; my whiny mom had her pussy boyfriend. Mom and Dad separated by the time I was ten. My sister was older, lucky her, she got out early; I just wandered in and out. It was like I was their punishment.

Mommy would say to Daddy, 'It's your turn—don't you dare tell me you're going out of town. I'm going to send him by taxi, so you better be home.' Then when I was 16, I messed up my knee. I'd just gotten my first job ever, as a courier. I was really looking forward to the job. Busting that knee ruined my life. It's taken years to get past that, but the knee is good now. I'm good now."

James looked down and traced the design on the third-hand Persian rug Caleb had in his room. He knew Caleb was looking at him, waiting for him to say something.

James looked up at Caleb. "Sorry your life sucked," he said. "I bitch about everyone wanting a piece of me, a bite out of me. I'm their candy, licking my face, nuzzling my neck, ugh." He reached up and grabbed at Caleb's stockinged foot and started biting his toes.

Caleb tried to pull away, but James held onto him. He growled and bit his next toe and twisted him onto the floor. Caleb grabbed at James' hair and pulled hard, and James pushed his head into Caleb's arm pit. They grappled on the floor playing, neither wanting to hurt the other. Caleb finally got James in a headlock, and James pretended to choke, groaning and flailing about. Caleb started laughing and tickling. "Gotcha!" he yelled. James turned in his grasp and mimicked kneeing Caleb in the gut.

Then James pulled out of Caleb's grasp and laid flat on the floor. "I give. I give," he said laughing.

Caleb laid flat on the floor too, laughing and shaking his head. "Looney tunes, you be so looney tunes, James Holden." He scrambled onto the chair and roughed up James' hair.

"Feel my pain?" James said.

Caleb laughed again, "I feel your pain. You're a pussy too, just like my family. Loved by two Moms and I didn't get loved by anyone. You are everyone's sweetheart."

"Old women love me," James said, his face twisting. "But I'm not good at dating. How about you?"

"I'm a 'fuck up' with women," Caleb admitted. "I was 'in love,' got her pregnant. When her brothers came after me, I left her high and dry. Ever since, I've picked up loose girls at the bars, one-night stands; that's OK for now."

"That bad business, getting a girl preggers. That's another reason I avoid women, they scare me. Some of them want to get pregnant I hear. Did you think that you might have been set up by her?"

"Damn it, James—I be the man." Caleb stood and thumped his chest. "It is always the man's fault—got it?"

"But you go to bars? What about those women?"

"I go back to their places, and they don't even know where I live, but I'm careful. I don't drink much, and I don't go home with drunk women, either. I pick up older, responsible looking… Hey, I've only done it twice."

They both laughed.

I haven't gone to the bars much, never picked up anyone," James admitted. "I want a woman in the worst way, but I want to skip the 'getting to know you' thing. How does that happen? Why can't a woman just appear out of nowhere and sweep me off my feet?"

"Ever had a woman?" Caleb asked.

"If you're asking if I'm a virgin, I'm not. I had one taste of what it could be like. I had sex with Sandra's daughter, Laurel, once. Growing up, Sandra, my second mother, acted as if I was one of her children. When Laurel started flirting with me, Sandra got so mad at her. Chuck saw it when I wasn't there. Sandra doesn't know the truth; no one knows it happened, but Laurel and I got it on, once, years after we had quit flirting with each other. I was just out of high school and she was probably twenty-one. There was a big party at her house, it was right before she got married! The folks were gone, and she got drunk and was really pissed at her fiancé."

Caleb just shook his head. "Why was she marrying someone and having sex with you?"

James shook his head, too. "We were drunk, she was mad at the dude, she fucked me to fuck him over, end of story." James raised his pointer finger. "Except," he said. "Except, she fucked me over as much as she ever did him. She hasn't looked at me since." James shook himself out of his mood, jumping up to show off his biceps. "I'm Antman," he shouted.

THEY HANDLED the stronger smoke better as they used it more frequently and started walking to bars to listen to music or driving to small theaters to watch independent films. James and Caleb spent time together until classes were out and Caleb went back to New York for the summer. He was going to try to be a bike courier again. He planned to be back at Augsburg the first part of September.

10 / JAMES FINDS RANDALL

After the cookout, James stopped by Spooner's several times a day for a week looking for Randall. He was down to his last dredges of the weed. He finally registered for classes after his mother called and reminded him that she was still paying for his tuition and books. Good, he thought, she can pay. She's the one who wants me to do this. Chuck helped him move the big items: table, desk, futon, and two armchairs he'd found at a secondhand store near Grand Ave.

He took Willow to the movies for their second date. The date went smoothly until the goodbye.

They parked at James' favorite lot with the view of the river. Willow wordlessly pushed away from a clumsy grope to her right breast on James' part. Still, she held his offending hand after the incident and leaned over for more kisses before she suggested that he take her home. She hopped out of the car as soon as James parked it at her house. She got out and didn't even look back at him as she trotted to the door.

James sat with a twisted set to his mouth, watching her half dance to her door. She wasn't making this easy on him. Was he supposed to ask for permission before touching parts of her body? He didn't know.

ON SUNDAY, James readied himself for a pastry run to Spooner's. It was raining, but he wanted pastries with a good cup of French roast using his new single cup server.

The expense of living in an apartment surprised James. He'd gone through nearly half of the $10,000 from his savings account in three weeks. The $10,000 plus a few thousand from his summer job was supposed to last the whole academic year, and he was burning through it. The handsome retro armchairs cost $250 a piece.

If he found the dope he wanted, it would cost hundreds for a month or two's supply, depending on how much of the stash would be straight marijuana and how much would be laced with opium. How much of his stash would Caleb be smoking? He hoped Caleb would buy his own dope this semester.

Throwing on jeans, t-shirt, running shoes, and a light hooded rain jacket, he stepped outdoors. The rain wasn't cold yet, but the air had a seasonal tangy dead leaf smell to it. He looked for 'Help Wanted' signs in business windows as he ran to Spooner's.

Entering Spooner's, stomping and shaking rain off his jacket, James gazed around the weather darkened coffee house and recognized Randall Sagan, slumping over a tall mug in a back booth. Seeing how wasted Randall looked, James rushed up, crossing his arms like a railroad warning sign. "Don't get up for me," he laughed. "Looks like you are crashing."

Randall looked up with a scowl, but recognizing James, he sat up straighter. "James Holden, isn't it? Chuck told me you went to Augsburg. I did, too, for a couple of semesters." His voice trailed off.

"You weren't sitting here waiting for me, were you?" James teased.

"Of course not," he said. Randall's look turned arrogant. "I don't wait for anyone these days, James. They wait for me."

"Well, I'm glad I found you," James said, lowering his voice. "I'd like to be a customer."

A shadow of a smile passed over Randall's face. "Do you want to sit down?"

James remained standing. "Hey, how would you like to see my new place? It's almost around the corner. I'll buy some pastries and make you a real cup of coffee."

Randall clasped his fingers together and pulled his arms high over his head, stretching from side to side. "Chuck said you hung out here. I'm surprised we haven't run into each other."

James looked around the big room. "Yeah, I guess neither of us are very observant."

"I am," Randall said. Then he put a finger to the side of his nose and with a quick sniff said, "Want to get high?"

"Your wish is my command," James answered with a slight bow. James selected a few pastries, and they walked out of Spooner's together.

Randall pointed out his ride.

"You got a Lexus?" James nodded his approval. "This is a good-looking car."

Randall nodded and rushed between raindrops to his car. James waited for the sound of his door unlocking and jumped in.

James asked, "Can you find 1824 W Currant?" Randall nodded.

"Still smells new, doesn't it?" Randall said. "It's a smooth, comfortable drive, and it doesn't create a lot of attention from the wrong kind of people. It's a middle-aged professional's car."

James felt the soft tan leather of the interior. "Chuck said that you were dealing, but I didn't know it was this lucrative."

"It's as lucrative as you want to make it James, my boy. The marijuana market is still excellent. It's in flux, of course, with all of this legalization shit happening, but with our line of additives we're able to outdo and undercut the legal shit. But there are other revenue sources in my business. You have to diversify, like any business. I'm gaining capital, and I don't plan to be dealing drugs into my thirties. Oh, I'll probably launder money, keep my hand in that profitable cookie jar."

James was all ears, excited to be getting the low down on drug business.

"What's this about you locking up the frat house?" James asked. "Is that what you do? Capture a market here and there?"

Randall lifted his eyebrows, tilted his head at James and nodded, acknowledging James' smart response. "That's part of it. I've got a market at a number of campuses in the Twin Cities. That has been my bread and butter. As long as you stay on your own side of the street, provide a good product, you can do well with very little hassle from the authorities; it's hardly a felony for selling small amounts anymore. The risk isn't that big, and the money grows on trees."

"I guess I never really thought about it as a legitimate business with smart young people at the top. Here we are, at my place. Park in front of the porch, and we will go around to the back."

"I'll tell you more about business some time. Are you interested?"

James surprised himself by nodding "Yes."

Randall walked into James' place and looked around. "Nice floors. I like the kitchen area. What does a place like this cost?"

James lied a little. "Nine-hundred and I get a parking place in back."

"Good price if it's with utilities. It's got good light and some privacy, awfully small though," Randall commented.

Randall, the Egg, James thought. What an arrogant son of a bitch. "Choose a place to sit, the rocker or the armchair."

Randall plopped down on the comfortable armchair, one leg up on an arm, "Make yourself a cup of coffee. I'm still working on this latte, and I'm not quite ready to eat anything. I partied last night. Coke keeps you going like the bunny energizer." He gave his genitals an admiring feel. "Chauncey 'rented' me his new girl, not far from here in fact. We went to her room at the Day's Inn and fucked for hours. She knew her business all right. Chauncey is training her right."

"A pro?" James had gotten up and was standing by his coffee maker, half turned to listen to Randall. He thought of the women he'd seen on the street, the tall young girl.

"Yes, a pro, but like I said, she's young, and Chauncey cleaned her up good for me—stilettos, nice dress, black lacy Victoria Secret underneath—you get the picture. I wore a twenty-dollar lamb's skin rubber; I went through four of them last night. I'm not going to get some disease and lose my dick over a fuck, that's for sure."

James thought about the girl he had seen on the street. He wondered if she wore Victoria Secret. He hadn't heard dirty talk like this since high school. It didn't offend him, and it didn't turn him on. It was just juvenile.

"So, you want to get high? Looks like you're toking on the roaches," Randall said, nodding at the ashtray on the table.

"That's how close I am to being out of smoke. That's the end of my roaches. Feel sorry for me?"

Randall shook his head.

James continued. "I'd love to try out what you have. I like my reefer, but what else do you have with you?"

"I don't have any reefer. Do you like heroin?"

James looked amazed at Randall. "You use heroin?"

"It's the way to even out after a cocaine binge. It brings you down gently. Want to try some?" Randall was already reaching into his pocket and pulling out a folded foil.

"Heroin? It's the word! That's the big leagues." James heard that tons of people were giving it a try; kids got hooked on it back in high school. People died of overdoses on the News all the time.

"I suppose you've heard some of the press," Randall said. "They say it is as addictive as sin. It's a sin, they say, just like they said about Marijuana in the 1950s. But it's not true. The majority of users aren't addicted. You only hear about the idiot addicts."

"That's the thing about drugs; either you use them or they use you. You have to be the boss. I have fun with coke, a little heroin, maybe once a month. Oh, I might do a line or two of coke if I'm really stressed, but that doesn't happen often. I'd rather party like I did last night and be done with it for a while, for weeks. I've been using it, not abusing it for years."

James didn't want Randall to see him 'hemming and hawing.' Would it do any harm to give it a try? He turned back to the counter and watched the coffee pouring into his mug. His hand shook as he added cream. He looked at the mug he'd purchased when he bought the coffee machine. A big yellow mug with a smiley face. He felt a tug in his insides, almost nausea. Then again, life is short. He might never get another chance to try heroin. Yesterday he was excited about shopping for a coffee maker; today he was trying heroin. His hand was steadier now.

By the time he sat down in the rocker, Randall had pulled James' end table in between them and had laid out four lines of powder on a little mirror. Randall leaned over and sniffed two lines quickly through a rolled $100 bill.

He offered the other two lines to James.

"Go ahead—have a couple of lines. You'll like it." James took the bluish $100 bill. It felt stiff and reminded James of play money or foreign currency.

The powder hit his sinuses, and James sneezed. He sniffed in a few times and his sinuses settled down. He snorted the other line and waited. It didn't take long before the dope hit his head with a gentle jolt. His head swelled like a balloon and then that changed and he relaxed, relaxed, relaxed.

So, this was heroin. James looked around. It's all here, he thought, shiny and bright.

"Hey, my man," he said out of a deep tunnel somewhere in his head. "I like this high."

After a while, James was aware Randall was talking; his voice was part of the background, soothing to James. James nodded at Randall and went back into his high.

Slowly, he came back from wherever he'd been and looked at Randall in astonishment. "How long was I gone? Was it forever?"

"Not long. You're enjoying your little morning high."

"I'm gone, really gone," James said. "I'm sorry."

After what seemed like hours, James mumbled, "Do you want that coffee and a pastry now?"

"I have to get moving. I got a stop to make and then I'm taking a long nap. I go see my folks for dinner tonight, and I don't want to look as wasted as I feel."

From a faraway tunnel in his head, James said, "I'd like to be a customer. Can I buy some reefer?"

"I don't have any on me—I told you that," Randall said. "But here, take the foil, the rest of the heroin." He picked up the foil and tossed it closer to James. "Have some fun. Let's meet at the coffeehouse on Thursday. Are you free?"

"Sure—when are you going to be there?"

"Sometime late afternoon, wait there for me. I'll bring you some smoke."

He walked by the nodding James into the bathroom. He closed the door, checked his medicine cabinet (nothing interesting there), and snorted a finger of coke from a vial in his pocket. Goddamn it, he thought, I have to get moving!

Randall walked out of James' place without saying goodbye, berating himself for his unprofessional behavior. He had to take care of business today. Someone on his team hadn't called in and the cover guy couldn't make the first pick-up. Randall was forced to do a hospital pick-up himself. He was due there in less than an hour. He hopped into his car, checked both ways, and drove off slowly. One of the rules he drilled into his crew was never work stoned. "You'll get there on time," he told himself, then added, "Don't speed." Damn he was tired, tired and stoned.

These pickups were part of Randall's new revenue source. It was a tremendous opportunity afforded to him by one of the bosses as a reward for doing well with his other product lines: marijuana, designer drugs, and heroin. But there was no room for error in this business. The bosses were dangerous, more dangerous than law enforcement. Randall could lose more than his business if he failed the bosses; his life could be on the line.

The new revenue source was simplicity itself. Randall's team was staffed with hospital employees and drug users. They filled out regular applications and were usually recommended for the job by one of the current members of the team. The application was similar to any application for a mid-level job. Applicants had to be in a position to know the protocols for collecting and disposing unused and expired opioids. The applicant needed to be able to describe the facility's protocols for giving medication and how placebos could be exchanged for opioids. To keep the job, they needed to be able to provide a minimum of a couple hundred pills a week.

Middle class people loved pills. The usual history was an injury or chronic pain. Nothing worked like opioids for chronic pain. But big pharms' pushers, prescription writing physicians, were being watched these days. Customers weren't satisfied with the knock off pills from Mexico and other sources. If they got good pills, even half good pills, they'd pay up to $50 a pill. Randall had a growing number of health facilities, extended care facilities, and hospitals in regular rotation.

The bosses, who were arranged in a number of tiers above Randall, got nearly half of Randall's take. He paid his dealers out of his take, but because the profit margins were huge, Randall could afford to pay the bosses and his dealers and still make a good profit.

If he could advance another tier, he would be in the rarified air of the low risk profit makers. In the meantime, Randall needed good middle men and dealers. Finding and keeping them kept Randall busy.

Dealers faced tremendous risks. The risk of incarceration was not the highest on the list. The highest risk was addiction, then came the risks of violence from clients and other dealers.

Randall hated doing these exchanges himself. He was breaking another rule of business. He was several rungs removed from the hospital employees. If they ever met him, it was under his assumed name, Jay. The first rule was absolute secrecy about the players above your own rank.

Randall's thoughts kept coming back to James. He knew James. They both had roots in St. Louis Park. He assumed James worshipped him. James and Chuck were smart and careful and not addicts. James would be someone Randall could use. James seemed to be interested in the business. Randall could tell James was already interested in several of the products.

AFTER RANDALL LEFT, James headed for bed. When he finally woke up, it was mid-afternoon. He felt good, relaxed, but for some reason he wanted to call his mother. He called her while still sprawled out on the bed.

"Hi Mom—it's me. Do you miss me?"

"Yes, James. I do."

James cleared his throat. "Mom, I'd like to do some laundry tonight at your place. It's been over two weeks, and I'm getting grungy."

"I'd love that, and, son, it is still 'our' home. Come for dinner? There is a new Sherlock Holmes on Mystery tonight. How does salmon, mashed potatoes, and salad sound?"

"Great—I'll be there about 6."

James called Willow next, and she answered on the third ring. "James, hey there."

"Hey there yourself. How's your weekend been? You had dance classes yesterday, right? I thought about stalking you and then accidentally bumping into you again."

"If you'd 'bumped into me', I might have had to show you a couple Taekwondo moves I know."

"I thought you were the Tai Chi type." They both laughed. He was right, she loved Tai Chi. She was pleased he remembered that about her. They were getting to know more about each other, and talking came easier.

"Do you like riding bikes?" James asked Willow, thinking about how he'd brought his bike from home.

"Do I like to bike ride? I can still do corners without hands." Willow bragged.

"I want to see it. What's your schedule? Are you free tomorrow? I don't know the paths around here. Can you give me a tour of the neighborhood?"

"I've lived in this neighborhood my whole life; I can give you a tour."

James' tone changed. "Hey, I love your voice, Willow, the way you say my name. You're one sexy chick."

"James," she warned. "I want to be sexy to you, but I want us to get to know each other. You don't need to tell me I'm sexy; I know that."

That put a hitch in his gait. "I'm teasing, Willow. I don't want to offend you."

"Maybe I should hang up on you."

But they kept talking. Willow absently played with colored clips at her desk, James playing with a hair band he'd found under his pillow.

JAMES PARKED IN FRONT, found the door unlocked, and walked in. "Mom, I'm home," he yelled out.

"I just got home myself," Ellen said as she came in from the bedroom hall with a big smile for her son and they gave each other a little hug.

"What have you been up to this weekend?" he asked.

"I went to brunch and the arboretum with a new friend. I'm trying to become a social butterfly."

"Who is the friend?" he asked, looking toward the kitchen and basement staircase, eager to get his laundry started.

"Her name is Carmen, a new acquaintance, a social worker. We attended a conference together this fall and noticed each other. She suggested we go to the arboretum before the fall flowers fade."

James was impressed. "You actually made a date with her? Too bad she isn't a guy, then I'd be really excited."

"Oh, she's fun—she has the best sense of humor. Maybe you'll meet her someday."

James searched her face. "I'm glad you have a new friend. Kind of like me meeting Caleb?" Ellen nodded.

"How has your week gone, James? Have you registered for classes?"

"Yes—classes start a week from tomorrow. I've only got one more week of vacation. I'm glad I walked off the stupid job—oops," he said, putting a hand over his mouth. "I didn't tell you that, did I?"

"I assumed you had at least talked to them about leaving. That is irresponsible, to walk off a job you've had for three summers." Ellen thought for a moment and decided not to confront his lying as well as his irresponsibility. "Are you looking into getting a part time job closer to where you live?"

"I've been offered a job tutoring if I want to take it," he lied. "Or maybe I'll start selling cell phones with my friend Randall."

"Randall? I haven't heard you talk about a Randall. You mean working at a kiosk somewhere?"

"No—this is something else. I'm not sure the logistics of it, but there are bunches of start-up mobile companies now that the government broke up the monopoly on the phone business." He made all this up as he talked. "Randall is a guy that Chuck and I know from way back in middle school. He is making a bundle selling these cell phones. He said he might need some help."

"Well, as long as it all is legal. Be careful not to get into a scheme where you have to put money into the business or where you work on straight commission, schemes where the guys on top make all the money and the little guys take all the risk."

How did you get so smart, Mom, James wondered? He'd been thinking about working for Randall, and what would be the risk? If he could make sure he wouldn't have to hold drugs or meet customers, it would be an easy way to make some money. Drugs are a growth industry; he knew that much.

James and Ellen had a pleasant evening eating and watching PBS Mystery while James folded his clothes. James was antsy to go home and try one more line, this time listening to jazz.

PART 2

LIFE GOES ON AMID THE OPIOIDS

11 / JAMES AND CALEB GET HIGH

James enjoyed Monday's long bike ride with Willow. They both could handle busy city streets as well as the hilly intricate trails in cloistered Fort Snelling Park where white stucco barracks from WWI still stood at an old man's attention among ball fields and a small golf course. All attractions vied for views of the roiling waters where the Mississippi met the equally impressive Minnesota River. James remembered bike rides and cross-country skiing there with his mother when he was a kid; Willow rode there with school-mates and her papa.

After Snelling Park, they stopped at the Mississippi Co-op, bought take out delicacies, and ate picnic style on the banks of the Mississippi River, sharing plastic forks. They leaned against each other, nudging each other, and ended up throwing bits of uneaten pita at each other before being overrun by a flock of geese.

Wednesday, James lolled around, took a run and showered, and laid back on the futon, thinking about a nap. But suddenly he sat back up—he was still completely out of marijuana and antsy. He thought about how complicated his life had gotten. Dating Willow was different than he'd hoped. They'd had three dates, but still she didn't fall into his arms. There was some chemistry between the two of them, but she was standoffish. Why hadn't the sex thing just fallen into place?

Finding Randall was more than he expected. He had to admit the heroin was exciting, but it couldn't be a regular thing. He told himself it could not be a substitute for marijuana. Randall made the drug business sound profitable and easy, but was it safe?

Caleb was supposed to be back from New York, but James hadn't heard from him. Way down the list was starting classes next week; James didn't want to think about classes. He'd see Randall again tomorrow. He decided to text both Caleb and Willow.

To Willow: "Thinking about you, but then, I'm always thinking about you."

To Caleb: "Are you back in town? I'm living in town, on my own, and I want to show you my place."

Willow texted him right back: "Keep your dirty thoughts to yourself, James. Ha, ha, ha."

"Movies on Friday? I'll pick you up, maybe meet old Gram?"

"It's on, but pick me up at work about 6 p.m. I'm not ready to get my nosy folks involved."

James texted a thumbs-up.

Caleb called instead of texting back. His voice was rushed. "Hi, I'm back. That's great news about you moving out, James. I knew you had to get away from your mom's place. I'm half-crazy from splitting time between my mother and my dad's places all summer. Surprise! They both missed me and wanted to spend 'quality time.' I worked the summer courier job, and my knee held up great. I got strong legs, superhero legs."

"Sounds good Caleb, but I have to tell you, I like living alone, having this place. Everything is turning around for me. Lots of things are happening. Want to come over and see it? I've got something for you to try. Oh, I met a girl, too. We're dating—three dates—can you believe it?"

"Can I share her?"

"Shut up, man. She's solid."

"And are you solid? Tell me where, when, and how to get to your place."

"You can walk over. I have my bike if you ever want to use it. My place is less than a mile from you. Come on over now, if you want to.

Two hours later, Caleb walked into James' place, grinning. "I was trying to visualize the kind of place you would find." He looked the place over. "This is much better than I imagined. You said it was small, but it's plenty of space. In New York, this would be going for mega moolah."

"Yeah—I'm kind of proud of the place. Do you like the chairs I got at your second-hand store?"

"I'll comment after I try them."

"Sit in the arm chair; it is the guest chair. Want some coffee? I've got a little Keurig; I'll make you a good cup."

They sat with their mugs of coffee with cream, both leaning on their knees with their elbows. Caleb asked about the girlfriend. James thought a minute before speaking. "Willow's an exotic dark princess, but her name is Scandinavian, and her dad is Mexican American, but he isn't her biological dad. She is smart, starting at the U, and she is into dancing, like big time dancing, not pole dancing."

Caleb laughed and nodded. "Is it casual?"

James shrugged. "All new to me. We're moving kind of slow; I think she is ah, well, inexperienced, if you know what I mean. God, what should I do? Really, I'm lost."

"Relax, James. Let her lead on the sex. If you relax, hug, enjoy her, it will turn her on. It'll come naturally. She sounds real."

"That's what I'm doing, going slow," James said. "Didn't even kiss her on the last date. I was letting her think about that."

James' knees started to jangle, so did Caleb's. James was thinking about Willow but also thinking about getting high. He thought Caleb probably wanted to get high, too. They always got high together.

"Do you like this sound track?" James asked. He'd put on some tunes he knew Caleb liked.

Caleb nodded.

James wanted to be cool like Randall had been. He brought out a piece of glass he had found at a construction site nearby and laid the foil of dope on it. "I got something from a friend. Well, he's not really a friend, not like you, my man. It's a guy I knew way back in junior high. Chuck said he'd run into him at the frat house. His 'franchise' whatever that means, supplies drugs to the fraternities at the U. Anyway, Chuck said I might run into him at Spooner's, and I did. He came over and turned me on to what he had. He is way connected now, a supplier. This is the real deal, heroin."

James thought Caleb would be excited. Instead, Caleb put his head back against the headrest and got quiet. His eyes were moving back and forth; he was thinking and chewing the inside of his cheek.

James had never seen Caleb look, what? Scared? It shook James up. He was wondering what he had done wrong. Was this a bigger deal than he thought?

"What's wrong man? I didn't mean to offer you anything you don't want. It's no big deal if you don't want to get high. It's OK with me." James put the mirror down against a leg of the coffee table and the foil back in his pocket.

Caleb's lips pressed together, so tight his mouth paled. He was sure doing some heavy thinking. James waited, wanting to give him time to think through what he had to say.

"I've had some history with opioids; I never told you," Caleb said. "It started when I broke my knee. I got a load of pain medication, got into some stuff, some oxy. It took the pain away, all the pain. Then I was stupid and re-injured the knee, more opioids, of course. I wanted more than I could get and then I had to start buying it from the streets. I stole, too, faked a robbery and stole my mother's jewelry. They found me out and sent me to treatment.

Last year, I did a lot of thinking about whether I was really addicted. We smoked a lot last spring, and I didn't get into craving for marijuana this summer. I didn't use once in New York this summer—even though I was stressed by family shit. I think I'm OK if I keep my rule: Don't buy drugs.

I'd like to get high with you, but again, I won't be able to pay you back. I am not going to start buying shit."

James thought how Randall had talked to him about heroin, how Randall said 'either you use the drugs or the drugs use you,' how Caleb seemed to have a plan on how to use drugs without them using him.

James said, "Be straight with me. Tell me if this could cause you a problem later on—I don't want either of us to get into something that is going to cause us problems down the line."

"I'm not hiding anything from you. I don't want you to think I just hang out with you because you get me high. I'd like to try this, James, but I'm not going to keep doing it."

"Hey, I'm glad to share what I have with you, but I don't want to get you into any addiction. If you're not sure you can handle drugs, don't do it. You know what I'm saying?"

"I'm not worried about handling drugs. We were smoking opium in our joints sometimes, weren't we? As long as I don't buy anything, I'll be fine. I just want you to see the whole picture. Do you understand where I'm coming from?"

"I guess so. Well, do you want to try this stuff or not?"

"Hell, yes I want to try it. Let's do it."

James laid down the lines like Randall had done for him and gave Caleb a clean rolled twenty. Caleb drew hard and sniffed then snorted the other line. He gave the bill back to James and closed his eyes, coming home to something he loved. James followed him into that void.

Sometime later, dusk, James turned on a few soft lights and brought out snacks, and they munched and talked quietly. They talked about ordinary life; they were students preparing for a new semester. They were going in different directions. James was questioning his choices, not entirely sure the 'Discipline' of engineering was the right choice for him, but he'd put so much into it already. Caleb was excited about getting into several writing classes his sophomore year. He'd be able to write short stories, several a week, and he wanted to fold them together into something larger.

It was like they'd talked yesterday instead of three months ago. They listened to each other. Caleb's thoughts stretched James' intellect. Caleb appreciated that James could follow his abstractions and see application for his ideas.

They didn't talk about being high. The high lived separately inside them, rubbing and purring against their legs and moving up their bodies as if it was alive within them.

When Caleb started shuffling around, getting ready to leave, James separated the left-over powder in the foil and put half of it into a foil packet for Caleb to take.

Caleb took it and laughed. "You're saving me from myself?" he said and pocketed it.

12 / JAMES STARTS WORKING FOR RANDALL

James waited for Randall at Spooner's, at a small table in the back on Thursday as planned. He sprawled out on his chair, watching the lone students with buds in their ears, long hair over their eyes, writing like mad on their iPads. Is that me, he wondered, or have I changed? James felt more like a risk taker now. When Randall finally showed up, dressed like a young business exec, he didn't have the marijuana that he had promised.

Randall had all the power, the drugs, and James was pissed and hissed at Randall. "What do I need to do to get some marijuana? Will you help me out or not, Randall?"

"I'd like to meet you again on Sunday morning. I'll stop by your place."

"OK, but will you have some marijuana then?"

"I'll have marijuana for you, and I'll have a proposition for you."

"Is it dealing? I don't want to do that."

"It's not dealing. I'll drop by your place on Sunday, 9AM? I might have something I need you to do for me on Sunday afternoon."

"I need to know what you want me to do before I can commit to doing it," James said.

"Trust me on this, James. If you don't like the work, fine, maybe I can find something else for you."

"Can you tell me a little more about what I would be doing, so I can think it over?"

"I have a meeting, been waiting to hear from the brass almost all afternoon. There might be a shake-up in the business. We'll talk Sunday. I'm sorry about the marijuana, but here take this on me." Randall handed him another foil. "It's called 'brown sugar.' It's good Mexican stuff, better than what I gave you."

With a handshake, Randall was gone, and James was left holding the foil.

ON SUNDAY, RANDALL WAS AT JAMES' place on time. He was wearing dress pants and a sports jacket and carrying a briefcase.

James answered his door and motioned for him to sit down.

"Want a mug of coffee?" he asked.

"Why not," Randall said. "You have cream?"

"Half and half—why are you so dressed up?"

Randall walked over to the oak table and picked up the cat-like salt and pepper shakers, shaking a little salt out. "Remember my sister, Andrea? Wasn't she in your class? She got married yesterday. Today there is a brunch, opening the gifts. I have to be there by noon."

James shrugged. "I didn't know many of the girls in my class. She was out of my league." James smiled to himself. He did remember Andrea, and she was in a clique that didn't interest him. They tried for 'valley girls,' and could have been a vision on a screen —she was that two dimensional and unapproachable.

"Do you have a girlfriend?" James asked.

Randall pocketed the salt and pepper shakers and studied James. "What's with all the questions?"

"Just wanting to know you." He thought Randall had talked nasty about women last Sunday. He wondered if Randall even liked women. James noticed Randall put the salt and pepper shakers into his pocket but decided he'd just let Randall's action play out.

"Dating women? What can I say about it? I'm a drug supplier, right? Maybe I'll be rich someday. Then, when I quit dealing, maybe I'll get married and have a family like everyone else. I can't be with any woman I would want to marry now. I get it on with women who want to party, to get high. We recognize each other at the clubs. But one way or the other, you end up paying for those women, too. I have a list of names. Then, once in a while, I use a street prostitute—the young ones are fun."

James wondered, again, how that would feel, paying for sex. "Where do you live?"

"I've got a duplex off of Grand Avenue. But remember you never come around unless I invite you, understand?"

James nodded.

Randall continued. "OK, let's get down to business. I'm offering you a courier job. Want to hear about it?"

"I have to tell you, I'm scared. It's happening too fast."

"Put your big boy pants on, James. If you're careful, there will be no problem, got it?"

James nodded.

"Remember last Sunday? I had to leave and do a pick-up because the courier didn't show up. That courier not only failed me, he also ran off with a batch of pills and a lot of money. The boss blames me. I failed him. I have to pay the boss's take for that day out of my own pocket. Further, the boss wanted me to put a hit out on the courier, but I'm not ready to get anyone killed. See how serious this business is? I need to replace that courier with someone I trust. I want your help James."

James felt fear raise the hairs on his forearms. He blew air out of his cheeks and rubbed his arms, then asked, "What would I have to do?"

"It's simple. You exchange opioids for money with a staff person at a medical facility. Then you put the packets of opioids into a keyed large mailbox at the main post office. I'll give you a key to the mailbox. We change mailboxes often; it's super safe."

Using his fingers, Randall enumerated the rules:

1. Never give the name of any of us, including your name, to anyone you meet. Don't talk to or acknowledge the guys giving you the packages.
2. Never be high or hung over when you're working.
3. Always wear light colors, beige, grey, a loose jacket, a reversal jacket is best, and a cap. No insignias.
4. Absolutely trust your instincts; if it doesn't feel right, walk away.

"If you tell anyone my name, I'll have to kill you," Randall said seriously, looking hard at James until James got a serious look on his face. "I probably wouldn't kill you, but that's the way all the bosses talk. Remember my code name is Jay."

James almost laughed at the 'reversal jacket,' but he kept a straight face. This is a movie, he thought. I'll just play my role.

Then Randall opened his briefcase and pulled envelopes out, and it wasn't a movie anymore.

"Here, this is yours." Randall handed the first envelope over to James.

"Give me back one of your hundreds." James handed him a hundred-dollar bill.

Randall opened another compartment of the briefcase, put the bill in it, and pulled out a tightly wrapped parcel of marijuana. The warm light brown flowers inside the parcel were covered with an oily resin. James' eyes widened.

"Is this as good as it looks?" he asked.

Randall nodded and dug out three more envelopes. "One for each drop. Your contacts have already texted; everything is a 'go' for today's meets.

James nodded numbly.

"OK, first St. Ann's Residence." James knew exactly where it was.

"Go to the Walgreens around the corner at exactly 12:00 p.m. The men's room has two stalls and a urinal. Make sure no one is in the first stall. Rap on the second stall and say: 'one, two, three.' The other guy answers the same way. He'll lift the package over the stall, and you grab hold of the package, passing the envelope of money over the stall. That's it, the exchange."

"Can I write this down?" James asked.

"No. Don't act like an idiot, James."

"Ready for number 2?" Randall asked.

"Are you asking me to poop in the stall?" James asked.

Randall laughed and pretended his finger was a gun pointed at James' heart. "POW," Randall said and blew on his finger.

"St. John's Hospital in Bloomington, know it?"

James nodded 'yes,' again, numbly.

"Unisex handicapped bathroom on the second floor by the cafeteria entrance, 2 p.m. Wait until no one is in the corridor then rap on the door three times. He'll rap back three times. You rap back, again, three times. He'll open the door; you hand over the envelope, and he'll hand over the package. Slip it inside your jacket."

"What comes next?" James asked.

"3:30 at the Pinehurst facility out north of City. Rd. C and 280?"

"That one's unfamiliar."

"It's huge, limestone, four stories—you can't miss it. Circle around to the back, and you'll see a sign, Lot C, Employees only. In the end corner of the lot look for a Red Rav4, one of those cars with a spare tire on the back. Drive by and wave if you see a big woman eating her lunch. If all is fine, she will wave back. Pull up next to her, and roll down your window."

Randall laughed at the confusion on James' face, "Ok, write notes on a scrap of paper. Eat it when you're done."

James gave him a dark look but went to his desk for a pencil and a scrap of paper. He wrote down what he was afraid he would forget. Randall grabbed the slip of paper, read James' notes, nodded, and returned them.

"Did you try the brown sugar?" Randall asked.

"I just finished the other stuff, gave some to my best friend."

"You say where you got it?" Randall asked.

"Of course not," James lied. "I'll never use your name."

"Good. I have to get going now. If you do well, I'll show you how to party. We'll have a real party." Randall reached into another pocket of the briefcase. "Here is your burner cell and your mailbox key. Keep the key somewhere in the trunk of your car, off of your key ring. Keep the phone on your person, take it to the bathroom when you shower. I've programmed two numbers, J (me) and D. D is lead coordinator on this new pharmaceutical business. He's worked for me for years. If the cell rings, always answer ASAP. When you're done with the pick-ups, go home and call D. You, by the way, are T. When you call D, just say 'T is done' and press off."

James wrote a quick note. "Got it. But one more thing about my friend, the guy I shared the heroin with. He goes to Augsburg, too. I just wanted you to know that."

"If he is a stand-up guy, great, it's your dope. But no names, now, you hear me?"

James nodded yes.

Randall turned away from the door and started walking

through the apartment. "Do you have privacy? Where is the landlord?"

"He is right next door, lives with a woman, but I can't even hear them having sex or talking. The guy said not to bother him with little things and that he would give 24 hours' notice before going into my place."

Randall looked around for a hiding place for James. He pulled the futon away from the wall and pushed aside James' small dresser. Then he headed for the bathroom. James could hear him whip open the shower curtain, open the vanity.

He told James to come into the bathroom. "Keep the heroin out of sight; hide it behind the toilet—stick the foil up from the bottom, between the tank and the wall. Don't worry about hiding marijuana, but keep the strong stuff where no one is going to look. Don't leave any tattle tale marks." James nodded.

"Call D if anything goes wrong. Just say, 'T's asking you to call,' and he'll call you back on another phone."

Randall finally left, James shouting out to him, "Keep the salt and pepper shakers."

He realized he had to hurry. It was almost eleven. He had an hour until his first meet.

Driving to his first meet, James tried to put his fear behind him. But his mouth was so dry he started to cough. Then he realized he was driving like a 16-year-old kid, he was jerking along the freeway. He fretted the afternoon away, feeling self-conscious and acting self-conscious, making his drops.

James was back to his place from the post office close to 5:30 p.m. and he remembered to leave the cryptic phone message for D: "This is T. I'm done."

He was cold, and he wanted to feel warm and clean again. He

ripped off his clothes and headed for a long shower. Then he remembered he needed to call his mother and bow out of his plan to have dinner and watch more TV with her tonight. He put his robe on and called her.

"Hi son," Ellen answered. "I'm at Sandra's. I'm just about ready to come home and start our supper. Ralph and Chuck are at a Twins game, extra innings, we're listening on the radio but mostly talking."

"You two getting a little buzz on?" James teased.

In fact, Sandra and Ellen were finishing a second pitcher of Margaritas, but they were also in the midst of an intimate conversation. Sandra, to her great relief, was honestly admitting the extent of her marriage problems to Ellen. Ellen had listened to the whole gory story of Ralph's infidelity. She was preparing to get honest about meeting someone special (Carmen) when James' call interrupted them.

"Put him on speaker phone," Sandra demanded. "What's this about a new girlfriend, James?" Sandra asked, bending her head down toward the cell phone. "How did you meet? Who is she?"

James took a while to respond. Do I have a girlfriend? He thought about that. Hadn't Randall just told him it didn't work, having a girlfriend and being a dealer? Who am I? He wondered.

"You told Sandra that Willow is a girlfriend?" James accused Ellen. "We are just dating, Sandra, no name calling. But I'll tell you one thing, she is the nicest girl." His heart fluttered and sank. Willow was going to be a good woman, too good for him.

He continued talking to Sandra. "Nothing much has happened between us. We went to the State Fair. She knows the Fair like the back of her hand, just like us. That was fun. Her dad owns Joe's Café; it's a popular Mexican restaurant on University, a couple of blocks off of Dale. She's a waitress there—that's where I met her. She's starting at U of M this fall. She's a dancer and, I got to say it —she's very good looking. But get this—her name is Willow Gunderson-Reyes." James laughed and said, "I can't imagine she is related to your Gunderson's, but maybe somewhere down the line. We've gone out a few times, and she hasn't given up on me yet."

Before Sandra could reply, James said, "Hey, Mom, I'm calling to say I'm beat. I spent the day with Randall; I'm starting to work the cell business. Can we reschedule my visit for next week?"

"Fine—I'll stay here with Sandra until the boys come home. Goodbye James."

13 / CHAR AND SANDRA ARE SISTERS?!

After the call, Ellen put her cell phone in her pocket and looked over at Sandra with a smile on her face. Sandra was ashen.

"What happened?" Ellen said, "Did a ghost walk by and I missed it?" Sandra was staring into space with a horrified expression. Ellen wondered what had ruined Sandra's day; she hadn't had her chance to ruin Sandra's day. Sandra had been so happy; they'd been getting along so well! Was it something James said? Ellen felt sad seeing her friend lose her happy glow. She finished off her margarita, sucked on the last ice cube, and looked sideways at her friend.

With tears in her eyes, Sandra explained. "James' new girlfriend is my great-niece. She's my sister Charlene's granddaughter. You were at my mother's funeral—Charlene had her granddaughter, Willow, with her and her husband, Joe Reyes."

"Oh, my God," Ellen exclaimed. "You're right, that was your sister's granddaughter's name. I love the name, Willow. At the funeral, Charlene did introduce you to her husband and granddaughter. I was watching you and then I kept an eye on them most of the time. Charlene was looking over at you whenever you weren't looking at her. Then she was gone."

"I didn't make the effort to talk to her," Sandra confessed. "I was surrounded with local people who wanted to comfort me, and I took the easy way out. Every time I looked in her direction, she was looking away from me."

"You didn't have much of a chance to talk to her, Sandra. Charlene didn't even stay for lunch after the funeral. She was avoiding you more than you were avoiding her."

"This is too much; I'm going to pray about this." Sandra folded her hands and lifted them up beneath her chin and implored the heavens: "Oh, God, help me!"

"God isn't here—I am," Ellen said, "Talk to me! How did you know Charlene's husband owned Joe's Café?"

"Can you imagine seeing my sister at my mother's funeral after, what? Thirty years incommunicado? I hadn't seen, heard from, or talked to Charlene since I was nine or ten. She never came home after she bolted off following high school graduation. Our brother Denny drove her to the bus, and she left the farm forever. He stays in contact with her, I guess. But he doesn't talk about her to me."

"Why not?"

Sandra looked at Ellen and shook her head. "I'm not ready to talk about it. I need to take a hot bath with candles and essential oils and pray. I'm speechless for once."

Ellen sat silently with her friend for a few minutes and then excused herself.

"I'm sorry, Ellen. Please, just leave, but I'll talk to you tomorrow."

MONDAY AFTER WORK HOURS, Sandra banged on Ellen's door and rattled the knob.

"Yoo-hoo," she yelled. "Where are you?"

"Just a minute," Ellen yelled. She was changing out of her work clothes. She zipped up her jeans and hurried to open the kitchen door. Sandra walked in.

"Do you want a glass of wine?" When Sandra just nodded, Ellen poured them each a tall glass from the refrigerator box.

Sandra paced the small kitchen clutching her wine glass. "I almost called you at work, but I waited, and as soon as I saw your car, I came over."

"Let's sit outside while we can; fall is in the air." Ellen grabbed a cloth to wipe down her deck table, and they sat outside, Ellen looking expectantly at Sandra.

"I bit my tongue to keep quiet after Ralph came home. He shouted at me through the bathroom door, and I told him I was taking a long soak. I was crying. I'm so afraid that Charlene still hates me, and now we're going to be in-laws."

"That's so exaggerated, Sandra. First, two or three dates don't mean marriage." Ellen looked hard at Sandra, who didn't appear to be listening.

"Listen to me," Ellen said in a loud exasperated voice. "How can a ten-year-old sister's fears drive her sister away forever?" Ellen waved her hand in front of Sandra's face. "Stop it Sandra—you're being a drama queen."

Sandra's shoulders dropped, and she finally really looked at Ellen. "OK, I'm a drama queen," she said with tears in her eyes.

"Sandra, keep looking at me; now, listen to me. It was obvious at the funeral that neither of you knew how to approach the other. I was watching you both. Your sister was not looking angry when she snuck a peek at you; she was looking sad."

Sandra nodded. "Well that's how 10-year-old Sandy felt when Charlene didn't even say goodbye to her; she felt sad."

"You two are having a terrible case of emotional impasse. Let's do something—how about casing the restaurant, Joe's Place, right now?" Ellen suggested.

Sandra's eyes got wide, and, slowly, a wild smile spread across her face, "BFF, let's do it. You better drive, or I'll get chicken and just drive by the restaurant as I did before. After Mom's funeral, I was gung-ho about getting reconnected to Charlene. I asked my brother if he had met Joe, and he said he'd even eaten at their café. I drove by it several times but I couldn't summon the courage to go inside."

Ellen headed back into the house. "I better change," she said.

"Just put on your high-end leather jacket. I love you in that jacket."

A look of mutual conspiracy brought grins to their faces.

"I wonder if Charlene works there, too." Ellen speculated from the kitchen door before heading to her closet to find her jacket.

"Wouldn't that be a kettle of fish?" Sandra said. "I'm not ready to casually run into Charlene."

They made a plan as Ellen carefully drove to the cafe. Sandra had memorized the route.

Sandra was surprised how quickly they were getting to the café; part of her wanted to tell Ellen to stop and turn around. She told Ellen, who usually drove too slowly for Sandra's taste, to ease up on the gas pedal. "You peek in and make sure the coast is clear before I go into the place. I'm just saying, I won't go in if Charlene is in there. You don't understand what I did to her—I'm so ashamed!"

"The folks sent her away to Aberdeen, South Dakota to have a baby out of wedlock when she was a junior in high school. I heard my folks talking while she was gone. Charlene was pregnant with a black baby. My dad was outraged at Charlene and angry at my mother, too. I don't know why; I guess Mom wasn't mad enough at Charlene to suit Dad. But how did she get pregnant with a black boy? There weren't any black kids in my grade school. I guess after the baby was born, Charlene held him for two hours before social workers took him away. She came home, cold and distant. I took Dad's side, and when Charlene came home, I spied on her, and I didn't want her to touch me."

"Oh God, Ellen, I've never thought about it and certainly never said it, but I thought she was ruined. She started smoking at the place they sent her. If I caught her smoking, I'd run and tell Mom or Dad. I was only in third grade, but I hated that Mom cried in her room, and Dad seemed mad at all of us. I'm like my dad. You know how mean I can get. I've been mean to you too, haven't I?"

Sandra looked out her window. They were driving in the heart of St. Paul now, down University Avenue, and she was looking out her window at the diversity of people in Minnesota. Here, near downtown St. Paul, people of all colors and ethnicities walked to shops and the light rail and the bus on the busy commercial streets. She spotted two dark-skinned little kids holding the hands of a blond woman. The three swung their arms in union. Sandra's heart cried out for her sister.

Ellen was thinking. Was Sandra a mean person? "I don't think of you as a mean person, Sandra. That was a hard time for your family. Charlene having a black baby out of wedlock in 1970 in rural Minnesota. Your family was reacting to the 1970s community mores. You've changed your attitudes over the years, haven't you?

Sandra looked at Ellen, crossly, out of her red eyes. "I've changed," she said. "But that's who I was, an icky little girl. I'm haunted by my past."

I'll soon find out how much you've changed, Ellen mused, thinking about her own growing relationship with Carmen.

"Remember Charlene's granddaughter at the funeral?" Sandy added. "She had the longest skinny legs and those big dark eyes. She had a lovely brown skin tone; I bet she is a beautiful young woman. The person I am now would love to welcome her into the family. At the funeral, I wanted to get to know the little darling; she was wide-eyed, afraid of all of us strangers. I'm sure she sensed her grandmother's discomfort; I didn't know how to reach out to either Charlene or to Willow. That was one time I didn't act on my instincts. My instinct was to march over and kneel in front of Willow and talk to the child. I'm living my regret for not doing that."

"We are here, Sandra," Ellen said, pointing to the cafe and parking the car on the street nearly in front of the cafe. Wipe your face, and touch up your makeup. Let's get going."

Fifteen minutes later, the two women were peeking in the plate glass window at Joe's. They could see the well-lit interior from the window without creating any attention. It was an informal place, clean and utilitarian. It had wooden booths along the walls and chrome tables with matching black padded chairs in the center. The floors were refinished wood, and the walls were sandblasted bricks. The ceiling still had the original tin tiles.

On a Monday at 6:30, the place was less than half full. Each table had an electronic jukebox with old standards and current popular choices. Someone had chosen to play Ella Fitzgerald singing "Lullaby of Birdland."

An older waitress in a white blouse and black pants waved them in and indicated to seat themselves.

"I can't believe it," Sandra said as they slipped into a booth. "That was one of my sister's favorites when I was a little girl. She taught me the lyrics." Sandra started singing along in her fine alto:

"*Have you ever heard two turtle doves*
Bill and coo when they love?
That's the kind of magic
Music we make with our lips when we kiss".

"Charlene would buss me on the lips after we sang the chorus. You can imagine how a little girl would like that."

"I'm so jealous. I wish I'd had a big sister's love. Look around, Sandra, this is your kind of place. I'm glad we came." Ellen was enjoying everything more these days. She had come to a startling self-revelation, and her dysthymic depression seemed to be lifting.

A young waitress came to their table with a damp terry cloth and was about to wipe down their table. She was close enough to hear Sandra singing along with the chorus of the song. She stopped in mid-motion and stared at Sandra.

Sandra stopped singing. "Am I that bad?" she asked the girl.

"No—you sound like my Gram. It's a special song between us."

Sandra knew immediately that this was Willow. "Is your Grandmother Charlene Gunderson?" Ellen asked.

"How did you know that?" Willow asked.

"This is your great-aunt Sandra," Ellen excitedly pointed at Sandra; Ellen was as excited as Ellen got.

Willow studied Sandra and saw her Gram written all over her, the oval face and round blue eyes, pretty—how pretty she was. She was a younger, heavier, more feminine Gram.

Sandra hoisted herself out of the booth. Getting out of a booth is not easy when you're excited, but she made it out and put her arms around the girl and hugged her tightly, pinning her arms to her sides. Willow struggled a bit, almost pulling away, looking around to see if anyone was staring at them, but then she let go and let her aunt give her the kind of hug she had been getting all of her life, the kind of hug that told her she was loved and protected.

Where have you been? Willow wondered as she gently pulled away.

"I'm so sorry for throwing myself on you; everyone tells me I have no boundaries." Sandra backed away and dropped her arms. "But that song, 'Lullaby of Birdland,' your grandmother sang it to me when I was a little girl. Oh, what a small world this is." Sandra bowed her head. She was ashamed of herself; she hugged so easily, cried so easily. She felt tears forming in her eyes. What a fool she'd been to stay away from this child over pride and a family feud.

"That's OK," Willow said quietly, patting her aunt's arm, her AUNT! "Can I get you salsa and chips?"

Willow's kindness helped Sandra recover some composure, and Sandra smiled teary eyed, giddy with all she was feeling.

Willow turned to Ellen. "Would you like chips and salsa?"

"I'd love chips and salsa, guacamole too?"

Willow nodded. "Of course, I'll be right back. Mild?" she asked.

"Thank you—that would be great," Ellen answered. Willow took another astonished look at Sandra and spun away, all business, but almost running into the kitchen to tell her papa what had just happened.

"What should I do?" Sandra pleaded with Ellen.

"You're doing just fine. She let you hug her, didn't she?"

"I guess so. I'll try not to overwhelm her," Sandra said, wiping the tears from her eyes.

"Just be your loving self. I wish I could jump up and hug people. I wanted to hug her, too."

That helped Sandra. She looked over at Ellen and chuckled. "Isn't she the dearest girl you have ever seen?"

Ellen chuckled. "Yes, she's dear to us, but now don't overdo it. She's not a child. She is a young woman. Here come the chips."

Sandra swiped guacamole onto a chip and put it all in her mouth. She munched and swallowed while Willow looked back and forth at the women, wondering what she should say to them.

"Yum, this tastes so fresh, do you make it all here?" Ellen asked.

"Yes—the chips, guac, and salsa are all made right here."

Sandra scooped salsa and guacamole on another chip and popped that into her mouth, chewing and swallowing. "I love the salsa, too."

"Do you want menus?"

They both nodded, continuing to look at Willow with a

fascination that made her uncomfortable. "I'll get you menus," Willow said with a hesitant smile for her aunt and for Ellen.

As Willow walked away, Sandra whispered to Ellen, "She smiled at me, did you see that?"

"Yes. It's going to be just fine."

After a plate of burritos, black beans and rice, Sandra asked Willow, "Is Joe working tonight?" Willow nodded. "Could you ask him to come over to our table?"

Willow almost ran back to the kitchen. Joe was standing near the swinging half door, discreetly watching his daughter flutter around her great-aunt's table. She had rushed to him as soon as she knew who she was serving and twirled around him, letting him know what was happening. He was thinking how overwhelmed Char would be to know Sandy was here, and he was waiting for an opportunity to greet the women, to let them know how welcome they were.

Joe waltzed over to the table from the kitchen. He smiled at both women. "What an unexpected pleasure!" Joe said. "You're Sandy?"

"I'm your sister-in-law, Sandra Dahlberg. Do you remember me? We met at Mom's funeral, but I was so overwhelmed at the funeral. I didn't really talk to either of you. I am so sorry for that. All I can say for myself is that, well, I'm sorry. I loved all of your food, the combination of cumin and fresh cilantro in the rice, divine." Sandra looked over at Ellen. "This is my BFF as the kids say, Ellen Holden. She was at the funeral, too." Joe and Ellen smiled at each other.

He turned back to Sandra and said, "I don't know if I would have recognized you if Willow hadn't told me who you are, but your beauty is like my wife's. I'm very pleased to have you eating in my restaurant. As far as the funeral, I don't remember Char making much effort to talk to you, either. She was overwhelmed, too, I think. Funerals are hard, all the emotions."

Then Sandra surprised them all by saying, "This has got to stop. Please tell Charlene 'hi' from me and tell her how pleased I am to find you and Willow again. If I can have Charlene's cell number, I will call my sister and tell her myself."

Joe had a wonderful smile full of white teeth and he looked so pleased. He was pleased knowing how Charlene cried on the way home from the funeral as much for losing her sister as for losing her mother.

He turned to Willow and asked if she had the bill and a pen. She did, and he wrote Char's number on the back of the bill.

"Here is the number. Dinner is on Willow and me, right Willow?" He reached over and gave Willow a sideways hug. Willow nodded in agreement.

"Can we bring you anything else? We have great fried ice cream," he said.

Sandra looked at Ellen, who shook her head no. "I guess not," Sandra said, sounding a little disappointed. She looked at Willow. "I can't tell you how happy I am that we finally met again." And being Sandra, she dug her way back out of the booth and swooped over and gave the poor girl another huge hug and Joe a bit of a hug, too.

ON THE WAY HOME, Sandra chatted about plans to call her sister and about how handsome Joe was and how beautiful Willow was. Ellen drove home quickly, half listening to Sandra and wondering if they should have taken Joe's suggestion and eaten a little vanilla ice cream. Her stomach was churning from excitement and the slightly spicy food, and she needed her antacids.

Parked at Ellen's garage, Sandra summed up her experience with an exclamation: "I nearly dropped my drawers."

"That would have been a sight," Ellen mumbled.

"What?" Sandra asked distractedly and continued to speak her thoughts. "Calling Charlene is going to be hard. I'll talk to Ralph about it. I think he'll be pleased I finally took the initiative. Of course, I'll call both the girls, too. I want the right tone, not too apologetic. Kimber is so diplomatic; she'll know the best way to handle it, and Laurel will be angry if I don't call her, too."

As they parted company, Ellen said, "I'm so glad all this is happening, Sandra. It's bringing us together again, too. But you're not going to abandon me, now that you have a real sister, are you?"

"Ellen, you know how much I love you. You are my soul sister. I mean it when I say Best Friends Forever." Ellen reached up to Sandra, and she hugged her hard.

Joe called Char and told her not to go to bed early; he and Willow would be home about 10:30, and they had some news for her. She tried to get him to spill the news on the phone. "Not so fast Grandma," he said. "You need to hear this from your granddaughter."

"She's not getting married, is she?" The new boyfriend, they'd had all of two, three dates, was Char's new preoccupation.

"It is nothing about that. We will be home soon."

Char watered the plants, put a load of whites in the washing machine, and cleaned the basement window by the dryer vent. She looked at the time; it still wasn't 10:00. She turned on the television and surfed like Joe did when he was nervous.

Finally, they were coming through the door. Joe first then the door banged closed the way it did when Willow announced her arrival. Char met them at the door. "What's going on?"

"Willow, you tell your Gram what happened tonight."

Willow had a big grin on her face as she pulled off her jacket and hung it on her entry hook. "Gram, your sister Sandra came to the restaurant for dinner and jumped up and grabbed me and nearly knocked me over."

"Oh, my God," Char exclaimed. "She's only seen you once. How did she know who you were? Nearly knocked you over, was she drinking?"

"Does she drink?" asked Joe. "You never told me that."

"I don't know if she drinks; I doubt if she drinks too much. One of the boys would have let it slip if she were a drinker, I think."

"Hey, stop the drinking thing. She wasn't drinking, was she Willow?"

"They both had a beer with dinner, that's all."

"How did we get on the topic of their drinking?" Char asked.

"You started it," Joe and Willow said in unison.

"I'm confused—did she come for dinner? Who was she with? Why did she come to Joe's after all these years?"

"She never said why she came for dinner at our café tonight." Willow answered. "Here is how it happened. I had played 'Lullaby of Birdland' on the Juke, and when I went over to serve them, she was singing it, and I said, off the cuff, my Gram always sang that song to me, and her friend said something about me being Char's girl. She jumped up and hugged me and wouldn't let me go, saying she was my Great-Aunt Sandra. Then they ate and then they asked if Joe was here and you tell the rest, Joe."

"Well I went out there, all friendly. It was Sandra and her friend, Ellen, I think. Sandra said this woman was her BFF. I gave them dinner on the house. Sandra was complimentary about the food."

"That was it, wasn't it?" Joe asked Willow.

"No, Papa, Sandra said she wanted to talk to you, Gram. She asked for your number and said she was going to call and apologize for not being nicer when she saw you at Great Gram's funeral. And then what did you say, Joe?"

He gave Willow a little pissed look and said, “I said that you hadn’t gone out of your way to be nice to her, either.”

“Thanks, Joe,” Char said absently.

“I know, I know, it wasn’t my place. Sorry about that, Char.”

“You’re right. I wasn’t nice to my little sister at our mother’s funeral. I’ve been so ashamed of myself for cutting ties with Mom and Dad. Sandy was an innocent child, caught in the middle between people she loved. I cut her off like I did Dad. I felt betrayed by both Mom and Dad, but I mostly blamed Dad when they sent me away as a teenager, but that was over 40 years ago.”

“I’ve been over the anger through working the program, but that shame, the shame of what I’d done, I’ve never gotten over that. If it weren’t for my brother Denny keeping tabs on all of us, we wouldn’t know a thing about what was happening in Sandy’s family.”

Char sat back down on the couch, and Joe and Willow sat down on either side of her.

Joe said, “I gave her your number, so expect a call from her.”

“I’m glad she came in,” Willow said. “She liked me. She didn’t even seem to notice that I’m black.”

“You stop that talk right now. Having black blood is a gift of the highest order,” Char said, putting an arm around Willow. “She saw that you are beautiful, and she couldn’t stop from jumping up and hugging you. Isn’t that right?” Willow nodded yes.

“She looks a lot like you, Gram. She is a little heavier, shorter, a little younger, but put the two of you together, anyone could tell you’re related. Gram, you’re the prettiest.”

Char looked at Joe embarrassed. She hadn’t been fishing for a compliment.

“I agree you two are sisters; there is no doubt about that, and you’re always the best-looking woman in my book. I hope you want her to call. You do, don’t you?”

“I’m stunned. I’m excited, too. But that doesn’t answer your question. Yes, I want her to call. I'm already impatient; I want her to call now. Can you two imagine? My little sister wants to talk to me after 40 years of silence?"

"This is going to happen, Char," Joe answered.

"Thanks to you two." Char hugged them both at once. "Our family might get bigger. Is that OK with you two?"

Joe nodded yes but that got him thinking about his side of the family, wondering if he should make more effort to connect with his boys and his brothers. He hadn't invited his brothers or his children to the small ceremony when he and Char got married. They had gone to his mother's funeral, too, and hadn't stayed for the church lunch afterwards. None of them were getting any younger. Maybe he'd talk to his sponsor, Father Dave, about making a real connection with his kids.

Later that night, in bed, both Char and Joe tossed and turned for what seemed like hours. Joe outwaited Char, and when she finally breathed those deep, regular breaths with just a hint of a snore, he carefully extracted himself from the twisted bedclothes, put on his slippers, and went downstairs for a cup of warm milk.

He thought to himself, his family had loved him, hadn't they?

14 / JOE'S STORY

Joe thought of himself as about as Mexican as Char was Swedish/Norwegian. They were both several generations removed from the 'old worlds.' His grandparents, Miguel and Ana Reyes, came north as migrant workers to pick beets in the fertile Red River Valley of North West Minnesota. They traveled to St. Paul, Minnesota and settled in the small Hispanic community already established in West St. Paul.

By the time their children were adults, Miguel and Ana owned a small café in West St. Paul. Their son, Jose, carried on the traditions of Papa Reyes, and by the time Jose's oldest son, Joe, came of age, the café became a restaurant and was a very busy place.

Joe was the 'Golden Boy.' No one understood why he drank so much. He knew the gossip about his drinking, but he didn't give it much thought. He was glib, good looking, and hard-working, all the makings of a young entrepreneur. When he was 24, he got 19-year-old Janice Orvis pregnant. Joe's father and brothers as well as Janis' father, pressured him into marrying her. By then, Joe drank excessively almost daily. But both families hoped for the best—that Joe would settle down after he got married.

Joe got so drunk the night of his wedding, he couldn't

remember if he had sex with his new wife. He vowed he would do better, and he did drink less for a while, but an incident at work gave him reason to tip a few beers then to buy a bottle and to not make it home at all that night.

He didn't make it to his first son's birth, either. He started celebrating in advance and ended up at a poker game that lasted all night. On the night his first son was born, he lost what his family had given him for a down payment on a house in Cherokee Heights, West St. Paul.

Joe's mother, Renee, felt awful for Janice and her first grandchild and convinced Jose to put up more money for the down payment on the house. That angered both of Joe's brothers to the point that they confronted Joe and told him to get some help for his drinking or quit working at the family restaurant. Joe went to treatment and stayed sober for over a year. By then, Janice was pregnant with their second son, Raymond.

When Joe started drinking again, he put a lot of energy into drinking responsibly. He discovered that if he only drank beer, he didn't have blackouts. If he didn't drink on an empty stomach, if he didn't drink before 5 p.m., and if he drank beer at home on the weekends, his drinking was fairly manageable. But if he started drinking whiskey or drinking anything at a bar, he was playing with fire.

Drinking hard alcohol led to occasional blackouts. Janice was afraid of Joe when he was in a blackout. Whenever Janice heard the car jerking to halt a certain way in the driveway late at night, she anticipated a blackout and herded the boys into the unfinished basement, unscrewing the light bulbs so Joe couldn't follow them down there.

Joe loved his boys and built them an elaborate wooden play set for the backyard. He took them to Twins games and taught them to throw baseballs and footballs.

But he couldn't understand why they became timid if he raised his voice when he was coaching them to play ball.

"The boys act just like you," he said to Janice. "You're all a bunch of wusses. Jesus, they wet their pants if I tell them to stand still and listen to me. They won't look me in the eye. What nonsense have you put in their heads? Why are they afraid of me? I've never hit any of you."

"You're pulling on my arm right now!" Janice said. "If you hit me or the boys, and you know you've hit me in a blackout, I'm leaving you and you won't see any of us again."

Joe walked away and didn't come home that night.

Not long after the birth of their third child, a girl, Joe lost control because Janis talked back to him when he complained about the baby crying. Joe split Janice's lip. Janice finally had enough. With the help of her mother, she moved the children to California to get emotionally and physically away from Joe.

Joe missed his boys and Janice terribly and that was reason enough to continue drinking. A year later his dad died, and his brothers squeezed him out of the restaurant.

He lived with a woman, another miserable alcoholic, for a few years. They did the best they could. He worked construction jobs in the summers and took unemployment insurance over the winter months, and they spent a lot of down time at the bar.

Three years had passed when Janice brought her new husband, Dwayne and Joe's four-year-old daughter, Jenna, back to Minnesota to visit her mother. Janice called Joe and told him that she was in town with Jenna. She and Dwayne agreed to meet Joe at Como Park by the Merry-Go-Round so he could see Jenna. Joe had every intention of following through with the visit, but on the day of the visit, he stopped at a bar for some liquid courage before going to the park.

Janice, Jenna, and Dwayne waited two hours, but Joe never showed up. Janice tried to call him, but he didn't answer his cell.

Dwayne took Janice and Jenna back to her mother's and asked Janice what bar Joe frequented. Dwayne said he just wanted to meet Joe.

Joe was three sheets to the wind when a big man in a white t-shirt and chinos walked into the bar asking for Joe Reyes. Joe nonchalantly raised his forearm with a drink in his hand. The man identified himself as Janice's husband and asked Joe to follow him outside. Joe swaggered out of the bar with the stiff, fragile strut of the practiced intoxicant. Janice's husband met him in the alley and beat the hell out of him. Joe didn't fight back; he didn't even protect himself. He was taken to the hospital with broken ribs and missing front teeth.

Before taking the first swing, Dwayne said, "Joe Reyes, you disgusting excuse for a man, if I can help it, you'll never see Janice or the kids again."

JOE ENDED UP IN ST. Joseph's hospital. Three days later, he was still lying in a hospital bed. He was lying quietly, eyes closed and sober, wishing a cold beer was on the dinner menu. Joe shifted and turned and half opened his eye lids. A priest sat quietly by his bed.

Father Dave had worked at a hospital-based treatment program for years. He was retired now, but he still volunteered at the hospital to visit patients identified as problem drinkers. On this day he'd asked the nurse if Joe Reyes was one of the Reyes boys from the well-known restaurant. The nurse nodded.

Father Dave sat by Joe's bed patiently, waiting for Joe to wake up. "Are you awake, then?" Father Dave asked.

Joe nodded without really looking at the priest. He didn't really need someone telling him what an asshole he was. Joe knew what an asshole he was.

"Relax, Joe. I'm not going to tell you something you already know. I hope to tell you something you don't know—by the way I'm Father Dave. I've been to your family restaurant and enjoyed the food."

Joe didn't respond.

"Is it OK with you if I tell you a little about myself?" Father Dave said.

Joe nodded yes and turned to stare up at the ceiling.

"I went to seminary to commit my life to God and service to others, but as you know, things don't always go the way we plan. I hadn't planned to become an alcoholic."

After finishing his own long, sad history, Father Dave asked Joe to look at him. "Only another alcoholic knows how it feels to watch people you love lose hope in you," he said.

With some effort, Joe turned on his side and looked at Father Dave. The priest didn't look sad. His eyes were twinkling; he was smiling. Joe turned away disgusted. How could this priest look happy after taking twenty years to sober up?

"Are you thinking that you're different from the rest of us drunks, Joe? That you have to keep drinking and suffer for the rest of your life? Or do you think you can beat it, lick this disease?"

Joe shook his head. "No," he said. "I'll never lick it."

"It doesn't matter if you're born with a silver spoon in your mouth or if you've never eaten off of silverware. If you are the one, maybe one in ten, who takes a drink and then the drink takes a drink, then the drink takes the man, you're an alcoholic, but you don't have to suffer with it. Do you know that, Joe? Do you know you can be an alcoholic and not suffer?"

Joe shook his head. He was an alcoholic and he'd have to suffer with it.

"Are you an alcoholic, Joe?"

Joe nodded again, miserably.

"Son, if you can honestly admit you're an alcoholic," the priest said with feeling, "you have just taken the first step toward never drinking another drink of alcohol. The next step will help with the suffering."

Joe had been in AA, and he tried to think. What was the second step?

"Do you know how many years it took me to practice that second step? It took me over 20 years to believe I could recover."

"I was lying in a hospital bed just like you. I'd been to treatment three times when a man I had never met came into my room and told me that if he could do it, if he could recover, so could I."

"Son, I'm telling you, if I can do it, if I can smile now, so can you."

Joe shook his head; he was an alcoholic. Being an alcoholic was terrible, how could he recover? "What is that second step you're talking about?"

"I came to believe a power greater than me could return me to sanity."

"What is that power, Father? Is it God? I don't believe in God."

"Joe, the power and light of God is many things. One gift of God is an attitude, a belief, a way of life. You can choose to face life with an open heart instead of a fearful heart; you can choose love over fear. The choice is yours. Listening, respecting, loving, be it love for a field of flowers or for a flock of birds—a forest of trees or the love of a friend. Compassion for a drunk on the street. Love versus fear, Joe. Love for all of God's creations, including ourselves."

Father Dave left Joe with the AA Big Book and promised to visit him the next day. Joe watched the old man walking out of the room. What was that second step?

15 / JOE, CHAR, AND WILLOW

Three years later, Joe Reyes still studied the second step. AA had become a power greater than himself. AA was a group of alcoholics with the wisdom to help him shine light on the dark alleys of his past. His sponsor, Father Dave, helped him. Meditation helped him. Meaningful work and long walks in nature helped him.

He was sober and managed a café in St. Paul called Day by Day. It was a breakfast and lunch place owned and staffed by people in the AA program.

One of Joe's customers intrigued him. She was an attractive tall blond woman, cordial, well dressed and older than most of the people who frequented the café. He asked around and found out her name was Char Gunderson. She'd been in the AA/NA program for years and still sponsored young people starting the program. She had discovered the back booths of the café were perfect for her weekly meetings with those she sponsored.

She was always multitasking at the cafe, using her iPad, reading or writing notes as she waited for whomever she was meeting. She laughed a lot, like so many of the grateful people Joe met through

AA. Her laughter was contagious. Joe wanted to be that way. He was too serious, too focused on digging himself out of the hole he had gotten himself into.

Char noticed Joe, too. He was older and seemed to be a good manager. He was willing to chip in, clean tables or to wait on customers if the place got busy, and she saw him take the time to listen to young wait staff, commiserating with them when they seemed overwhelmed. She sensed a kindred spirit in him. He was probably a lot younger than she was, but the perceived age difference worked well for both of them, allowing them to chat easily without thinking either would be attracted to the other.

When Joe had the time, he would slip into the booth across from Char and they'd chat. Over several months, they started sharing more real parts of their lives. Joe discovered that Char was raising a granddaughter the same age as his daughter, Jenna. Char told him she lost her only daughter to AIDS and how she couldn't touch on that deep pain. He commiserated, told her how he had lost his children when his ex-wife moved them to California.

The more he got to know her, the less he thought about her as an older woman. One day he asked her, "How can you be a grandmother? Did you have Rainey when you were 15?"

Char laughed. "No—I was in my twenties."

"Oh," he said wondering exactly how old she was.

"Do you want to know how old I am?" she asked him, chuckling to herself. "I'm over 50."

"I'm in my forties," he said, feeling like a kid, wanting to say he was almost 41.

"Early forties I bet," she kidded.

"I'm surprised we have so much in common, you being an educated woman and all," he added.

"An older, educated woman you mean. I appreciate intelligence more than education," she countered. "You are a good looking, younger, intelligent man and all. Your smile just shines."

"My beautiful false teeth you mean," he said.

For the rest of the day Joe's thoughts went back to their exchange. She *likes* me, he thought. They had been talking for months now, and he knew she liked him, but now he knew it was more than that. She was flirting with him. That truth surprised him. Even more so, he liked it.

Several days later, Char came into the restaurant and sat down at her usual booth. She ordered coffee and waited to see if Joe would find time to come and sit with her.

He did and after pleasantries, he said, "I wonder if you'd like me if you knew who I really am. I only have three plus years of sobriety, and I'm not very social outside of work or a meeting."

"You're perfectly social to me. If you'd like to visit us some time, Willow and I would like the company.

"I'd like to meet Willow," he said.

He liked the old house Char had rehabbed and filled with comfortable furniture, and he loved Willow. She was the daughter he hadn't been able to raise. She was a serious little girl, and he wondered if Jenna was like her. Willow brought out the jokester in Joe. He couldn't help wanting to pull her pigtails a little bit. He could tell she loved his attention, and the second time he came over, he gave her a hug when he left. During the third visit, she asked if she could read to him, and she sat close to him like she did to her Gram and read from her second-grade reader.

"You're a great reader, Willow," he said and then pretended to fall asleep.

Willow punched him. "Joe, wake up! This is the best part." He pretended to be startled awake to listen again. Willow shook her head. "I've got better books; I'll go get some." She raced upstairs to her room.

"Now you've awakened the beast." Char laughed knowing how much Willow liked books.

Willow came back with her arms full of books. "You choose one," she said.

"That will be hard—what if I like them all?" Char shook her head at him, warning him that he was getting himself in deeper.

"I tell you what, Willow, let's start with you telling me a little about each of these books, just so I can choose. We aren't going to get through them all tonight, but I'll be back, and I promise I will listen to them, one book at a time." He looked to Char; did she want him to keep coming back? She was smiling and nodding, rubbing her pressed palms together.

Char watched Joe's interaction with Willow. If she did bring a man into their life, it was going to be someone she absolutely trusted with Willow. Char hadn't been with a man for years. She thought she was done with romance. She was a dried-up post-menopausal woman now. She tried dating after she sobered up, when Rainey was the age Willow was now, but three tries hadn't worked out and that was enough for Char. Two of the men had competed with Rainey for Char's attention, and the other man had been too interested in Rainey.

Joe continued to visit and sometimes stayed into the evening after Willow was settled in bed. He sprawled out on the armchair watching TV while Char puttered around, up and down, doing laundry, paying bills, making calls. She wasn't comfortable enough in his presence to do what she would have been doing if he wasn't there, writing stories on her iPad. Her writing transported her, and she couldn't go there with company in the house.

She came to trust Joe with Willow, and she was attracted to him, but she didn't know how to proceed.

Joe was as sexually introverted sober as he had been sexually indiscrete when he had been drinking. He liked being with Char and Willow, he liked being in a family setting, and he enjoyed helping out with dinner or doing some little chore Char found for him to do, but he wasn't sure how to move their friendship forward.

They kissed at the door, but Char didn't relax into their kisses. Joe wondered if it was because Willow was asleep upstairs. He hoped it wasn't that Char just wanted to be friends.

He tried another approach. He called Char on the spur and asked her what she had planned for that afternoon.

"I don't have anything planned, why? Do you have time off?"

"I'm going to be running some errands; can I stop by after lunch? I'll bring dessert."

She said that would be great. He arrived with flowers and a box from Café Latte.

"Is that chocolate cake for me?" she asked.

"You told me you loved it, so I bought you some, but let's put these flowers into a vase." He stood behind her in the kitchen as she prepared the flowers.

"Something is up," she said, "What is going on with you?"

"I'm right here, Char," he whispered in her ear, and as she turned to face him, he leaned against her, taking her in his arms. "This is what is up," he said, rubbing himself against her. "Let's go upstairs and see what we can do about it."

Char laughed, pleased, and led Joe up her familiar staircase. They chuckled at their awkwardness, not wanting to let go of each other but not moving quite in unison either. Joe led her into her bedroom, and they rolled upon the bed, already wrapped in each other's arms.

After that afternoon, Joe scheduled several afternoons a week to spend with Char while Willow was in school. After his first unstoppable sexual energy ebbed, he started thinking of ways to make sure Char was as satisfied with their sex as he was.

"I'm not going to come unless you come, too," he told her, and he kept his word. He readied her slowly and waited her out, licking her and touching her and telling her how beautiful every part of her body was until she couldn't stand it anymore and begged him to enter her. Char came to believe that Joe loved her body. She relaxed and was able to write with Joe in the house.

WITHIN MONTHS, Joe moved into Char's house. He took over vacuuming and did most of the weekly shopping and some of the cooking on weekends. Char did laundry, dusting, cleaning the kitchen and bathrooms and all the other 'hidden' things mostly women do, picking up, sorting, changing towels and linens, deep cleaning. The three of them set the table and did the dishes together.

They worked together, rebuilding Willow's self-esteem when she was hurt by insensitive kids at school. Willow loved dance, and they took her interest seriously, finding her the best classes available. Joe was willing to go to dance recitals, and the three of them went to Twins baseball games together.

Char wanted Joe to play Scrabble with her. She had played scrabble for years with her good friend Sally and wanted to share the game with him. After being trounced game after game, he suggested they try cribbage. He trounced her and trounced her until she cried.

They found other games they played more equitably, and Willow played games with them, too. They gave her a stake at first so she wouldn't feel so cheated when she lost, but by the time she was 12, she was winning against them without needing a stake.

Joe and Char hadn't lived together a year before Char started politicking Joe to buy his own restaurant. Their first conversation on this subject started one afternoon while Willow was at an after-school dance class. Char brought lemonade and chocolate chip cookies onto the porch where Joe had just finished watching a baseball game. Char couldn't have found a better afternoon to broach the subject. Joe was elated after a rare Twins win over the Yankees.

Char sat down on the edge of her chair and said, "I want us to buy a cafe, Joe."

"I don't have that kind of money, Char. You know I need to get a better job and really start saving."

"I want that cafe, now," she said standing up. "I'm into my fifties; I don't have time to fool around. Let's buy a restaurant."

"And how are we going to do that?"

"We'll put a mortgage on the house; this neighborhood has gentrified, and this house is worth many times what I paid for it. That's how we are going to do it."

Joe jumped out of his seat. His anger went up into his eyes, and it scared her a little, but not enough to stop her. She'd seen small signs of his anger before, but she trusted that he wouldn't touch her in anger. When they first dated, he told her about his abuse of his first family; he promised her, and himself, he would never use physical violence again.

"If you won't do this with me, I'm going to get a loan and start a cafe without you."

"Char, you're breaking my balls. I'm the man here," he said and raised himself up, hovering over her and pointing to his chest. "Are you sure you want a man? Maybe you want a eunuch. Is that what you saw in me? Is that what you want? Do you think I'm your boy?"

Char raised to full height, too, and held her own. "'Breaking my balls,' really Joe? A line from a Robert De Nero movie? Please just let me tell you my idea."

Char stepped back and took a deep breath. "I want us to finance the restaurant with equity from the house because I want you to support us. I'll be your banker. We can be equal partners. We will write it up legally, and you will pay our household good money. I'm going to be almost without income once the paper downsizes. Newspapers are starting to fail across the country. Will you support us? It will all be legal."

Joe regained his composure, rocking back onto his heels and moving a few steps back from Char. "Do you know how many new restaurants fail? My brothers are always on the verge of losing our family restaurant. What makes you think this can be different?"

"You tell me. Why do you think they are in trouble?"

"Well, I think they put too much money into ambiance and grew too big. They wanted a trendy, high style place, and they didn't want to do 'hands on.'"

"Don't they say location, location, location, Joe?"

Joe shook his head. "I'm from the old school. I think good food and good service is what makes a restaurant successful. I'd use as many fresh ingredients as possible, provide excellent service, and let the restaurant develop an authentic reputation."

"Then it wouldn't take an arm or a leg to start? If we moved into a failed business like on University Avenue?"

"I'm not sure how much money it would take. I'd have to do figures, maybe go to that Small Business Institute. Stop it, Char; I know what you are doing," Joe said, taking a few steps back from her.

"Do you believe in me," she said, closing the gap between them. "Do you believe in me the way I believe in you?"

"Oh, Char, you are such a ball breaker."

"No—I'm not. I'm being your partner. You chose me, and you knew what you were getting. You got a woman who is your equal."

"Good God, what have I gotten myself into?" he said, but his anger had faded. He shook his head in resignation. He thought she was probably more than his equal at a lot of things, but he believed in her, and his love for her kept surprising him. It kept growing, and he knew he was growing with it in ways he had never imagined. He reached for a cookie.

After a cooling off period, Char broached the subject of a restaurant again, and Joe said he was thinking about it. Char said, "If you're willing to think about it, then I'm making an appointment for us to go to the bank." He had been thinking about it and had decided that if she brought it up again, he would do it. He was sure he could make it work.

They decided to tell Willow about their plans; they were buying the restaurant together, but Joe was going to have to do all the work. Willow looked at Char and said, "But Gram, why should Joe have to do all the work?" They laughed and said that Char was going to be a silent partner but that the restaurant was going to be a family affair. Then Willow asked them, "Why aren't you married if we are a family?"

Joe's joking answer was, "Your Gram never asked me."

Joe could tell Willow was disappointed in his answer. He thought Char looked a little disappointed, too. Joe had thought Char was too contemptuous of marriage to ever consider it. He was open to the idea. If they were going to be partners, why not seal the commitment? The more he thought about it, the better it sounded to him.

Joe wanted to make the proposal into a big deal so she couldn't off handedly just say something like "Not yet," or worse, laugh him off.

He bought her a band with three nice sized diamonds

embedded in it, one for each of them, and asked her if she would like a romantic night on the town. She said she would love it. On a lovely spring evening when the lilacs were in bloom, Joe took Char to a white linen tablecloth restaurant and after dinner, for a ride in a horse pulled carriage. As the horse clopped along the quiet downtown neighborhood filled with charming old houses and canopied elm trees, he took out the velvet lined box and opened it.

Char looked at the ring with its three stones and looked up into the smiling, earnest face of the man offering it to her. She nodded and grabbed onto him, pushing her face into his chest, hiding her tears. When she regained her composure she asked, "Are you sure you want to marry an old maid like me?"

He laughed, "What do you mean an old maid?"

"No one has ever asked me to marry him. No one has ever wanted to make an honest woman of me."

"Char, you're a beauty, inside and out. You never gave them a chance. The only reason I have a chance is that you are too old to out run me."

She looked down at their hands, his warm, tanned hands, one holding a beautiful ring and her long thin, slightly aging ones. She listened to the uniform clip-clop of horses' hooves. They swayed in the buggy, moving in and out of the moonlight on the quiet tree lined street.

She felt so young at heart, so loved in this moment. "In my heart, I'm sixteen, Joe, and I always will be. Will you promise not to break my heart?"

Joe had fleeting thoughts of the heart he'd broken, but that was not the man he was tonight. "I want to share my life with you. I love you, Char. I promise I won't break your heart."

WHEN WILLOW WAS 12, Joe's daughter Jenna visited her

Minnesota grandmother. It was agreed that she would spend some time with Joe and Char and Willow. Joe had exaggerated the similarities between the two girls in his mind. Char and Joe were hoping the girls would spark up a friendship. It didn't happen.

Joe took them to the YMCA swimming pool and left them to swim for a few hours. Jenna spent the time flirting with the life guards. Her behavior embarrassed Willow, who didn't want to flirt with older boys.

They tried going to the Mall of America together. Jenna wanted to shop until she dropped; Willow wanted to go to a double feature. They weren't speaking to each other when Joe picked them up. The visit was a bust.

Later Willow asked her Gram, "What is wrong with me? Why am I still such a little girl? I'm bigger than Jenna, two months older, and just as smart, but all the boys ignored me and stared at Jenna."

Gram said, "Come on sit down by me." They leaned against each other.

"Everything comes in its own time, OK?"

Willow sighed. She wished she were still little enough to sit in Gram's lap.

"Remember the story of the Ugly Duckling that I told you, and I told your mother, and way before that your great-Gram told me?"

"Tell me again, Gram," Willow asked.

"Here is today's take: A gaggle of young ducklings lived and swam together in the middle of a very blue pond. The yellow, downy ducklings splashed and played as if they were the only little birds in the pond and paid no attention to a bigger grey young fowl, swimming alone at the far end of the pond…"

After the story, Gram asked, "Do you want to sing the song with me, Willow? The song the Trumpeter Swans sang to the grown, no longer feeling ugly, little swan?" Willow laughed and shook her head.

"Come on, Willow, sing our song with me."

"OK, Gram, if you insist. *Oh, when the saints come marching in, oh when the saints come marching in*…Don't rush to grow up, little swan," Gram added at the end of their song. "It takes time to grow into yourself, to discover your specialness."

16 / SISTERLY LOVE

Char was in an AA meeting when she felt her cell vibrate in her pocket. She reached down and held on to the last feel of the vibe, feeling her sister calling her. She waited until after the meeting, offering goodbyes and good luck all around, and in the parking lot, she took the phone out of her pocket.

"It's me—your sister," the voice message said. "Please call me back if you're willing."

Char coughed hard twice and cleared her throat while walking to her car parked at the far end of the church's asphalt lot. She turned around to make sure she was alone, walked around to the passenger side, opened the door, and sat down, leaving the passenger door wide open. It was a warm fall day; a fresh breeze cooled the hot interior of the car. Char took off her blue windbreaker and folded it, laying it on the seat next to her. She wanted to put her head down on her windbreaker and ignore this call. Instead she sat on the edge of the seat and remembered the day she left home for good.

No one had come out of the house to wave her goodbye. Her brother Denny drove her to the bus stop. She sat rigidly next to him as he picked up speed and the farmyard faded from view. Char stared out her side window at the soft, Irish green early summer leaves filling out the cottonwood trees that lined the farm's gravel lane to the country road. She'd loved walking the lane to the mailbox with her Dad. The little girl in her cried, but the eighteen-year-old young woman had already hardened herself to a new reality. She abruptly shifted her vision to the road ahead.

Char lifted her cell to her ear and hit 'call back.' Sandra answered on the second ring. "Thank you for calling back," Sandra said. "Your 'Hello, this is Char' message sent shivers up my spine. We sound so similar, that Southwestern Minnesota lilt."

Char agreed. "Um, we do sound similar. Willow and Joe were so excited when you showed up at the restaurant. Me too, when I heard about it. How did this happen? After all of these years?"

"I've been thinking about family lately," Sandra explained, forgetting all about James' part in it all. "I've had visions of our Grandma Gunderson in her garden—remember how she used to lean over, shaking her finger and showing her big loose panties while talking to her plants? We'd giggle, but the plants did what she told them to do."

Char laughed. "Now Grandma Gunderson had the Swedish lilt. She liked things orderly—we had to mind our Ps and Qs, but she could be silly and loved to sing songs with us. I remember her holding me and rocking me and singing to me when I was getting to be a big kid."

Sandra added, "She always said, 'You're never too big to be loved.' I was that way with my kids, too. I sang them the songs Grandma and Mom sang to us. Now my girls are singing the same songs to their babies, and so am I. I've got three grandchildren, two girls and a toddler boy and am expecting a fourth. My youngest son, Chuck, is going to Medical School in Duluth next fall."

"My granddaughter started at the U this fall."

"I loved meeting Willow. She is beautiful. She is more precious than I remember my girls being at that age."

"I think of her that way, too—precious. I used to think it was because I lost her mother, my daughter Rainey." Char's voice broke, and she cleared her throat.

"She's special, Charlene. I can't imagine what you went through losing Rainey. I'm so sorry, so sorry I wasn't there when you went through that."

"I would probably have pushed you away. I was so focused on raising my granddaughter and on my career. We've both been busy raising children and having careers. Perhaps we have time now to get to know each other. I still can't believe it; I am talking to my sister.

"You're a writer, so accomplished. I'm starting to read your blog."

"You are? How did you find it?"

"I researched, found it on the net," Sandra explained.

"I'm not so accomplished," Char said. "All the mistakes I've made? I've just forged ahead in life, consequences be damned, I guess. As for writing, a recovery blog isn't very creative. 'Trying' is the operative word for my writing."

"Charlene, I can't wait to see you. I'd love to have you and Joe and Willow over for dinner. Do you eat meat? Ralph and my girls, Chuck too, are excited to meet you all. But I guess I'd like it best if we could first get together alone so we can talk from our hearts. I need to ask your forgiveness. I was a little princess and so mean when you came home from having the baby. Remember how I spied on you and tried to catch you smoking or doing something wrong and tattled to Mom and Dad?"

"You were eight Sandy. Let it go. When can we get together?" Char asked.

Ouch, she's blunt like me, Sandra thought. "Will you come to see my house?"

Both wanted the other to see her home first.

Char said, "My home is the portal to my soul".

Sandra said, "My garden tries to live up to Grandma's."

It was agreed that they would meet at Sandra's. She was the baby sister and got her way.

Two days later, Char arrived on time, wanting to appear casual but respectable in high end slacks and buffed leather ankle boots, a shiny Hermes silk scarf looped around her neck. She hadn't reached the door before Sandy came tearing out of the house, throwing her arms around her sister. Thank God for the wrought iron railing or they may have toppled each other over. They hugged for a good long time, both of them with tears in their eyes, holding on to each other.

Char pulled away, holding Sandy's upper arms with her hands. Yes, Sandy was her own image, younger, a bit shorter and rounder. They were well preserved, handsome women. Char was surprised to see that Sandra was wearing makeup, so suburban of her. But she was dressed in soft worn jeans and a soft blouse hanging loose, and she was shoeless. Char liked that. She studied her feet. Yes, she had the same long hammertoes as Char.

Char didn't get a good look at the front rooms of the house. Sandra was in a rush to show off her garden. She offered the living room, family room, dining room, bedroom corridor and stopped for a moment in the lively red toned kitchen before they were out the back-patio doors leading to the magnificent garden. The season was ebbing, but still, the greenness, the scent, the straight, productive rows, all evoked farm life. Sandy's garden was the continuation of a long family tradition.

"My God, this is fantastic Sandy. I want to take off my shoes and run through the rows, feel that black soil between my toes again. Have I died and gone to heaven?"

That was the right thing to say. "Come on, take off your boots.

The grass is prickly cool, but the soil is still warm—let's do it." The boots and the socks came off, and Sandra led the way into the rows. She explained the raised beds, and Char picked cherry tomatoes and tomatillos and the last of the green beans, stuffing them in her mouth as she tried to keep up the conversation while simultaneously enjoying the taste of red, yellow, and green trophies from the garden.

The luncheon was a success. They ate seafood salad and warm rolls on the deck and drank a pitcher of iced sweet tea. They talked and talked.

At one-point Char asked, "What did you mean when you commented that Willow seems more precious than your daughters were at her age? Are you thinking I am overprotective of her? I'm asking because I am afraid, I am overprotective."

"Oh, no, Charlene, I'm thinking we were negligent in raising our girls. Kimber and Laurel grew up so quickly. Ralph and I laughed that they were 15 at 12 and so on. But maybe they needed more sheltering from us. Then again, maybe they were pushed by their peer group into being so precocious. They were preteens in grade school, dating, already talking about sex by the time they were 13 or 14. I feel badly about how quickly they grew away from me."

Sandra changed the subject. "I had a lot more fun raising the boys. The boys were not at all alike; Chuck was a search and destroy little boy, all raw energy but loving, too. James liked problem solving; he was always thinking, how does this work, can I take this apart and try putting it together? I loved their relentless activity, and I felt more needed by them."

"Boys? Where did the second boy come from?"

"Oh, you don't know about James, do you? He is the son of my friend, Ellen. Ellen and I met at college and stayed roommates until I married Ralph. She was with me the other night when I met Joe and Willow at the cafe. She was at Mom's funeral, too. When Ellen got married, we were pregnant at the same time, her for the first time, me for the third time. James was born first; he was colicky, and I helped them at first, having James sleep over with me several nights a week when I was too pregnant to sleep anyway. I just loved James from the first time I saw him. Then, after Ellen's divorce, Ralph and I helped Ellen buy the house next door to us," Sandra said, pointing to the little gray bungalow. "I half raised James."

Sandra thought for a minute. Was this the time to share about her abortion? About her feelings that James was the baby she'd lost?

Char interrupted her thoughts. "I'm looking forward to meeting all of them. Tell me about Ralph, Sandy."

"Do you mind calling me Sandra? I've been Sandra my whole adult life."

Char nodded. "Please call me Char now, too."

"Well, then, Ralph. He's a doctor, a proctologist. He is very conscientious. He's the kind of doctor everyone loves, even though he's working on their butts."

Char chuckled. "And you're happy together, right?"

Sandra began with a drawn out "Well—"

"That's OK; you can tell me if you want; I don't want to probe. I just assume married folks are happy because Joe and I are so happy, but then we didn't get together until I was over 50."

"Joe is so good looking, and he looks so young."

"He is young, well, not young, but a lot younger than I am—almost12 years younger."

"My God, he's younger than me! You must have good self-esteem to be married to a man that much younger."

"We've been happy together. Oh, we've had a few bumps along the way."

"Ralph is nearly 10 years older than I am. I think I admired Ralph as much as I loved him; I put him on a pedestal."

Sandra paused. Char chewed on the end of her straw and waited for Sandra to get out what she had to say.

"Char, Ralph had an affair. He was almost sixty years old! I was in denial until my friend Ellen said it out loud. I am still so mad at Ralph, even though the affair ended two years ago, and I'm just getting over being mad at Ellen for saying the obvious out loud. I've festered with that anger for two years, but, now, we've started marriage counseling, and I can't, I can't—" Sandra dissolved into her pain.

Char jumped up and put her arms around the shoulders of her sad sister, tucking her head against Sandra's neck, embracing the solidness of her.

Sandra finally pulled away. "Do you mind if I talk about this? It is personal and embarrassing."

"That's life—personal and embarrassing. Of course, I want to hear all you have to say," Char said and plopped back onto her deck chair. Almost angrily, she said, "I'm your sister. I love you."

Sandra looked skeptically at this stranger, her sister. "OK, I'll have to trust you on that. I mean I have to trust that you mean it when you say you love me."

Char nodded; her eyes wide open, ready to listen.

"I'm scared to death I'm going to lose Ralph. He has begged for forgiveness and I've said the words 'I forgive you' and I meant the words, but I can't forget." Sandra looked up at her sister and cast her eyes down again. "I'm frigid in bed. You know, I lay waiting for it to be over. He tries less and less, and we can't talk about it. I'm sure I'm sending him into the arms of yet another woman."

Char squirmed and sat back in her chair. She felt bad for her sister but couldn't help empathizing with Ralph.

Sandra was waiting for Char to respond to her.

Oh well, Char said to herself. Tell her the truth. "If I betrayed Joe and he couldn't forgive me for, I'd want to just kill myself. Well, maybe that is a little strong, but I'd be in such pain, having hurt him that much."

"Don't put it that way, Char. You've never met Ralph. He seems like he is doing fine," Sandra snapped. Ellen was more sympathetic than this sister of hers. "So, you think it is my fault? I didn't do anything but raise his children, cook his meals, clean his house. I worked so hard to be the best wife."

"Too bad we can't live in the past," Char commented. "I'd love to see my baby sister happy with her Ralph."

"I'd love to be happy with 'my Ralph,' but he is a traitor."

"Do you love him?" Char retorted.

"You don't give up, do you? Everyone loves him, OK? That's part of the problem—he is such a wonderful man—we do all love him, but how could he do this to me?"

"How could he not be perfect? Is he serially unfaithful?"

"No. He's not, but I'm sick of this conversation. You act like I'm the bad one here, and we just got reacquainted. Sandra looked suspiciously at her sister and continued the conversation. "I've told all. What's awful in your life?"

Chars eyes opened wide again, and she looked at her mirror image—the wide, round eyes just like hers—and chuckled. Sandra chuckled, too; she didn't know why. She grabbed the outstretched hands of her sister and squeezed them tight.

"Things are good now, Sandra, but if you had known me when I lost my daughter, you would have seen the most miserable creature. I wanted to rip myself open and give her my blood. I certainly was 'a ragged set of claws, scuttling across the sands of empty seas.'"

"Oh, darling, I can't imagine. I complain about Kimber and Laurel, but if anything happened to one of them." Sandra's eyes glistened with sympathy.

"Tell me about it, Sandra. If it hadn't been for that baby girl, Willow, I don't know how I would have survived. But that darling little girl with her brown eyes looking up at me with such hope, such wonder, she saved me. I'd hold her tight, and we would rock and rock. Oh, I hope I haven't ruined her, too. My first baby I gave up for adoption, my second wasted away in front of my eyes; you don't know the anxiety I feel for Willow."

Sandra grabbed Char's hand. Life is a long dusty road, she thought and said to her sister, "Think about the incredible length of life. All the mountain peaks and valleys. Me, I prefer living in the abundant plains. I like poetic images, too, Char. We are so much alike. Last week I was thinking my antidepressants had failed me. My kids had left me, and probably my husband would, too. I don't want to burden you, but I need more in my life, more than once a week volunteering at a homeless shelter, going to church on Sundays, more than my garden. I need family and friends. I hope you won't get sick of me, Char."

Char smiled broadly. Don't worry, Sandra. I'm not going to leave you again. I need you as much as you need me."

"We should go home to visit Dad, Char—so you can forgive him."

"Where did that come from? My God, just throw it at me in one fell swoop." But then Char smiled; she was already feeling connected to Sandy 'Sandra' again. She felt halfway home already.

17 / BROWN SUGAR

James hadn't heard from Caleb for over a week, and he worried how Caleb had handled using the heroin he'd given him, so he called, even though it was Caleb's turn to get in touch. "It's been almost two weeks, Caleb. I thought maybe you dropped out and went back East,"

"I'm here. Getting used to being back in classes. Writing a lot. Why? What's happening?"

"Well, I got a part time job. Guess what I am?"

"I give up—just tell me."

"I'm a courier."

"Now you got my attention. What the hell are you talking about?"

"Come by my place, and I'll explain. I'd rather talk about it in person."

"OK. If you're free, I'll come by now. I was just going out to get something to eat. Want a pizza from the Top Hat I saw near your place?"

"Bring some Coke, too?"

"Coca Cola, yes. Cocaine? Ain't got none."

Caleb bought hot wings, too, and it was quite a feast. They talked about classes starting while they ate. James burped twice and wiped his mouth, throwing the last piece of crust back in the big pizza box and moving it from the coffee table to the kitchen counter.

"Want the last of the Coke, Caleb?"

"Nah—I'm ready to hear about the 'courier' job."

"Remember me talking about Randall, the dope dealer? He came by a couple of times. Anyway, he lost a courier, and I took the job." James explained the job to Caleb.

"I've done it twice. No problem. $100 a drop and as a bonus, he provided a nice stash the first week."

"The dope we just smoked?" Caleb asked.

"Yeah. After that heroin, it's a relief to smoke plain old weed. I got to admit I like the powder, but it sends me off the deep end. I'm so gone, on another planet. I feel strange using it alone. How about you? Did you handle it OK?"

"I threw it out," Caleb lied.

"What? Threw out that great shit? If I'd known you were going to throw it away, I wouldn't have given it to you."

"I agree with you; I don't want to use it alone."

"Randall left some more heroin for me, but he says it is stronger, and I certainly didn't want to try it alone."

"What's it called?"

"Brown Sugar. I mean it's still heroin—supposed to be good."

"I've heard of it. You didn't even try it?"

"I'm a wuss."

"I'll try it with you."

"You will? Are you sure?"

"I'll do you a favor and try it with you."

"Don't do me any favors, Man." They both laughed, busting each other over who really wanted to try it.

James went to the bathroom and brought the stash out from underneath the toilet. He'd put it in a little plastic bag to protect it from the sweat of the toilet. He took the foil out of the baggie, and it seemed dry.

Caleb was standing up when he came back, pacing.

"You scared?" James asked.

"No. Are you?"

"No. Let's give it a try."

James put down thinner lines and passed the money straw. Caleb snorted and sniffed and did it again.

"My God!" Caleb said, throwing his head back. Now he remembered. His body cried out in memory—rushing, tumbling, and shivering. His mind closed, and he lay in the womb again.

James snorted his two lines. He waited for a reaction, and wham; his stomach flipped and lurched. He staggered to the bathroom and threw up in the toilet. He waited, threw up again, and staggered back to his chair.

They were both gone, floating away into their highs.

Caleb's hollow voice startled James. "What?" he mumbled.

"That girl, you still seeing her?"

"Willow, pussy Willow."

"Don't," Caleb said.

"Don't what?" James mumbled.

"Don't call her that."

"What are you talking about? What did I say?"

"Don't be hurting that girl, James."

"You haven't even met her. You're worrying about a girl you haven't met?"

"Treat her good," Caleb chided.

"Hey, man, I'm good to her. I'm just dating her—movies, a bike ride—we went to the Fair. You're talking strange, man. I don't hurt girls, women. Why would you say that? I'm meeting her Gram."

James reached over to push at Caleb, but it was too much trouble. "What a high, Caleb. What decibel is this?"

"High decibels, very high, righteous shit, James."

"I'm going to lay down," James announced. When he woke, Caleb was gone.

18 / WILLOW FEELS SEXY

James arrived at Willow's house on time. He checked his cell, 7:01 p.m., and walked up the porch. He took a closer look at the exterior of the house. Wood beams separated the upper floor stucco from the first level brick. He pegged it as a 1920s prairie style home on a block of comparable homes, urban intellectuals. Gentrified homes.

James wondered what Willow's grandmother would be like. He had gotten the impression that Joe was Hispanic, but he didn't think Willow looked all that Hispanic. Maybe she had an Island heritage, but she talked like a Minnesota girl. He figured Willow's grandmother would be some dark-skinned beauty.

Willow had been kneeling on the old sofa, watching out the window for James. He'd been on time for all their dates. That showed her that he liked her and he hadn't disappointed her yet. She jumped up when she saw him and ran to the door, paused, and then opened the door, startling him. He drew back a bit to take in her beauty. She was wearing a very short skirt that showcased her dancer's legs. Her shiny black hair was up, exposing her long neck and square shoulders.

"Hey," he said. "What can I say, you're looking good."

"Hey, yourself, James. Welcome to my home." She opened the door for him, and he walked into a vestibule with a mirrored coat closet to one side. She opened the door into the living room, and he walked into a home that didn't replicate the early 1900s—it was the early 1900s. Heavy dark woodwork and floors, beige walls, Mayfield Parrish prints, Tiffany lamp shades, and a mirrored mantel above a brick gas fireplace. The home evoked calm. He felt like he was in a comfortable museum room: something out of an F. Scott Fitzgerald book.

"What do you think of the place?" she asked. She watched him, the awed expression on his face, and knew her home impressed him. She smiled at him. She wanted to impress him, wanted him to think highly of her and her family.

"I'm watching you, too, you she-devil," he said. "You can tell I'm impressed."

They smiled at each other, and James heard some rummaging in the kitchen.

"Gram is finishing dishes. Joe's at the café—I think I told you that."

"You did. Is she coming out to meet me?" he said quietly, sincerely wanting to impress the woman who lived in this house.

"Gram—come meet James," she said loudly. "She is making a grand entrance,"

Willow whispered. "She wants to impress you, too."

James looked at Willow and gave her a rabbit wrinkle with his nose. Then Char walked in. He looked at her incredulously. She looked so much like Sandra that they could be sisters.

"So, you are James," she said and smiled a very familiar smile. "I'm Char—the very protective Gram of Willow." She offered her hand, palm down.

He looked at her hand, should he shake it or bow down and kiss it? He wasn't sure what to do. He looked over at Willow; she was silently laughing at her gram's imperialism and James' confusion.

He wiped his palm and took her hand gently and looked into her face with a crooked grin. "You look so much like my second mom; I think you must be related. Sandra Dahlberg?"

She dropped his hand and put her hands on her hips. "You're James—Sandra's boy?"

"Sandra," Willow gasped. "She's my aunt."

"Sandra's got a sister I don't know of?" James asked. "You're Sandra's niece? No," he said. "No."

The three of them grinned stupidly at each other.

"Would that make us 'kissing' cousins, James?" Willow said wickedly.

Willow and James looked at each other and grinned. Char chuckled nervously. "Sandra and I are just getting to know each other again. You've heard the story about us losing touch for 40 years?"

"I'm the last to know, I guess," James said bewildered. "But I've been to the Gunderson farm; in fact, I have the porch table from Grandma and Grandpa Gunderson's farmhouse in my apartment."

The women looked at him again. Willow said, "You mean you've spent time with my great-grandparents, and I didn't get the chance? I almost got there once, for Great-Gram's funeral. We just went to the little country church service." She frowned at her Gram.

"I guess so," James said, shaking his head. "It's a great farm, Willow, horses and everything." Willow put her hands on her hips, pouting at Char.

"Sandra thinks highly of you," Char said. "She calls you her second son."

"She should. I spent as much time with Sandra and her family as I did with my own mother. Mom worked a lot, and I stayed at Sandra's.

Sometimes my mom would have to take me home kicking and screaming. That was when I was really young—I mean I haven't done any kicking and screaming for a while." He grinned, remembering what a brat he'd been. "Sandra is the best. Chuck and I are the same age, and he's my brother. I didn't spend as much time with Ralph, he'd be coming home from work about when Mom got home."

"I was over to Sandra's just this week," Char said. Sandra said she and your Mom have stayed friends since college."

"They made a commitment to share with me; they keep telling me that. I'm divided between women, how do you like that, Willow?" Willow turned to James, a waning smile on her face. "Sandra and my mom are going to be blown away by all this. They don't know I'm dating your granddaughter, do they?"

"I'm not sure, James. I haven't met your mom, and as for my sister Sandra, I've just had one long and beautiful afternoon at her house, playing in her garden. She pointed out your house."

"I hate being left out!" Willow said. "First James has been to my great-parents' house and now you, Gram, have seen James' house before I have. That's enough Gram. James isn't interested in all of this."

"Are you kidding? I'm very interested. Mom and I don't really have any family other than the Dahlberg's. They adopted both of us. You'll love Chuck, Willow. All the girls love Chuck—hope you don't like him better than me."

"Don't worry, James. I won't let you pawn me off on Chuck."

"I won't pawn you off on anyone, Willow." James thought for a second about Caleb's interest in getting to know Willow.

Char added, "You're sweet, James. I see why Sandra likes you so much."

He grinned. He thought Char was probably a lot like Sandra. He knew how to stay on her good side, how to stroke her ego.

"I think I met James' mother," Willow spoke up. "I bet she was the friend with Sandra at the restaurant." She turned to James. "Is your mother small with dark hair and dark eyes?"

"That's my mom. We don't look alike, do we?"

"Sort of, in the eyes." Willow remembered how pleased Ellen had been to meet her. "I liked her right off."

"I haven't met her," Char said. "What is her name?"

"Ellen Holden. She is a psychologist," James revealed.

"Well, that would come in handy around here, wouldn't it, Willow?"

"Gram, I don't think we need a psychologist! Between you and Papa, I've gotten plenty of 'help.' Why make James think we are crazy? He can find out for himself."

James looked back and forth and only saw teasing between the two of them. He was hoping they weren't crazy. The introductions were crazy.

"Enough," Char said. "You two run along to the movies. I don't want to make you late."

James and Willow looked at each other and nodded.

"I love your home, Char. I'm into old things, women, too." He ducked when he said that, thinking that Sandra would softly hit him on the head for that one. Char just looked at him and laughed, thinking I know your type, all talk. All talk was fine with Char.

He had a lot more to say, but Willow was pulling on his shirt. He gave up and followed her out of the door to the car.

"Hey, I was getting it on with your Gram," James said, putting the car into gear.

"I know, but I want this to be about us. Let's find some place to sit and talk or walk for a while. I want to get to know you better, cousin."

He laughed. "Don't take that too far, honey, or we'll lose our tantalizing edge here."

"Can you believe that?" Willow said. "Us being almost family? It's strange, but it's OK. God, you should have seen Sandra when she came into Joe's Cafe and found out who I was—she put a stranglehold on me." They both laughed.

"I've been held in a stranglehold by Sandra lots of times. But what about us? You still like me?" he asked.

"I like you more than you know, James. I'm falling for your charm. But watch it with Gram. 'I'm into old women?' Gram is married to a man who is 10 years younger than she is, so I wouldn't go too far with the 'old' stuff."

HE DROVE them to his favorite parking place where they could watch the wide river slowly moving south. The setting sun shone on the sandstone bluffs across the river; the bluffs sparkled with gold flecks that reflected like stars into the water. They both watched the few minutes of breathtaking beauty while the sun sank below the horizon, and the river became its nameless dark flow again. James reached for Willow, and they kissed deeply. The little car was uncomfortable; the console between the seats kept them apart.

"Can we move to the back seat?" he asked awkwardly. She nodded, and he slipped out of the car, trying to rush to her side to open her door, but she was out of the door and propping the front seat up before he could reach her.

They laughed and squirmed into the back seat.

"Um," he said, rolling his tongue on the ridge above her lips, enjoying the salty taste. Laurel was fading into the background; Willow was real. She played with his lips with her teeth, tasting, nibbling then probing his mouth with her tongue.

Back and forth they probed, tasting, testing each other.

The street lights came on and brightened the parking lot. They slipped down to a half lying position in the car.

Suddenly, Willow sat up and pushed away from James. "I need

to talk to you about something, James. You're not going to like it, but can I be honest with you?"

"Anything, Willow. I'd do anything for more of those kisses."

"You smoke a lot of weed, don't you?"

He looked at her. She saw the frown, the anger in his eyes. He pushed away from her.

"Why do you say that?"

"Why are you so defensive?"

"I asked you first. Why do you say that?"

"Your car smells, James. Your shirt smells, James. I'm not stupid."

"I'd never accuse you of being stupid. What is wrong with smoking dope, for Christ's sake? I do it honestly. I run five miles almost every day; I'm in the engineering/architectural program at Augsburg, and I get excellent grades. I started a few years ago and, yes, I smoke almost every day. Can you live with that?"

"Boy, you're defensive about that."

"If you had a mother like mine on your case, when you were only doing a little toking after finishing your day, you would understand why it bothers me so much."

"It would bother my Gram, too. She is AA through and through. She did a lot of drugs when she was younger, and Joe is a recovering alcoholic. I was raised to fear and respect what alcohol and drugs do to a person."

"Maybe you should give it a try. I've learned so much from smoking dope, about really hearing music; I've expanded my consciousness. I'm not the uptight suburban boy who plays games at a fraternity and just tries to get laid."

Willow reached over and kissed him quickly on the cheek. "I like you James. That's why the weed smoking bothers me. I don't want a stoned boyfriend who can't take me seriously. I'm not that kind of girl."

James kissed her back, hard on the lips. He wanted her to

understand him. “And I’m not that kind of guy, Willow. I’ll be good to you. Please give me a chance, but give me a chance as I am, don’t start by trying to change me.”

“Hey, I just wanted you to know that I ‘know.’ I want you to remember, buster, that I’m as smart as you. I get high, too. I get high dancing. I can’t explain it like you did, but I go beyond myself and defy gravity—fly away. I get high just riding a bike, and now, starting to make love to you, is one of the best highs I’ve ever had. I’ll say it, James. I think I’m falling for you, too.”

They kissed again, leisurely, as they had earlier, exploring each other’s eyes and noses and mouths and silly ears. She loved smelling him. There was more than just the pot smell: he smelled clean. His skin was smooth, his facial hair still soft, his chest hard, and his arms strong. She sniffed his underarms and bit the skin there, making him squirm and laugh.

He thought she was a wonder. He kissed the crook of her elbow and up to her shoulder and on to her gorgeous long neck. She was totally smooth, her skin soft, and her scent intoxicating.

“You smell good. What is it about you?”

“It’s me! And maybe the Opium body powder I borrowed from Gram’s stash.”

“I know all about opium,” he said, letting it slip out.

She ignored the comment. “What’s the next step for us, James? I don’t want to wait long. I want to have you naked. I want all of you.”

She’s fast, he thought. What’s happening here? He looked outside. He hadn’t necked with a girl in the backseat of a car, but he’d watched a dozen movies about some pervert attacking a young couple in a car, in the dark.

“Honestly, Willow, are you ready for all that? Are you on birth control? I’m not ready to be a father. Have you done it with other guys?”

"No. I'm not experienced, but I can get a prescription for the pill this week. I'm ready, James."

"I don't know—are pills effective immediately? I'm not taking a chance with our lives here, Willow. Find out if we have to give the pills time to work."

Willow sighed. "We aren't going all the way tonight. I just want you to know, I'm choosing you."

"I want you, too, and I have a place of my own to take you to, and I want to lay down with you. Oh, God, do I want to lay down with you. Do you think you should talk to your Gram and tell her what we want to do? I don't want to sneak around. You're more to me than that. I want us to be upfront with your folks."

"Well, jeez, let me think about that, James. I know that's what I'm supposed to do, talk to Gram before I have sex, but ick!"

"I'd never talk to my mother," James admitted, "but I don't want to get you pregnant, us pregnant, and I'm a lot older than you. I want to do right by you."

"You think you're a lot older than me? Two years? What makes you say that? Do I seem too young for you?"

"No. You don't seem young to me, but we're almost in the same family. If we're mature about this, we can stay over at my place, and we can really have some fun. I can't wait."

"Too much thinking—I want to taste you again. I want to make you really hot and ready for me, OK?" She reached down and rubbed the front of his pants.

That worked for James.

19 / ELLEN'S TRUTH

Midweek, about nine at night, Ellen was already in her pajamas, reading in the living room when the phone rang. "Hi, Ellen. It's Carmen."

After a few pleasantries, Carmen came to the point. "Let's get together. Are you free tomorrow night? For a late supper? I know a great pub, O' Henry's. It is handy, in between our neighborhoods."

Ellen paused. They hadn't met during the week and not just for a meal. Was Carmen wanting their friendship to become more intimate?

"Mid-week usually finds me free. The fall weather is great for a walk, too. OK," Ellen said. "Let's do it. Tell me about the pub. Is it a busy noisy place?"

"If we meet at 8:00, the pub will be pretty well emptied of diners, just a few locals at the bar. We'll find a high booth for an intimate talk."

That sent shivers down Ellen's spine. Was she pleased? Perhaps I am, she contemplated.

"See you there, pal?

"Yes," Ellen answered casually, feeling far from casual.

ELLEN WASN'T able to settle down to sleep. She didn't even try. Pulling sweats on and zipping a hoodie over her pajamas, Ellen headed out for an evening walk to wear off her nervous energy. The evening air was refreshing; she felt nearly chilly in just a cotton hoodie, but within a few blocks of fast walking, she was warm and comfortable.

Carmen had instigated their first 'date' to the Arboretum, and they discovered they both loved strolling down flowered paths. After that first planned date, they'd gone to an action movie of Ellen's choice and then to a disturbing feminist play of Carmen's choice. Carmen had laughed off the painful politics while Ellen shuddered in horror, watching women attempting to appease angry representatives of God and other difficult men in their lives.

Ellen wondered how Carmen could be such a joyful woman with such far left-leaning politics. She somehow seemed to take pleasure in the simple things of life instead of ruminating about the horrors so close to home. A child dancing on the arboretum path sent Carmen dancing, too; a fairly good beer and a meaty sandwich sent her into rhapsodies. Carmen was talkative but not intrusive, playful and accepting of Ellen's shier nature.

But the tenor of this last phone call was different.

Ellen shied away from friendships with women she met through work. She hadn't let many people into her life, other than Sandra's family and to a certain extent, one coworker, Elliot Pearson, who was gay.

Elliot enjoyed giving Ellen the male perspective in raising James, and over the years, she'd invited Elliot and his partner, Ron, to come over to meet James. Several times Elliot and Ron brought their little fishing boat and fished at a lake nearby Ellen and James' cabin in Wisconsin. Ellen had laughed at them when they came to fish with huge hooks and very sturdy fishing line. They'd surprised her, catching a sturgeon weighing 25 pounds. She and James were very impressed.

But for twenty years, Ellen's focus had been her work, paying off loans, graduate school and the house down payment from Ralph, and raising James.

Ellen loved long evening walks in her neighborhood, block after block of similar houses, lights coming on and off, upstairs and down, as families moved through their evening rituals. Walking by strangers' homes comforted Ellen. She enjoyed the imagined common domesticity she believed most families shared. At this hour, we all have our 'readying for bed rituals,' she thought. There, in the two-story tutor, someone was finalizing the clean-up of the kitchen and turning off downstairs lights. Lights were coming on in all four upstairs bedrooms. The kids were brushing teeth, getting last drinks of water, climbing into beds, and, perhaps, saying their prayers.

Next, in the one-story bungalow, gray light bounced off a large entertainment center. The curtains were open, and Ellen stopped for a moment, mesmerized by flashes of a movie she'd enjoyed.

We are creatures of gentle habits, she thought.

In her own life, aside from the gift of being given a son to raise, she had taken minimal risks. She had chosen a structured life of well thought out goals, education, and career. She was successful in her career, guiding clients to take risks in small increments, to slowly practice change, and she was proud of her work.

But now, this woman, Carmen—Ellen had to admit—she felt attracted to her. She was attracted to a woman. She thought about what this might mean and began humming a ditty from childhood:

"I'm looking over a four-leaf clover,
that I overlooked before...
No need explaining the one remaining

Is someone I adore..."

The longing had started; she'd felt it before, but she'd run from it, had only acted on attraction once. The longing started in the heart region then moved to the groin. Exquisite and awful. Don't, she'd warned herself. Don't go there. She stopped walking, looking around to be certain of her privacy. She put her arms together at her gut and rocked. Breathe, she told herself, and she felt the tension lessen. She walked on, safely back in her head.

In this day and age, she thought, even Sandra would react better to an introduction of a lesbian into their lives than she did nearly thirty years ago when they were roommates and JJ came calling. Times change. Gays and lesbians were now free to marry. Still, personally, this was not a small risk. She was older now, in her fifties; would a let-down, a doomed attraction be worse in middle age? Calm down, woman, she told herself. Don't be a fool. Perhaps she was making up this big attraction.

THE NEXT EVENING, Ellen and Carmen met outside the diner. The supper rush was over, the diner nearly empty. Carmen led the way to a high booth, up a step, in a glassed-off corner of the quiet pub. A faux gas lamp from the garden area cast half-light through the glass and onto their profiles.

Later Ellen could not for the life of her recall the waitress or recall ordering steins of beer and sandwiches, or the taste of the beer, or the eating of the sandwiches, or their chattering about daily events.

Coffee was served, milk was added, spoons were set aside, and Ellen looked up and turned her eyes fully on Carmen then sideways onto Carmen. Carmen was sitting squarely across from her, elbows on the table, manicured fingers intertwined and resting on her chin.

Her veils had lifted, and she let Ellen see her as she was, a beautiful mature woman: a woman content with herself, a woman attracted to Ellen.

Wow, Ellen thought. She's swept me into a movie. Me, little mouse me, sitting across from this woman, this very out lesbian.

"I've been thinking about you," Carmen said. "And I keep hoping you're thinking about me, too."

Ellen tried to look more directly at Carmen but couldn't quite make herself do it. "Yes. I have been thinking about you but about me too," Ellen answered. She continued; her eyes downcast. "I took a long walk last night, thinking about our get together tonight." Then she took a deep breath and looked directly at Carmen.

Carmen dropped her hands down and looked at the table.

"You are an out lesbian, and I am not," Ellen said. "I chose another path, not an altogether happy path, but I've plowed along, enjoying my work and my son and my chosen family. My world has been safe. The word 'out,' much less the word 'lesbian, frightens me. Doesn't that connote outcast? I've worked all my life to fit in."

Carmen's brown eyes saddened. "When I started meeting other out lesbians, we occasionally talked about our attractions to 'straight ladies.' We'd all had our painful experiences with women who were attracted to us, sometimes even had sex with us, but in the end, chose to return to the straight world, date and marry men, go back to husbands, or sometimes just never get involved with anyone again. Lots of hearts were broken over 'straight women,' including mine, but here we are, older, wiser. Do you agree, we're wiser, Ellen?"

Ellen looked down quickly, thought a moment, then looked back up and nodded. "I'm both—older and wiser. I love peeking at you, Carmen, at your wild mane of hair falling as it will. I think of you as 'cat like,' and because I'm such a mouse, you scare me. OK, I'm going to say it. I'm scared but awfully attracted to you."

Carmen tried for a beatific smile, somewhat succeeding. "Do you have plans for the weekend? Should we get together? You haven't been to my house, Miss Mouse, or met my domestic cat. I promise he'll only purr. I'll make an early dinner and then we can walk around my neighborhood."

"OK, Carmen. I'd love to see your place, meet your cat. And let's go for a walk now before it's my weeknight bed time."

Carmen laughed. "Aren't we getting old? I'm so glad we've cleared the air between us. And you?"

Ellen vaguely nodded her agreement.

Carmen slipped her arm through Ellen's and pressed against her once or twice as they matched strides down a quiet unexplored neighborhood street.

THIRTY YEARS AGO, after graduation from St. Olaf College, Sandy easily talked Ellen into finding a place together in the Cities. Sandy's dad offered to pay their first three month's rent. With their four-year degrees, they both applied for professional positions but supported themselves in the meantime working at a temporary agency.

Sandy got a real job in the fall as an assistant buyer for Dayton's, the big department store downtown. After she got the job, she wanted to look the part of a wholesale buyer and started getting $50 haircuts and highlights and wearing expensive, smart business women's clothes.

Ellen was offered and accepted a social worker position in Child Protection. The work opened her eyes to parents and children's social suffering—things she never knew existed in Minnesota. She second guessed her own orphaned childhood; being taken in by older relatives hadn't been half bad.

Both women loved their work.

With a fairly good salary, Sandy wanted to find a more expensive apartment. Ellen preferred their affordable duplex, close to the river's biking paths. But Ellen had a hard time saying no to Sandy, and off they moved to the suburbs into a huge complex of apartments. Their apartment had a half-raised ceiling and a balcony overlooking a complex of swimming pools.

Ellen had listened to Sandy's stream of consciousness talk about Terry, her hometown boyfriend, all through college. Terry, gentle soul, was still in the picture, visiting often on weekends. But now, Ellen listened not only to Sandra's Terry stories but also to Sandy's stories about her boss, Rocky.

Sandy had disliked Rocky when she first met him. She derided his beltless tight bell bottoms and his blousy shirts that exposed a hairy chest. He was from Boston, and she could mimic his flat 'A.'

She'd overheard him say, "I like hiring farm girls. They have good work ethics from being up early to milk cows." But she had no problem interrupting the men's conversations. "I've been coming to Dayton's department store to shop since before I could talk, and my family always stayed at the best hotels. I'm not a goddamn milk maiden."

After that, Sandy became Sandra. "My family could probably buy and sell his family," she lamented to Ellen.

Her disdain for Rocky did not last. He genuinely liked the feisty young country woman with a good work ethic, and ultimately, he seduced her. But Sandra didn't talk about her sex on a couch with Rocky to Ellen. Sandra was embarrassed about giving in to him after she had demeaned him, and besides, Ellen would be loyal to Terry, who happily spent part of his weekend visits verbally sparring with Ellen and the rest of the weekend engaging in robust sex with Sandra.

Sandra was gaining entrance in the artsy scene, while Ellen

spent time at REI, buying active sports clothes and equipment for hiking, biking, and skiing with new friends from work. They remained good roommates, giving each other space but saving Tuesday nights to line dance together at the Medina Ballroom. Disco was the in thing, and they both loved to dance. Ellen loved Abba, and Sandra loved the Bee Gees.

Ellen was developing friendships among her coworkers. She especially liked JJ Sandberg, who worked in Child Protection, too. JJ was an outdoorsy woman who winter camped. She invited Ellen to give it a try, and Ellen agreed. Ellen gave sex with JJ a try, too.

One evening when Ellen came home from work, Sandra was sitting in a darkened living room, crying into a wad of Kleenex. She tried to talk but got choked up and started crying again.

Ellen asked, "Did someone die? Is everyone OK?"

Sandra shook her head. "Everyone is fine; I just can't quit crying."

Ellen asked Sandra if she wanted tea and Sandra nodded. The sounds of Sandra's crying softened and then quieted. Ellen brought in a tray with cups and a teapot, sugar and milk, and set it on the coffee table in front of them. Sandra looked pathetic. Ellen sat down next to her and said, "Here, cry on my shoulder." Sandra let Ellen put her arm around her, and Sandra leaned, heavy and wet against her friend.

"I'm pregnant," she said. "I don't know who the father is. It could be Rocky, or it could be Terry, and I don't want either of them, and I hate me. I forgot my pills at my folks; it was past the middle of the month, and I was sure I was safe. What am I going to do? Rocky is just a fling, and I don't want to marry Terry and become a farmer's wife. What a mess I've made out of my life. I'm going to have to get an abortion, aren't I?"

The abortion was a sad day for both of them. Ellen found out from a woman at work about an abortionist in St. Paul. She got the information, Sandra made the call, and they went together. When they got home, Ellen filled the hot water bottle, and Sandra curled up in bed, her face to the wall.

Ellen had never seen Sandra so subdued. She still went to work, but the joy was gone. She called Terry and told him that she had made the decision to stay in the Cities and not marry him. He was angry and hurt by her rudeness and called Ellen asking for an explanation. Then Sandra called Terry and told him she had met someone else. He finally lost hope and quit calling.

Ellen was torn between having her own life and being home for Sandra. Sandra was depressed and didn't like it when Ellen went out socially. Ellen accommodated Sandra and spent less time with her friend JJ.

Finally, JJ asked Ellen why she was avoiding her, and Ellen told her the truth about her roommate's abortion and depression. JJ asked if she could come over to their place and meet Sandra. She would bring Chinese and beer and the three of them could play cards.

Sandra wasn't excited about having Ellen's friend over but then changed her mind and said, "Of course, let's have her over. I've got to get myself out of this depression. I've finally made an appointment to see a shrink at the HMO. I hope he gives me valium. I can't stand the way I feel."

JJ came over with Chinese and two six packs. As soon as she was inside the apartment and had taken off her jacket, Ellen could tell J.J. was making a statement. She was wearing a tucked in man's shirt, men's pants, thick belt, and heavy boots. Her short hair was slicked back. Out of the corner of her eye, Ellen thought she looked sexy but not in front of Sandra.

Still, they all knew the same card games and settled on playing three handed hearts. Sandra was more her old self, trying to "shoot the moon" almost every card hand and gleeful when she won.

Ellen was happy seeing her two friends were doing well

together, and she was bolder than usual, showing off her prowess at cards, too.

The next morning, drinking coffee and eating leftover Chinese, Ellen asked Sandra if she liked JJ. Sandra gave her a serious look and said, "You know what she is, of course."

Ellen knew where Sandra was going with this but wanted her to say it. "What do you mean?"

"Well, she's a dyke. It is obvious—short hair, wide belt. I think she was wearing men's pants and definitely a men's shirt. Didn't you see the shoes she had on? She was in drag. She is a diesel dyke. Rocky took me to a bar one afternoon to watch the diesel dykes with their women."

"Those are mean words, Sandra. How can you be so nice to her face and so mean behind her back? She isn't that butchy at work," Ellen countered. "She dresses like everyone else."

"Then why was she showing off for me? Ick, Ellen. You don't run with people like her, do you? You're not going to do that to me, to us, are you? That isn't you, is it? You're not 'attracted to her,' are you?"

"What if I was?"

"Then everything between us is a lie, and I'll have lost my best two friends—both you and Terry. I can't even talk about it." Sandra stomped out of the room and slammed her bedroom door."

Ellen went to her bedroom door. "Talk to me Sandra! I'm not all that attracted to her, but I think JJ is a very nice person."

Sandra mumbled and slowly came out of her bedroom. "I'm sorry; I overreacted. But you seemed so comfortable with her, that's all. I mean, you brought her over here. She acted like she was courting you. You don't have to lower yourself to that level. The right man will come along. You believe me, don't you?" Sandra pleaded with her eyes.

Ellen took a minute, looking at her best friend, the woman who befriended her when she was so out of place at that Lutheran college. "It's so hard for me to believe that I will find a man. I'm just not meeting men I'm attracted to."

"You'll meet the right man, trust me," Sandra promised.

That's how things remained between Sandra and Ellen. They remained extremely attached, and Ellen never did meet the right man.

PART 3
THE FAMILY GROWS

20 / ELLEN AND CARMEN GET IT ON

Ellen arrived at Carmen's near twilight on a windy fall day. The exterior of Carmen's house was white stucco with a red tiled roof and long, multi paned black metal windows. Later, she remembered the wrought iron door knocker and the sudden gust of red maple leaves mixing with the sounds of Gershwin's "Rhapsody in Blue" as Carmen opened the rounded plank door.

Carmen welcomed her inside with a slight bow and sweep of her arm. The front room was as Ellen anticipated, noisy and bright. The interior walls were white with groupings of paintings everywhere. The old, dark polished wood floors were bare.

Primary colored acrylic unframed paintings fought for room on the walls, but a black and white framed photo of two happy women dominated the mantle of the classic 1950s brick walled fireplace. Two white down couches with a long plank bench between them faced each other in the center of the room.

Ellen knew James would love this room. She studied the black and white photo, obviously Carmen and her partner Susie. They looked so happy and relaxed, leaning into each other with an apple orchard in the background. Ellen's heart ached for Carmen's loss.

"Tell me about Susie the artist," Ellen said.

With a sweeping gesture, Carmen explained Susie's art as best she could. "As you can see, she had an eye for focusing on one aspect of a busy setting," Carmen said, pointing to a few of her favorites. "Urban sprawl with a focus on a colorful street dancer, a busy interior with a solitary woman looking out a window, and a wall of books with a cat appearing to read the book titles. All these were juxtaposed."

Ellen focused on Carmen's favorites then continued looking at each painting, shaking her head and smiling in amazement. "Susie had intensity in her eyes," Carmen said. "She was like a camera. Sometimes she would stop when we were walking and pull at me to stop, too. Then she'd slowly move her head from left to right, always from left to right, and when she found what she had seen in a glance, she would take time to memorize the image. I'd watch her and guess what she found so interesting. Later, she would show me a quick drawing of what had stopped her in mid stride. I loved those moments, walking with Susie."

"James is artistic, too," Ellen said. "He is doing Anime now. He says images and stories come to him while he's running. He would love seeing this art."

"I hope he visits soon; I want to meet your lovely son, and I noticed you are a good photographer, Ellen. That day I picked you up for the movies and you rummaged about for your jacket, I studied the spontaneous pictures you've taken of James. You caught him in mid-movement a number of times, and I got a sense of what you love from your photos, besides James, I mean. Biking, fishing, camp fires, I learned you love being outdoors."

Ellen lowered her head to hide her blush. "You didn't say anything about the photo gallery when you stopped by our house." Ellen looked shyly at Carmen's profile. Did she really mean what she was saying, or was she trying to make Ellen feel more equal to the love of her life, to Susie?

As Ellen continued to study the art on the walls, Carmen turned down the music and opened a bottle of wine. She brought snacks from the kitchen, and they sat together on a couch, feet up on the roughhewn coffee table, drinking wine and nibbling on cheese, salmon, and crackers.

Ellen noted to herself that if they were to be together, she wouldn't compete with a dead woman. Ellen's mouth felt suddenly dry, and she moved her teeth back and forth against her inner lips, not wanting to continue the conversation with a dry mouth.

"Oh, we were in and out of your home so quickly, and my mind was wandering when we were there. I was liking everything about you," Carmen said, finishing her thought.

The deep couch seductively rolled them towards each other; their arms and thighs touched, sending jolts through Ellen. Was this passion or fear, she wondered.

Panache, the large yellow tabby, hopped on the couch and walked across Carmen to inspect Ellen. He looked deeply into her eyes with his own yellow, wise eyes before settling himself in the nest of their limbs and purring between them.

Dinner was delicious. Ellen ate with more appetite than usual. She had seconds of eggplant lasagna, garlic bread, and salad. They chatted, becoming ever wittier as the wine bottle emptied. Carmen said, "I love the smell of garlic on a woman's breath. How about a little night cap in the living room? I have a good brandy opened."

Ellen nodded and raised up from the large, embroidered dining room chair, folding her patterned cloth napkin carefully and leaving it by her empty white plate. They moved back to one of the deep couches in the living room. Carmen brought their aperitifs and sat down next to Ellen. They sipped and swirled their brandies.

"Should we take an evening walk?" Carmen asked.

"Should we finish our brandy first?" asked Ellen.

"OK," Carmen said and finished her brandy in a gulp.

Ellen laughed, setting her near empty snifter down. "Come on, let's walk."

THEY WALKED arm in arm along the old neighborhood's uneven sidewalks, catching each other before tripping and laughing. Ellen gasped at the splendid homes of the urban wealthy just blocks from Carmen's more modest West Minneapolis neighborhood.

After they were back inside, Carmen locked the door behind them, gathered their coats, and hung them on well-placed hooks before saying, "Good—that's done. Can we go upstairs to bed?"

ELLEN LAUGHED NERVOUSLY and suggested they clear the dining room and do the dishes. Carmen shook her head, and Ellen allowed herself to be led up the stairway.

Carmen hopped onto the high bed and put out an arm to invite Ellen to follow her. They clumsily lay down, fully clothed, and faced each other on the bed. Carmen circled Ellen's heart with her finger tip. "I think I know the way to your heart."

"Well," Ellen said, still nervous. "What do we do now?"

"Oh, it comes naturally," Carmen responded and quoted FDR. "The only thing to fear is fear itself."

Sex, indeed, came naturally, slowly, and satisfyingly. They loved each other until the early dark morning hours. Ellen woke up with the light, entangled in Carmen's limbs, Carmen's curly head of hair tickling her nose.

Ellen felt comfortable beneath the weight of her new lover's body. She loved this bed, she loved being with this woman, and she was ready to get up. She tried to disengage herself, sneak out of bed. Carmen stirred.

"Tell me again that you love being with me, naked in bed," Carmen asked.

Ellen rolled on top of Carmen, lying with all her weight on her, toe to toe, and hugged her deeply. "I love being naked with you, but I'm ready to get up and explore your house."

"I've got a long robe hanging behind the door. Throw it on, if you will. Don't trip on the hem going down the stairs. I've done it myself, and I'm taller than you."

ELLEN DID as she was told, holding the hem up and walking barefoot down the stairs, looking at the series of black and white photos that lined the staircase. Most of the faces and many of the settings were unfamiliar, but Carmen or Susie showed up regularly.

Ellen was overwhelmed and wanted to be where she was most comfortable, outdoors. She bypassed the scene of last night's dinner and made a beeline for the back door and deck she had noted the night before. The wet deck tickled her bare feet. The air was cool; Ellen could see her breath.

Ellen felt girlish and safe in Carmen's long robe and in the fenced in backyard. She pantomimed "I'm a little teapot," raising her head and blowing steam from her mouth. Then she drew a heart on the deck with her big toe. Dawn was breaking; the pink sky was graced by horizontal orange flares announcing the rising sun. It was going to be one of those October days that belied the cold days ahead. Today would be blue sky, warm sunshine, and gusty wind—piles of dry fallen leaves. Kids' weather, lovers' weather.

She looked at the well-used lounger sitting on the deck. She surmised that this is where Carmen sat for five years, mourning her wife. Ellen was tempted to lie down to feel and smell the essence of sadness. Ellen wondered how Carmen could appear so happy after experiencing so much loss.

Finally, Ellen went back up the stairs and carefully replaced the robe behind the bedroom door. She sat naked on the edge of the bed, looking at the floor and feeling almost as uncomfortable as she had approaching the bed last night.

Carmen sat propped up by pillows, obviously still comfortable in bed. "Come—you look cold. Let me warm you." Indeed, Ellen was cold and worried, sitting naked on Carmen's bed. Carmen grabbed her by the waist and gently pulled her back under the covers and lay against her, sharing her warmth, rubbing her arms and hands and tucking Ellen's cold feet between her thighs. Ellen was starting to relax when Carmen leaned forward to whisper in her ear. "Do you want to go to church with me? I'm excited to show you off to my friends."

"Church?" said Ellen with obvious disappointment; she had expected an appeal to spend the morning in bed. "We haven't talked about religion. I assumed you were like me, spiritual, not religious."

"It isn't what you might think; it is better. I'm a Unitarian, and I sing in the choir; they'd miss me."

Sandra had tried and tried over the years, encouraging Ellen to go to Lutheran church with her family. Ellen drew the line there; she was not religious.

"Would I have to sit by myself?" Ellen asked.

"No—we in the choir just get up and go to the front when we sing then go back to our families."

"So now we're family?"

"Kind of, I guess," Carmen said and looked longingly at Ellen.

Ellen sighed. If she were to be with Carmen, the relationship would come with maintenance and embarrassment. She thought about how self-centered she had been most of her life. She could have put more into raising James, and she was disappointed in herself for hiding her sexuality. But could she change? Become more open? I better try; she told herself.

"Carmen, I'll go to church with you."

Carmen smiled appreciatively. "Let's cuddle for an hour or two and then I'll make you coffee with cream and heat up the scones I bought for us yesterday."

ELLEN FOUND the church service to be tolerable; the hour went by quickly. She hadn't envisioned Carmen's strong, clear voice. How little she knew about this woman.

After church, people milled around, moving outdoors into a garden area with stone benches and tables and chairs surrounding a small pond with a gurgling fountain. Ellen tried to hide her discomfort by letting Carmen charge ahead while she followed. A tall blond woman and handsome dark eyed man walked up to them, smiling at Carmen, ready to hug her, but she turned away from them and motioned for Ellen to come forward before turning back to her friends.

"Ellen, these are my good friends Char Gunderson and Joe Reyes; Char and Joe, this is my new special friend, Ellen Holden."

Joe and Ellen recognized each other immediately from the evening at the cafe with Sandra. Joe reached out his hand, and when Ellen took his hand, he pulled her in and gave her a half hug and a pat on the back.

Ellen steeled herself and didn't pull back from him out of embarrassment. Now Sandra would hear about her relationship with Carmen. Once again, she had no separation from her critical friend Sandra.

Char and Carmen drew back with wonder and looked at Joe.

"This woman, Ellen, is your sister's best friend," Joe explained to Char.

"You're James' mother?" Char asked.

Ellen recognized Char. "Yes, I was one of the many at your mother's funeral."

Char reached out and gave Ellen a big hug, wrapping her arms around her in the familiar way Sandra did. After Char released her, Ellen patted her arm. Then Joe gave her another hug. She patted his arm, too.

"Let's sit down," Char said, and they followed her to a nearby empty table.

After sitting, Carmen said, "What is this? You all seem to know each other. I'm on the outside." Char grabbed Carmen's hand and said, "You go first Joe. You were the first to meet Ellen again."

"She, Ellen, I mean," Joe smiled his apologies to Ellen and looked at Carmen, "came to our restaurant a few weeks ago with Char's sister, Sandra. Char and Sandra hadn't been in contact for many years, and, Ellen, weren't you the one who figured it out?"

Now it was Ellen's turn. "Sandra and I knew that James' new girlfriend, Willow, was Joe and Char's girl, but we had only seen Willow once, at the funeral, when she was just a little girl. We knew from James that Willow worked at Joe's Café, and we went there to snoop and to have dinner. We were served by this beautiful young woman who we decided must be Willow. In fact, I told Sandra, 'that's your niece.' My impetuous friend, Sandra, jumped up and smothered Willow with hugs."

"That's where I come in," Charlene interrupted. "A few days later, Sandra called me and I went to her home for lunch and was introduced to her fabulous garden. Sandra and I danced through the garden barefoot and reminisced about life on the farm. We both admitted that we are more like our outspoken Swedish grandmother than we are like our sweet Norwegian mother. Now, Sandra and I, with Joe and Sandra's husband, Ralph, are going to visit our father. It's been over forty years since I've been back to the farm." Char's hands fluttered with anxiety.

"But there is more than that. Char. Tell them the rest, about James," Joe coaxed. Ellen's ears perked up. She was anxious to hear what they had to say about her son.

"Ellen, I met your James," Char said then turned her attention to Carmen. "Ellen's son James is dating Willow. I met him on Friday. We talked. He's full of fun—I like him."

Carmen gave Ellen a pleased look and added, "I know Willow, Ellen. I've known her for years."

"James was such a gentleman," Char said. "He had no idea that Sandra and I were sisters. But he put two and two together, the Gunderson name and the physical similarity between Sandra and me. He said Sandra is like his second mother. Willow teased him. 'We are kissing cousins,' she said. Willow is very observant and says what she thinks." Joe nodded reflectively at that comment.

Carmen wanted to get a word in edgewise. "Well, I guess I have some catching up to do. I hate being left out. I'm confused, but I'm sure I'll get it all straightened out." She looked around for reassurance.

Joe offered it. "I don't know Sandra, yet, either Carmen. And I haven't met James. We're the in-laws, outlaws, whatever, in this extended family."

Ellen shrugged. "Sandra and Ralph have always considered James and me part of their family. Before Sandra married Ralph, Sandra and I were roommates. She picked me out as her friend when we were in college and has never let me go, and I'm very grateful for her shared parenting of James."

"I'll say the obvious: there are changes in our family dynamics going on here," Char said. "James and Willow just getting to know each other, Sandra and I are just getting reacquainted, and I guess you two haven't been seeing each other all that long, either."

Carmen and Ellen looked at each, grinning. Carmen said, "We are new to being together. I can't speak for Ellen, but I trust my instincts, and I'm very happy to have met this woman." She grabbed Ellen's hand.

Carmen added, "There is this joke about lesbians. On the first date lesbians check out each other's houses, and by the second date, they know who will be bringing the U-Haul with her on the third date."

"Well, I never," Ellen said, laughing nervously.

Char and Joe looked back and forth at the two women and then looked at each other, remembering their own good fortune in finding each other. Joe linked Char's arm and said, "Love is contagious, women. Thank you for sharing it with us."

Carmen smiled at her church friends. "Your blessings mean so much. Thanks, Joe; thanks, Char."

"Neither Sandra nor James know about our new relationship," Ellen said. "Please let me be the one who tells each of them. Obviously, I need to do it soon."

"I hear you, Ellen," Char said. "I'm glad you said that out loud. We'll definitely keep tight lipped about you two, right Joe? I'm excited by all this synchronicity. Our lives are weaving together—it's like being rural again, where everyone knows your business. I hope our new friendships and family blend."

21 / ELLEN COMES OUT TO SANDRA

Ellen got home about 5 p.m. after eating left-overs, loving again, and napping at Carmen's. On the way home, she drove almost carelessly, singing the chorus with Abba on one of her favorite CDs. '*See that girl, watch that scene, digging the dancing queen.*'

She thought about the 'sweep and move around movement' while line dancing with Sandra thirty years ago. Oh, she felt young again—hopeful, heart full.

As she drove into her garage, she shook her head in disgust. Her home was a place to read and sleep, not to live and love. Ellen wondered if James would come home tonight to do his laundry. Although James was reticent about sharing details of his life, Ellen sensed he was more at peace with himself and was doing well. He wasn't complaining about classes. He had started a part-time job, and he was guarded in his revelations about his new work, but it seemed important to him, and, of course, he was dating. She could hardly believe how quickly he had moved into action, finding a new life for himself. But then, so had she.

Her cell dinged as she entered the house. It was Sandra.

"Can you come over for leftovers? I'm hanging out alone. Ralph got called in to consult about someone's rectum, I presume. I'll set out a smorgasbord of goodies for us."

Ellen answered evenly: "I'll check with James, if he isn't coming by, I'm free. I'll tell you about my weekend, too."

Ellen called Sandra back. "James isn't coming tonight, so I'll be over ASAP."

"Good, put on a hoodie," Sandra said. "We're expecting frost overnight—there goes the garden. Let's have a drink and watch the sunset on the deck before eating."

"Summer has segued to fall so beautifully this year," Ellen said to Sandra. "I'll wear my warmest hoodie and get right over. I'd like to hit the scotch tonight."

"I've got scotch, Ellen."

"OK! I'll be over soon."

Ellen marched over to Sandra's with new found resolve. She would be a true friend, opening up to Sandra in a way she should have done all those years ago.

Two slung back chairs faced the on-deck gas fireplace. The nearly invisible flame quickly glowed bolder as the sun set. The women dug into the bowls of mixed nuts and candied ginger and drank from the tall glasses of scotch and soda.

Diplomatically, Sandra asked, "Do you want to go first?"

Ellen declined, knowing that she wouldn't have Sandra's full attention unless Sandra shared her news first.

"Kimber's baby is going to be a boy. They didn't really want to know, but on the latest ultrasound, the penis was very obvious. They are terribly excited, and I suggested that I take the girls yesterday so they could do some shopping for the baby. Tally and Kenzie and I had a great day together, even Ralph got involved.

The girls are into dolls big time, so I asked them to bring their American Girl Dolls, and I got Kimber's Big Girl doll. Twenty plus years ago, I made oodles of outfits for Kimber and Laurel's dolls. The three of us played for hours. I brought out soft stretchy material, and we each cut out new scarves for our dolls. Then we put them through their paces on a parchment runway Ralph made for us on the deck.

Ralph was the judge at the end of the runway, making foolish commentary as we walked our dolls past him. Then he got bored and left to wash his car. He surprised us with three kinds of gelato: chocolate, mango and strawberry. 'My girls', he called us. I was so touched by his thoughtfulness, Ellen." Sandra's eyes teared up.

Sandra looked at Ellen for affirmation.

Ellen nodded for Sandra to continue.

"I've got so much going on, Ellen. Char is influencing my life already. She is so much like me. She's very smart. Did I tell you? She quoted TS Eliot when she visited me." Sandra stopped talking and looked hard at Ellen. Something was different. It wasn't a new haircut. Ellen was listening attentively, or was she? She was eating nuts, smiling and nodding for Sandra to continue her story.

Ellen noticed Sandra's pause and said, "I couldn't be happier for you and Char. I'm hoping to get to know Char, too. Have you talked to her today?"

"No. Why do you ask?"

"I ran into her today."

"Ellen, did you go back to Joe's Cafe without me?"

"No. I met her at church."

"Church? You met Char at church? I didn't ask Char about religion; I assumed Char was an atheist like you. How in the world did you and Char meet in church?" Sandra pulled back in her chair and uncrossed her knees. Suddenly, she was uncomfortable. She looked hard again at her best friend. What was the change in Ellen?

Ellen leaned forward, a gleam in her eye.

Had she found God? Sandra wondered.

"I'm not an atheist," Ellen said. "Why do you say that? I'm an agnostic. But don't distract me. Remember me mentioning a woman named Carmen—we'd met at a conference a few months ago and since we've been socializing?"

"Now you're going to church with her?"

"This once I did."

"How did that happen?"

Ellen drew a deep breath, looked at her more than half empty drink, and finished it off in two long swallows. "I stayed overnight with her last night, and this morning we went to church. I slept with her. She is a lesbian, and I guess I am, too."

Sandra closed her open mouth and leaned forward, trying to read Ellen's expression again. The sun had set, and she couldn't see Ellen's face as well.

"I'm dumbfounded, Ellen. Aren't you a little old for this sort of stuff? Your son moves out and you jump into bed with a woman? I mean I always knew you were a little in that direction. It's a continuum, isn't it? You're in the middle, kind of bi-sexual, aren't you?"

Ellen felt a rush of anger and bounced up to leave, turned around, thought twice and settled back into her chair. She would not allow Sandra to intimidate her about her sexuality. She would not allow anyone to define her sexuality for her. "Is there an expiration date on falling in love? Don't you want me to be happy? Or do you want me to try a 'nice' guy again?"

"You married Jay. I didn't ask you to do that," Sandra snapped back.

"Jay was a nice man, and the decision to marry him was mine. Sorry Sandra. I shouldn't blame you," Ellen admitted.

"The truth, Sandra, is this: I've been attracted to women all my life. And, now, my time has come. When I met Carmen, I was attracted to her, and best of all, she was attracted to me, too, and I didn't shy away from her. I just liked her too much."

"So, this Carmen is going to be part of our lives now?" Sandra said quietly. She got up and stood in front of Ellen with her arms outstretched. Ellen got up, too, and Sandra pulled her close. Ellen put her head on Sandra's shoulder. They hugged and rocked in each other's arms.

When they settled back down, Sandra wanted to know the details. "What did she say? What did you say? How did you get the message across to each other?"

"On our first date, to the arboretum, I asked if she was a lesbian. Sandra, I knew it. I knew she was a lesbian, and I wanted her to know I knew it. Something let go inside of me, and I didn't care anymore."

"I asked you if you were lesbian way back after that JJ came over, and you said no."

"God, you don't forget a thing, do you? You even remembered her name? You only met her once. Since you brought it up, I'd like to talk about that time JJ came over to visit. You were so negative about her, about lesbians. What was I supposed to say? Tell you that maybe I was a lesbian, too? I wasn't in love with JJ. Truth told; I was more concerned about what you thought of me than I was about what she thought of me. You were my best friend, my everything."

"Don't put that on me, Ellen. I would never have stopped being your best friend, even if you were a lesbian. I might not have liked it, at first anyway, but I would have gotten used to it."

"I didn't know that. You are my family, Sandra. I couldn't risk losing you." Ellen's eyes brimmed with tears.

"How did I get the power to keep you from being who you are? I'm putting that back on you, Ellen."

Ellen felt a rush of dislike for that little girl in her who cared too much about what people thought of her. "Oh, shut up, Sandra. I mean, I get it. You're right—I can't blame you. I wish I could blame you for me marrying a man I didn't love, for having a baby I wasn't sure I wanted, but I made those decisions; you didn't make my decisions. Today I vow to you, Sandra, I will be honest. I've been depressed most of my life, I guess. There is a name for it, dysphoria. It doesn't affect work; you can still function, but you live with a general dissatisfaction with life. I've known that about myself forever, but I never examined it in myself, even though I'm a psychologist. I'm a tricky devil; I can outsmart myself as well as I think I can outsmart others."

Sandra interrupted, "If I hadn't been so selfish, if I'd been thinking about you, I wouldn't have been hateful about JJ. I'd have tried to help you find a girlfriend. I would have pushed you in that direction. But, especially right after the abortion, I was so remorseful, and I guess I was afraid of losing you to someone else. During those months after the abortion, you were my life's blood, Ellen."

"Enough of this, Sandra. You don't have to apologize to me. I didn't want to be with JJ. I wanted a woman more like you. Now I've found her."

"How did you know she was the one, Ellen?"

"It's standard psychological fare, Sandra. It takes 14 seconds if the elements are present for two people to be attracted. First, the eye contact, then the smile, and finally the voice. If all goes well, 14 seconds and it is a done deal."

"Don't go all psychological show off on me. I bet she came on to you, didn't she?"

Ellen nodded. "This is how we met. I almost sat down by her without really looking at her in a big room of people at a Continuing Ed workshop. But instead of sitting right by her, I left a seat between us to give her more space. 'Hey,' she said, leaning over and whispering to me. 'Sit by me. If this bores us, we can play Hangman.' That's all it took. We introduced ourselves and spent the day together."

"What is she like?"

"She's full of life, attracted to me—so far, so good. She is full bodied, a mop of brown, graying hair, almost as curly as James' hair.

She is irreverent and funny. She was with a partner named Susie Gilmore for twenty plus years. Have you heard of her? She is a renowned local artist, but she died of cancer. Their house is really artsy. Carmen hasn't been with anyone since Susie died five years ago. She's been too scared to try again. She's already made me promise not to die before her. I'm excited to have you meet her."

"This morning, after I spent the night at her house, she asked me to go to church with her, the big Unitarian church in Minneapolis; she sings in the choir. After the service, she wanted to introduce me to her friends. It was all going too fast for me, but then the friends ended up being Char and Joe. We sat in the garden of the church, the four of us, and talked. Carmen spent many a Sunday afternoon at Char and Joe's house after Susie died, eating Sunday dinner and watching sports on TV with Joe."

Sandra was astounded. "I know you're not just saying that, but what are the chances? What's that word you use, synchronicity? That you would be connecting with Char before I would get a chance to introduce the two of you? When Char and I had lunch, we didn't get down to talking about religion, but she shared that she lost her daughter, Rainey, to AIDS. My heart broke for her."

"Was Rainey Willow's Mother?" Both women leaned forward, heads nearly touching.

"Yes. Rainey had a difficult pregnancy and died when Willow was an infant. I bet she would have lived today, but 18 years ago, more people were dying from complications associated with AIDS. Char said that caring for baby Willow was what kept her sane after Rainey died. She just held on to Willow for dear life. Willow is fine; she didn't pick up the HIV virus. The doctors knew to do a cesarean section to prevent blood exchanges."

Ellen was the first to pull back and relax some. Sandra looked at their drinks and asked Ellen if she'd like another. Ellen nodded and Sandra busied herself, lifting ice cubes out of the insulated bucket with long tongs, pouring the scotch and adding a topping of soda.

They both switched knees and dug their rears deeper into their sling chairs, taking several swallows of drink and reaching for the biggest piece of candied ginger, slapping each other's fingers as they always did.

Sandra switched the topic to James, "Do you think our double mama's boy will man up for a sweetheart like Willow?"

"Come on, Sandra. Don't be mean. James has turned a corner. He seems happy, taking care of business. He set up housekeeping, carefully shopping for furniture and all. And, he found a responsible part-time job. But he's not even twenty-one; kids make relationship commitments later in life now, especially college kids, certainly not at eighteen and twenty."

"He's working? Great," Sandra said. "He's taking care of business. He's finally growing up."

"I just hope he stays focused on his education. I would be terribly disappointed if he didn't."

"Be satisfied if he is productive and happy, Ellen. It's too late for us to control the direction his life will take."

"Can I change the subject?" Sandra asked.

"Sure. I'm done."

"I'd like to talk about sex for a minute." Both women squirmed and sat straighter in their chairs again.

"Sandra, I'm not giving you details of my new sex life!"

"I know you better than to ask you any sex details, much as I would like to know. If you want to share, I'd love hearing about it."

"No."

"OK, then what I want to share is about Ralph and me. Char said some things that reminded me how much Ralph and I love each other. Char thinks I'm breaking Ralph's heart by not letting go of his transgression. She also knows what it is like to be the older person in a relationship. Joe is twelve years younger than she is. Can you believe it? It's more than the age difference between Ralph and me.

Char has me thinking I'm part of our marital problems. Perhaps I need Ralph's forgiveness as much as he needs mine. Perhaps I took him for granted when I was so wrapped up in the kids. For two years, now, he has faithfully come home to a frigid wife. Well, that has to change, slowly, but change it will. Already I'm asking him what he'd like for dinner."

"I'll parrot your words, Sandra, 'You never listen to me.' I gave you the same advice as Char did, to look at your part in your marriage problems," Ellen said, smiling.

"Untrue, Ellen. I listen to you. I just don't always take your advice. I took Char's advice because she is so much older than Joe, so she has better insight into Ralph. And why would I listen to you for sex advice? You have never wanted to talk about sex. You've said more tonight than you have in 30 years of friendship. Anyway, my life with Ralph is starting to get on the right track. Next up, I want to meet Carmen." Sandra started to rise. She was getting hungry for more substantial food but she thought of something else she wanted to know and settled back down, crossing her knees again.

"One more thing, Ellen—now don't get mad—I'm going to say it so it doesn't stand between us. Did you ever think about us being lesbians together?"

Ellen looked at the fire burning bright then back at her friend.

"You were Terry's girlfriend when I met you. You befriended me and that was what I longed for. Lesbians have women friends just like heterosexuals have both men and women friends. You were the first person I truly loved, but I never considered us as possible lovers. Did you?" Ellen's eyes twinkled.

"Well, not until now. Maybe I'll give it some thought. I've got bi-sexual potential."

"I think I would have picked up on that during our 30 years of friendship. But don't worry. I won't let my relationship with Carmen spoil our friendship. We're still BFF's, right, Sandra?"

"Absolutely, BFF. Let's get inside, eat a real meal. Hasn't this sex talk made you hungry, too?" Before Ellen could ponder that, Sandra was headed to the kitchen.

Ellen followed with the empty snack bowls. "Sandra, tell me the details. How are you and Ralph going to bridge this gap between you?"

22 / JAMES' WORLD SPINS

Monday evening, Willow closed her bedroom door and hopped on the bed, put three pillows behind her head and called James in comfort.

He recognized the humming ring he'd set for her and answered with a grunt, "Ugh."

"Hey James—how did work go yesterday?"

"I explained the new phone system to a bunch of maintenance workers at a hospital." He flipped his phone and snatched it from the air, thinking, am I a good liar or what?

"Doesn't sound like too much fun, but beats McDonald's, I suppose."

"Hey, don't dis my work. It's good money. I knew Randall way back in junior high, so it's kind of fun working for him. I was on the junior wrestling team for a year when I was thirteen, and he was on the varsity team. As far as work goes, I'm adding another shift on Thursday afternoons."

"I bet you were a cute, skinny white boy at thirteen. Long legs, big feet, and red fuzzy hair, the 113-pound weight class." Willow rolled over on the bed. She was feeling a deep tingling sensation she'd felt before but not while talking on the phone to James. This was a scary first. She wanted to touch herself, but she felt awkward thinking about touching herself on the phone with James. She pulled a pillow between her legs and rolled over to her side.

"Sounds like you were there," he said. "Sharp elbows and knees—that was me. But some of the girls thought I was cute."

"How do you know anyone thought you were cute, James?"

"Well, Chuck's sister teased me, flirted with me."

"Umph," Willow answered, trying to think back to when she was thirteen. Had anyone beside her folks thought she was cute?

"No more teases about little James," she said, rolling onto her stomach and wiggling her butt in the air. "I know what I'd do to distract you. I'd dance for you—I can twerk better than Rhianna." She twerked on her bed as if to prove her point.

"You can do that? Vibrate like that? You do that, a good girl like you?" James flapped his legs open and shut. He remembered Willow touching his penis, and he touched it now. He lay there touching himself, quietly.

"You don't know what I can do, James. You're quite the sexist. You don't think us girls get a feeling for sex before we have it? I'm thinking maybe you're the naive one. How about next Friday? Gram wants you over for dinner. Gram told me to tell you that she can make chicken like my great-gram did. Did I tell you that Sandra has plans to get Gram back to that farm come hell or high water? I'll be going there too, of course, but later, not the first time when Gram and Great-Grandpa get reacquainted. I don't like that you met my great-gram, and I never did." Willow twerked again.

"Damn, I got to go," James lied. "I see Caleb's head in my window. I'll call you back tonight, Willow." He hung up and attended to his urgent needs.

James called Willow again, several hours later. He was sitting at the table wondering again why Randall took his salt and pepper shakers.

"Hey again. I won't keep you long, but I got to' know, did you talk to your Gram about birth control? Will she and Joe be mad at me when I come to dinner, mad about us having sex?"

"No. She liked that you and I are talking about it before just doing it. She said something about us being 'mature.' And, yeah, I got an appointment next week. It takes more time to get an appointment than I thought it would."

James sat on the kitchen chair, squirming, his long legs wiggling and jutting out from the table. "You talk so easily about sex. I thought girls were supposed to shy about sex."

"Gram signed me up for a sex education class years ago. The program was supposed to help teens become comfortable talking about sex before they had sex. One of our assignments was to go to a pharmacy and buy a form of birth control. It was scary, but we went in pairs, so it wasn't so bad. We had to show and tell afterward. On break, we girls snapped rubbers at the boys and tried to hit them in the crotch. That took a lot of the mysticism out of being sexual."

"Ouch, Willow. I just reflexively put my phone over my boy. When I was a teenager, I'd have ruined that class for everyone. Whenever I got embarrassed, I made a joke of everything. I'd probably have farted or something.

"You mean last year, when you were a teenager, James?"

James laughed.

"That's OK, James. I was a teenager when we were together last week. I used the word love. I'm sorry I said it; it just slipped out. I take it back."

"I loved hearing that word from your beautiful, oh so full lips; I really did."

"Talk to me, James. Tell me anything. I just want to hang on the phone with you. Is that OK?"

James made himself more comfortable. "Yeah, I'll tell you almost everything. My friend Caleb just stopped by for a book he'd left here. I want you to meet him sometime. He turned me onto jazz—we have these deep talks about life and stuff."

They talked on; they had a lot in common now: family, classes, biking, movies, music. Willow felt a familiarity with James that she'd never known with anyone—boys or girls.

Caleb came over Tuesday afternoon to snort a couple more lines of the Brown Sugar. James was eager for another heroin jolt. Caleb was in a great mood, and James didn't get sick from the heroin this time. They nodded out at first then James staggered up and got them both a beer. They ate a bag of chips and salsa and talked some, hanging out, listening to sounds, both pulling back into their high unexpectedly. It was strange, other worldly, floating, then landing, only to float some more.

While studying at home the next morning, James looked up from his tightly written, hardly decipherable calculus notes. He took in the outdoor scene from the big pane of window, the fall scene he'd imagined the day he'd moved in.

Dry yellow leaves drifted in the breeze across the lawn. The sturdy, straight trees were sentinels now with empty branches. For the first time he could clearly see the backs of the houses across the alley; big gray garbage containers and smaller blue recycle bins lined the sides of the houses. He delighted in the new landscape, thinking how each season brought a new harmony to this landscape. Soon he'd be seeing a thin snow cover and then mounds of snow riddled with man-made paths.

He started daydreaming about last night's Brown Sugar. It had been absolutely mesmerizing. He swiveled around in his desk chair, taking in everything about his small space. All his heroin use had been in this space. Today would be a perfect day to get stoned on

Brown Sugar, take a chair outside, and sit in his backyard, nodding off with the warm sun on his face.

Without further thought, on that bright Wednesday morning, James brought out the heroin and snorted a few lines alone. He would never have guessed he would use heroin like a casual high, like he used marijuana. Heroin was a righteous high, he thought, and James followed through with his plan, nodding off outside on a perfect day.

LATER, James drove to his mom's for dinner and to do his laundry. His laundry bag was bulging again. His mom wasn't home from work when he arrived, so he took his laundry downstairs and started the first load.

He heard Ellen popping the stubborn backdoor open, and he took the basement steps two at a time up to the kitchen to say 'Hi' to her. Since he'd moved out, spending a few hours with Ellen worked out fine. He didn't feel she had any control over him now.

She was placing a large carton on the table. "Mom, I'd have carried that in for you. What is it?"

"It's for you, son."

He looked at the picture on the box. "It's a microwave?" he said with excitement. "I really need one. Using an oven for frozen burritos sucks. Thanks Mom; this is great!"

"It's your housewarming present. I hope this small microwave won't take up too much space in your kitchen?"

"No. It'll be fine."

"I froze three packets of macaroni and cheese for you to take home with the new microwave. How about grilled tuna and cheese sandwiches for dinner tonight?"

James nodded his pleasure.

"Would you help by making a salad, James?" He nodded again.

Ellen set out the cutting board and her one sharp knife for James. He showed his style by cutting up tomato, green pepper, and carrots. First, he washed his hands like a surgeon, raising them high to wipe them dry. He tested the sharpness of the knife and set to work: pull with the fingertips and cut. Pull, cut, pull cut, pull cut. He liked making a rhythm with his cuts.

"So, what's been happening with you, Mom?" James asked as he performed vegetable surgery.

Ellen finished putting together the sandwich ingredients and buttered bread and began to fry sandwiches on a low flame. She moved closer to James, watching him make the salad. He felt her presence, put down the knife, and turned questioningly to her.

She'd tried rehearsing the right words: 'I met someone' (too vague) or 'I've always loved women' (too revealing). Finally, she blurted out, "I've been dating."

He looked at Ellen with genuine interest. She had a grin on her face, nearly ear to ear. She couldn't help grinning nowadays; she was happy.

"Who is the lucky guy, Mom?" he asked.

"It's not a guy, James. I'm dating a woman."

James dropped his arms to his side, staring in disbelief at her. "Are we really having this conversation, Mother?" he asked. He looked around, sensing the presence of someone else in the room.

She plowed on ahead. "I told you that I met a woman, Carmen, at a workshop. She is a marriage counselor. We started seeing each other, and now we are admitting that we are, in fact, dating."

"Dating," he repeated. "You're dating a woman? Is she a lesbian?" He was confused.

"Yes. I'm dating a lesbian, James, and she is a very special woman. I think you will like her. When I first walked into her home, last weekend, I thought of you. She has the kind of home I wish I could have given you." Ellen looked away from him with glazed eyes.

"If you say so," he mumbled, wondering what she meant by that. The washing machine dinged. "Saved by the buzzer. I'll put my next load of clothes in and be back in a minute," he said, glad for the excuse to pull himself together. He felt protective of his mother, afraid for her, afraid for himself, too.

His quiet, proper mom, dating a woman? He put his first load into the dryer and threw his second load into the washer. Then, he went into his nearly empty room, taking comfort in the reflective galaxy he'd glued to the ceiling. He rummaged in his closet for his winter jacket and boots. With no more excuses, he went back upstairs.

Ellen was humming an old song James vaguely remembered, something about a dancing queen. She had that smile on her face. James thought she looked pleased with herself. Pleased with herself! He thought the only times he'd seen her this pleased with herself were when she'd caught a good-sized walleye.

"I see you decided to take a warmer jacket from your closet. Good idea, but your room is still your room. Keep your extra clothes, sports equipment, whatever, here. This is always your home remember that, OK?"

"Thanks, Mom. I don't have room for much at my new place. I've got a ton of jackets and winter clothes, boots and skis, more than I realized, downstairs." He sat down at his place at the table.

He looked up at the old chalkboard near the back door where his mother left notes. His name was still in cursive, underlined, on the top of the board. He fingered the raised ribs on his blue plaid placemat. The navy blue in the placemat matched his blue rimmed dinner plate and his large blue rimmed milk glass. He had grown up here, eating dinner with his mother. He wasn't ready for his mother to date, much less date a lesbian. The wind had been knocked out of his sails.

They ate quietly together. Ellen chatted about Carmen's architecturally interesting neighborhood and Panache, the cat, and Carmen's art-filled house.

James was uncharacteristically quiet.

23 / JAMES COMES TO DINNER

Friday James arrived at Willow's for dinner and checked his car clock while he parked. He was right on time. He'd attended morning classes and studied at the library for a couple of hours before driving home and getting in a run. He enjoyed a long shower and moved right along to get to Willow's on time. He wore a pair of semi-dress black trousers and a white long sleeve cotton shirt. He hadn't shaved for a few days, and he thought he looked good. He smoked a joint with the windows open on the way over. He was pleased by the quality of the marijuana from Randall, but it was only 'every day stuff' after the heroin.

It was good to see Willow at the door; she puckered for a kiss, and he obligingly kissed her, peeking over her shoulder for Char or Joe. She led him into the living room. He walked in, feeling more comfortable than he had the first time. He sat down on the couch and patted the seat next to him for Willow.

"Where are they?" he whispered.

"You don't have to whisper," she said in normal tones. "Gram is picking up Joe; his car is getting new brake liners today. They'll be here in a few minutes."

"It smells great in here. I hope there is plenty of chicken for me. Come here my little chicken bones," he patted the couch again. "I like thighs," he said. She sat down, wondering if that patting of the couch was bordering disrespectful, but he quickly put his hand on her flesh where her short skirt ended, and she was distracted by the shiver that went up her thigh.

"I'd say stop that, but when you hear the door open, you'll be all good boy again, right?" They kissed again, more deeply. "I just love kissing you, James. Give me another." She nibbled on his lower lip.

James pulled away. "Don't bruise my lip; has your Gram said anything more about you starting the pill?"

"She was still flustered, rubbing her hands together like she's washing them when we talked, again, about you and me. I told her I was the one who should be flustered. I thought it went well, all in all. She is glad I'm 'so honest.' She was speechless for a minute during that first talk, but it didn't last long. Now she's acting all accepting. She asked what I see in you."

"Thanks, Char," James said, rolling his eyes and laughing. "Well, what do you see in me?"

"I told her I thought it was time for me to experience the great mystery of sex and that we are attracted and I feel safe with you. I am safe with you, aren't I?"

"I'd never hurt you or let anyone hurt you, Willow. I suppose it's scary out there for pretty women. I bet men are on your tail a lot."

Willow thought for a moment. It was a bummer the way some men were. Could she tell him the truth about it? Then she thought, why not? Who needs him if he can't handle the truth in her life?

"Yeah, take a beautiful thing, like me, and try to make it ugly—what's that about? Most guys are great, like you. They flash a smile or even whistle, and I just give them the frown I gave you that day we met on the street, but there are those predators out there, too.

Many of them. I'm on alert, getting off the sidewalk and into the street to avoid dark areas or to avoid odd acting guys. I move away, keep my body language neutral—maybe even act a little subservient. Isn't it awful that I have to do that? Then there is the subtle and not so subtle racism, in school and in the streets," Willow said. "I know you didn't mean anything but healthy hunger the other night when you said something about my 'full lips,' but, one day in high school, a girl who actually liked me asked if I ever tried wearing lipstick, using it to line the insides of my lips. She said it might 'normalize' their size. Yes—she said that to me. Living in a too white world."

"You got a little rage?" James said, teasing, yet wondering sometimes what he was getting into with Willow. He had pegged her as easy going, after all the kissing she had done with him the other night and all the talk about being attracted. Now she was telling him how she really sees the world.

"Do you still want me?" she asked James, reaching up to read his eyes. He looked at her, into her dark lively eyes.

"Feel me and decide for yourself," he answered.

They heard the door open and true to Willow's prediction, James straightened up considerably, glad for the loose pants he was wearing.

"What are you kids up to?" Char asked as she came around the dining room corner.

"No good," James mumbled.

"Welcome, James." Char added and Joe followed her into the living room.

James walked over to shake Joe's hand. "Nice to meet you, sir."

"You can call me Joe. Pleased to meet you, too, James. But remember, I'm not as nice as Char." Joe's smile belied his words, but James got the message and nodded seriously that he had gotten the warning.

The chicken fell off of the bone; the gravy on the mashed

potatoes was rich and lumpy with chicken drippings. Char added sides of beans and beets from Sandra's garden and hot home-made rolls. She passed a divider of mixed olives, pickled crab apples, and raw carrots and celery. James ate like no tomorrow, and Char and Willow kept filling his plate.

"This is the way we ate on the farm every day, and no one was heavy. Amazing, isn't it?" Char said.

James mumbled while chewing. "The chicken, gravy, all of it is great, Char."

"Do you know I've met your mom a few times now?" Joe asked.

James felt a rush of blush. How much did they know about her? He let Joe's comment drop.

For a while they sat digesting. Joe asked James about his classes. James gave the standard answers for those sorts of questions; he tried to feign enthusiasm, but the conversation faltered.

"We have dessert, too, James. Do you have room for blueberry pie and ice cream?" Char asked.

James nodded. He never got too full to turn down dessert.

"I'll get the pie and ice cream." Joe got up from the table.

James was more comfortable after Joe left the room, "This is like being at Sandra's for a holiday. I loved eating at Sandra's, and I loved going to the farm. This meal has Grandma Gunderson written all over it. My mom is mostly vegetarian. Sandra talked her into serving me meat when I was growing, but Mom never got into things like gravy."

"I enjoyed watching you eat, James. It's fun to have a young man around, and it's great that you know my sister and her family so well. Sandra just loves you."

"I know she does. Ralph has always been good to me, too. I went to their cabin with the rest of the kids during the summers, when I wasn't up north with my mom. We'd water ski; Ralph played cards with us, stuff like that." James realized Char was looking at him strangely, and he just stopped talking and looked back at her.

Char kept looking at him like she expected something from him; he didn't know what. There was an awkward silence. "What's going on Gram?" Willow said agitatedly.

James wasn't expecting this. He thought Willow and he would eat and run; he wished Joe was back with the pie and ice cream.

"I just want James to know us a little better. Do you know what kind of a family we are?"

"You're a lot like Sandra's family, right?" he asked.

"Yes and no. Joe and I are both in recovery, from alcohol on his part and drug addiction on mine. How do you think that affected you, growing up, Willow? Having your folks take sobriety seriously?"

"Gram, I don't know what to say. I don't want to get into some deep discussion about drug use." Willow put her cloth napkin on her plate and turned sideways, away from Char, toward James.

James felt pinned under a spotlight. "My mother drinks a little," James offered, starting to feel uncomfortable.

Char lifted her head and continued without looking at either of them. "I've been thinking a lot about when I was young and I left the farm. I was on my own in Minneapolis by the time I was 18. I was an angry, alienated kid and gravitated toward other young people who felt the same. We were part of a counterculture that didn't like the materialistic way our world was moving. We wanted to be completely different from the people who raised us. We wanted to be simple and loving and back to the earth. We believed that marijuana, other drugs too, helped give us a vision of how the world could be. Drugs were our way of being unique and special. What does your generation think about using drugs?" Char turned her focus onto James.

James' ears burned. Had Sandra or his mother talked to Char

about his marijuana use? It was probably his mother, he thought. He felt sweaty.

Willow was uncomfortable, too, and changed the direction of the conversation, "James," she said loudly. "My Mother had AIDS when she was pregnant with me, and I could have been an HIV in vitro. I wasn't—I didn't get AIDS or anything else, but when I was growing up, there were rumors in my school about me, and kids were told to stay away from me."

He looked at her incredulously. He tried not to squirm. He realized he was jiggling his knees and tried to relax, get a grip.

Willow turned to her Gram. "Do you ever wonder if Rainey's pregnancy with me killed her?"

Char looked at Willow, her head jerked back, her eyebrows raised. "Of course, you didn't kill your mother. You saved her."

"Explain that. How did having me save my mother? It killed her, didn't it?"

"Rainey was going to die whether or not she had you. AIDS was just a plain killer back when you were born. You gave her shortened life meaning. She didn't die right after you were born. She saw you, she held you, she saw what a beautiful baby you were and knew, as I did, what a beautiful woman you'd become."

Willow looked intensely at her Gram. "I love you Gram, but having James over to dinner is not about you. James doesn't have to endure your drug history the first time he comes over for dinner. We need some time alone; can we be excused from the table?"

"What about pie?" Char said. Then she called Joe. "What is taking you so long? The kids want to get going."

Joe stood in the doorway between the dining room and kitchen, looking uncomfortable, "I had to search for the ice cream. You left it in the downstairs freezer, Char."

Willow got up and so did James. "We want to go, Gram. We want some time alone; is that OK?" Willow got up from the table and walked out of the room.

James thanked them both and scooted out with Willow, who grabbed their jackets and headed for the door. Minutes later they were parked where they had parked the week before, in the empty lot by the river.

24 / JAMES AND WILLOW

James and Willow sat quietly on their own sides of the car, listening to the inky water rolling down the river on a dark night. James wondered if he was paranoid or if it was true that the whole family was gossiping about his marijuana use, disapproving of him. First his mother then Sandra confronted him, even Chuck was negative about his marijuana use. Then Willow had said something last week, and now Char sounded as if she were the expert on drug use and the counterculture. She is full of bullshit, he said to himself.

Willow was sitting on her side of the car wondering if James would run away from wanting her now that he knew about her mother's AIDS. It took all her fortitude not to open the door and escape into the night. She was glad she was wearing flats with decent heels for running.

James finally turned to Willow, frowning. "What was going on there? Did you say something to her about me smoking dope? Was Char getting ready to confront me about my marijuana use?"

"I didn't say anything to Char or to Joe about your dope smoking. Is that how much you trust me? I would never do that, invite you over to be confronted by my Gram. I could shoot her."

Willow twisted her body further away from James, towards the side window.

James could hardly hear her as she continued speaking softly into the window. "I said all that about my mother, Rainey, to get Char off her rant about drugs and to give us a chance to get out of there. I'm so sorry, James. I'm totally embarrassed that you had to find out about me that way."

James knew she was quietly crying. His burner phone started to ring. James straightened up and reached into his jacket pocket. "I'm sorry—this is my work phone. I've got to take this call. I'll be right back."

James jumped out of the car and shut the door, moving to a big oak tree just beyond the parking lot. He leaned against the tree, shifting fallen leaves with the toe of his shoe and watching Willow hunched against her window as he answered the call.

"What's happening?" he asked.

"James? I said I was going to get back to you today, right?"

"I'm kind of' in the middle of things, Randall, uh Jay. I'm with Willow," he said, "but she can't hear us."

"OK. I need some more help. You'll need to add another stop on Sunday."

"I'm not sure about this," James answered cautiously.

"Get sure, James. It's going to happen. Tomorrow at 3—see you then. Your place."

James twisted around and looked at Willow. She was leaning on her door like she was getting ready to open it. "This is going to be it, Randall. No more surprises, right? I haven't even started the new Thursday runs."

"Right. Just be home tomorrow at 3."

James walked back to the car feeling low, feeling lower than he had since leaving home. Everyone wanted a piece of him, Willow, Char, Caleb, Randall, his mom—no one was on his side.

He got back in the car and closed the door and rubbed at a

scratch on the dashboard. "This car sucks. Now the sound system quit working," he said, slamming his right fist into the dashboard. Willow visibly jumped.

She asked hesitantly, "What's up with work?"

"I've got to increase my hours for Randall on Sunday. I'm starting to hate working for him. Randall thinks he owns me now."

"James, don't be mad at me."

"I'm not mad at you," he said. "I'm pissed at Randall." James kept messing with his dashboard, now feeling under the dashboard for a disconnected wire.

"James, look at me," Willow demanded. He reluctantly turned to look at her. Her eyes were red from crying.

"I'm sorry," he mumbled. "I'm an asshole," he admitted, wishing he hadn't made her cry. He moved over a few inches and wiped a tear from her cheek with his thumb. They reached out for each other simultaneously and held onto each other as if they each were alone in a very cruel world.

"Come back to my place," he asked. "I want to be alone with you."

James drove quickly to his place and jumped out of the car after he parked and hurried around to open Willow's car. They held hands walking around to his back door. James guided Willow up the few steps and into his small space. He excused himself to turn on a soft study lamp on his desk and turned to look at her apologetically, sadly. He'd wanted to be happy, to usher her in with pride, but he didn't have it in him.

"Here it is—my home," he said, taking her jacket and his jacket and throwing them over a dining room chair. "Can I get you something to drink?"

"Now don't get mad at me, James. I have to call Gram and tell her that I'm with you and I'm staying here tonight, OK? I just don't want to go back there; I'm pissed at her."

"You're willing to spend the night with me?" That pulled James half out of his funk. He grinned and walked over to give her a quick hug. "Yeah, call her. I'm not mad at her, just sad that everyone thinks the worst of me all the time."

"Not everyone, all the time, 'poor James.'" Willow had some of her tease back. She called and said what she had to say. James listened, trying not to be obvious but really wanting to know what Char had to say.

"Um, yeah, I know, um, no, yeah, that's right, OK. I don't have to be at the dance studio until 10. See you tomorrow—love you and give Joe a huge hug. I love him."

"What did she say?" he asked.

"She reminded me that I can't start the pills until after my next period starts. Does she think I'm an idiot? I know we can't have the real thing tonight, are you OK with that?"

"I promised you I wouldn't do anything to harm you, and I meant it. Just having you here when I'm feeling so low, I can't tell you how good it makes me feel, and having you spend the night with me? Nothing could be better. I kind of like our anticipation of sex. You know what I mean?"

James put on his Bose and poured two glasses of diet coke and ice. Willow sat on James' lap in the big armchair with her head on his shoulder. Their moods lightened. They kissed as they listened to soft, sexy jazz. Before they laid down, Willow used James' toothbrush. They threw off most of their clothes and jumped into bed in their undies.

"Isn't this fun? Like a slumber party," Willow said. "I didn't go to slumber parties. As you know now, everyone was afraid I'd give them AIDS."

James reached over and kissed her deeply. "You are the healthiest looking woman I know. Hey, if you have AIDS, give me some." Willow winced at his response, but he was smiling.

"We get to feel each other, don't we?" she asked.

James carefully took off her bra and caressed her breasts. "Hello

Erma," he whispered to her left breast. "Hello Zelda," he said, kissing her right breast. He nudged and touched and licked, moving down to her belly button, but he stopped himself and laid his head on her bare stomach.

"I don't know what to do with this hard on," he mumbled. "Sorry, but it is all I can do not to rub against you."

"Tell me what you would like me to do." Willow touched his penis, and he twitched.

"I'm a wuss, Willow. Can we turn off the light?"

"Sure, then let me feel you," she answered.

25 / CHAR'S PERSPECTIVE

Joe and Char were in bed, too. Joe on his back, his arms raised, hands under his head. His elbows defined his territory on the bed. Char lay on her back over on her side with her arms stiffly at her sides. The room was dark.

Joe was mad, and Char hated getting the cold treatment. The evening had droned on. Char cleared the table and did the dishes. Joe didn't offer to help. He sat in the living room watching TV and eating seconds of blueberry pie, changing the channels at will, as if Char wasn't there.

"Joe, we promised each other we would never go to bed angry. Why are you so mad at me?"

"You tell me what I'm mad about," he said. "You know everything."

"You're mad because I tried to talk to James about drug use."

"Your object was to get him to 'share' about his use; we all knew it. The two of them scampered away like mice, and now she is staying overnight with him. Did that work out the way you wanted it to, Char?"

"It wasn't planned; it was spontaneous. I already told you I'm sorry. What else can I say?"

"What in the world were you thinking? James was starting to talk about his life and was happy being here with us. Then you asked him what he thought about Willow coming from a family in recovery. Why did you do that?" Joe's muscles twitched. He could hit her. He never would, but this was one of the times he wanted to.

"I heard it in his voice, Joe, the reedy sound of someone who is stoned. He was stoned tonight, and I have a sixth sense that he is a fairly heavy user. Why would someone smoke marijuana before coming over to dinner at their new girlfriend's house? Someone who medicates anxiety with marijuana."

"I didn't hear anything strange in his voice; you're hearing things, Char."

"I know that voice; I've heard it many times. Post-adolescent recovery is my specialty. I've heard that reedy tone for 35 years, listening to kids who think no one knows they're stoned. James had been smoking marijuana tonight."

"I can't say this nice, Char. You picked a hell of a place and time to do a confrontation. Even if you are right about his smoking tonight, you didn't have the right to jump right in there and start confronting him without talking to me and Willow about it. I'm so mad at you. Now Willow is over at his place, and you told me she isn't even on the pill yet. Why do you jump to conclusions? You're hunches, your impatience will push our daughter right out of our home."

"I trust Willow, Joe. She loves us. We have to stop thinking of her as a fragile child, stop babying her."

"I treat her like a baby? Now it's my fault? Char, you crack me up."

Char slapped her arms against the mattress. "I give. OK—I acted like a modern-day Carrie Nation dragging a prohibition placard like Jesus dragging his cross. Is that what you want me to say? Please, Joe, let it go. I don't know what got into me. Sometimes I really don't know why I do the things I do."

He could tell she meant it. His anger dissipated some, but he wasn't quite ready to let her off the hook.

"You can be selfish and petty and over confident."

"Thanks a lot, Joe. Thanks for reading my inventory. Can you give me a break?" Char's voice cracked.

He chuckled. "Now that I've hurt your feelings, I'm feeling a lot better. Good night, Char, sleep tight, after you get your flaws in order." He rolled over, pulling most of the covers with him.

CHAR PULLED HALF the covers back to her side and rolled over closer to Joe, she lay listening to his breathing slowly change until she knew he had finally fallen asleep. Now she could think. She didn't question herself about whether James had smoked marijuana before coming over tonight. She knew she was right about that. She just wasn't sure how habitually he smoked. She suspected he had a problem, but she acknowledged her suspicions were intuitive rather than based on facts.

Willow's response to Char's attempt to discuss marijuana was another puzzle. Why did Willow choose that moment to start revealing her painful truth about her mother's AIDS? Why had she initiated running out of the house? What did Willow know about James that she hadn't told her? Was Willow already worried about James' drug use after dating him for a matter of weeks? That wasn't a good omen.

Still, Char liked James. She enjoyed sponsoring young men. When people new to the AA/NA program liked the program, they asked someone in the group to sponsor them, someone they could call if they'd support and to help them work through the basic ten steps. Young men often asked Char to sponsor them. If she had time, she gladly worked with them. They'd meet weekly for several months, working toward recovery.

James was tender and loving like so many boys she'd met. She respected his forthrightness with Willow about sex. Willow said he wasn't sexually experienced either, yet he took the risk to talk with Willow about sex—that's not what Char's generation had done.

Back in Char's day, parents put out firm expectations that kids should speak no evil, see no evil, and do no evil. When the kids experienced dreaded sexual attraction, sex became an unplanned eruption of their repression.

Talk about arranged marriage, she thought. How many women her age got pregnant after one or two indiscretions with a boy they didn't know how to say 'no' to. Hopefully, times were changing; young people were finally talking about sex.

Times are changing in terms of social marijuana use too, she admitted. James isn't someone she met in AA; he's Willow's friend and her sister's boy. She had no right getting in his face about his use of drugs. She needed to get to know him better before making any assumptions or judgments. She should have been patient, to be there for him if he asked for help.

She turned and nestled against the broad back of her husband, putting an arm around him, lifting herself up to kiss him in the ear before trying to drift off. She lay there for what felt like hours, tossing and turning. Finally, she got up and went downstairs to heat a cup of milk and eat another small piece of her very good blueberry pie made from her mother's recipe for Crisco pie dough and the small, oh so flavorful, frozen blueberries from Costco.

Selfish, petty, over-confident, and impatient, she repeated her husband's inventory of her faults. It could be worse, she chuckled to herself. He does put up with me, the poor darling.

She wasn't angry at him. In their years together, she could read him as well as he could read her. They liked each other, accepted each other. She knew he would wake up in the morning with a big hug for her and feel a little contrite for having been angry. He was so afraid of his anger, and he needn't be. He wasn't that angry drunk who had once terrorized his family. But changed as he was, he still had to live with his shadowy past.

Char knew she was living under a shadow, too. How hard it was to forgive ourselves. Thank God for AA and the ten steps. Char wasn't always the woman she wanted to be, but she could accept the woman she was, most of the time, and she usually acted in a way that she could accept. She'd learned how to make amends and how to accept the things she couldn't change. But, living with herself wasn't always simple.

At 18, angry and ashamed, she'd left home, away from the father she believed condemned her. She took a cardboard box and a big suitcase on the bus to Minneapolis, emptying her savings account and carrying nearly five hundred dollars hidden in her pockets and shoes. She met Sally, the dear friend she'd made at the unwed mother's home, at the bus terminal downtown. The bus terminal was nasty. People loitered around, looking destitute and lost. She wanted to get right out of there and see the place she was going to live.

Sally and Char wrote to each other after they left the home for unwed mothers without their babies. Sally hadn't finished high school like Char did. She got a waitress job and was living in a house with three boys about her age. Sally had encouraged Char to move to Minneapolis and live at the 'house' when she graduated from high school. Sally promised Char could share her room for free until she found a job. Sally carried Char's suitcase, and Char struggled with the big box on a city bus to Sally's house.

"What do you have in that box? It sure is heavy," Sally asked.

"It's the typewriter I got for Christmas two years ago."

"Your folks bought you a typewriter? What are you going to use that for?"

"I'm going to college. I'm going to get a job and take night classes."

"What type of job are you thinking you'll get?"

"I'll try to be a newspaper reporter or work for a publishing company. Something interesting like that," she said optimistically.

"Good luck with getting a job like that."

"Different strokes for different folks. I know you're waitressing. I can't do that work, taking orders and finding my way around a restaurant; I'm too clumsy. I'll have to find something that exercises my mind."

"Maybe you could be a secretary or something like that. They use a typewriter."

Sally thought Char's ideas were too ambitious, but Char was optimistic and bold. She'd been a good student and co-editor of the school newspaper. Even during her last year, coming back after almost everyone knew she'd had a baby, she'd gotten on the honor society.

They got off a city bus and walked less than a block to Sally's house. It was in the West Bank area, not far from downtown Minneapolis. Sally explained that it had been called Snooze Boulevard when her Scandinavian immigrant grandparents lived there. Now this area over the Mississippi from the main campus of the University of Minnesota was called the 'West Bank.' Thousands of young people lived near the 'West Bank' whether they were students or not. The housing was cheap, and there were numerous bars nearby that catered to students and hippies, as well as bikers and old drunks. The area became the Minneapolis hot bed for hippies in the late 60s and 70s.

The house wasn't bad. It was a sturdy old traditional with four bedrooms up, near Cedar and University Avenues. The house was quiet when they arrived. Char hadn't ever been in a house so sparsely furnished; mattresses lined the living room, but at least it was relatively clean. Later she discovered Sally did most of the housework for the boys, and soon Char was helping her. They put Char's stuff up in Sally's bedroom. Her room had a double bed and a single mattress on the floor. Char knew which bed was going to be hers. She dumped her box on the mattress.

"What now?" Char asked. "Do I get to meet everyone?"

"Everyone is at work. Maybe Johnny is at the bar. Want a beer?"

"Not now," Char said. "I'm just getting my bearings. Is my money safe here?"

"I doubt it. We have a lot of people coming and going. Don't keep anything you think is valuable here."

"I saw a bank from the bus, not far from here. Could I start a checking account, put my money there? What do you think, Sally?" Char asked.

"I think, just don't keep it here. Let's see what else you have. The typewriter is probably safe. That's an awfully nice jacket you have on." She was looking at Char's fairly new natural rough suede jacket with fringes along the sleeves and pockets.

"What can I do with it? It's already too warm to wear. I'm just wearing it because I didn't want to carry it."

"Put it under my bed, behind the dirty clothes I keep under the bed. If you have anything else really nice, put it behind the dirty clothes."

"Are we safe here? No one is going to come in and rape us or anything?"

"No. The only time that things go missing is when we have a big party. As far as rape, the guys we live with are fine. If they get too drunk and start groping, just yell at them and push them away —keep them in their place. They'll protect us from strange guys. It's pretty safe. Oh, but, keep your rings on."

That was Char's introduction to Minneapolis.

She got a job at a bookstore downtown. The pay was bad, but Char loved books, so she was happy at work and willing to live cheaply. Lying on the mattress not far from the bed where Sally was having sex with her boyfriend was uncomfortable at first as was the traffic in and out of the house on the weekends.

Mostly the weekend company was laid back on weed and beer and wine. They laid or sat around, listening to loud rock and roll or rhythm and blues in the communal living room. The kitchen was reserved for talk. Sometimes people who knew people who knew people came roaring in, wild on speed balls or cheap wine. Then there would be loud shouting matches that scattered the crowd. No one seemed to get hurt.

Men and women wore bandanas to keep their long hair out of their eyes. They wore bell bottoms and psychedelic shirts and cheap homemade jewelry. Many of the girls switched between pants and long peasant skirts and soft revealing tops. Almost everyone smoked pot and cigarettes. Char already loved cigarettes and soon gravitated to pot smoking, too.

After several long months of this communal living, Char moved into a room in a boarding house a block from Sally's. She still partied at Sally's occasionally but loved having her private place. She was identified by her rough suede jacket; everyone loved it. She wore it in the summer too—it was hot weather but a cool look.

Char was a bit shy around the guys at first. Sally was right; the roommates didn't bother her unless they were drunk, and they weren't offended if she didn't want to sleep with them. There were plenty of girls who did want to sleep with them. Sally's Johnny was a sexy, sweet young alcoholic. That first summer, Char was still smarting from her painful experience of getting pregnant in high school and stayed away from seductive men, gravitating instead toward the long, raw boned, quiet men who, like her, enjoyed conversation and drugs in the kitchen.

The first fall in Minneapolis, Char started a pattern she followed for several years: night classes, a fulltime job, and parties on the weekends. Smoking cigarettes was her constant vice. She didn't buy marijuana often; she just waited for the parties when the guys brought their drugs to be shared.

There wasn't a defining moment when Char became less reserved and fully joined into the hippy lifestyle. It just happened. She became known in the community; she experimented with LSD and peyote and started drinking to intoxication once or twice a week. There was general consensus among the young, liberal hippies in the seventies that the Vietnam War sucked and their parents' generation sucked. The pride in the country's nearly forgotten victories over fascism and communism was lost to these young people. The hippies challenged classism, sexism, racism, and nationalism.

Family ties that bind, were broken. Family became those you lived with and shared your beliefs. Sex, drugs, and rock and roll were tasted and then feasted upon. Char wore a black felt slouch hat and a navy pea coat with bell bottoms like Janis Joplin.

As the drugs became passé, Char began having casual sex with men. She wasn't going to let anyone disappoint or hurt her; she remained standoffish. Janis Joplin ripped through her soul. Once, stoned on LSD, listening to Janis with a like-minded man, Char commented that Janis's throaty voice was more than sexy; it was the blueprint to a woman's orgasm.

Sally wondered why Char didn't find a main squeeze. "I don't know, she said. "I haven't fallen in love, and I don't want a 'ball and chain.'" Sally still had her main squeeze, Johnny. When Johnny was on a drinking spree, Sally sometimes slept around, but she always went back to Johnny.

Finally, the party grew old. Char was sick of it. Sally and Johnny had their first baby and got married. In the late 70s, Char became pregnant with Rainey. She wasn't sure of her baby's father. It could have been the nice guy who wanted Char to settle down with him or the former athlete she felt a kinship to. She liked them both, maybe loved them in a way, but she wanted this baby much more than she wanted either of them.

Sally and Johnny helped Char out. Johnny was trying hard to control his alcoholism. He was kind hearted to both Sally and Char. Char lived with them for the last month of her pregnancy and for the first months after Rainey was born. Then Char rented a big house in St. Paul. She found a couple of suitable roommates, hippy guys who didn't mind her lifestyle, and she lived communally again. This time, though, she ran the show, and the guys helped with housework. Rainey was a beautiful, healthy baby with brown round cheeks, large black eyes, and thick hair. She was a good baby, and everyone loved her. Char took Rainey to a black hairdresser when she was a year old and started learning how to work with her hair.

When she was a toddler, Rainey loved passing joints back and forth between the adults as they sat in the living room or on old lawn chairs on the porch, listening to music, talking about discontents and politics, reading *The Whole Earth Catalogue* as a blueprint for simplifying their lives.

Char had little patches of garden for herbs and easy vegetables. She made her own yogurt and granola and tried to be a vegetarian. She'd gotten a job with the newspaper, answering the classified line that helped the customers write their 'To Sell' ads. The paper offered a flexible schedule and cooperative daycare for Rainey. Char was able to put a down payment on her house.

Monday was still Char's night out. She liked the 400 Club along Cedar Ave. when the weekend suburban gawkers were back to work. She'd arrived with a couple of dollars, just enough for cigarettes and her first drink. The hippy men greeted her with big smiles and bought her drinks all evening, offering pot and cocaine —some hoping for an invitation home for the night. Char was one of the many 'Queens of the Silver Dollar.' She 'ruled a smoky kingdom…' as the lyrics go, and she was happy with her life until Rainey started gnawing at her conscience when she was about five.

"Momma, don't smoke that stuff."

"Why not?" she'd ask Rainey crossly.

Rainey couldn't answer her. But Char knew that she zoned out when she was stoned. Char loved Rainey tenderly, but smoking marijuana settled her, relaxed her, and she could not quit smoking it. It wasn't any more than a glass of wine, was it? She compared her habit to Johnny's drinking and thought she was much more in control than he was.

On the other hand, Char kept her heroin use well hidden from Rainey. It was a guilty pleasure done in the company of her friend Raymond, who worked on the ore boats. When he came to shore after his ten day shifts on the Mississippi, Char shared heroin with him before he went home to his wife and three small children, living on a patch of land in the wilds of Wisconsin. She teased Raymond that he kept his wife pregnant and barefoot.

Char reasoned that she used marijuana to feel normal, to right the ship, to keep her anxiety and depression at bay, but truth be told, Char was on a roller coaster of exaggerated ups and downs. Most days she wished she could just do some deep cleaning of the house and get those lingering smells of smoke out of her hair and off her breath. She was sick and tired of the effort to be normal. The thrill was long gone.

Rainey saved Char's life when Raymond and she overdosed on heroin. She was not only Char's daughter; Rainey was her guardian angel. Rainey's vigilance woke her mother up.

Raymond and Char were slowly dying in her bedroom, and the six-year-old child, waiting for her mother to walk her to the bus stop, walked through the forbidden closed door and pulled on Char until she fell out of bed. That was Char's wakeup call.

Two days later, Char called Sally and asked if she could bring

Rainey over after school. She told Sally that she'd made an appointment to see a counselor at an outpatient treatment program she found in the yellow pages. She admitted to Sally what had happened.

The counselor asked her all kinds of probing questions about her drug and alcohol use. Char hated the intrusive, though kindly woman, who asked shocking questions about her sex life as well as her drug and alcohol habits. Still, Char answered the questions nearly honestly. Her answers surprised her. Her alcohol and drug use were much more extensive than what she admitted to herself. The counselor left her alone in the room for a while then came back and told her to sit tight—a treatment group was starting in half an hour.

Char bit the bullet, called Sally, and cried while explaining she was starting treatment that day. Sally said, "Go for it. Rainey is fine with us. Pack her bag, and she can stay with us for a few days, if you want a little time to sort all this out." Before Sally hung up, she said, "Hey, I'm with you. I'm so sick of Johnny's using, but I'm sick of my own use, too. I hope Johnny and I can sober up, too. We can't go on like this. We have to put our children first."

Char came to drug and alcohol treatment a blond wild-haired hippy with a beautiful peasant skirt and silver rings on her fingers and another in her nose. Her hair was clean but unkempt, her sandaled toe nails painted black. She looked around at all the alcoholics and druggies in her group and smirked. She wasn't like them; she was special, special because she'd been hurt, special because she understood the world in a way these people didn't, special because she could make it on her own.

But before long, she was crying and hugging and part of something larger than herself. She was part of another 'special' group of people, a humbler group for the most part, a wiser group for the most part.

26 / LIFE GOES ON

James and Willow touched and tasted each other almost everywhere that first night at his place, but they didn't have coitus. Willow told James to change the sheets the next time she came over.

James ran over to the coffeehouse in the morning and brought rolls back and made cups of coffee and wanted to serve Willow in bed. She appreciated his effort but wanted to get up to enjoy breakfast at her great-grandparents' table. Willow absentmindedly followed the textured grain of the wood with a finger-tip. She loved wooden tables; she'd done her homework on Char's oak dining room table all her life. She wondered if Gram had done her homework on this table. Willow looked at James. She wished she had known him when they were both children; she wished she had brothers or sisters or at least knew her cousins.

James was talking about making his place more private. He thought he should have some curtains for his big window. Willow shook off her personal thoughts and looked over at James.

"Do you have a tool kit, James?"

He shook his head.

"I've helped Gram put up curtains at the homeless shelter. I learned a lot about curtains."

"Would you make curtains for me?"

"I'd help you—we can make them together. You're family, James. Joe gave me a tool kit when I was about 14. I even have a drill."

"How about next Saturday, Willow?"

"I've got dance practice on Saturday mornings, remember? And next week I have a tryout for a regional dance troupe on Saturday morning as well. But I could come over at lunch time." She waited to see if he would make the connection.

"I'll make you lunch," he said and she smiled gratefully. "Then we can shop and make curtains," he added.

"Brilliant idea!" she responded.

James drove her home so she could shower and change and get to dance practice by 10. He gave her a long kiss when he dropped her off.

Char and Joe were drinking coffee and reading the morning papers in the sunroom off of the kitchen when Willow slammed in the side door.

"You're going to break the glass, Willow," Joe said with resignation.

"How about a good morning?" she answered.

"How was your night out?" he asked.

"It was fine. No. We didn't have sex, happy?"

"I'm happy," Joe said and looked over at Char. "Are you happy, Char?"

"I'm happy you are home. I trust you, Willow. You're a lot more mature than I was at your age. I'll give you that," Char said.

"I've got practice at 10, and I need a shower. Any more questions for me?"

Char looked at Joe, but he didn't say anything. She could read him. He wanted her to shut her mouth, so she did.

Willow looked pointedly at Joe. "I'll see you at the restaurant at 5?" Joe asked.

"I'll be there. See you both later." Willow ran upstairs to shower.

After hurrying to catch the light rail, Willow had a few minutes to think about the night before. Being in bed with James had been fun, but sitting on his lap, listening to music and playing with each other's hands, she had felt closest to him. Her feelings toward James were changing. Sitting at his table, thinking about family, she wondered if maybe she felt more like family than lovers with James.

Why is sex so loaded, she wondered? What if we become lovers —would that change me? Would I still just be my own person? The truth was, she felt disappointed in James. She always asked him about his classes and his work and his family. He answered her questions, but he didn't often reciprocate with questions about her life. It hurt that he hadn't commented on what she had said at dinner about her mother dying of AIDS or about what had happened to her in grade school. His comment about her looking so healthy didn't reach inside her and give her real support. She wondered if he just didn't know how to be a boyfriend or if he just didn't care to put out the effort to be her boyfriend?

As Gram liked to ask, "What's the difference between ignorance and apathy?" Willow had learned the answer. "I don't know, and I don't care." Willow chuckled. Then she thought, maybe James was a guy who didn't know the difference.

After Willow had slammed out again, Char asked Joe if he thought Willow seemed OK.

"I think so. I'm glad you are seeing it my way and not making more of a big deal out of things that aren't about you."

Char didn't like it when Joe patted himself on the back. Still, he had helped her see things differently, and she acknowledged that.

"After you went to sleep last night, I gave it some thought. I'm coming from the seventies. Those days, when a person was using a lot of marijuana, it usually meant a problem. But that's old-fashioned thinking. I'd better hustle my way into the 21st Century. The USA is legalizing marijuana left and right; obviously norms have changed. I guess most of us don't think there is anything abnormal about marijuana use. James seems like a good kid, and he's gotten a strong endorsement from Sandra. We've met his mother, and we know Carmen has good taste. I'm determined to have an attitude adjustment."

"Once again, when you make up your mind about something, you run with it," Joe said. Now I'm the one who is cautious. I didn't like the way Willow hustled him out of here. What was that about? The more I think about it, maybe you did kick the hornet's nest. I'll have a little talk with her after work tonight. Ask her why she didn't want her boyfriend to get to know you better. Running out of the house like they did, that was rude, too."

"When Willow gets upset, she listens to you better than to me. She seems to discount my opinion, but if Papa says something, she listens. Thanks, Joe."

James ended up making an additional stop for Randall on Sunday. This stop, however, was a fifty-mile drive both ways, and now he was working nearly eight hours on Sunday. His new Thursday schedule of stops involved a lot of driving, too. He'd ended up missing his Thursday study group. He didn't really like that class, anyway. It was his most advanced Engineering class and used a lot of applied math. He was taking an advanced applied math class at the same time. Friday morning, James decided to drop the Engineering class, just making the deadline for dropping the class without penalty.

He decided he deserved a reward for dropping the class and called Caleb to celebrate with a couple more lines of the Brown Sugar. They ended up at Spooner's listening to the same band he'd listened to on the night he met Willow.

27 / MAKE LOVE NOT WAR

Friday night James dropped Caleb off and was home by midnight. Saturday morning, he cleaned in anticipation of Willow coming for lunch. He swept the floors, cleaned the bathroom, and put clean sheets on his bed. The new microwave fit on the end of the counter perfectly. Before she arrived, James took a walk around the block and smoked a joint. He didn't want the place smelling like dope when she arrived.

Willow had had a great morning at the dance studio.

The visiting choreographer tried to make the dancers comfortable by following a familiar workout routine. He outlined a performance to a piece of music, then the dancers tried the movements, first without music, listening as the choreographer snapped a tempo, then with the music. Willow was blessed with rhythm, excellent control of her body, and a presence on the stage that could not be taught. She excelled.

During break, Hattie Goldberg came over to talk to Willow. Willow had been a little put off when she found Hattie was in this dance class. They'd been in all the same dance groups in high school, and Willow didn't want to bring her past with her to college.

"Hi Willow," Hattie said. "I wish I had your talent; you are dancing so light hearted today."

"Oh, thanks, Hattie," Willow said and continued stretching out a small tightness. She didn't feel like talking to Hattie.

"Earth to Willow," Hattie teased.

Willow stopped and turned her attention to Hattie. "I'm sorry —do you want something?"

"Yeah, I want something. I want to invite you to lunch with us after practice."

"And who is this 'us?'"

"My brother, Isaac, you remember him. He's two years older than us? He was watching us dance earlier. I'm not going to play any games for him. He wants to have lunch with you but doesn't think you will remember him. Do you want to have lunch with us? If you want to go alone with him, that's OK, too."

"Isaac? He never talked to me."

"You never paid any attention to him, but I remember him trying to talk to you twice when you came over to listen to my dad's collection of Broadway musicals. Isaac could have been in another room for all you cared."

"I was completely absorbed in the music. We danced, too. I don't remember him trying to talk to me. I remember seeing him, but I was there to play with you."

"Well, can you come to lunch?"

"No. I have to help a friend put up curtains. Tell your brother if he wants to get to know me, he can't hide behind his sister. He'll have to call me. You have my number, don't you?"

"I have your number, Willow. I'll tell him; he'll be disappointed. I thought it was a dumb idea. I like the idea of making him call you; I wonder if he will."

"We better get back to work," Willow said and walked away from Hattie, ready to dance again.

Hattie looked at Willow's straight back and shook her head.

Willow didn't know how hard it was for guys to approach her. Willow was tall and beautiful and haughty on the dance floor; it made her almost as unapproachable as she had been when she'd been a skinny mouse in junior high.

AFTER DANCE TRYOUTS, Willow drove Char's Toyota to James' place. She basked in the success of her tryout performance and drove slowly through residential streets, gradually coming down from her performance high before visiting James.

Kids were playing football in the streets, old people were raking leaves, the sun was shining—all was well in St. Paul. What a morning she'd had but now, but as she headed for James' her enthusiasm lessened.

Last week, riding home with Joe after work, he'd bluntly asked, "Why did you leave the dinner table when James was over? Did you slam out of the house to protect him from your Gram because you think he has a problem with marijuana?"

She answered honestly. "I don't know if he has a problem. I suspect he smokes a lot of dope. He's sharp; he gets a lot done, and I don't want to get too judgmental. Gram pissed me off. I know she was trying to be sneaky, verbally sliding in the back door to get him to talk about his marijuana use."

"Thanks for your honesty, Willow. I don't always like the way Char puts things, but I always know she has nothing but love in her heart for you and for James, too. When we talked later, she said she had overstepped her boundaries and was sorry."

Willow, feeling less enamored and less protective of James, said, "Gram can try to 'save' him, if she wants."

Joe said, "I'm sure Char will talk it over with you before she says anything more to James about his drug use.

Willow said, "Good, maybe one of these days she and I can talk about James."

Now on this crisp, sunny autumn day, Willow was feeling in charge. She liked that Hattie's brother had shown interest in her. She didn't remember him as anything but a good, scholarly kid. She parked the car, hoping James had cleaned up his place.

She was surprised when she got there. The apartment looked clean and smelled like good food. They hugged and kissed, but Willow wasn't desperate to make a good impression on James. They had both acted a little goofy when they first met. Smitten was Gram's old-fashioned word for it. She was relieved he seemed more relaxed too.

"You promised lunch, but I didn't think you would make it. Hey, thanks because I'm hungry."

"The chili is hot, and the nachos are in the microwave."

"I've been dancing for nearly three hours; I'm starved."

"I've got beer or coke or milk. What would you like?"

"I'll have one of each. I'm kidding, a pitcher of water and a glass of milk. I'm really thirsty."

James' nachos were basic, but Willow loved the sharp melted cheddar and mild chilis. The bean chili was all right with dollops of sour cream and shavings of chives. All and all, it was a good lunch. James was expansive—this was what he had imagined, entertaining a beautiful woman.

As they sat at the oak table after finishing lunch, James squirmed a bit and then said, "I've got something to tell you about my mother, Willow. She told me something unbelievable. Now don't make fun of her or me, but what is about the last thing you would ever think that your Gram or my mother would do?"

"Get arrested?" James shook his head.

"Get fired?"

"No. No—this is it," James said, pausing dramatically. "Out of the blue, big smile on her face, she said, 'I'm dating a woman.'"

James watched Willow's reaction. She lifted her head and looked around, rolled her tongue against her teeth, deciding how she felt about that.

"OMG. I would never have thought of that. Was it really out of the blue? Think James—didn't you see it coming? Has she always dated men? Does she have women friends who are gay?"

"No. Just stop it," James said. "She is a very professional person. I never saw it coming. I was speechless. I was doing laundry and the buzzer went off, so I ran down into the basement right after she told me and rummaged around for a while. I couldn't think of a thing to say. I still can't think of anything to say to her. What should I say to her?"

"You should try asking questions when people tell you something big," Willow suggested. "You didn't ask me anything when I told you that my mother had AIDs and I could have been HIV positive and that she died," Willow said, her voice raising with each word.

"Amazing," James answered. "Years ago, Sandra gave me the same advice. She tried to coach me about asking girls questions about themselves. I figure people will tell you what they want you to know."

"That's a terrible, lazy approach to relationships," Willow said. "You put it all on the other person. When I told you the most awful thing about my life, my mother's death, how the kids treated me, you didn't ask one question. You are hard, James, hard." Willow felt herself getting hot. She realized she was still mad at him about that.

"Hey, I'm the one who has a lesbian mother. Talk about not giving support—don't start on me," he said, defensively, looking like a little boy, and they both chortled.

What is it about James? Willow wondered. It was so hard to stay mad at him.

"So, you got a lesbian mother, James. I love it. It is sort of sexy, really. It is a real conversation stopper or starter. Now you know what to say to girls to make them look at you twice."

"Stop it! You met Mom. She is not sexy. But I did have a fantasy about her and her new lesbian lover in bed. Do you want to hear it?"

"Maybe? This is either going to be good or very bad," Willow said, laughing.

"Well, there they are, naked in bed, propped up with pillows. The covers are up to their chins; only their arms are out of the covers. They are holding hands, laying there quietly, watching TV together. They pass the popcorn back and forth. Mom is holding the remote control, but that's as far as my mind can go."

He looked at Willow with a gleam in his eye. "I promise I'm not thinking what she will be doing with that remote later on." Willow laughed so hard, she let herself fall on the floor, and James rolled onto the floor on top of her, growling. They started wrestling, and James was surprised by her strength, but laughing like they were, neither could get a good grip on the other.

Finally, Willow sat up, still on the floor, still giggling, "You have an awful imagination. I don't know if I'll ever be able to look at your mother in the eye with a straight face. You are the devil."

He sat by her, getting his breath back. "I just added that last part to make you laugh. I really never go there in my mind about my mom. Well, I guess I just did. Uh, oh, broke a taboo—Oedipus, Electra, one of those?"

That got them laughing again.

"This isn't half as funny as your story, James, but kind of on the same street. Do you want to hear about when Char and Joe got together when I was about seven or eight?"

"Bring it on," he encouraged.

"I was this serious, smart little girl. I'm sure, now, what was happening; they were having sex in the afternoons when I was at school. Of course, I was in love with Joe, too—that's Electra, for you—and jealous of their time without me—the center of the universe.

When the bus dropped me off after school, I'd look for Joe's car. If it was in the driveway, I'd run to see him. When I got into the house, they would be sitting separately, Gram on the couch and Joe on the armchair. They both looked like they'd just run a marathon. They had this blank look on their faces. I could smell a rat.

Somehow, I knew it had something to do with Gram's bedroom. I'd run upstairs and into her bedroom. The room smelled strongly of her perfume. I'd peek under the bed because I thought whatever they were doing, they were doing it under the bed. I just couldn't figure out what it was. I'd crawl under the bed and lay there trying to figure it out.

"Later, when Joe moved in with us, I asked if I could sleep with them. Gram delivered the sad truth: they loved me more than anyone, but they loved each other, too, and in a way I couldn't always share. Broke my little heart!"

The little girl's look on Willow's face was priceless. James felt tender toward her and scooted over to her, grabbing her and blowing on her soft spots, the neck, the underarm. She laughed again, and it started all over, rolling on the floor, teasing each other, laughing together. Willow crawled on all fours, butt in the air, pretending to sniff something out under his bed. James got his phone out and took a pic of her with her ass up. When she turned around and stuck her tongue out, he took another pic and another pic and another pic. She pulled the phone out of his hands and took a series of pictures of him. Then they did selfies together, laughing, hamming it up. She sent all the pics to her phone.

"Now we are really in each other's lives," she proclaimed giving him back his phone.

"Aren't you glad we are so sophisticated?" she asked, and that set them off being goofy again.

"Good grief, James. How can we people even do it, be sexual? It makes us look and feel goofy, even fancy artsy movies with men's butts in the air and women waving at the camera with their legs and feet up? Gram says the anthem of the 1970s was 'make love, not war.' Think of it, the huge difference between all the goofiness and vulnerability it takes to be sexual and all the hardness and meanness it takes to make war."

She laughed. "Real sex is a big deal, isn't it? It demands that we be vulnerable. I'm proud of my Gram's generation for making that point. Let's be 'make love not war' kind of people, OK?"

"You'll have to discuss that with my friend Caleb, the philosopher; he would have a lot to say about it. But I agree. I want to be a fool for love."

They sat there, holding hands, liking each other. James asked if she'd like to lay together; he wanted that. But Willow was set on hanging curtains.

Buying the fabric and rods was fun. They played house at Ikea, where James also found some water glasses like the ones at his mother's and a number of other kitchen items. Willow picked out long curtains of light yellow and blue squares on a white natural fabric. Putting up the curtains was fun too. All in all, they did a fairly good job. They laughed at the slight slant along the long curtain rod, but neither of them cared enough to straighten out the mistake. They were hungry again and agreed to eat at a Chinese place near Joe's Cafe.

They walked over. James smoked a joint on the walk, and Willow wasn't bothered by his smoking. She was letting go of her concerns over James' smoking, not because she approved of his smoking, but rather, she wasn't as invested in James as she had been last week. She liked him now. She grabbed his arm as they walked. The young, anxious girl in her who had told James she 'loved' him when they made out a few weeks ago was fading from her memory.

When James asked her to stay overnight, she said no. She was tired. Her schedule was grueling. She was dancing three times a week, taking a full load of classes and studying, and still working fifteen hours a week.

James tried to seduce her into staying, but she just wasn't responsive to his kisses, and he finally gave in and believed her that she had run out of juice.

28 / CHAR GOES HOME

Ralph and Sandra arrived Saturday at 9:00 AM sharp to pick up Joe and Char in their charcoal BMW. The plan was to stay overnight at Katie's Bed and Breakfast close to the farm. The Gunderson brothers' wives would make a big Sunday dinner the next day. Joe wheeled their luggage out of the house, and Char followed with an overnight bag. Willow came outside with them to greet her Aunt Sandra and to meet her Uncle Ralph.

"Do you think that's enough for an overnight?" Joe rolled his eyes apologetically and pointed his head back at Char before seeing another equally large if not larger suitcase already in the trunk. Ralph and Joe looked at each other and grinned.

"I can travel with just underwear and socks; how about you?" Ralph added.

"No pajamas?"

Ralph wiggled his bushy eyebrows and tapped his imaginary cigar. "Groucho Marx here. Pleased to meet you." Joe reached out to shake Ralph's hand.

Ralph took his hand in both of his and pulled him in for a hug. Joe smiled sheepishly. He liked the guy already.

Char and Sandra vied for the favored seat in back, the one behind the passenger, the better to get the driver's attention. Sandra won, and Char sat behind Ralph. Char and Joe looked out the windows as their familiar neighborhood faded, both wishing they were spending a quiet weekend at home.

It was hard for the sisters to hear the men's soft voices in the front seat thus giving Ralph and Joe a chance to get acquainted without interference from their wives in the backseat.

"I'm sorry I haven't made it over to your restaurant," Ralph said. "Sandra said the food was great. How is the restaurant business in this recession?"

"The restaurant is busier than it ever has been. I like a busy place, and I've kept the prices reasonable, focused on fresh ingredients and prepped on the premises. That's how you keep people coming back for more."

Ralph nodded. "I like authentic food. Sandra raved about the food, the service, and the price—thanks for picking up the bill."

"Well, I'm not sure how authentic it is. I'm about as Mexican as Char is Scandinavian. I've been blessed with the ethnic good looks," he said as he flashed his toothy smile, "but we use a lot of cheese at Joe's Cafe and keep things a bit bland. That's the way the customers in our neighborhood like Mexican food."

Ralph looked over at Joe, trying to tell if he was putting him on or was serious about the food.

"OK, tell me the truth. Is your food authentic Mexican?"

"It's Minnesota Mexican. Have you spent any time in Mexico? There is regional Mexican food in Mexico, too. Have you had a chance to explore the Mexican cuisine? The Moles` are regional. I often do a unique daily special, using a regional mole` or make Mole de Olla, a soup. The specials go fast. All of us, the employees and I, often take the specials home for our families." Joe squirmed in his seat, wondering why Ralph was so persistent about Mexican food. Was he some kind of a gourmet or sort of a racist?

"I'll make sure Sandra drives over and gets us a special," Ralph responded. "We've taken vacations to coastal resorts. We fly in, though, and we haven't explored the countryside or interior. The food has always been great. How about your family, Joe? Do you take regular trips to Mexico?"

"We fly here and there, and, of course, I always taste the cuisine, talk to whoever speaks English. Willow speaks pretty good Spanish. She took an intensive near Mexico City between her junior and senior years. The interior of Mexico is gorgeous, green and mountainous. My grandparents were from the desert near the Texas border. They traveled all the way to Minnesota in a caravan to pick beets in NW Minnesota. They liked it here in the North Country, and so do I."

"I'm sure our experience of Mexico would be way different if we traveled with an authentic Mexican-American like you. My family has Scandinavian roots like Sandra and Char's. I grew up in a Minnesota town south of the Cities. I haven't traveled much; I'm kind of hoping the four of us can do some traveling together." Ralph glanced over to Joe, eying him sincerely. ``

Joe looked straight ahead but smiled broadly, thinking the four of them might have fun traveling together.

"Now, what do you want to know about proctology?" Ralph said seriously.

Joe looked at him. "You're putting me on, I hope."

Ralph laughed heartily and told Joe a joke. "A man came for his first proctology appointment. He was told to wait in the examination room. He looked around for tools of the trade. On a stand, he saw K-Y jelly, rubber gloves, and a beer. About this time, the doc comes in. 'Hey doc,' the man said. 'I can understand the K-Y and the gloves, but what is the beer for?' The doc goes back to the door, opens it and yells at his new nurse: 'I said a butt light, not Bud Light.'"

Ralph whooped with laughter; Joe chuckled with him.

"Laughing at your own joke, aren't you, Ralph?" Sandra chimed in. That led to more light hearted laughter and the beginnings of an understanding between the two men. They both were married to Gunderson girls; they had that in common.

They drove in silence for a while, Joe gazing at the empty landscape, farm fields, huge rounded metal structures clustered on the large farms. Sandra explained the containers were silos, storage containers of mixed grains to feed cattle or for storage of crops the farmers were holding to sell later when the market price was right.

Later on, Ralph asked Joe if he wanted to hear about his first visit to the farm. Joe nodded.

"Sandra and I had been dating for about two months. I was already in love with her and pleased when she invited me to meet her family. Her dad was nice to me, her mother even nicer. You know they always say you can tell the girl by her mother; little did I know I was marrying the granddaughter of a hearty Swede, not the pretty daughter of a sweet Norwegian mother."

"I heard that," Sandra yelled from the backseat.

"Mind your own conversation; this is 'guy' talk in the front seat."

"Joe," yelled Sandra. "It wasn't as bad as he makes it out to be. He's exaggerating."

"Is a broken leg, exaggerating?" Ralph answered.

"It was just a hairline fracture," she added. "Six weeks in a boot, you weren't even admitted to the hospital."

"You took me to the hospital? I thought it was the veterinarian clinic."

"Ralph tries to be a big City Snob—why did I marry him?" Sandra asked her sister.

"Shush, Sandra—I want to hear the story. Let him tell it his way, please."

"Promise to shut your mouth, Sandra?" Ralph asked.

"Oh, OK. But you exaggerate."

"That's your perception, farm-girl. We had a very good first evening, the folks and Sandra and me. The brothers were out courting. We slept in separate bedrooms, but, of course, Sandra snuck into my room."

"Stop teasing me—stick to your story, Ralph," Sandra chided.

"The next day, after a very good chicken dinner, I got a tour of the farm from Sandra and the brothers."

"Tell them what you were wearing. You didn't even bring regular clothes with you."

"I'd been in a rush coming from the hospital, and I guess I wanted to impress the folks, being a doctor and all. Don't parents want their daughter to marry a doctor? Anyway, I did have on good pants and my car coat instead of my pig calling jacket."

"It was a long 'car' coat; don't forget that part."

Ralph reached back and tried to slap Sandra. The car swerved over toward the median.

"Watch the road!" The three yelled in unison. Ralph complied.

"Anyway, we got around to the barn, and I was surprised that they had horses. I like horses. I said I'd done some riding, and the brothers challenged me to get up on one of the horses. They put a bridle and saddle on that horse so fast I couldn't think of how to get out of it."

"Oh boy," Char commented. "I've seen my brothers do this to their townie friends."

"You got that right. I got up on that huge horse and they led me outside. Denny slapped its rump and off the horse and I went, a hundred miles an hour. I couldn't even find the reins; I gave up and threw my arms as best I could around the neck of the beast."

"He looked just like a picture of Ichabod Crane, headless, coattails flapping, bouncing up and down," Sandra explained.

Char and Sandra started to hoot. Joe had too much empathy and looked back crossly at Char.

"All of a sudden, I see a fence coming up. The big mare just raised herself up and turned on a dime and I flew, literally flew off of her back and landed between rows of stubble over the fence! Need I say more?"

"Oh, my God, my sides. I'm going to pee my pants," Char said helplessly laughing.

"What horse did they put you on?" Char asked.

"Rainey," said Ralph.

Char's laughter abruptly stopped. "Rainey? Rainey was still alive?"

"Our Rainey?" Joe asked, "Our daughter was named after a horse?" He always thought of Rainey as his, too.

"She was the one in the family I loved the most, at the time Rainey was born, I mean," Char said and turned to the window to hide her feelings.

Sandra patted her back. "There, there, that's OK, Char. Rainey was the best horse we ever had. She loved Char. We all loved Rainey, but if Char was in the barn, Rainey just tolerated the rest of us and neighed to Char, a low special soft neigh. Rainey had a good life, Char. Denny and Lyle's kids absolutely loved her. She gave rides and ate apples and enjoyed the pasture up until the time of her death. She was 36 when she died."

Joe reached back with his hanky for Char to wipe her eyes. "Is it clean?" Char asked. "I'm going to tell on you, Joe; he handed me a hanky once that he had used to wipe his hands after cutting up hot peppers."

"Oh, my God," Sandra shrieked. "You didn't."

"It was such a fluke. I don't go around wiping my hands on a hanky," he said, trying to explain. Too late—now he was the butt of a joke or two.

Conversations and revelations followed easily and the time went quickly. Joe marveled as they passed the small city of Mankato and entered the flat farmland of Southwestern Minnesota—huge fallow fields in squares of wheat colored stubble or bare black soil.

"This is 'Black gold,' Joe," Char explained. "Some of the best loam soil anywhere in the world. Two generations ago a farmer's family lived on a quarter section of land; now most farms are at least four times that size. That's a whole section of land, a square mile. Our father farmed a whole section by himself when we were growing up. He was one busy man."

Joe watched the mega farms, little fiefdoms, rolling by. Char pointed out the remaining Sear's farm houses, some 100 years old, but most of the farms were newer brick and lathe McMansions with huge grain silos rising stories into the sky, along with classic barns, additional pole buildings for implements, and some acres of trees and meadows for grazing.

Leaving the four-lane highway behind, they traveled on empty tar roads, bypassing small, dying villages and a few larger towns that were little more than huge school complexes, homes, a few shops, and golf courses. They finally turned onto a smaller tar road and a few miles later, slowed at a swinging wood sign announcing the Gunderson's. They turned down a gravel lane lined with trees and drove the half mile to the farm. Several silos framed a huge white barn, a large mid-century ranch house, a remodeled Sears house, and all the rest of the buildings and pens and gas tanks and other equipment needed for a large farm operation.

Denny, Char. and Sandra's oldest brother had taken over his father's farm. Denny and his wife, Paula, and Grandpa Gunderson lived in the newer McMansion behind the grove of trees. Denny's son, Joel, and his family lived in the restored original farmhouse. Char looked for her childhood favorite. The large grove of trees she and her brothers had used for their homemade tree houses remained, though the grove seemed diminished. The corn and soybean fields encroached almost to the house on two sides. The paddock for the horses, surrounded by a wide white fence, remained. In early November, the weather was surprisingly mild, and the paddock was still green and lush.

CHAR TRIED to regulate her breathing and relax her jaw as she prepared to face her father.

Sandra hoped out of the car. Two barking dogs and Denny rushed out of the house. Sandra and Denny hurried over to each other to hug. Sandra ushered him over to Char's side of the car, and he opened the door and offered his hand to help her out of the car. They hugged deeply. Char put her head on her little brother's shoulder and felt his strength and calming presence. He had been a good boy, and now he was a good man. He had been the peacemaker who drove Char to the bus station when she left the family and had always kept in touch with her over the years.

He pulled away from his big sister to get a better look at her. "You're looking good, big sister."

Char patted his shoulder. "You remember Joe." The men shook hands, and Denny said, "Welcome."

Ralph and Denny shook hands and clasped each other's shoulders.

"Dad is excited to see you, Charlene. We shouldn't make the old man wait."

Char took a deep breath and walked toward the door. As she got closer, the door opened and an old, diminished man wearing bibs, a plaid jacket, and a John Deere cap walked carefully down the two steps. He looked up, spotted Char, and motioned to her with a smile on his face.

"Charlene," he said. "Come here; give your dad a hug."

She walked steadily toward her dad and put her arms around him. He hugged her, and they rocked in the embrace. Everyone gave them room, fearful that they would wobble and fall, but they didn't. Char and her Dad walked arm in arm up the steps and into the house while the rest stood there, tears glistening in their eyes. Joe turned away to wipe tears from his eyes.

By the time the others came into the house, Char and her dad were sitting close on the couch. Dad whispered to Char, "You've always had a place at our table. All these years, we've been waiting for you to come home."

Char looked closely at her Dad. His rheumy eyes were still bright blue. He looked back at her, examining her eyes, too. She remembered his smiling eyes; she had his eyes.

After introductions and re-introductions, Paula and Sandra set the table for lunch. All the grandkids and their babies were coming for dinner tomorrow. For dinner that night, the four Gunderson children and their mates were going out to the steak house down the road, still owned and operated by Max Hendricks, who, in alphabetical order, sat behind Char in school for 12 years. Dad was staying home; he liked to be in bed by 8:00.

After lunch, Dad asked Char if she would like to take his daily walk to the mailbox with him.

"I'd love that, Dad," Char answered.

As they walked, her Dad said, "I remember us walking before the boys started coming along with us. You hopped and skipped and asked the names of everything. 'What's this? What's that?'"

"Those are my happiest childhood memories, Dad," Char said, taking his hand and gently lifting his knuckles up, rubbing them against her cheek, as he'd so often rubbed his knuckles along her cheek when she was a child. Her heart sang, and she picked up a little skip to her step as she walked hand in hand with her dad.

PART 4
ARMAGEDDON

29 / CALEB WANTS MORE

Caleb reclined in his armchair, feet up on his bed. He'd snorted the last of the second batch of Brown Sugar that James shared with him. He'd floated on an island of pure contentment. But, too soon, he became restless, back to reality. His attention turned to the empty foil lying on the bed. He picked up the foil and licked the minute residues of powder then rolled the foil into a ball and flipped it across the room missing the waste basket. The big bummer, the last taste of a good product.

Of all the drugs he'd used as a teenager, booze, of course, and pot, and hallucinogens, and uppers, and downers; nothing satisfied him like heroin satisfied him. He hadn't let on to James just how mind altering, life altering, going back to heroin was for him. How could he keep his use of heroin in check?

He was hoping he'd attained the maturity to use heroin without becoming addicted, but was that possible? The pluses were; he was more mature, twenty-three, and had found his purpose in the writing program at Augsburg. The AA program and his sponsor had given him tools that improved his self-awareness and he continued to monitor his behavior through a nightly routine of re-examining his day to day life. He'd stayed sober for way over a year until he stopped going to AA and met James and started smoking a little marijuana.

When James offered him heroin, he believed if James could do it, use heroin, so could he.

He'd pegged James as a smart pothead from the suburbs, the perfect companion for a free marijuana high with now and again. But as he got to know him, Caleb witnessed an innocence and blasé good-will in James that seemed ironically heroic to Caleb. James just went with the flow and Caleb believed James' way of being would protect James against the dark forces at play in the world.

Caleb hoped if he stayed in James' light, he could protect himself too. He wanted to use opioids as a tool to help him write profound literature for his apocalyptic generation.

William Burroughs and Hunter Thompson were 'beat generation' writers Caleb admired. They danced on the edge of the dark side, embracing drug use and alcohol binges during their adventures through life. They transformed mid-century literature by writing in a stream of consciousness about their amoral lifestyles. Caleb reasoned he was living in an amoral American society, he should continue those authors' work, tumbling around, searching for something to hold on to.

He was beyond pessimistic about the earth's future. The current damage to the planet, by carbon emissions, deforestation, deep water mining and the burgeoning population, spelled doom. One professor presented a graph that showed that environmental destruction had gone past the point of no return, the world, as we know it, would be devastated within the next twenty-five to forty years. Caleb wanted an opioid boost to keep writing in this tangled storm of living in a world of hurt.

Returning to opioid use was going to be a new, demanding lifestyle. He hoped he was up to the challenge. He would start a new life today.

On this early November Saturday, stoned out of his gourd, he staggered out of his room into the hallway and held onto the railing down the stairs. He opened the outer door to cool, clear fall air. Leaves were whipping down the street in a high wind. Trees were barren. The autumn blue sky was an empty blue as empty as the world was becoming.

There's an apocryphal lesson in watching the seasons' change, Caleb thought, he'd write about that. Down the concrete streets he wandered in short sleeves, oblivious to chill. Along the warren of alleys, he traveled, lost in his imagination of living in the post-apocryphal world.

By Saturday night, Caleb readily admitted he wanted to get high again. Still, he had written a couple of chapters and that was all he really had wanted to accomplish this week. His writing was on task.

Damn, he thought, if James doesn't call me, I'll have to call him. He hated the idea of asking James for more heroin, but with $2000 in the bank and $1000 for expenses from dad, he had to get more money coming in for heroin, he vowed he wasn't going back to lying and stealing for heroin.

When he called James, he would ask about meeting this dealer and getting himself a job in the business too. James had called the guy, what was it, Randy, Randall? Something like that, then reverted to 'Jay'.

Caleb put aside his worry about the addictive consequences of heroin use, he just needed a way to pay for the junk. If he could get a job with James' dealer, he would all set.

He wanted to call James tonight, it was early evening, but it was date night and James was probably out with Willow. He called anyway.

"Hey dude, what you up to?" Caleb asked.

"Hey, back at you, I'm not doing anything, Willow left, she's got a life of her own, I guess, anyway she didn't stay like we planned. I don't understand her, I make us lunch, we put up curtains together, we fall over each other laughing, I finally got some pics of her on my phone and then she leaves."

"I'm sorry for you, but if you don't have plans, want to do something with me?" Caleb asked.

"Sure, I'll pick you up, maybe we can go to a movie."

"You pick me up and get me high, and I'll pay for my own movie, how does that sound?"

"You're my date now?" James teased. "You sure don't measure up to Willow, but I'll roll a couple of joints and head over to your place. I'll text when I get there."

"I'll be waiting at the curb. I'll be the one wearing lipstick."

"Wait till I tell you about the latest development in my dear old Mom's life. She is unbelievable."

"I'll be waiting for you, but I'm wearing pants, is that OK?"

"What a disappointment. See you soon."

Caleb was leaning on a boulevard tree. He waved when he saw James and angled his car and reached out his hand, "I want to see the pics of Willow."

"Don't you want to get stoned first?"

Caleb settled into the passenger seat and shook his head, "give me the phone, you can start the joint." James delayed the joint to show off his favorite pic of Willow, the one with her butt in the air, looking under his bed. Caleb loved the one where she laughed with her mouth open, showing her full set of beautiful white teeth and the one from a more sober moment, looking as if she were searching James' face.

"She has good teeth on this one and she's searching for your soul on this one. Did she find it?" Caleb said.

"She's deep" James allowed, "I don't know what she sees in me.

But isn't she something? She almost said 'love' once, but then she took it back. Damn."

"Women have a lot of expectations you know." Caleb kept looking at the pics.

James finally asked, "What about the pics of me? You aren't looking hard at them."

"Oh, I see you all the time. Will you send Willow's pics to my phone?"

James complied and said, "You got to meet her. I've mentioned you today. She was spouting off about love and war; she thought it took more guts to make love, than it took to make war, something like that. I said she would like talking to you about philosophy."

"Hum, a woman's perspective, but then women are right about lots of things," Caleb commented.

"She can twerk, she's a dancer."

"I can bullshit you, James, but honestly, I envy your courage, taking on this one. Be good to her. OK? I thought I was in love back in the day. Having someone who loves you, I miss that."

They were still sitting in the car by the curb at Caleb's rooming house. James commented that it had gotten dark. Caleb kept looking at Willow's pictures.

James knew Willow would be saying, 'ask him to tell you more about his lost love' but James lit a joint instead. "Here man, something to lighten your spirits."

They smoked casually, watching cars and people go by, commenting now and then, trying to make each other laugh.

Caleb took a deep breath, "I want to meet your dealer, James. I want to see if he has some work for me too. I'm tired of mooching off of you."

James finished the joint, spit on the little roach and popped it into his mouth, "You and me haven't talked about my 'job' much. It isn't a piece of cake. I'm living with anxiety and I'm paranoid. I keep looking around, if anyone even looks at me, I think they are undercover cops. I get a feeling someone standing right behind me, and I turn around and no one is there. I panic and start sweating. Does that sound fun?"

"Don't worry, James. I ended up in Juvie for a few days and the stories I heard there, the stupid risks those guys took to land there? None of the smart guys or kids from money were in there. It was all poor, dumb, scum bags on the nod in there. Did I tell you that my Dad called the police to come get me? He let me sit there for a few days before dropping charges against me."

"We're smarter now, James, and we don't need the money, or the dope, we just want it. Remember that, we want it, not need it. Besides, even if you did get busted, it would be a first-time offense. Stay smart, from what you told me about Jay, or whatever his name is, he is smart and cautious, stay with him."

"You're saying all the things Jay said. I guess you're right. Being a little paranoid is probably smart. But I'm anxious, and of course I can't get stoned before I do the pickups. I wonder if I will ever get used to those feelings?"

"You will. So, will you introduce me to him?"

"Sure, I already told him I had a standup guy who was sharing the smack with me."

"Good. Did you get any more of it?"

"No, not yet, I got a couple of lines left."

"When do you think I could meet 'Jay'?"

JAMES AND CALEB ended up going back to James' place and finishing off the heroin.

Caleb head bobbed and he talked slowly from a hollow place in his head, "Man I got to say, I didn't believe when you said Willow was a ten. But she's got that something special." Caleb leaned back against the chair and took out the pictures of Willow again.

They were silent for a while, gathering their scattered thoughts. James wanted to talk more about his paranoia but wasn't sure Caleb wanted to hear about it.

"Where did she come from? You met her on the street you said, what kind of family does she come?"

"She's Sandra's great niece, that almost makes her sort of a cousin of mine. I didn't know that of course, seeing her on the street. Then I met her grandmother, her Gram, who looks just like Sandra. First, I almost fuck my sister, now I'm after my almost cousin. What is wrong with me? How do I pick them?"

Caleb tried to register what James was saying. "She doesn't look like she's related to you. You didn't fuck your sister, you don't have a sister, you told me that. Where is your family from?"

"We're from Lake Wobegon. You know where that is?"

"Uh? Oh, the Garrison Keillor home place. His radio show was the only reference I had to Minnesota when I moved here. Then I met you, straight out of Lake Wobegon."

James rolled his eyes, he wasn't taking the bait, "Willow's mother had AIDS when she was born, but I don't like anyone talking bad about Willow. I don't know what I just said. Forget what I just said."

"Then why do you say it to me?" Caleb went back to dreaming about Willow. So did James.

JAMES MADE it through his exchanges on Sunday, smoked a joint, took a long shower and called Willow. She was cool to him even though he tried hard to hold up his end of the conversation. He tried to engage her in some phone sex play but she didn't respond to that either. He was at a loss. The conversation ended up unsatisfactorily.

MONDAY WAS COLD AND RAINY. James was bored. He skipped his Monday seminar and decided to run in the rain with a hooded slicker on. He ran about four miles and stopped at Spooner's on the way home and sure enough, Randall was sitting in the back booth he favored.

James shook out his yellow slicker and walked over to Randall, his wet shoes squeaking at every step. Randall was wearing a black leather jacket, dark grey shirt and black pants. James thought this was Randall's mobster look. Randall looked up noticing James' squeaky shoes and shook his head and they both laughed.

"You know what you should be? You should be a mailman, rain or shine."

James didn't know if he should sit down, as wet as he was, or just say hi and go home.

"I'm drenched but I always feel good after running. Now I can go home and take a hot shower and open a book and fall asleep."

"Get yourself some coffee. I'm glad to see you," Randall added.

"OK," said James and he came back shortly.

"How was yesterday, is it becoming old hat for you? Doing your pickups?" Randall asked.

James looked around before responding. Two ditzy girls were huddled a few booths away, no else was within ear shot.

He sat down and responded quietly, "Every time is a little easier. I'm not quite as paranoid. I had a talk with my friend Caleb, the guy I told you about. He's been in Juvie in New York and he said that the only guys there were idiot junkies. He said that I shouldn't be paranoid about handling a few drugs."

"You didn't tell him about our operation, did you?"

"First rule, no names, and no, I just said I was working with a friend who knew the drug scene. Told him I've known you for years. He's an honor student in Philosophy, does that sound like someone you have to worry about?"

"I'm not worried about the police, we got them covered, or the DEA, the bosses say there aren't any stings in the forecast, but how do you know he can keep his mouth shut?"

"Chuck met and liked Caleb, call Chuck, who's a better judge of character than Chuck? Or you could call Caleb's mom and dad, like the Mafia, get to know the family. You could get references from his summer job too. He was a bicycle courier in New York city (Not the same kind of courier service I'm doing of course)."

"I've already put myself out there for you, James, and now you want me to put myself out for your friend."

"You did help me out and I'm telling you that you can trust Caleb."

Randall toyed with the idea of using James' friend. He knew the bosses played him against his nemesis Popeye. Popeye had been pissed when Randall got the new opioid business instead of him and had retaliated by bullying Randall about his cocaine use.

Randall believed in the adage, 'keep your friends close and your enemies closer'. He liked the idea of having someone he knew working for Popeye. Maybe this friend of James would be just the right guy. He knew that Popeye was looking for another front guy to help with money laundering. Randall made his decision.

"Call this friend of yours right now and ask him for his Dad and Mother's names and telephone numbers and a reference from his summer job. I'll call his parents and his reference. I like the idea of calling the guy's parents."

Before Randall left Spooner's without offering soaking wet James a ride home, he invited both James and Caleb to his place Saturday night for a little private party, just the three of them. "Be ready to rumble. We'll have ribs and chicken. Then we'll watch the 'pay for view' octagon games, and I'll invite a couple of 'ladies of the night' for you two, I got my own lady."

Randall verbally gave James his address with a warning, “don’t write it down and never come by without an invitation, don’t even drive by the block, understand?” James nodded.

Randall looked sharply at him again, “Did you understand? Did you hear what I just said? Don’t go over there uninvited and no names?” James nodded sincerely. For a parting gift, Randall slipped James a little foil package.

30 / WILLOW BREAKS IT OFF

When Char and Joe got back from the farm on Sunday, they found a subdued Willow lying on the couch watching 'Funniest Home Video' reruns.

"Hi honey, are you feeling OK?" Joe asked.

She shrugged her shoulders and asked how their weekend had gone. She sat up and greedily looked at the pictures Joe brought back from the farm and commented on Char's wide smiles and Great-grandpa's lively eyes. But then her head sagged and she looked sad again.

"What's wrong," Char asked more persistently.

"If you got to know, I think I'm going to break up with James. I like him so much and he'll be mad and Sandra's whole family will hate me," she slouched, putting her head sideways against the couch and sighed.

Char moved a little closer to her and said, "You didn't promise to marry him. You have the right to decide what kind of a relationship you want with him. Sandra and I thought you were getting a little ahead of yourselves, you haven't dated that long."

Willow sat up and turned to her Gram, anger flashed from her eyes, "You weren't there, what do you know about it? You two", she glared at Joe too, "are gossiping about me. Jeez, how do you think that makes me feel?"

"What do you expect us to talk about?" Char answered defensively, then apologized, "Oh, I'm sorry, Willow, it's just that Sandra and I are becoming so close and I've wondered if this thing between you two was more about finding 'someone' rather finding 'the right someone.'"

Willow gave her gram a long warning look before continuing, "He thinks I'm in love with him. I led him on. I told him I wanted to have sex with him and now I want to take it all back."

"Feeling sorry for someone isn't a reason to have sex with him. I did that and it led me down a very sorry path. If your feelings have changed, he should know as soon as possible. He's a big boy. He'll get over it."

"But he'll hate me. I want to meet Chuck and Laurel and Kimber and their kids and spend time with all of them too. I want to be part of this family like you are."

"Don't whine. Tell him the truth and really mean it if you want to be friends. Tell him we'd still like him to come around here too. I won't bring up drugs ever again. Let him know we think of him as part of this family too."

"What do you think, Papa, is it OK if James comes around if we end up being friends?"

"I don't care, bring it on. I won't chase him away."

Char chimed in, "I'm happy that you want to get to know your cousins better. You were impulsive with James, no harm in that, and now I'm thrilled you want to act responsibly. We talked on the way back about having Thanksgiving with Sandra's family. You can meet all the cousins then, sooner if you want."

Willow signed, "Thanksgiving is coming up, I got to' talk to James soon. Do you think it is OK if I wait a few days before talking to him, to think it through?"

Char nodded 'yes.' Joe just shrugged his shoulders.

Willow jumped up and gave her Gram and Papa hugs, "This a weight off my shoulders. I think I'm going to do a hot bath now with candles and incense so I can get a good night's sleep. Do you mind if I go up?"

They both shook their heads no. Char and Joe needed a little time to process the weekend before heading up to bed. After Willow was safely upstairs, Char and Joe turned to give each other a double high five.

WEDNESDAY, late afternoon, Willow trudged upstairs to call James. She thought he'd be home from his Wednesday classes. She sat on the edge of her bed feeling anxious.

"Hi, James, how are you? Done with your grueling class day?"

"Hi, Willow. I'm glad you're calling. Yes, I'm winding down on the futon, trying to get the energy to microwave a few burritos. Jeez I hate thinking of going to work tomorrow."

"Tell me, what do you do that is so awful?"

"Steal money from geriatrics, I don't want to talk about it. It sucks."

"When can we get together, have a chat."

"Is that a euphemism for what I hope it is?"

"No, I'd like to talk something over with you."

An alarm went off in his head like the time she blindsided him with the talk about his smoking marijuana. He shifted his posture and sat up leaning against the wall.

"What are you up to now?" she asked.

"I told you I'm trying to unwind."

"Why don't I come over and bring us something to eat, I can get take out from Joe's Café."

"Can't you put it off? I'm tired."

"No, I'll be over in an hour, rest your eyes." Willow was over in less than an hour.

They ate quietly, James snapped a few chips Willow's way, but she remained solemn, letting the chips fall away from her pressed lips.

"What's up?" he finally said when their plates were empty.

"I don't want to have sex with you after all", she blurted out. "I suppose that means we won't be dating."

Surprisingly, James didn't get angry or sad. He almost looked relieved.

"I'm surprised. You don't look upset." Willow looked at him quizzically.

"I'm surprising myself here too. I must be maturing," he said cynically.

"I don't like the part about being tangled together, having expectations of each other, do you?" Willow asked.

He nodded. "Living on my own is hard enough, but living up to your expectations? If you don't want me the way I am, I guess it's over."

She nodded. "Saturday when we played, we had such a good time, just being friends. It was a wonderful day, wasn't it?"

James sadly nodded his agreement.

Willow slammed into the house waking Joe who was half asleep on his recliner with the remote in his hand. He was stubbornly waiting for Willow to get home. Char was half asleep lying on the couch.

Willow loomed over them with a young person's energy.

"How did it go?" asked Char, sitting up and patting a place next to her.

"It went well, much better than I expected it to go. James was in agreement with me. I'd been trying to think of the perfect lie and then the truth turned out to be easy."

"Let that be a lesson for you," Joe commented.

"Please don't make this into a 'learning moment', papa."

"Sorry, I couldn't help myself," Joe jerked the recliner into the sitting position.

"I'm worried for James, Gram. He was blaming himself, 'I'm not a good guy', shit (oops, sorry) but saying shit like that, he was taking it all wrong, it's not about him being bad. It's more than the marijuana. There's something more, I wonder if he doesn't think he is doing well with the part-time job. He is so edgy. I think he was relieved that we were breaking up. What do you think about that?"

"Sandra described him as mercurial."

"Speak English please," Willow protested.

"Moody. I thought you had a better vocabulary than that!"

"I do, I just don't use it!" Willow insisted.

"You've got so much on your plate. Getting involved with a complicated, unhappy man is not what you need."

"You're quick to judge him, Char," Joe said. "Isn't that the way young people are? Complicated? The world may be their oyster but it's hard to get that oyster out of the shell."

The women looked at him. "That's a pearl of wisdom, Joe." Char teased.

"Oh, you two," I'm going up to my room and closing the door for a little peace and quiet." Willow waved them off as she headed for the stairs with a "good night."

"I love you," rang out from both Char and Joe.

Joe leaned forward on his recliner to conspire with Char, "Well, tell me what you really think is going on." he asked Char.

"I don't know what's up with him. But do you ever wonder why we haven't done anything about Willow slamming that back door? She's been doing it for years, how many years? without us doing anything about it?"

"Now that you bring it up, yeah, it's strange that neither of us laid down the law. You know she is going to break that beveled glass one of these days."

"I'm thinking back on when the slamming started. I think it was way back when we first got together and she would come home from school and tear in here to see you. Remember?"

"We'd be sitting here, feeling so good but waiting for the onslaught of our favorite little girl, slamming her way into my hearts."

"I'd be feeling the same. We sure have some good memories don't we, Joe?"

"Last weekend was one of them." He got up and walked over to sit by Char on the couch. "I loved meeting your dad. No wonder you're such a good woman, you've got good roots, Char." He put his arms around her and pulled her close to him and kissed her on the cheek.

"Tell me all about the weekend again, Joe. Be my camera. Start with Ralph, what do you think of Ralph?"

31 / JAMES AND CALEB AT RANDALL'S PARTY

James picked up Caleb to go to Randall's party. Caleb was wearing an open collar white dress shirt and the old bomber jacket he had found in the trash behind some rich people's house. He'd had to mend a rip in it. Somehow the mend worked, Caleb looked trendy. James was dressed down in worn jeans, navy T, and heavy grey hoodie.

James shook his head, "Even with a lousy job of mending, your jacket is cool, you disgust me."

Caleb laughed, "I'd rather disgust you, than turn you on, huh?"

"Shut up, you couldn't turn me on if we were the last two people on earth. We'd have to find a goat, right? Light the joint." James tossed a joint over.

Caleb laughed and lit joint. "I'm looking forward to this party."

"We're only young once, right? But remember, do it Randall's way, I mean Jay's way. Jay, Jay, Jay. I got to get this right in my head. He's the same guy he was back in junior high, 'my way or the highway'. Be careful around him, hear me?"

Caleb chuckled, "Sounds charming. Hope it's worth my time."

"My bet is on Randall, Jay I mean. You'll be kissing his ass like I do."

"Hey, I don't kiss ass."

James eased the car into a parking spot around the corner from Randall's place.

"Hey, SpongeBob, maybe you'll finally stop sponging on me."

They got out of the car both discreetly looking in both directions.

"What can I say?" Caleb answered and shrugged his shoulders, "Beggars can't choose."

"I'm sorry. SpongeBob just came out of my mouth like a burp, not on purpose."

"You're right, I sponge, I like the name, James, SpongeBob will be my code name. What's your code name?"

"I can't remember if I have one. Oh, yah, it's T. But they all know my name and they know where I live." James said in a spooky voice.

That, plus the weed, broke them up and they were still guffawing when they stumbled to the door and rapped.

A burly looking guy in jeans and tee shirt opened the duplex door a crack. "What you want?" he asked. They could smell meat frying from the open door of the downstairs apartment. It sounded like kids were playing inside the place too.

"What's going on?" Randall shouted from the head of the stairs.

"Your knuckleheads are here," the guy shouted back.

"Send them up, Sammy, they're friends."

Sammy shook his head in disgust of Randall's friends and opened the door wide enough for them to squeeze in. Then he shut it, locked it twice, and motioned up the staircase.

The place wasn't far from Willow's house, right off of commercial Grand Avenue. James sighed again thinking of how he and Willow had just called it off.

Caleb gestured for James to go up first.

Randall stood in the doorway of the second floor flat. After trudging up the stairs, James made quick introductions, "Jay, Caleb, Caleb, Jay."

They nodded and sized each other up. They were about the same size. Randall swaggered back into his apartment thinking he was better looking and, for sure, better dressed than either of these guys. He was wearing a maroon dress shirt and pressed black slacks.

He stepped aside and ushered them in, pride written all over his face. He had huge mounted deer antlers that served as a coat rack. "Put your jackets on the deer sheds. Got them from a kid who shot the twelve point in Wisconsin".

The front room was large, square, painted grey, with leather couches and a couple of big men's chairs and some chrome and glass and a red Persian rug over the refinished wood floor. A big aquarium took up most of one wall.

"Jeez, this room is bigger than I thought it would be, judging from the size of the building," James commented.

"I opened up the front porch, over here, James, look at the job the contractor did. It almost looks like it was always one room."

James nodded his head in appreciation walking over to where the wall between the rooms had been removed. "I like that you kept the porch windows wide. I hate remodels when they cut back on the size of the windows. Totally fine upgrade."

James zoned in on a tune, he recognized one of Randall's favorites, "Ah, ah, you're in trouble" the lyrics rang. Randall played the same rap in his car.

Caleb walked over to the aquarium.

"I've seen some good aquariums at restaurants, dentist offices, but nothing like this in someone's home. I'm counting, I'm up to 10, how many species do you have? What's that big blue baby?"

"That's Nicky. He's a Neon Blue Discus. Great color, huh?"

"Makes me want to lie down on a white sand beach, or 'swim with the fishes, nah, nah, nah.'" Caleb rapped to Randall's tune.

"I got a drug that'll do the same for you."

"What's this little spotted leopard one?"

"I've got a chart over there, to the left. A guy comes by and tells me what I need and I buy it. I've had Nicky the longest, he's my dawg."

Randall turned to face both of them, "Smell those ribs? Want a beer?"

James and Caleb both nodded and Randall yelled into the hallway, "three beers, Norma Jean."

Minutes later a small blond woman, bare foot in a geisha styled robe, came trotting in with a tray of imported beer, cheese, and crackers.

Randall made introductions, "Norma Jean, this is James and Caleb." After James and Caleb took beers, Norma Jean sat the tray down and turned to Randall. He wrapped his arms around her, leaned down and kissed her passionately on the lips. She kissed him back, morphing from a servant girl to a passionate woman in front of their eyes.

James' eyes widened and he looked over at Caleb who was watching the action with his eyes pinned on the woman. He turned to James and gave him a nod with raised eyebrows, as if to say, what did you expect?

Randall traced his fingers down her chin to where her robe closed, leaned into her body, and kissed her again before letting her go with a pat to her butt.

"Isn't she lovely?" he asked.

They both nodded and took a swig of their beers.

"Norma Jean, bring the mirror, we're going to get stoned before we eat."

Norma Jean stood as tall as she could in the middle of the room, "Can you ask nice, maybe a please, Jay?" She put a hand on her hip and waited.

"Please, then, please just do it."

She sashayed out of the room and Randall explained, "She's showing off, giving me shit because 'college' boys are here. You're a couple of nice guys, right James? Are you going to be a nice guy and pass on the women tonight?" Randall asked as he made himself comfortable on the big chair and motioned for them to choose a couch.

James looked a little embarrassed but shook his head no.

"What? I couldn't hear you?" Randall taunted him.

"I'm not going to pass."

Caleb looked over at James.

"What about Willow? What's up, James?"

"We are having second thoughts, I guess. I'm not waiting around for her."

"What about you, Caleb, you waiting on a virgin?" Randall asked.

"I'll decide after I see what you got to offer."

"You'll like my choices. They're clean, they work the streets sometimes, but I know the guy who runs them. He treats them good and keeps them clean. He's not into beating them with hangers or anything, as far as I know."

James and Caleb glanced at each and Caleb couldn't help grinning. Partly because he knew James was such a horny dude and partly because 'Jay' was great fodder for his book, but mostly because James and Willow might be breaking up. She was too good for James.

The evening progressed. The loaded weed came out, the music went down, the UFC championships came on, the ribs were eaten, finally the junk came out with a little hard case, a spoon, needles, a lighter, a rubber tourniquet, the works. Caleb made up a fix for James and carefully found his vein, slapped it a couple of times, put the needle parallel to the vein and pulled up a little blood before gently injecting it into James' vein.

It was immediate, James melted into the couch, his facial

muscles sagged. He faded in and out, floating, his eyes opening and closing, his ears doing the same.

Sometime later, he awakened to a strange heaviness along his thighs and groin. He opened his eyes startled, a naked woman was crouched on his lap, groin to groin, undulating her hips slowly, back and forth against him.

"You're coming around, then," she whispered in his ear, her smooth cheek against his, her hair, astringent and prickly, tickling his nose.

"Argro u?" struggled out of his mouth.

"I'm here for your pleasure," she whispered.

Despite his initial reluctance, James felt a stirring in his loins and reached for the snap on his pants. She pulled herself up and half holding on to the back of the couch, helped him pull his pants down around his ankles. She put a rubber on him and they were doing the ageless dance he dreamed about at night.

"God, god, god," he murmured.

"Are you praying?" she murmured back.

He swung her down to the floor and kicked off his shoes and struggled out of his pants, trying not to let go of her, and pushing himself into her, over and over. She lay there quietly, legs spread, and let him have her. He thought he was done several times but he started up again. He was all body, no mind. Later, he wouldn't have known if he had come or not if it weren't for the wetness and the smell of semen mingling with the other scents.

Finally, he rolled off of her and flopped on the rug next to her slowly becoming aware of the room. The faded blue on the muted big screen spread a soft light in the darkened room, the coffee table dug into his shoulder and butt. Then he looked at the woman, who was pushed against the couch, lying on her back. He looked at her profile, touching her classic pert nose and rolling his fingers along her soft lips. Even in the semi dark he could see her heavy eye makeup and dark lip gloss, smudged, clown like. He wanted to find a cool wash cloth and gently wipe away the makeup to really see her. He put his arm around her waist and snuggled against her, cuddling her. He wanted to cry, he wanted to be here and he wanted to be out of here.

They must have slept, when he awakened again, there was daylight and he could hear Randall and Caleb murmuring in the background. They laughed, jarring him more awake, and the woman stirred next to him. He held her closer, wishing for the guys to go away. The guys were over by the fish tank. He heard another woman's voice.

"Angie, get up, I know you're not sleeping, we got to' go, now."

She stirred again and he held her tighter.

"Lemme' go," she murmured and brushed her cheek against his face, against his nose and mouth.

He let her go and as she raised up, he watched her, looked at her body.

"What's your name?" he asked.

"Aren't you listening? I'm Angie."

He looked at her face when she talked and recognized her, she was the girl he had seen on the street, the night he met Willow.

"I saw you near University Avenue, about 11:30 p.m. on August 15." He told her.

She looked at him as if for the first time, and now she too might remember him if she saw him again. She stooped over and kissed him tenderly on the lips, "Bye, James," she said and both girls walked out the door.

James knew he would see her again.

He rolled over on his stomach.

"Time for coffee James, then you got to go home." Randall had walked over and nudged James' inert foot with his shoe.

"I'm not getting up with you guys looking at me. Move away from me, give me a little privacy, will yah?"

Randall laughed. "You don't like being a porn star, James?"

"Come on, get me a coffee, will you?"

James lay silently on his stomach, with his head on the floor, until he heard Randall and Caleb step away and go towards the kitchen. Assured they were gone, he hustled up and dressed. He stuffed his shirt into his pants and sat on the couch, rubbing his face, taming his wild hair with his hands.

"Here, mate," Caleb had a mug in his outstretched hand.

James tasted it. Good coffee with lots of cream, not too hot, the way he liked it. He gulped it down.

He looked at Caleb, "Thanks, I needed that, I think I got run over by a Mack truck." He coughed, grinning foolishly at Caleb and looking around for Randall.

"Jay's getting some coke. He thinks we need a snort to make it home."

Do you want to do it?" James asked.

"God, I'm done in," Caleb said. "But I don't have to drive, maybe you should snort a line. What do you think?"

Randall came in sniffing, with a couple of lines on a little mirror. "Here's a taste for the road."

"OK," James reached for the mirror and snorted a line. His head jerked back and he waited a minute until the high settled in. "One more, OK?"

Randall nodded and James finished it.

"I like her," James said.

"What did he say, Caleb? Did I hear right? Did he say he liked her?"

"That's what he said." Caleb answered

"James you're so predictable. But I like that about you, I'm counting on that. James, tell me about this guy, here," he pointed to Caleb. "What am I getting with him?"

James looked over at Caleb, "Smart, interesting, experienced with drugs, in control of himself. You're getting the real deal."

"Sorry, I don't need you Caleb."

Caleb looked crestfallen. Randall laughed, "But I know someone who could use you. Do you want to meet with him?"

"Tell me what he needs," Caleb asked. "I want some easy money, but I won't do just anything for it."

"He needs a pretty boy to do some money drops for him."

"Sounds interesting if the money is decent and I don't have to use a bicycle. Oh, I can't drive a car."

"That's not a problem," Randall assured him.

Caleb and James decided to get some breakfast at the St. Clair Broiler on their way home.

James' knees jiggled as he drank his second cup of coffee.

James asked, "What was the name of your girl? I didn't really look at her."

"You were so out of it, I got to choose first. But I'm a nice guy, I took the one who looked the most experienced, she was a little older and had a lot of butt on her. I was thinking 'this lady knows how to dance' and she did. Her name was Ellie. I thought you'd like the baby blond. She's almost as tall as you, you could go toe to toe."

"I saw her on a street corner last summer, Caleb. It was the night I moved into town. I'd gone to Spooner's After Dark, and listened to the "Light Rail", the group we heard a few weeks ago. I left after a few sets, walked around looking for Saturday night action. I saw Angie on a side street and walked by her, my first 'walk by a prostitute' and I had a quick thought about paying the price to spend time with her but I didn't know where the whores took you if you were walking, if you ended up in a bed or pressed against a brick wall. It was all too sordid. She was too sordid for me back then. That was the same day and night I ran into Willow twice. She was waitressing at her dad's place at University, Joe's Cafe, and we started talking."

"She works at Joe's Cafe? I've walked by there but never gone inside. What's the scoop, what happened between you and Willow? Just last Saturday, you were thinking this might be the girl for you."

"Do you really think I can have a girl like Willow and get into what we're into?" James blushed, "She pegged me for a doper about our third date. I know she would start nagging on me if we got too involved. I don't want to be owned. I don't know about her, but I know the family she comes from, and those women own you."

"Yeah, that's been my experience, if you let them under your skin, ouch, big trouble. I'm with you, I just want to get done with Augsburg, no woman. And now I have a chance for easy money too. Has Jay/Randall ever talked about this Popeye?"

"No but what did you think of Randall?"

"He's a little edgy, like you said, wants things to go his way. I didn't particularly like him but wow, SpongeBob got invited to the big show."

"How are you doing, James? Can you stop singing, 'can't get no satisfaction' for a few days?"

"God, I just remembered, my rubber came off. Now I'll get a VD, won't I? Hurry up, eat the eggs, Caleb, I got to' get home and take the longest, hottest, soapiest shower ever.

32 / CALEB AND POPEYE

Caleb and James were talking on the phone. Both of them half lying in their armchairs, feet dangling, listening to their competing sounds as they talked.

"Thanksgiving is coming up. What you got to be grateful for, Caleb? Tell me about the big bucks you're starting to get working for Popeye."

"First let me tell you about Popeye. I meet him downtown, he's black wearing a bold green plaid suit. One of the first things he says to me is, 'Jew boy, your family into counting money?'"

"I thought about the anti-Semitism. I shook my head sadly and said to him, 'just call me SpongeBob, and I'll call you Popeye'. He looked hard at me and finally gave me a thumbs up. 'I want you out front, meeting the public. You do that for me?'"

"Then I asked him directly, 'am I going to be the front man, dropping off money at places that launder it?' He said, 'You ask for a particular guy and leave a full briefcase and bring back an empty one. That's it. I want you to look like a high-end salesman to those rich boys. Don't say one word more than you have to anyone. Dress like the man, business suit, good shirt, new shoes, haircut, everything.'"

"I went to Good Will and found a cashmere dress coat to die for plus a good suit and a couple of ties, one yellow with blue dots and one blue and red slants as if I belonged to some downtown club. I looked for shoes but couldn't find any that fit so I had to put out my own cash for shoes and wrinkle free dress shirts, (yeah, pink), and new socks. Wait until you see my GQ razor haircut. You get the picture."

"Say something, James, what do you think of all that?"

James had moved to the refrigerator and was taking out a package of mac and cheese his mother had frozen for him. He put it into the microwave thinking that now Caleb could write a couple of chapters for his book about Popeye.

"That was a mouthful! My only question, how much is he paying you? It sounds better than waiting in shit holes for someone to throw money at me."

"Yah, but it takes time too and I ride with someone called 'Little' who chauffeurs me around in a black Mercedes. I sit in the backseat and have to listen to his rap sounds breaking my eardrums."

"So how much is he paying you?"

"$750 a week. It takes about four hours, three days a week. How much are you getting?"

James said, "I work six hours plus twice a week and provide my own ride. I get about $1000 per week."

Caleb changed the subject, "Popeye doesn't deal opioids, he's all about cocaine and uppers. It's a strange arrangement. Popeye supplies Randall with coke and Randall supplies Popeye with heroin for their personal use."

"How did you figure that one out?" James asked.

"I listen better than you."

"I keep wondering who their handler is," James commented.

"My best guess is whoever bosses them is probably invested in some of the places I drop the money."

"Where do you pick up the money?" James asked.

"The places surprised me. Of course, it's got to be places where a lot of cash flows. Dell's Food Marts, city and suburbs, 'Big Z's' Pizza Palaces, a couple of 'big box' stores, some fast food franchises, some corporate offices I've never heard about. We're talking thousands of dollars per place. I'm sure I'm not the only one doing drops."

"I still don't get it," James said. "You drop stacks of money to company offices, what do you give back from the companies?"

"Well, I got a chance to look into one of the empty briefcases I pick up when I drop the one with money in it. There were checks in it made out to various companies I'd never heard of. Get it? The dealers own some phony shell companies that get checks for doing work for these big stores, work that never gets done."

"What kind of work," James asked.

"Probably interior and exterior maintenance, legal work, travel, any expense a big company can write off."

Caleb baited James, "I'd rather be chauffeured around doing laundry than hanging in public toilets like you do. Which reminds me, you said you were going to see that Angie again, did you?"

"Don't be mean, Caleb." James growled. "I did go back to where I met Angie last summer and there she was, shivering in a short skirt and a vinyl jacket. It must have been 35 degrees. She was wobbling on wedges just like I remembered her."

"Ah, the poor girl, a victim, like she didn't make some bad choices."

"Don't judge what you don't know, asshole, she's a good kid. Anyway, I had to pay $250 but it was late and I got to take her back to my place for a couple of hours. I warmed her up. You'll be pleased I wore my rubber to the end this time. We like each other. She liked my place. We snorted a couple of hits of brown sugar. It's almost gone again. I'll have to see Randall; I mean J and take some more abuse to buy another supply."

"But the truth is, I like Angie. I was hoping she got to go home after I dropped her off. I gave her a couple extra $20's to put where he wouldn't find it. She said her pimp always has eyes on her. I stalked her spot last night and just watched him. He laid low in a warm Toyota while she froze. He didn't leave once, stayed in his spot, running his engine, while someone picked her up and she was gone for over an hour. I only stayed a few hours. It was cold and I couldn't give myself away by keeping the car running. He didn't let her warm up in the car once when she was standing out there."

"God, James, what a sick fantasy. Be careful with that pimp. How about your prick? Do you have pustules yet or maybe a hot red spot?"

"You sure know how to shrivel a guy's equipment."

"You drop Willow and pick up a prostitute? What's going through your mind?"

"I didn't drop Willow and I'm not 'involved with Angie'. I just like her."

"I worry about you, bro, you could get hurt and I'm not talking about your feelings. Now you're messing with a pimp? They'll show you a world of hurt. She chose this guy and she chose this profession, didn't she?"

James changed the subject, "Do you want to come to Sandra's for Thanksgiving? You can have a look at Willow, she'll be there. Hands off though."

"What do you take me for, I don't grope women and don't hang with prostitutes. You sure you want me to come to your family Thanksgiving?"

"Hey you're like another brother, you met Chuck. Laurel is his sister, the one I had sex with – damn that just came out of my mouth- you forget I said that, Caleb, promise me you'll forget that."

"I can't forget what I already know. But I promise I won't even look at her. Will I get to meet the lesbians too? I mean your mom and Carmen, and, of course, the second Mom, Sandra. I know the cast of characters, the women in your life."

"Never call my mother and her partner 'the lesbians' again, they are Ellen and Carmen and I'm having dinner with them next week and making the best of it. Jesus, you're insulting today. Tell me again, why do I like you?"

"Cause you need someone who knows the whole sordid truth about your life, the same as I need you. Yes, I want to come to Thanksgiving. It's a sociological anomaly, your Lake Wobegon. Fodder for my books."

"If you write about us, you better disguise us good. You got your own anomalies, poor little rich boy, you know that?"

"I'll pretend you're all living in the Fjords somewhere in Norway."

James was silent for a minute. "Well, let's get together this weekend, I want you to show me how to shoot up again, that was an unbelievable high."

"I'm free."

33 / JAMES MEETS CARMEN

Carmen was fastening the clasp on the pearl necklace she'd given Ellen. They were dressing in preparation to meet James for dinner. Carmen complained, "I don't know why we're going out to eat. I wanted you to invite James over here for casual dinner."

They both looked into the mirror at the effect a necklace had on Ellen's scooped neck universal black dress. Their eyes met, Ellen looking up a bit, Carmen looking slightly down. The bond between them was deepening. The divide between them lessening.

"That's exactly why I didn't invite him over here, Carmen. It takes time before either James or I feel comfortable with new people. I let you choose the venue, a downtown steakhouse. It sounds fun, especially because it has memories for you."

"I loved going there with my family when I was a little girl. I can't believe it is still there. Murray's has a lot of memories for me."

"I don't think James will be impressed by a steakhouse. I'm a nervous wreck. I'm such a different person when I'm with you, Carmen. Here I am, half moved in with you before my son has even met you. Please, don't overwhelm him with our intimacy. What has happened between us, has been incredibly fast. Now he's coming home to do laundry in what must feel like an empty house. He already has abandonment issues."

"I know you're anxious, but trust me, I'm eager to meet him and to start getting to know him. A step-son, I love the idea."

Now we're getting married? Ellen looked down. Was Carmen joking? She's moving too fast for me in too many directions. Ellen worried about that for the umpteenth time. She wondered if Carmen would drop her as fast as she picked her up.

They were meeting James in downtown Minneapolis. They arrived first and waited for James; Carmen told yet another story about Murrays. She'd had her first legal drink there over 30 years ago. She had ordered a martini to be sophisticated and it tasted terrible. Did that stop her? No, she slugged it down and ordered another.

Back then, the old waitresses dressed in black and white and seemed like from another time, the 1940's or earlier. Carmen wondered if the waitresses still swept the linen tablecloths free of bread crumbs with butter knives. The small club with its wheat colored fabric walls was nearly empty on a raw Wednesday evening. James quickly found his mother and walked across the room not stopping to check his jacket. She stood and they loosely hugged.

"I've never been into one of these retro places." He looked around at the dark warm wood and fabric walls and nodded his approval. Then he settled his eyes on Carmen.

They both started to speak at once and then both hesitated, waiting for the other to say something.

"Do you want me to make the introductions?" Ellen asked and they both turned to her and nodded.

"James, this is Carmen, Carmen, this is James." Carmen put out a manicured hand and James held it for a moment, it was soft and warm. "I was telling your mother on the way over how lucky she is to have a son. I never had that blessing. Tell me all about yourself, starting with Augsburg. What's it like? I've never been on the campus, but I've driven by of course. The buildings are substantial, business-like."

James looked astounded at his mother wondering how she managed to find these outgoing women, Sandra, and now Carmen, when his mother was so quiet? He looked back at Carmen.

"Augsburg is OK. I'm sick of it though, I can't wait to be done. I don't know if I'm learning anything applicable. It's all a scramble in my mind. Do I really want to be an architectural engineer? Most of the professors are nerds, pens in the front pocket type of guys, don't show much personality, if they have any."

Ellen looked at James then looked at Carmen. Carmen had gotten more out of her son about his college experience in one question than she had gotten out of him in two plus years.

Carmen nodded at James, her eyes sparkling, "That's how I felt when I had to face making a career decision. It is hard to have a curriculum that prepares you for life and prepares you for work too. Have you thought of a semester off campus, Europe? South America?"

"Mom has pushed me towards getting the 'Keys to the Kingdom', credentials, you know, so I can make big bucks, fast."

Oops, Carmen thought, I'm getting into class issues. She remembered that Ellen had come from poverty and had struggled to become a professional. Ellen had been forced to focus on academic success. Carmen had the luxury of a family that could foot the bill and would bail her out.

Carmen turned back to James, "Ellen brags about you, James, she tells me you've got artistic talents plus an academic mind, that is special."

"You do?" he said, smiling hopefully at his mother.

Ellen nodded. "And he's great wielding a knife, cutting up vegetables, making great salads."

"I had Willow over for lunch, Mom. She was really hungry. I made nachos with chilis and sharp cheddar cheese. I also made bean chili from Sandra's recipe and served it with sides of sour cream, grated cheese and I had assorted olives in a bowl too."

Ellen and Carmen nodded their approval.

Carmen said, "I'd be thrilled if you'd come over to my place and we could all cook together. I want you to meet Panache, my cat, his fur matches your hair. He's the closest I have to a son."

James laughed.

"Mom, did you hear through the grapevine that Willow and I decided not to date?"

"I did hear something about it, but no details."

"Nothing bad happened. I mean we didn't hurt each other's feelings, anyway, not that much. We are going to be friends. I took it like a man. Hey, we're both still young. It just wasn't the right timing, I guess."

Ellen nodded her approval.

"Are classes and work stressing you, James? You're looking drained." She looked at his strawberry blond hair. He had the beginnings of a halo around his head. She'd liked it that way when he was young but he'd been wearing it almost buzzed on the sides the last several years, keeping it tamed down.

"I'm not drained. I'm fine. My hair needs a cut, all right? I'm not going to start wearing it in an afro or anything."

"You're still coming to Sandra's for Thanksgiving, aren't you?"

"Yah, I want to bring my friend Caleb. I already called Sandra and asked her, she's fine with it. I've talked to you about him, haven't I?"

"He's the writer, isn't he? I suppose now that your near campus, you're spending even more time together?"

Turning to Carmen, James explained, "Caleb is writing a novel. I call it a doom and gloom novel, apocalyptic stuff."

"I'll look forward to meeting him." Carmen answered.

"How is the part time job working out?" Ellen asked.

I'm getting the third degree here? James shrugged with disinterest.

Carmen changed the subject to football, then the weather, it was supposed to be a hard winter. It had already snowed, then melted, twice.

The three chatted pleasantly.

James ordered the 'butter knife' steak and loved it.

Carmen was hoping that Ellen would open up a little more about their relationship, now that they were moving in together, but she didn't. Still, Carmen was pleased that James seemed comfortable with their relationship. She studied the interaction between Ellen and James. She saw a softening in Ellen's features when she looked at James. She thought there was a lot of love between them but quite a bit of parental worry on Ellen's part and adolescent defensiveness on James' part. They checked out just fine with her. She liked James and she loved Ellen.

34 / FAMILY SUPPORT

Sandra had been first to suggest they gather their families together for the Thanksgiving holiday and she suggested she hostess the event. Char and Joe and Willow usually shared the holiday with Char and now Joe's longtime friends, Sally and Johnny. But this year Sally and Johnny wanted to go to Rhode Island to be with her daughter and her family, and it freed Char to start a new family tradition with Sandra's family.

Almost all of Sandra's growing family, including the new grandbaby, Andy, were coming to Thanksgiving dinner. Then Char's family of three and then Ellen and Carmen, and finally James and his friend Caleb. The only conspicuous absence would be Laurel's husband Brian who decided to go to his parents. Sandra had her suspicions that Laurel and Brian were having marital problems, but Laurel hadn't confided in her mother.

When Sandra called Ellen to invite her and Carmen to the holiday get together, Sandra confronted Ellen. "Why haven't you introduced me to Carmen? You've been dating for months now, haven't you? And you're seldom home any more. Have you moved in together without even introducing Carmen to your best friend?"

Ellen paused before answering. "Do you want the long version or the short version, Sandra?"

"Both, of course," Sandra responded.

"The short version, and it is true, is you and I have both been busy. The months have flown by, right?"

"Right, I'd have confronted you sooner about not meeting Carmen if I hadn't been so busy, but that doesn't let you off of the hook. Why haven't you introduced us? You know I want to meet her, and you know I'll always make time to meet her."

"Sorry, Sandra, you do always make time for me. Truth is, I too have been wondering why I haven't made the effort to introduce you two and I think I've thought it through.

Carmen is too important to me. I'm afraid if I introduce you to her, you'll read me, you'll see I've fallen in love with her, Sandra. Then when she dumps me, I'll be so ashamed that you saw it all coming. I'm waiting for that other shoe to drop. I'm waiting for her to discover the real me, the boring, fearful, plain-Jane Ellen. How can I be enough for her? The love of her life, her wife was an artist, they traveled the world together. I've been to Mexico twice. This relationship is doomed to fall, it can't last."

Sandra hated to admit when she didn't understand something, but she didn't understand this. "Aren't the two of you getting closer as you spend more time together?"

"Yes, I guess so, but she always wants to take the next step, move in together, then she talks about marriage. I feel pushed, she must be bored with what we have if she keeps wanting to take another next step, right?"

"You mean she never wants to do the same thing twice?"

"Well, no, but she is so full of thoughts of new possibilities, let's go to Europe, Turkey, then let's retire early and volunteer for the Peace Corp. I can't keep up with her."

"You're just scared, Ellen. Carmen sounds alive, interesting, like me. I'd say 'try to relax and enjoy the ride' but I know that's not your style. How about me inviting you and Carmen and Char over to our house, just a girls' brunch, maybe Carmen will be more comfortable if Char is there. At least then I'll have met her and have formed my own opinion."

"Hum," Ellen answered. "Promise me that you won't bring up my insecurities. If I'm comfortable, I'll try to ease into talking about relationships. Please, Sandra, don't make me sorry I confided in you."

"I promise, my lips are sealed. In the meantime, enjoy your time with Carmen!"

THE NEXT SATURDAY, Carmen and Ellen arrived at Sandra's for brunch. Carmen and Ellen had tickets to the University of Minnesota's Gopher football game and were bündled up in flannel lined pants, two layers of sweaters and winter boots. Their warm jackets, team colored wool scarves and ski caps were left in Carmen's black BMW. They could only stay an hour or so before leaving for the game.

Sandra opened the door for them, "Well, aren't you two cute, all bundled up for outdoor sports." She hugged Ellen, then swooped in to do the same with Carmen and was surprised to get an equally warm hug back from her. Sandra looked at Ellen's new girlfriend with pleasant amazement. Carmen appeared open and warm hearted, she also openly looked Sandra over and said, "Ellen's right, we are nearly the same size." Sandra smiled broadly; she liked the comparison although knew she was just heavy set, not voluptuous like Carmen.

Sandra was about to tell Ellen to take Carmen into the kitchen and pour her coffee when the door popped open and Char arrived. There were hugs all around and explanations of the sport wear and questions about Joe and Ralph and the kids as everyone moved to the kitchen. Sandra shared that Laurel and Roy were coming later, Laurel wanted to meet Carmen too.

Ellen had prepared Carmen for an onslaught of questions from Sandra. Carmen assured Ellen she was fine with anything Sandra threw out at her.

Sandra served bunch. Coffee was poured, homemade scones, egg casserole and fruit cups appeared, and Sandra sat down.

Char was leaning into Ellen explaining her read on the 'break up' between James and Willow. She thought it was mutual and friendly.

Sandra cleared her throat and Ellen looked up at her and Char sat back in her chair, allowing her sister to lead the conversation.

"Carmen, thanks for joining us, I've been dying to meet you. You know Ellen and I are best friends from college days, roommates in our post-college, pre-marriage days, neighbors and both 'Mom' to James."

Carmen responded, "I know Ellen adores you Sandra and I'm sure I will too. I already love your sister (smile to Char) and Joe. They were true friends to me when Susie died. Susie and I had been together for twenty-three years. I was overwhelmed by grief for several years. But then look who walked into my life?" She turned to Ellen.

All eyes turned toward Ellen.

Ellen swallowed and looked at Carmen, "I sometimes wonder, what did you see in me when I walked into your life?"

Sandra was surprised by Ellen's directness. She drew back and just listened.

"Well", Carmen began with a gleam in her eye, "there was an initial attraction of course. Who wouldn't be attracted to a lovely well-presented woman, nearly my age, who agreed to play 'hangman' with me during a boring presentation?"

Ellen nodded agreement. "We had an immediate connection.

But my question is, how do people maintain long intimate relationships? I haven't. Do you, friends, have any advice for me?"

Char jumped in, "Well I put Joe through the wringer, second-guessing him, waiting for him to leave me and he just wouldn't do it. After he told me he loved me, I asked him to tell me that every day. I was that insecure, but he did keep telling me he loved me and he acted like he loved me and now I'm certain he does love me."

Sandra jumped in, "Ralph and I were attracted to each other and we both wanted children. We got what we wanted, three and a half lovely children, the children further bonded us and completed our lives. But we've had a rough patch. Ralph let his career become too important and I let our children become too important. But we're making it through those trying times and I'll never take our marriage for granted again. And, mark my words, neither will Ralph."

Ellen smiled and nodded at Sandra. She knew whatever Sandra wanted; Sandra got.

Ellen looked at Carmen, "You're optimistic about our future, Carmen, what makes you think you will continue to love me?"

"Oh, Ellen," Carmen said with an earnest look, "I bet I know where you're coming from. You think my life with Susie was so exciting, Susie being an artist and you worry that I'll be bored with our life together?"

Ellen nodded yes.

"Ellen, my dear, Susie was an artist and she was an exciting person and I loved her. But I'm not an artist, I'm a marriage counselor. I love working to help people grow and I love being with someone who understands my work as well as you do. You appreciate how exhausting it can be to help others. You understand my need to rejuvenate. I look forward to spending time at your cabin, swimming, reading, even learning to fish. I want a full life with you, Ellen, our way. Walks, some books, some sports and television. We'll take our special trips, but this is our life! I'm very excited to have you and James and Sandra and Char for my family. My parents are living in Arizona most of the year and I don't have much of an extended family. This will be the best Thanksgiving ever."

Carmen's admiration for Ellen and happiness in her new life shined in her eyes.

Sandra looked one by one at Carmen, Ellen, and Char, "Our lives keep getting better. Thanks for joining the family, Carmen."

CARMEN AND ELLEN bustled out shortly after the soulful brunch. Char was about to put her coat on too but Sandra pulled her back.

Char looked expectantly at her sister, "What's up, sis?"

"Laurel is having some marriage problems and I've told her how insightful you are, with your recovery blog and all. she is hoping to get a chance to talk to you."

"Me?" Char asked, "I've only briefly met Laurel, I don't remember what Laurel and I said to each other."

"You said something when you met her that got her attention."

Laurel arrived with Roy in tow. Char beat Sandra to Roy and asked him if she could help him with his jacket. He looked at his mom and she encouraged him to let Char help him. He raised his arms to Char and she picked him up, twirled him around, took off his jacket, and kissed his smiling face.

"Remember me?" She asked him. He shook his head 'no' and she explained, "I'm your Great Aunt Char."

Sandra was hovering nearby and Char handed Roy off to his Grandmother who swept him into the kitchen for a treat.

"You two get acquainted", Sandra said from the kitchen doorway, "Roy and I are having a snack, right Roy?" Roy nodded seriously and grabbed his Granny's face, encouraging her to keep moving to the kitchen.

Laurel was surprised by her faith in her new Aunt. They'd only met once but they'd both rolled their eyes when Sandra mentioned how happy she was that her daughters married young. Laurel thought her early marriage had been a mistake. Laurel hoped she could open up to Char.

Comfortable with Sandra out of the room, Laurel and Char sat down, one on the couch, the other on a nearby swivel chair. Laurel leaned in, arms on her knees, and swiveled closer to Char. She didn't mince words, she told Char that she wanted to go back to graduate school to get a master's in early childhood development, but Brian wanted her to keep her administrative assistant job full time, because they were financially over-extended. Laurel admitted she had started her marriage with expensive material tastes, but now she had a change of heart.

Their new McMansion in the exurbs felt impersonal to Laurel, the high walls and raised ceilings painted in beige and off-whites were cold. They couldn't agree on a warmer color scheme and also couldn't afford an interior decorator or a professional painter for the house's high walls. When they bought the house, they hadn't budgeted upkeep costs for the large house and expansive acreage. They hadn't budgeted their long commutes or the cost of Roy's nearly ten hours a weekday of daycare. Laurel wanted out of this empty materialistic lifestyle.

Brian's response to their grinding weekday schedules was to buy a motorcycle for the weekends. He found an expensive one he loved and bought it without consulting Laurel. Although Brian made an excellent salary, the more he made, the more he spent.

Laurel wanted a sweet bungalow or small mid-century ranch house in a real neighborhood. Char listened and nodded her empathy.

"You're not the first young couple to get into the materialistic trap. Good for you, girl, for wanting out of it. Most of us go through a period of buying things, hoping to find the answer to our existential angst. I hope you and Brian can focus on communicating with each other; listening and sharing your dreams, asking each other what makes you happy that doesn't cost anything."

Laurel looked at her aunt crossly, "We've been to counseling, the five sessions our insurance would pay for," she laughed but shook her head, "No we are at cross-roads and have been almost from the day Roy was born. Brian thought a baby would be great, he wants everything, but he doesn't want to take care of a baby. Roy definitely put a damper in Brian's free and easy lifestyle."

Sandra had yelled out that she was cleaning up the kitchen and she and Roy were ready to join them.

Char suggested that they let Sandra into the conversation. Laurel called her mother into the living room.

Roy ran to his mother. Laurel picked him up, hugged him, and sat him on her lap, kissing his head, "as soon as Roy was born, he became everything to me."

She bluntly said, "Mom, things aren't going well between Brian and me. I've been wary of telling you the truth because I know you will blame me; you think Brian is perfect."

Sandra was still standing and now she put her arms on her hips and leaned in. "I've never said a word against Brian. You like him, I love him. That's my philosophy toward my son-in-law. It is not the role of the mother-in-law to criticize her sons-in-law."

She turned to Char, "Can you believe Laurel is somehow blaming me for favoring Brian when I'm just trying to be a good mother?"

Char stood up too, "Sandra, Laurel, I love you both. You both are doing your best in this hard situation."

Laurel and Sandra sidled a look at each other. Sandra apologized in her own way, "I know I'm not perfect, I'm sorry Laurel, you are a wonderful mother to Roy, I see your love for him all the time."

Laurel responded, "I try Mother, loving Roy is so easy for me, but I'm failing at being the wife Brian wants me to be. I'm stubborn, I can't love Brian the way he wants to be loved. He wants to be the head of the family. He's a good guy, works hard, makes good money. But he's like his dad. When we were dating, I teased him, I couldn't believe he was serious when he said things like 'I'll always take care of you.' He was crazy for me, but he also told me what I'd get if I married him. He was going to be head of the family. I took the wedding vows in his family's conservative church, listened to their crap about husbands and wives, but I thought I had him wrapped around my finger. This whole marriage has been one big mistake."

Sandra said, "I'm so sorry Laurel," and sat by her daughter, fearful to touch her, wanting to touch her.

Char sat down on the other side of Laurel and reached over and hugged her. Laurel put her head on Char's tall shoulder but reached out a hand for her mother to hold too.

35 / THANKSGIVING

Char and Joe arrived early. Char put the potatoes on the stove to be boiled. Later she would mash the potatoes and make the gravy and heat up her side dishes of sweet potatoes and green bean casserole when the turkey came out of the oven to rest before serving.

Sandra offered Joe matched bowls to set out his home-made appetizers, chips and corn and black bean salsa in the living room and the family room. Ralph set out Sandra's lefse with sides of soft butter and shakers of plain sugar and cinnamon sugar. Then the guys were free to start watching the traditional Thanksgiving football games.

Willow was driving Char's car over separately so she could leave for an open house at Hetty's and Isaac's. Their family did an annual 'after the event' buffet for all the volunteers of a huge dinner for the homeless.

Willow's several dates with Isaac were nearly the opposite of dating James. Isaac was interested in knowing Willow, her life, her ideas, her aspirations for a dancing career. He listened! And, although they'd kissed, Isaac didn't push Willow towards a sexual relationship and she was enjoying slowly becoming friends with him.

Sandra set the table with her best: lace tablecloth, white chinaware, sterling silver, and Waterford water and wine glasses. Sandra's 'Horn of Plenty' centered the table and overflowed with miniature gourds and small boats of mulled fruits. The extended dining room large enough for sixteen.

Char hugged her nephew Chuck for the first time. She saw a handsome young Ralph in Chuck. Kimber, the elder daughter, arrived with Tally and Kenzie, both grade school girls now, and her husband Paul carrying baby Andy. Laurel soon arrived with Roy. Kimber and Laurel joined their mother and aunt in the kitchen. Paul gravitated to the football game with Andy comfortably tucked in his arm like a football. Tally and Kenzie twirled in their new pinafore dresses and showed off their wide black bows fastened sturdily in their long blond hair. Roy wore black corduroys and a white dress shirt, and twirled along with the girls. Sandra sent the children into the living room to bother the men.

James and Caleb arrived at the curb the same time as Ellen and Carmen. After James introduced the women to Caleb, James and Caleb carried the women's pies and bottles of wine from the car. James pointed out the prices on the bottles of Zinfandel and Chardonnay to Caleb, and whispered, "That's Carmen, Mom's moving up from boxed wine."

"Note the haircut, Mom," James said when he first saw his mother. When Ellen and Carmen and James and Caleb arrived indoors, Sandra and Char peaked around the corner of the kitchen to say hi. Caleb and Char took one quick look at each other and turned in opposite directions.

James introduced Caleb to the men watching football in the living room. Chuck and James did their elaborate greeting. Tally and Kenzie ran to James and Chuck, wanting them to twirl them but Chuck and James had been warned by Sandra to show some decorum toward the girls in their good outfits. Instead, they devised a game to play with the girls in the family room. The boys pulled down cushions from the couches and supervised a game of "tight corner track" that they made up as they went. Caleb laughed out loud watching the action. Roy started to cry, wanting more attention, and Caleb grabbed him up and helped him through the paces. The action was soon quelled by Sandra who came barreling in and said they were still playing too rough play in the house.

"Girls," she said, "You have dresses on, show some decorum."

James and Chuck laughed, "Decorum, girls", then pointed at each other, "decorum gentlemen."

"I mean it," Sandra said sternly, and she got her decorum.

Laurel came in to see what the ruckus was and gave James a reprimanding look. James walked over to a little brown fridge behind the bar in the family room and got two beers and sat down by Caleb.

'Women,' Caleb mumbled, tasting his beer and giving James a nudge of understanding.

Char motioned to Joe to come into the kitchen. She led him out of the kitchen to the deck. They walked gingerly on the icy boards. It had started sleeting off and on and the temperatures were plummeting.

"Joe, help me. I don't know what to say." She looked absolutely spooked.

"What's wrong, honey?" Joe said.

"The boy James brought? Caleb? I'd sponsored him for months and then he just disappeared, remember me telling you about the young man I was so worried about? wouldn't answer my phone calls? How should I act toward him, here, at my sister's? I'm suspicious he's gone back to using. He was a serious heroin addict, Joe, he had made so much progress and now he's hanging with James."

"Ah, gee, honey," Joe said, at a loss for words. He reached for her and hugged her. They both took sponsoring young people in AA very seriously.

Then he pushed her back so he could look in her eyes, "Think, Char. Aren't you sort of' over-reacting? It's his choice to be in the program, not yours."

Char slowly came back from her place of disconnect. She took a couple of deep breaths. She felt the rough fabric of the sweater she made Joe to wear, a sweater she treasured from a shopping spree at her favorite consignment shop. Joe said it made him itch, 'so wear a t-shirt underneath it' she told him.

"This sweater is itchy," she said, "I'll take it back to the consignment shop. You're right again, darling husband. Caleb has all the right in the world to move on without consulting me. He looks fine. I promise you, Joe, and promise myself, I won't ruin my day over Caleb. I'll give him a wave to acknowledge I remember him. She lifted her head high; she was ready to go back to the party.

"OK," Joe sighed, "OK." He gave her a last little squeeze before leading her back inside.

Caleb was sitting by himself. Joe took the chair James had just vacated.

"Nice to meet you Caleb," he said. "I'm Char's husband and Willow's Papa. Char wants me to tell you that she loves you and that she will just give you a little wave for today. She is busy today getting to know this side of her family, but you have her number and if you ever want to call her, she'd love to catch up with you. We're both glad to see you here. Enjoy the day. I'm a little on the outside here myself, being an in-law, I know how it feels, being with someone else's family."

Caleb's shoulders noticeably relaxed. He gave Joe a genuine smile. "Thanks for that."

James was back. "Hi Joe, what's happening?"

"I'm just getting acquainted with Caleb, here. I'm glad you invited him. Here, I'll let you have your chair back."

James continued, "I love your chips and salsa, Joe. I want to learn more about cooking. I like getting around the kitchen, how do you make chips?"

"It's a trade secret, James," Joe said, "The women and men in my family have been making chips in restaurants for generations. It's in the blood."

"Caleb's been at your restaurant too. For a look at Willow, right Caleb?"

Caleb scowled at James, "Stop it, James. I just wanted to see the girl James thinks is the next best thing to sliced bread, as they say in Minnesota."

Joe got a kick out of that, and walked away laughing and shaking his head.

Willow was the last to arrive. She was wearing slacks and a short hooded three-quarter beige sweater and leather boots Char found for her at the consignment shop. She'd braided her hair and raised the braids into a high rounded bun. She was tall and stunning. She took the wind out of all the young men's sails. Joe looked at her in amazement. She was maturing so quickly. Willow made the rounds, acknowledgements to Ellen and Carmen (Carmen had been a frequent visitor at her home after Susie died), a big hug for her Aunt Sandra, introductions and slight hugs for her three cousins, and down to one knee for bigger hugs for the two little girls. James got his hug too, but Caleb was basically ignored.

The table was resplendent with turkey and giblet dressing and mashed potatoes, milk gravy, whipped sweet potatoes with a crispy marshmallow topping for the kid in all of them, green bean casserole with shoe strings on the top. Each place setting included a salad plate of green Jell-O salad with pimento olives (Char and Sandra's mother's favorite). Side dishes included cranberry/orange relish, raw vegetables and dips, creamed herring, and warm rolls. Pie desserts awaited in the kitchen.

After everyone was seated, Sandra and Ralph at the ends of the table stood and the family and guests rose from their chairs. Sandra and Ralph began singing the Lutheran grace and their children and Char followed their lead:

Be present at our table lord;
Be here and everywhere adored;
Thy creatures bless and grant that we
May feast in paradise with three. Amen.

Willow, sitting between Chuck and James, was amazed by their ability to sing in harmony.

She turned to James and purred, "You have a beautiful voice, James," then quickly turned to Chuck, "you too Chuck." She took each of their hands and added, "My cousins, I love being with you."

James and Chuck vied for her attention for the length of the meal, telling stories on one another and getting her to laugh. She made that disgusted face James loved, this time towards Chuck after he told a particularly gruesome story about mud wrestling.

Caleb sat on the other side of James and tried to get into the conversation, but James thwarted him, blocking his view of Willow. Caleb gave up and turned to converse with Paul, Kimber's husband.

Char purposefully sat between her nieces Laurel and Kimber and helped keep Roy at task and entertained and also took a turn holding infant Andy. She caught Caleb's eye and sent him a genuine smile. He nodded and smiled back.

Willow kept her eye on her girl cousins, Kimber and Laurel. Kimber was quiet and so competent with her children. She was surprised that Gram and Laurel seemed to know each other.

Sandra watched the others' interactions maintaining her role as hostess, jumping up, refilling bowls and platters, offering wine refills, making sure everyone had opportunities for second helpings. She also picked up on the intensity of the interaction between Char and Laurel. She smiled her gratitude to Char. She had such a hard time reaching that soft part in her daughter. Carmen sat between Joe and Ralph and hooted at Ralph's proctology jokes. Ellen sat on the other side of Joe and they talked easily to each other.

Before dessert was served, the men moved into the living room for more football. Char, Sandra, Carmen and Ellen cleared the dining room and did the dishes.

The big boys followed Willow into the living room and James found a soft jazz station on the Bose. Chuck took Caleb on a tour of the family photos on the walls telling him more stories about James and his adventures over the years. James and Willow took a minute to catch up with each other.

Willow started, "I had a second audition with a regional dance troupe based in Chicago. If I get accepted, I'll have an apprenticeship in Chicago and a stipend to pay part of my expenses."

"You'd be leaving Minnesota?" James asked glumly.

She nodded and James walked away from her and landed on a leather couch. Chuck walked over and laid on the other couch while Caleb sat on the floor, leaning into James' couch, the big boys all just wanted to close their eyes and digest.

Willow felt shut out and was turning to leave the room when Laurel walked in. The few times James had mentioned his 'almost' sister, Laurel, it was a cautionary tale about the 'cranky' older sister who was off and on, sometimes liking him, mostly not.

Laurel suggested they sit together by the corner game table.

Willow discretely looked at her watch. She should be leaving soon but followed Laurel.

Laurel led off the conversation, "How does it feel to have the boys fawning over you? Does that feed your ego? I couldn't believe them at the dinner table."

Willow was caught off guard and her first reaction were hurt feelings like the playground kids made her feel. But it was just a twinge; she didn't go to that little girl place much anymore.

Instead, she ignored Laurel's question and said, "I like your mom a lot, Laurel. She started this whole thing that got us together. Your dad is great, too. I loved it when he led you all in singing the blessing, in harmony! I've never heard a family singing together like that. I watched my Gram; she knew the words, too. It must go way back. You guys have roots that I never had growing up as a single child.

Anyway, I'm hoping we can get to know each other. But about the boys, they act like they're trying to feed my ego, but I think they're strutting for each other more than for me."

Laurel put her hand on the younger woman's arm, "You got that right, sister," and gave her a high five and the most genuine smile anyone had seen on Laurel's face in a long time.

Roy tottered in, getting sleepy, looking for his mother. As he rushed to her side, Laurel looked over at James and caught him smiling at the little boy. James quickly looked away, then snuck another look at Laurel. She was still looking at him with those cat eyes of hers, and he could feel the color rush to his face.

Tally and Kenzie burst into the room, too, with Kimber right behind her girls, "We got Andy down for his nap. Roy held him and kissed him so gently, didn't you Roy?"

Roy nodded, looked around the room and went over to Caleb and sat on the floor by him mimicking his position. Caleb brushed Roy's hair with a gentle hand and Roy snuggled against him.

Tally and Kenzie stood looking expectantly at Willow.

"What do you want to ask Willow?" Kimber prompted her girls.

Tally, the bolder of the girls asked, "Can we touch your hair?"

Willow laughed, "Why would you want to touch my hair?"

Kenzie blurted out, "Because it is so beautiful."

"Show your cousin Willow your hands girls," Kimber asked.

"Mom made us wash our hands with soap so we could touch your hair and not get it greasy, can we touch it?" Tally asked.

Now even the boys laughed.

"How thoughtful of you," Willow said with a smile, "Yes, you can touch my hair."

Both girls descended upon her and felt her strong, shiny black hair with their fingers, following the braids to the top of her head.

"Will you braid my hair?" Kenzie asked.

"Let me text a friend. I'd love to give you both French braids.

Willow texted Isaac: 'Be there in an hour, getting to know my little cousins, W'.

Later the pies were served. James and Chuck ate slivers of all the different pies, ala mode, as per usual.

"Shame on you gluttons," Willow teased and looked at Laurel who laughed with her.

Sandra caught that small interaction, Willow and Laurel smiling at each other. Laurel seemed lighter hearted. Sandra hoped things were would turn around for her younger daughter.

Sandra sent care packages back with James and Caleb. Enough food for both of them for several days. Chuck was staying home for the four-day weekend.

36 / ARMAGEDDON

On the way home, Caleb commented, "Even the men knew how to cook. Home cooking ended for my family when Baba died. After her death, we always went to restaurants for holidays."

"Was 'Baba' your grandmother?" James asked.

Caleb nodded.

James added, "Sandra knows how to satisfy us with rich foods, but I'm starting to appreciate my mom's healthy choices as I get older. What did you think of Ellen and Carmen?"

"Carmen was having a good time with the guys. I'd never had known either of them were, well, you know what I mean. Carmen knows her football, yelling at the refs and hooting. Joe seemed to know her and they were having a great time together. I liked Joe."

"What about my mother?" James asked.

"She was fine, maybe a little formal with me. You must have told her I majored in philosophy and creative writing. She asked about my writing, about my characters, my settings, she showed true interest."

"Did you tell her that your characters are all drug addicts?"

"My characters aren't all drug addicts." Caleb punched James harder than James was expecting. James rubbed his shoulder, driving with one hand.

James asked again, “What did you think of Willow and Laurel?”

Caleb answered honestly, “Willow is a ten. I liked Laurel’s looks. I loved her little Roy. Doesn’t she have a husband?”

“Yeah, she’s married. I told you about her, how I kind of loved her when I was a teenager.”

“She was mean to you, wasn’t she?”

“For a summer she liked me,” James said and sighed. “Yeah, she’s married, he’s as snooty as she is. He seems to look down on Laurel’s family. Doesn’t have the time of day for me of course.”

James talked on but Caleb retreated into his personal space, James wondered if he had fallen asleep.

“Caleb, wake up,” James demanded as he parked in front of Caleb’s brick building.

“Oh, we’re back? Do you want to share a hit with me? I got some good stuff from my chauffeur.”

“Not tonight Caleb. I missed my Thursday afternoon runs for Randall and have to do those runs tomorrow. Plus, tomorrow’s another ‘party’ at Randall’s. I hope Angie is there. I’d better chill out tonight.”

Caleb was staring down at James’ floor mat, he sat up straight, turned, and looked right at James. “I’m hooked, James. I don’t even care, I guess. You’re right about me, I’m all doom and gloom. I don’t want to live to see the grand finale, the death of Earth. Using the dope isn’t working, I’m already sick of that too. I’ve been using junk every day for the past two weeks and I want the next hit as soon as I shoot up. That’s why people overdose; there is no satisfaction, just a constant craving. I’ll use it again tonight; I’ll use it tomorrow. I’m lost, that fast.”

He opened the car door mumbling “Thanks, really, thanks for inviting me today,” and slammed out, quickly walking to his doorway.

James had been feeling satisfied and happy with the day. Now he was left with Caleb's pie tin of leftovers in his hand. He sat holding the leftovers for a few minutes. His mood plummeted as he drove home.

After James put all the leftovers in his fridge, he lay down on his bed and closed his eyes. He was angry and anxious about what was happening to Caleb, guilty too.

He was thinking about the first time they used heroin. He knew it was wrong. But did he listen to his instincts? No. He wanted Caleb to get high with him. Caleb knew so much about everything, but he was his own man, wasn't he?

James' feet jiggled. He smoked a joint but it didn't do anything for his mood. He wanted to do some junk, but now, after what Caleb said, he was scared of it. He got up to pace but he felt claustrophobic in the small space. He started thinking about the heroin he had and his new works. The heroin would be a simple solution to his compound feelings. His anger kept building.

He grabbed his keys, grabbed his money and slammed out of his place in his heaviest hoodie. No one understands me, he lamented. I'm just trying to be cool and have a little fun, then my whole life goes to shit. I can't stand being in my skin.

It was winter's sure darkness when he got into his car with $300 and headed for Angie's corner. There she was in the below freezing temperature. The sleet had stopped but snow was in the air. He drove up to her and signaled to her from his car, but she ignored him. He parked the car and walked over to her, "Are you avoiding me?" he asked her.

She shewed him away, "Get away from me, James." He just moved closer and said softly, "Angie, what's wrong?"

She turned her back to him, "Get out of here. You've caused me enough problems." When he just stood there, not leaving, she finally turned to face him, pointed at her face, and yelled, "Look what you've done. You're nothing but trouble. Leave me alone."

He could see the damage to her face. She'd tried to cover up her split lip and a black eye but he could see the damage through her makeup. She was beat up.

"You did it," she said, stepping away from him. "He found the money you gave me and saw you snooping around the next night. If you don't leave now, I'm really going to get hurt and you will too."

James was filled with rage. He knew where the pimp was parked, and he skipped over to the pimp's car avoiding the icy patches on the street. He tried to look into the car but it was too dark to see anyone. He beat on the pimp's window. The guy didn't respond.

"You motherfucker, if you lay another hand on Angie, you're a dead man walking," James yelled, still pounding on the window with the palm of his hand.

The pimp reacted. He opened the door so quickly and hard that James was thrown to the ground, twisting his ankle. James saw a knife in his hand. He was standing over James. "Get the fuck out of here. If I see you here again, she's dead. Not you, motherfucker, she'll be a dead whore 'walking', you damn fool."

James was trying to lift himself up but slipped back down, onto his back on the icy pavement. With his arms holding him up, he kept his feet free to kick out if the bastard came closer.

James yelled, "You fool, do you know who you're dealing with? I work for Randall; you know who that is. We know where you live and I can have the feds on you like this," he tried to snap his fingers but it was a useless gesture in the cold. "You're messing with the wrong crowd, Chauncey Sands, yah, I know your name. They got big eyes on you. They're waiting for you to do something dumb, like beating your whores, waiting to put you away. Bring it on," James said and pulled his phone out of his jacket. "This is being recorded, idiot." Then he yelled toward the phone, keeping it directed at the pimp. "Chauncey Sands is standing over me with a knife, you heard him, he just threatened to kill his whore Angie. Alert to all agents."

The pimp hesitated and James rolled away from him a few feet, still unable to get his footing. He kept the phone on Chauncey, "We are at University and Main." About then a passing car with a super loud muffler stopped in the street. A window rolled down, a Hispanic boy yelled from the window, "We've called 911, they're on their way."

Chauncey didn't even look up. He snapped his switchblade closed and raced back to his car. Angie and another girl were by the car and jumped into the back seats. They sped away. James didn't have time to register a description of the other girl. It happened so fast. He aimed the phone's camera at the fleeing car, hoping to get the license plate.

The guy who called 911 was still idling in his car, on the street, "Are you OK, man?" he asked.

"I'm fine, I'm fine." James said, finally scampering to his feet. "I don't want trouble," he said, brushing himself off. "I'm getting out of here before the cops come." He hobbled to his car and both cars took off before the police arrived.

Maybe they saved my life, he thought, but who's going to save Angie? He drove randomly around. He had no idea where Angie lived. He didn't know if she lived with the pimp or if she lived with some other girls. He remembered her saying that Chauncey loved her.

'Rumph', he said out loud. He was afraid she was going to get beaten again. He shivered at the thought, her bones breaking, her pretty face in ruins. He second guessed his impulsiveness at confronting the pimp, he didn't even want to think about what he had yelled at him.

James found himself over by Randall's house. He should call Randall; ask him how to get in touch with Popeye, Popeye was Chauncey's uncle. He needed to explain that he hadn't really recorded anything, he'd made the whole thing up. But he had recorded it. He stopped and looked at the video. 'Jesus, look at that knife,' he said out loud.

He thought Randall was probably at his mom and dad's for Thanksgiving. He wouldn't be home. James turned down the street where Randall lived thinking it couldn't hurt to drive by on Thanksgiving night.

He idled his car a few doors down from Randall's place and was about to drive away when he saw Randall's car pull up across the street. James turned off his car and jumped out, landing on his sprained ankle. He hobbled a few steps. He had to talk to Randall, explain everything to him.

He had to make this right. He stumbled and looked down, trying to get the damn ankle to perform naturally. He hadn't noticed another car parking behind Randall's. He took a couple of tentative steps and by the time he looked up, he realized that Randall wasn't alone. A guy was approaching Randall from the car behind Randall's and they were greeting each other. Randall looked around furtively as he greeted the other man and saw someone hobbling toward him.

James thought, it's too late now, and waved at Randall, and limped toward him. Randall ignored James and started ushering the other man up the sidewalk to his place. They were caught in the light of a passing car, and the other guy looked hard at James but continued up the sidewalk and into Randall's duplex.

"Shit, damn, holy roller shit." James turned and limped back to his car. He recognized the man as his employer at the "Sports Now" box store.

James made it home and sat in his armchair with his iced ankle up on a kitchen chair. He nearly chain-smoked marijuana, but it brought no relief. James' paranoia kept growing.

Did Randall recognize him? Did Alex Weatherly recognize him?

Alex was a son of the very wealthy Sam Weatherly who owned all the "Sports Now" franchises.

Alex was always at the annual work picnic sporting an unnatural tan and an awful pink golf shirt. And he had looked hard at James.

James hobbled up, used the toilet, and wrapped his ankle in fresh ice. The swelling was going down. James was familiar with ankle sprains from cross-country running days. He knew how to handle this sprain. When the swelling stayed down, he'd put warmth on it to help his flexibility.

He couldn't stop himself from going over and over the recent action. The best scenario was that he scared Chauncey. Knowing his name may have helped him, Chauncey flinched when James called him by his first and last names. Maybe he'd be afraid to hurt Angie again. That's what James wanted, wasn't it, for Chauncey not to hurt Angie again?

Damn, James remembered that Angie and Chauncey knew where James lived from when he brought her to his place. James checked the latch and the deadbolt and closed the curtains tighter, and turned off all the lights. He sat in the soft yellow glow of the nightlight in the kitchen. Someone could easily kick the door in if they wanted to. He looked at the time, 4:30 AM, it wasn't a reasonable time to call anyone. He wanted Caleb's read on all this. Should he call Randall? Was he making too much of the whole deal? He picked up another joint he'd rolled.

This stuff wasn't helping his paranoia. He threw the joint into the ashtray before lighting it. What else could he do? His mind went back and forth, is this a big deal or not? His sheltered life hadn't prepared him for threats of violence. Was Randall's warning, to keep away from his house, all that serious? How much of this was a game, and how much was serious? He picked up the joint from the ashtray, lit it and pulled the smoke deep into his lungs.

Finally, it was 6:00 AM, pre-dawn light flowed through the high kitchen window. He couldn't stay in the apartment another minute. He hobbled around, getting together all the money he stashed here and there, then grabbing his marijuana and his heroin and the works he'd been so proud of. He couldn't risk having anyone find the heroin or the works, that was hard evidence. He tied the laces of his winter boots tight to support his wrapped ankle, put on a clean pull-over and lighter colored hooded. He stuffed the pockets of his all-weather jacket and looked with regret at the books and the study materials on his desk. He slammed out, taking a quick scan of the backyard before exiting the entry door. He didn't see or hear anything. He limped quickly to his car. The street was empty. His ankle was sore but his gait was getting better.

He ended up sitting at a McDonalds, his hands in his hair, his breakfast growing cold. Man up, man up, he kept telling himself. I'm so fucking paranoid, he added looking around for the fourth time, his eyes resting on a tired, red eyed man who seemed to be looking his way.

He went into the bathroom and took a look at himself. No wonder that guy is looking at me, he thought, looking at his own red furtive eyes. He wondered who was on his ass. Or was he just being paranoid? He needed eye drops. He hadn't bothered to shave or brush his teeth. He decided to sneak back to his place and get his toiletries.

He parked the car one block over; these houses met the backyards of those on his street. He casually walked between houses to his backyard. He stopped at the back of his garage, hunched down, peeking around the corner, listening for voices. Feeling safe, he stood erect and walked around the garage. When he saw his door wide open, he turned and hobbled to his car.

EARLY THAT MORNING, Caleb was alone in his room. He was

wearing his favorite soft, fawn colored chamois shirt and soft jeans for comfort and sprawling in his big chair. He'd pulled out his heroin works and sat there looking at the high-end metal needle gauged perfectly for filling his veins.

Seeing Charlene had spoiled his taste for heroin. He thought about a saying he had heard in AA. 'Once you face your addiction, you might go back to using, but the thrill is gone.'

There is a lot of truth in that damn AA program he thought. Truth was, he wanted the junk but he didn't want to be a junky.

He dug through his bottom desk drawer and found the AA 'Big Book' Char had given him. He thumbed through the book until he came to the story he'd liked. It wasn't a complex, profound story, it was a silly story about a guy who liked to jaywalk. He didn't know why he liked jaywalking; he just did.

As the story goes, this guy was jaywalking and he got hit by a truck. He survived but was hospitalized with broken bones. He finally got out of the hospital, and what did he do? He jaywalked again, right out of the hospital, wham, he got hit by another truck. This happened to the guy over and over, would the guy ever learn not to jaywalk?

Caleb shook his head, he had been jaywalking again, playing with heroin, he knew what happened when you played with heroin, but there he was, down for the count again. He ached, wanting a fix. Last night he hadn't used, instead he took three over the counter sleeping pills and finally drifted off to a fitful sleep.

He'd woken up early. After a warm, then cold shower and a cup of coffee from his single server, the gnawing in his gut just grew worse. His mouth watered, his eyes were dry, and his skin crawled. He finally took out the heroin and gave himself a boost. 'God, this feels better,' he said to himself, nodding off a little, relaxing, enjoying it. 'This might be it,' he thought, 'my last taste of junk'. His door knob jiggled.

"I'm not here," he mumbled, the knob jiggled again, he said "go away," a little louder.

The door popped open and two guys walked in. They looked at him and laughed. "This will be easy," one said. Caleb started to protest, tried to rise, but the bigger guy punched him hard in the side of the head and he slid to the floor.

They rummaged around a little, dumped everything out of his backpack onto his bed and tossed his phone, his works, and the smack into the backpack and took it with them. They stood him up, one on each side and half walked, half carried him out, closed the warped door and walked him down the stairs and into their car.

JAMES DROVE his car to Minneapolis and parked behind the athletic building at the U of M. He was backed up to the building so he could see in all directions. He thought about painting his car. Now that was an idiotic thought. Did they want to scare him, beat him up, or kill him? His mind couldn't wrap around the trouble he was in. Breathe, he told himself, get it together, just do one thing.

He decided to call Caleb, warn him, they were in this drug shit together. He sped dialed Caleb. The phone rang six times and went to voicemail. "Call me bro, now!!" James emphasized.

"Shit," he said. The stupor from all the dope he'd smoked, compounded by the adrenaline racing through his body, numbed him out, he couldn't think. Of all things, he fell asleep.

He was awakened by a rap on his window. He jumped in his seat, his head hitting the ceiling of the car. He turned to face the music. It was a campus policeman. He motioned for James to roll down his window.

"Are you sleeping it off in there?" he asked, not unkindly. "Show me your license and registration."

"The time got away from me." James answered. He got out his

license and registration and handed them over. He looked around, at the sky, but couldn't judge the time by the cloudy day. It had started to snow.

"You wonder what time it is?" The officer asked politely. James nodded yes.

"It's nearly noon. Are you in any shape to drive?"

"I'm fine, I had beer last night. I was at a big Thanksgiving party, had a fight with my girlfriend, and just wanted a place to chill out. Guess I fell asleep."

"Get out of the car, let me see you walk around a little."

"Sprained my foot too, kicking my tire, but I can walk on it."

James got out of the car and walked a little gingerly but he showed he could walk a straight line using the faintly visible parking strips.

The officer watched him and took his time before nodding, "You look OK. You don't have far to go home." He handed back the license and registration, "Go home now, get some more sleep."

James started his car.

"Drive carefully."

"I will, thanks officer."

37 / WHERE IS CALEB?

James drove slowly onto the street, checking his cell for a text from Caleb as he rolled to stop. This isn't like Caleb, he thought. He tried him again, still no answer but his answering service was still on. This wasn't Caleb's way of doing things. When Caleb wasn't taking calls, he turned his phone off.

Now James worried that Caleb had overdosed. James hesitated, he was scared what he'd find at Caleb's and didn't want to go to his place alone. He needed backup. James bit the bullet. He called Chuck.

"Chuck, are you free to talk? Get free, I've got to talk to you, alone, now. Call me right back."

Less than two minutes later, Chuck called back. "Sup bro. You sound terrible."

"I'm worse than that. Where are you?"

"I'm at the folk's house. I just got up, what's happening. I'm standing on the deck; it's snowing hard here. What's happening? It's not even 10 a.m."

"I don't know where to start, but right now I'm worried about Caleb. I've left messages and he isn't calling me back. He always turns off his phone when he isn't taking calls. I'll tell you the truth, he is using heroin again; he's becoming addicted. He just told me last night that it's a problem for him again. See why I'm worried?"

"Again? He was addicted before? Well, why don't you go over there to see if he's OK, get over there now."

"It's more complicated. Don't start on me now, believe me, I'm in bad trouble, you got to trust me, I need help. Some guys might be watching for me, I'm afraid to go over there. Will you do it with me?"

"Are you into heroin, too?"

James didn't answer, he repeated the question. "Will you help me, please?"

Chuck sucked in a breath, "Where does he live? St. Paul? It'll take me half an hour, in this weather, to drive there, you're right, he could be in trouble, overdosing."

"You got to help me here, Chuck, please, no more questions."

"OK, I won't ask you any more questions until we know he is safe. I'm already back in the house, getting my keys, where do I meet you?

"In the Target parking lot on the corner of University and Snelling, I'll be watching for you. Hurry, man."

"I'm on it."

Chuck was there in just over twenty minutes. They hurried to Caleb's; the snow was accumulating fast. They parked right in front of the brick building. James had Caleb's key on his car key chain, he gave it to Chuck and slipped down on the seat. Chuck ran into the building, not bothering to look around. Caleb's door was unlocked, no one was there. Papers and books were scattered on the floor.

Chuck ran back out and told James to come back up to Caleb's room with him, that his room had been tossed.

They raced, in the snow, back to his room. "This is his jacket!" James picked up the jacket and went through the pockets. "His wallet!"

James opened the wallet and pulled out $500, showing it to Chuck. "He wears this bomber jacket all the time. Where can he be? Did someone take him?" James threw down the jacket and wallet. He grabbed the handle of Caleb's desk drawer and pulled it too wide open. The drawer fell out, pens, coins, miscellaneous junk rolled on the floor. James kicked the drawer, causing his ankle to buckle and he screamed in pain, pulling at his hair.

"James," Chuck yelled, "Stop it."

James stopped pulling on his hair and swung around, at a loss for what to do.

Chuck went over to the door, kicked and pushed the frame into better working order and locked the door. "You got to settle down, James. Sit down, take some deep breaths. I mean it." Chuck pushed him over to the desk chair and kept his hand on his shoulder as James held on to the desk and shakily sat down.

"Deep breaths. Slow your thinking down, James. I'm here, we can work it out." Chuck stroked James' back and felt James' breathing slowing down. "It's you and me Bro, we'll do some thinking. Does Caleb ever wander around without a jacket?"

James got his wind back and felt his body relax slightly. "I'd guess he does wander around, he talks about it, but not in a snow storm, not when the door was broken in, right?"

"Let's get back to the car and take a drive around," Chuck suggested. "We can talk while we look for him. I don't really feel safe here, do you?"

A subdued James shook his head 'no'. They left, relocked the door, and walked to Chuck's car.

They drove the Summit area, Chuck circling the streets and the alleys. It kept snowing in earnest. James faced the passenger window, watching the residential blocks go by, telling Chuck when to slow down, so he could look in the shadows and alleys, hoping for a glimpse of Caleb.

"Start at the beginning James. I'm listening," Chuck was

subdued too, hunched over the steering wheel driving slowly in the snow on the empty post-thanksgiving streets.

"I guess I wanted to live out some of my fantasies. I got this great place and met Willow and she liked me. Can you imagine that? Suddenly I'm a winner. Then I ran into Randall and he liked me too. He brings out the free heroin. What a fool, I just went along with him. I tried the junk, and then I turned Caleb on to it. He hinted to me that he had had a problem with drugs in the past, but I didn't pay attention, I wanted someone to play 'heroin' with. Then Randall offers me this part time job, good money to pick up opioids at a bunch of medical facilities."

At that point Chuck uttered, "Damn, damn," and raised his arm ready to hit James. He stopped himself, stopped the car and hunched over the steering wheel.

James shrugged, half raised his arms helplessly, and continued, "Caleb wanted a part time job too. Now I'm the stud. Randall introduces me to this prostitute and I try to be the big shot and get between her and her pimp. That was last night. Here, look at the video. James found the video on his phone and gave it to Chuck to watch.

Chuck looked at the video. He kept shaking his head and watching it over and over. "My god, he could have carved you. Where were you? The camera's moving around, near the ground."

"I was lying on the ground the whole time. I pounded on his window and he slammed opened the door and it threw me to the ground. It was icy. I sprained my ankle and I couldn't get traction to get up right away. How long is the video? Ten whole seconds or something like that? It seemed like forever."

Chuck couldn't help chuckling. "You're lying on the ground, yelling at a pimp, my god, what a home video. Damn, you made a mess."

James tried to smile but he couldn't. "They broke into my place this morning. I wasn't there but I came back and the door was wide open." James' lower lip trembled.

That sobered Chuck up. "That's the scariest part yet! Is that the whole story? Anything you haven't told me? I hope that is it, James. Working for a dealer, into opioids and heroin, oh, boy, you are in so deep, Bro."

"There's something else. I don't know if it's important but it scares me. I don't know how big these guys are, how interconnected. For all I know, they all know each other, but Randall knows this pimp. I yelled Randall's name at the pimp." James threw his hands in the air, there was still more.

"OK, something else happened last night. After that fight with the pimp, (it was a fight sort of – stop laughing at me - I was stuck on the ground.) Then that car stopped and the pimp drove away and I turned off the phone.

After that, all I could think of was 'I have to make it right with Randall', so I drove by his house, that's a really big no-no. Anyway, he was just driving up and I parked and was limping over and then I saw he wasn't alone. I recognized the guy he was with, Sam Weatherly's oldest son, Alex, - I've told you about them. Randall has warned me about the bosses. Randall said they would kill me if I got in the way. I thought he was kidding but he said those very words, seriously. What do you think?"

"Did they see you, talk to you?"

"Not talk to me. I'm not sure they recognized me. Alex looked really hard at me. I had a hoodie on. Everyone wears them."

"As well as Randall knows you, he could recognize you from the street."

"I was limping, but I kind of' waved at him. He just glanced in my direction. I know that doesn't help much."

"Good god, we better call the police, James."

"No, don't think about it! Randall says they have the police in their pocket. If I tell them the truth, they get to arrest me, don't they? Worse, they'll just tell the dealers bosses that I'm ratting on them. This whole story is off the charts, who is going to believe me?"

"You could ask for some protection." Chuck suggested.

"Come on, protection? They are going to ask me what I've been doing. Fighting with pimps, dealing drugs? Where would I start? Do I sound like a victim here?"

"Yeah, no, but James, you got that pretty red hair and that soft baby face. They'll believe you."

James reached over and tried to punch Chuck in the ribs, Chuck protected himself and turned it around, twisting James' arm until James cried, "I give, I give." Chuck let him go. Then he put his arm around James and gave him a quick hug. "I don't know what to say, Bro, you're in deep dodo."

It was early afternoon. No sign of Caleb. It was still snowing. "Where is he, he'll die out here, no jacket," James feared.

"I'll go back to his place and make sure he didn't come back," Chuck offered. "Let's trade places. You put your hoodie back up and get in the driver's seat, keep the car running, I'll just run up there and be right back down, one way or the other. Keep your phone out, ready to call 911. I'll do the same."

James waited while Chuck ran back up to Caleb's, thumping his hands on the steering wheel, watching it snow, looking around diligently. Chuck wasn't gone for more than a few minutes.

"Nothing has changed. I left a spitball up on the door, if anyone goes in it will fall off and we'll know someone has been there or is in there. Let's get out of here."

James drove away in the snow quietly. He drove the car around a couple of blocks, watching to see if they were being followed. They stopped on a tree lined street, parking between two cars and waited. There wasn't any traffic coming from either direction.

"What now?" asked Chuck.

"I've got another big problem, Bro. I thought of it when you were out of the car. I'm supposed to do deliveries for Randall today. It's usually Thursday but with the holiday, it was changed to late this afternoon. Got any ideas?"

"Well, I guess this is as good a time as any to see if Randall's out to get you. Call him, tell him you can't do the deliveries, let's see what he says." Chuck suggested.

"Got any good excuse I can use?" James asked.

"How about, 'I'm being stalked by a pimp and he broke into my place."

"Damn it, Chuck, no more jokes. How about something like 'I must have gotten bad turkey, puking sick, coming out of both ends' something like that."

"Seriously, I like it. No one wants to mess with someone when it's coming out of both ends." Seeing how shaky James was, Chuck grabbed his phone and asked him to point to Randall's phone number.

Chuck punched the number and put it on speaker so they could both hear the conversation.

"James, you OK?" Randall sounded worried.

"No, I'm not OK, I got some bug, I bet it was the turkey, puking and the runs. I can't do my pickups today. No way, sorry Randall."

"James, you got to come over here. I need to talk to you. Skip the pickups. That'll be OK, but I need to talk to you."

"What's this about? I told you I'm sick."

"Listen to me, get your ass over here you got some explaining to do." Randall sounded angry but shaky too.

"Randall, I'm scared to go over to your place. Sounds like you know what happened. God, I was just bluffing that pimp Chauncey and, I'm so sorry, I used your name. I'll do what I can to make things right, I'll give the pimp all my money, but I got to take care of myself."

Chuck was shaking his head no, trying to take the phone from

James, but James held him off, shaking his head, lipping, "it's my deal." Chuck stopped interfering and they waited for Randall to say something.

Randall took a while to answer. Both Chuck and James were thinking he was conferring with someone.

"Fuck it, **run James**, don't call the cops." Someone must have grabbed the phone, there were two pop sounds and the line went dead.

"Did you hear that? Did that sound like a gun, maybe?" James asked Chuck.

Chuck nodded, "I'm going to call 911, tell them to send an ambulance, I think it was pistol shots, what else could it be? The line went dead, oh what do I know."

Chuck dialed 911, "what's the address, James?" James told him the address and started the car. They raced and slid over to Randall's place. James called 911 too hoping that two calls would get better attention. When they got there, two police cars were just pulling up. James pulled the car in an empty space across the street, Chuck whispered, "stay in the car". When James started to open his door, Chuck whispered, "On my life, James, stay in the car!" James closed his car door.

Chuck walked casually across the street and up to the officers. They turned to him and he said, "I was getting out of my car to go to the Pizza Hut, he pointed down the street to a Pizza Hut, when I thought I heard shots fired, I think maybe the second floor."

"You stay right here," one of them said pointing to the curb and the two went up to the house, hands on holsters. They started knocking loudly and tried to open the front door. It was locked tight. "I'm going around back," one cop said and hurried around to the back. A second police car arrived. Those two officers stayed in their car.

The officer came from the back, "The doors ajar in the back, we can go up there."

Chuck waited at the curb, staying cool. Then he heard the radio spurting from the other police car. "Code grey, gunshot victim.........," it took all his resolve to stay put.

Chuck started feeling dizzy and walked up to the second police car with the officers inside.

"Can I go sit in my car? I'm the one who thought I heard shots fired. I was walking from here to the Pizza Hut," he pointed to the Pizza Hut on the corner. I'm getting cold, this is scary," he said. The officers asked where his car was, he pointed and they nodded an OK.

Chuck got into the driver's seat while James slipped over the console to the passenger's side. "I don't want you identified by the cops; this is getting way out of hand. Sorry I'm bossing you around."

"Here's our story", Chuck improvised. "You and I are friends, going to get pizza at the Pizza Hut, I heard the shots, you're not sure, it happened fast, you were still in the car."

"Simple enough," James nodded his agreement.

"There's the ambulance", Chuck pointed out, the cops in the second car got out to meet the ambulance. "They aren't looking over here at all, can hardly see over here in this snow, let's go, now." James ordered. Chuck started the car and they quietly drove off.

"Should we check Caleb's place again?" Chuck asked. James agreed and they stopped around the corner this time and both went in this time. The spitball was still in place.

They slammed back into the car, "Where do you think they took Randall?" James asked Caleb.

"I'm sure they took him to Ramsey. We can go by there. I might know one of the med students working there." Chuck turned at the next corner, headed toward the hospital. "You'll stay in the car this time."

James nodded, "Check to see if Caleb is there too."

Chuck got back to the car fifteen minutes later, mincing his steps to prevent falling in the deepening snow. His jacket hood was pulled up. It was nasty outside. The sidewalks were treacherous with falling snow over frozen sleet.

Chuck sat quietly. Then, he turned to James, tears in his eyes. "Randall's dead James, he was shot two times in the head. Caleb wasn't there."

"Did I kill him, Chuck?" James asked anxiously.

"You goddamn fool, this is not all about you." Chuck hit the steering wheel with his right hand causing the horn to honk. Then he hit it again and again, letting it honk on. "We're all to blame. Jeez, I sent you looking for Randall. He turned you on to the heroin, the asshole. But then he saved your ass. He's dead James, this isn't a fantasy, isn't a blame game."

James turned his head. His eyes were watering. He could feel the wet spilling over onto his cheeks. He kept thinking, 'Caleb too, and Caleb too'.

"Where are we going to go, James, we can't just sit here forever."

"Give me a minute," James said hoarsely, wiping his eyes and blowing his nose into the sleeve of his jacket before turning to face Chuck.

"Take me to my car, Chuck, I'll find a place to stay. I'll call you and let you know where I am."

"No, I'll stay with you, James, we're in this together, Bro."

"Take me to my car, god damn it all, or I'll get out here and walk."

"You can hardly walk in this ice and snow."

"Watch me," James started opening the car door.

Chuck knew him too well to argue and said, "OK, I'll take you to your car. But I'll tell you right now, I'm not keeping it a secret James. You can't get out of this fix alone. We need our family." Chuck started driving to James' car.

"Do what you think you should, but no police, do you hear me? Please, no cops." James started making a call."

"Who are you calling?" Chuck asked.

"I'm calling Jerome. No one would look for me at his place. His building is safe and his apartment is a fortress."

Chuck heard Jerome talking fast, "Jerome, James here. Can I come over to your place for maybe a few days? I'll bring some McNuggets, need some coke?"

"Thanks, no that's alright, I understand, I'll explain more tomorrow when I get to your place." James ended the conversation,

"Jerome is at his mom's until tomorrow but I can come and stay tomorrow. I can find a motel for tonight. I'll pay cash, I've got money on me."

"You can come to our place James. They won't expect you there."

"Right next to my mom's place? These guys aren't stupid. You got to promise not to call the police. Do you promise me that?"

"I get it about the cops, they could be on your ass about Randall getting killed too," Chuck nodded his understanding. "Everyone will understand after I explain things. From what's happened, these guys want to get rid of you, and Caleb, who knows? Stay sober now. Agreed?" James nodded. "Chuck, I love you, man." James hugged him, hugged him twice more before getting out of the car.

Chuck drove James to his car. James got into his car and rummaged around for a joint.

CALEB WAS TIGHTLY TIED to a metal support post on a concrete floor. His arms looped around the post before his wrists were tied. He was in a sitting position; his legs were on either side of the post. They'd used a heavy zip tie on his wrists. His wrists were tied so tightly his hands and half his arms were numb. His head lolled against the post.

He'd been in and out of consciousness. His head hurt terribly. They kept a pillowcase over his head and he couldn't see much beyond his feet. He had no idea why he was there. He had yelled a couple of times without response. Yelling caused so much pain in his head that he gave it up. He thought he must have a concussion from the slam to the side of his head. He knew he shouldn't move too much. He kept rubbing the plastic tie on his wrists back and forth against the metal pole but he was just too weak, he couldn't put much effort into it.

There was a high window letting in some light but he had no idea how much time had passed. It was an effort to keep his head against the pole. 'What would Pugsley do?' he mumbled wondering if he would ever see his sister again. Once in a while he heard movement in another part of the building, some sort of a warehouse, he thought. He knew he wasn't totally alone. Someone would come sooner or later.

38 / POPEYE'S DILEMMA

While Caleb languished, tied to a post in an empty space, Popeye sat in the front office of the warehouse/hanger listening to an angry voice on his cell. Aside from the fiasco at Randall's, he'd been on the phone since Chauncey woke him in the middle of the night. Now he was grunting 'yeah' and waiting to get a word in as the voice on the other end vented and raved. He didn't even know the guy, just that Alex had said to listen to him.

Finally, a pause and Popeye explained again, "Chauncey Sands, he's my cuz, we grew up together. He'd seen Holden hanging around, sniffing after one of his girls. But last night, Holden attacked him like a crazy, man, I told you what Holden said to him, 'you're a dead man walking', then Holden said, 'I know Randall', then, 'the feds is watching.'" He was on his cell talking to the feds, saying the names.

"Yeah, James Holden said all those things to Chauncey. Then about an hour later, last night still, Holden was over at Randall's place, stalking Randall. Alex was there too. Both Randall and Alex are pretty sure that Holden saw them both. Randall says Holden knows who Alex is too."

"I don't know why Randall brought him in, knew him back in grade school or something, then Randall pushes this other guy, Caleb Epstein on me, a friend of Holden's, Randall said he vetted him good. Anyway, I hired him and he was getting to know my operation too."

"Of course, I didn't know anything until Chauncey called, who do you take me for?"

Popeye wheeled away from his desk, wanting to ring this guy's neck, then planted both feet and wheeled back to his desk.

"Chauncey is the one who says Holden's got a video of the whole thing. Yeah, Chauncey threatened him with a knife. Holden must have some back up too, a car drives up while Holden is videoing Chauncey, asks Holden if he's OK. Then Chauncey hears sirens in the background, cops are on the way, what could Chauncey do? He got the girls to safety, called me."

There was some more ranting on the phone and another question.

"Hey, I told Chauncey to wait, don't do nothing until I called him back, but he got eager, knew where Holden lived. He went over there, early morning, and kicked the door in. He was going to surprise him, but no one was there, so he messed up the place, slashed some furniture, nothing much to take. I don't know if he had a plan of what he was going to do when he found him, beat him up? Kill him? With Holden saying, 'dead man walking', Chauncey wanted to hill him, he'd a cut him up then and there if that car didn't come and stop."

Then another question for Popeye:

"Oh, yeah, maybe he was drinking, both of them were probably high."

"Chauncey didn't call me until he got the girls settled down, he took them out of town. I told him to wait until I got back to him, but like I said, he was over to Holden's early morning, Holden wasn't there."

"The nest thing that happened, Sticky and Delbert picked up Holden's friend, Epstein, he's the one working for me, I told you, his name is Caleb Epstein, from NYC. Now he's here at the airport. He's hurt but alive, Sticky hit him hard."

"Yes, I tried to talk to Randall, told him to get Holden over there. But Randall had his own plan, D was watching for Holden and planned to grab him up when he made his first delivery. If he'd made that delivery, we would have had him. I went over to Randall's to wait for D or Holden to call."

"Holden finally called but Randall couldn't get him to come over. I pulled my gun out and pointed it at Randall's head, 'get him over here' I said. Randall looked at me, like I'd lost my mind, then Randall started yelling into the phone, 'run, James, get out of here, don't call the cops', I yanked the phone and he held on to it and I don't know, the gun went off, it popped him twice. It was over. I didn't mean to shoot him, the gun had a hair trigger, I'd never pointed it up close like that, right at his head. Still, Randall was a rat, maybe an informant. I never trusted him, but I've never killed anyone, I'm not a killer."

The other voice barked some orders and hung up.

Popeye started to throw his phone across the floor but stopped himself and sat there, staring at the wall, at the picture of his wife with his little son and baby girl, choking up. He kept repeating to himself, "I'm not a killer, I'm not."

He looked at the bottle of bourbon sitting on his desk and took a swig. Usually he kept the bottle in his bottom drawer, it was for sharing with other people. But today it was for drinking alone. Can a man be more alone? He thought. It burned down his throat and esophagus and down into his empty stomach. He shivered, but then a wave of warmth spread from his lungs to his arms and he was able to breathe deeply.

Popeye hated that Sticky and Delbert had been called to take care of it. They were killers and cleaners. But at least it will be over soon.

Popeye was a born and bred Minnesotan, too. He'd been a scholarship student at an inner-city Jesuit school in Minneapolis. He'd been 13 going on 30 when he had started at St. Jazz. He wasn't an athlete like so many of the brothers at school, but smarter than most and became the student manager of the championship basketball team. He kept the basketball team out of trouble, supplied them with the right drugs and they won championships. After high school he expanded his drug business. It was a natural choice of profession. Although the Jesuits did what they could to lead him in other directions, he'd seen too many black kids try and fail at college, and he didn't want to take that iffy road.

Dealing was embedded deeply in his family history and a perfectly acceptable way to make money, as long you didn't use too much of the product. That was the downfall of too many of the dealers in his own family. He wasn't going to make that mistake and for the most part he didn't. He was a natural manager. He took computerized business classes seriously and developed a very serious business plan in his senior year of high school. He understood the principles of multiple cost centers and diversifying and was on a comparable track and slightly ahead of Randall.

The Minnesota cartel brought in both Popeye and Randall. Both of them had independent, successful businesses but the cartel offered protection from the cops and feds, good muscle when they needed it, and a chance to live a near normal life. Chauncey had married up, a good, loving woman with an education, and finally had the family life he'd been denied as a child.

Popeye had to do his part to clean up Randall's mess. Popeye had another problem, his volatile cousin Chauncey. Popeye didn't want the kid hurt. He was just getting started. Popeye had nurtured the kid since Chauncey's mother died and he came to live with

Popeye's mother who worked two jobs and raised four kids after his dad overdosed.

Chauncey adored Popeye and wanted to follow in his footsteps, but Chauncey hadn't been cut out for dealing, his profits went up his nose. Popeye had a 'come to Jesus with him' and he had settled into handling the two whores just fine, until this happened. Popeye was glad Chauncey immediately got the girls out of town, but then he came back and broke into Holden's place. He got nothing there but probably scared Holden into hiding.

Popeye hoped he had the moral fiber to protect his cousin if the cartel went after him. He didn't think they would, but he wasn't certain.

Chauncey's phone rang. He recognized Sticky's voice. "You get Epstein ready to go and we'll pick him up in an hour."

Popeye heaved a sigh of relief. His part would be done in an hour. Epstein would be taken care of, he'd already gotten rid of the gun, threw it in the Mississippi from Lake St. He vowed to himself that he'd never own a gun again, no matter the consequences. All he wanted to do was go home, kiss his wife, hold his kids.

39 / CAN CALEB BE SAVED?

Chuck called home and Sandra picked up. He told her James was in trouble with some rough people. He told her to call Ellen and have her come over. Sandra, stunned, gave the phone to Ralph.

"What the hell?" Ralph asked.

Chuck debated how much to tell on the phone while driving in snow. "It's about James and Caleb. Dad, I'm almost home. Call Ellen, call Char, make sure Willow is safe." He hung up and let the phone ring when his dad tried to call back. He had no idea if Willow was involved in any of this, but he wasn't taking any chances.

Chuck kept an eye out for cop cars as he navigated the slick road, trying to make sure no one was following him. He'd gotten paranoid too.

When Chuck got home, Ellen and Carmen were on their way, they had been playing cards with Ellen's friend from work, Elliot, and his partner, Ron. Char insisted she and Joe come too. They dropped Willow at the Goldberg's until Char and Joe assessed the situation.

Chuck revealed to Ralph and Sandra that James was safe and

sober but in a lot of trouble, and Caleb was in trouble, too, and it involved heroin.

Chuck waited out his dad's anger and didn't reveal more. He wanted to wait until everyone got there to tell the whole story. Chuck kept repeating, "I don't want any hysterics here." He and his dad slid glances at Sandra.

"I'm less hysterical than you two, pacing like lions in the zoo," she said. She had a point. She was making coffee and setting out a smorgasbord of Thanksgiving leftovers as the men paced.

Ralph turned to Chuck, "I need to ask you one thing." Chuck nodded and Ralph asked, "Are you involved in this heroin, too?"

Chuck gave his dad a resounding "No, never, dad." That calmed Ralph down and answered Sandra's prayers.

CHAR AND JOE ARRIVED FIRST. Ellen and Carmen brought Elliot and Ron in with them.

Ellen waved her hands for attention, "This is Elliot and his partner Ron. I've worked with Elliot for years. The four of us were playing cards when we got the call. Both Elliot and Ron are former Army Rangers, they know James, and they've dealt with very unsavory characters. We thought their input would be invaluable."

After introductions, when Chuck finally had everyone's attention, he started from the beginning, the call he received from James. He emphasized Caleb's disappearance and Randall's murder, and minimized James' initial screw ups.

In the bedlam of questions following Chuck's explanation, his cell rang. He looked down, "Quiet everyone", he yelled, "it's James, I'll put it on speaker."

"James I'm here, I'm on speaker phone at the folk's house."

"Chuck, I just got a call. It was from Caleb's cell, but it wasn't

Caleb. It was a stranger who said, 'Caleb's in trouble, get right over to his place now.'"

Chuck interrupted James, "Calm down James. Stop driving, listen to me."

James yelled back at Chuck, "Did you hear me? Caleb's in trouble, now, I can't stop, I've got to go there, now."

"Wait," everyone screamed and once again there was general bedlam. James was already off the line.

Ron walked over to Chuck, "You know where Caleb lives?" Chuck nodded.

Ron continued, "Come with us, we'll take my car—let me drive."

They grabbed their coats and headed out the door. Char ran behind them without a coat and yelled at them to wait while she ran to her car, slipping and sliding in the new snow. Elliot walked after her and looked at what she had, he took it from her and off they went.

"What did you give him?" Ellen and Sandra yelled out the door at her.

"Two Narcan Injectors and a Taser."

"What the hell? Since when are you driving around with Narcan and a Taser?" Joe asked, sticking his head out the door too.

"I knew the Narcan Injectors would come in handy someday. This is pretty recent stuff you know. I bought them from my cop friend. I've had the Taser forever, in my trunk, Joe."

Joe shook his head at his wife.

Ron had already retrieved his Ruger SR9 from the trunk. Off they sped, Ron and Elliot in front and Chuck in the back. Chuck said he could make it in a little over 20 minutes. Ron assured him that he'd get them there faster.

JAMES, was already in St. Paul, sliding down the busy streets. It had quit snowing but there were six plus inches of accumulation. It was the first heavy snow of the season and James and everyone else had forgotten how-to drive-in snow.

The plows hadn't started clearing the side streets and it wasn't worth the extra time it would take to get on and off the freeway, so James slid along the residential streets, trying to drive fast but having to halt at the corners to avoid careless drivers sliding through the intersections. With an overly cautious driver in front of him, James settled down and drove less recklessly.

Chuck had rung him back, "James I'm coming with help. We're only ten, fifteen minutes out. Wait for us. Stay in your car."

James wondered who the 'we' were. He made it to Caleb's before Chuck and saw the light on in Caleb's room on second floor front. He didn't wait for the others to arrive. He double parked his car and ran into Caleb's rooming house. "Hello," he yelled, no one answered him. The place was quiet, the hall lights on the second floor were off. He didn't look for the light switch, he just ran up the dark stairway and hall in the dim street light to Caleb's room. He hesitated outside of Caleb's room. He didn't hear anything. He took hold of the door knob and started to turn it. The door popped open and someone grabbed his upper arm and pulled him into the room. He went down on his knees. He saw two burly strangers looking at him.

"It's him," the one said and the other fisted him on the side of his head, above his ear, and he went all the way down. He felt his coat being unzipped and saw what seemed like a huge hypodermic needle in the tough guy's hand, coming down towards his inner arm. He tried to pull away but another big hand smashed his head against the floor and held him in place. The needle went in his arm and almost immediately he was weak as a kitten. The tough guy put James' fingerprints on the needle.

"This is the place," Chuck shouted. "That's James' car, double parked." They looked up at the building and saw the lights go out on the second floor. "I think that's Caleb's apartment."

The whole place was dark now.

As they piled out of Ron's car, they could still make out James' footsteps dashing and sliding from the door of his car to the building. He hadn't been there long.

They pussy footed their way through the wet snow toward the doorway. Elliot was first. His arm went up and Ron stopped on a dime. Chuck, bringing up the rear, slid like a bowling ball and managed to spill all three of them.

"Everyone OK?" Elliot whispered, pursing his lips to hide his amused look as he got up and wiped the snow off of his jacket and pants. The other two nodded as they staggered upright and wiped themselves off.

"How do we get to his room?" Elliot asked Chuck.

"The second-floor corridor, where the light just went off, it's the second room on the right straight up the stairway, sir," Chuck answered. Elliot's lips pursed together again.

"Stay to the left side of the staircase, Chuck, stay back, be quiet."

They quietly climbed the dark staircase, Elliot checking to make sure Chuck was well back. Once up the stairs, they heard a sound at the other end of the hallway, saw a flash and a bullet whizzed by in their direction. They all went down to the floor. They heard steps clambering down the back staircase. Ron was first up and running down the hall, chasing whoever it was going down the back staircase. Elliot dashed to the open second door. There was dead silence in the dark room.

Chuck had his cell phone out with its flashlight on. He handed it to Elliot. Elliot swept it across the small room, two bodies were lying on the floor then swept the wall near the door and found the light switch.

"Turn it on, Chuck."

"Chuck," Elliot said louder and again pointed out the switch with the cell light. Chuck flipped the light switch and fortunately it turned on. Both Chuck and Elliot got down on the floor. Neither James nor Caleb moved. Elliot lifted up James' head and it flopped down.

"I'm almost a first-year med student, if there's no bleeding, they're probably drugged, it's probably an overdose."

Chuck rolled Caleb over. There didn't seem to be any blood. He had a terrible bruise on the side of his head, it ran down beyond his cheek. He was in shirtsleeves.

Elliot pulled the Narcan Injectors out of his pocket. "Do you know how to use these?"

Chuck nodded, "They're nasal injectors, I can use them.

He pumped Narcan into Caleb's nose, then rushed over to James. Elliot helped Chuck pull James' jacket off and again they didn't see any blood on him and Chuck injected the Narcan. Within seconds, James gasped for breath and moaned. Caleb remained silent. Chuck rushed back to Caleb and started CPR.

Elliot called 911, "What's the address, Chuck?" Then said into his cell, "Two overdoses, one's hardly breathing, we're at 911 Mission, second floor, the door is open, 'Code Grey, Code Grey.'"

"Stay with the CPR, Chuck, I'll check the hallways and find some more light. I'll be near, keep at it, you'll make a good doc."

Elliot had the cell's flashlight on and was checking for hall lights. He found some by the stairwell, and went down the back stairs. The back of the place had a dining area and kitchen, and a back door. There was a motion activated light in the back that exposed a broken lock, the door was open. A number of footsteps went in and out the back door, including, probably, a half-dragged Caleb. Elliot whistled shrilly and listened for a return whistle. Ron's two shrill whistles answered. He's a good block away Elliot thought. He must be following the intruders. Elliot wasn't worried about Ron, he knew Ron would be carefully looking for information, not confrontation.

Elliot went back into the building and checked the rest of the first floor, turning on more lights, making sure the front door stayed open. The building appeared to be empty. The goons must have chosen to break in the back door. He stood outside the front door, waiting for the ambulance.

Elliot was smooth. He led the EMT's upstairs and pointed to Caleb. Chuck was still working on him. James was sitting on the floor leaning over his own throw up. His mouth dripped yellow bile. One EMT felt for a pulse on Caleb and nodded, "Faint but he's alive." The other asked Chuck a few medical questions, and then asked Elliot, "Is he someone you know?" Elliot shrugged, "Not well." The EMT's put Caleb on a stretcher and wheeled him out.

Another stretcher arrived and they lifted James onto it. Although James tried to lift himself up, he was too weak, and he fell back onto the stretcher and his eyes closed.

Two officers in blue headed back up the stairs, shaking their heads. "Heroin overdoses? Where do these college kids get the stuff?"

The officers made way for the first stretcher on the landing, one asking, "Are they going to make it?"

"The guys who found them had Narcan, that might have saved their lives. A young guy was giving this one CPR, he's got a very faint pulse. We'll do what we can for him."

Chuck tried to get by the cops to go with Caleb's stretcher.

"Not so fast, kid," the front cop said, "Come back with us, show us what happened."

Chuck followed the cops and stood in the hallway as the second stretcher rolled down the hall with James on it. James looked unconscious.

Elliot was standing in the room, waiting for the policemen to come in.

"What happened here?"

Elliot went over and shook their hands. "Boy, you guys are fast. We've just been here a few minutes. I'll tell you what happened." Elliot had such an easy, friendly way about him that Chuck could see the officers visibly relax.

"This guy, Chuck," he pointed to Chuck, "gets a call from his buddy, James Holden, the guy on the second stretcher. Holden says that both he and the other guy, Caleb somebody, got some heavy heroin and were overdosing. These friends of Chuck's were supposed to meet us for dinner and I was going to give them a NA talk, instead, they're overdosing. This takes the cake. I've been carrying Narcan around for months now. There's a drug war out there, officers, some of us, in the program, have taken to carrying this stuff in our cars. Sad, isn't it?"

The officers both nodded. It made sense and the officers agreed there was a drug war going on. They looked on the floor, two needles, a kit, strewn about.

"Jim, run down and get a couple of report forms." The younger officer left and the older guy explained. "You guys will write out your story. Just write it all down, I'll check your IDs and if all checks out, you can be on your way in a matter of minutes."

Chuck called his folks while he did the paperwork and explained the bad news. Caleb and James were on the way to Ramsey. Caleb was in an extremely bad way, definitely going to IC. James would survive but was probably going to be admitted to the hospital, too. Chuck agreed to meet them at the hospital.

Ron was waiting in his car for Chuck and Elliot. "I didn't find the perpetrators or their car. They must have known I was behind them, suddenly, no tracks. Do you want to go to the hospital, Chuck? We'll give you a ride, but I don't think we'll stick around, there are too many of us."

"If James left his keys in his car, I'll take his car to the hospital. I'm so sorry I knocked you guys down in the snow."

Elliot and Ron looked at each other and they all grinned. Elliot thumped Chuck on the back, "You were great up there. We made a good team. Don't you think?" Chuck smiled with relief, and nodded.

40 / CONSEQUENCES

James stirred Saturday morning from a drugged sleep. His mother quickly got up from a chair near his bed and kissed him on the cheek.

"Oh James," she said, kissing him again and putting her head on his chest, listening to the sound of his steady breathing. She looked up with tears in her eyes.

James looked at her in shock as memory of the last 24 hours overwhelmed him.

"Mom," he said, "Is...is Caleb dead?"

"No son, they are doing surgery as soon as his swelling goes down, you saved his life, you and Chuck and Elliot and Ron."

"Elliot and Ron? Where, what happened?"

"They think it was two guys, they hit both of you on the side of the head, but Caleb earlier in the day, then they gave you enough heroin to kill you, but Chuck and Elliot and Ron found you and they gave you both Narcan. That probably saved both of your lives."

"Caleb isn't dead? Oh," James said as he faded back against the pillow and truly rested.

James woke up again, alone, in his small hospital room built for a single patient but holding two patients, separated by a curtain.

James' roommate, who got the bed closest to the bathroom, sounded like an old gurgling, spitting drunk. He kept calling hoarsely for the nurses' help, even though a nurse had just been with him. The nursing assistant stopped by James' bed asking if he wanted fresh water or juice and told James his roommate's story. The old drunk had fallen in the snow, passed out, and the police found him and brought him in with hyperthermia.

James shuddered; the old man ruined what little peace of mind he had gotten knowing Caleb was alive. James laid quietly, his arms at the sides of the bed, his eyes closed wondering what would happen next. He didn't want to see anyone, maybe Willow would be OK, his mother had been OK, but the rest of them? They must hate him.

When he next woke up, Char was knitting by his bed. My god, the worst of the bunch he thought. He closed his eyes again and hoped he could outlast her with feigned sleep; maybe Char would take pity on him and leave. I nearly died, he thought, couldn't they give me one day?

He gave in, he could tell she wasn't going anywhere, so he acknowledged her presence with a question. "What do you think of my roommate, Char?" James asked, nodding to the curtain, "Is he part of my punishment? Am I in hell?"

"Make him part of your hell if you want," Char said evenly.

"I'm thinking it was a cynical nursing staff that put this guy and me together, but it could be an angry God, I guess."

"It's what you want to make of it, James." Char answered.

"I'll probably get out of here this morning; they don't keep you one hour longer than necessary, do they?"

"You and Caleb had enough fentanyl in your system to kill an elephant. They had to give you a Narcan drip all night. You're young and physically strong, but you almost died, you know that of course."

"I don't know up from down. I've fucked up so bad in the past

24 hours, Randall is dead, Caleb near death. I should be the one who is dead. What about Caleb, got any news about him?"

Char shook her head, "He's in a coma, James. He had emergency surgery this morning, to release the blood build up in his skull. His Dad is flying out today or tomorrow morning, it being a holiday weekend, transportation is haywire. I stayed with him last night."

"Why would you do that?"

"Other than, I love the guy?"

"Love, you only met him once."

"No, we have past connection."

"NA?" James asked.

"Anonymous." Char said.

"You enjoy helping us royal fuck ups, don't you? I hate myself, god, I hate myself."

"I thought you might be feeling down."

"Down? Suicidal - more like that."

"Should I tell the nursing staff to put you on suicide watch?" Char asked.

"I'm too depressed to kill myself. It's a conundrum, too depressed to live, too depressed to die. I have some heroin in my trunk, I can shoot up when I get out of here, die that happy way, but, I'm too depressed, I don't even want to shoot up."

"Don't worry about that, James, your desire to use will come back when you're feeling better."

"You're really fun. I'll keep my dark thoughts to myself. Why are you here, anyway? Where's my mamas? They loved me."

"Your whole family loves you. Willow, Joe, Sandra, Ralph, Chuck, your mom, Carmen, me too. You know your mom's friend, Elliot? He and Ron were with Chuck when they found you at Caleb's, drowning in your own bile."

"Elliot and Ron? Why don't you all go fuck your selves or each other, some of you seem to like to fuck each other."

"Showing a little spirit? Trying to get rid of us? We're not going away. You're ours, we love you, we won't let go of you."

"What are you talking about?" he said angrily. "You hardly know me."

"I know you in a way not everyone in your family does. I know the addict you've become, the twisted guy who tries to do the right thing, but can't quite do it because another voice keeps whispering in his ear, 'drink me, snort me, smoke me, shoot me, do me, let me live high."

"Ick, you make me sicker and sicker." James squirmed in his bed thinking how to get this witch out of my room.

"I'll leave you with some advice, James. This is what is going to happen. You'll stay in the hospital another night. And, because it's the weekend, you'll get discharged before you get an appointment to have a chemical use evaluation. The social worker will set up an appointment for you on Monday morning. I suggest you tell the truth and accept the recommendation. You'll be going to court for possession anyway and if you're already in treatment, you'll make some points. The alternative will be involuntary, court ordered treatment and entanglement with the drug court.

Further, I suggest you try the AA/NA program as soon as possible. Joe is coming by this afternoon and he is more than willing to spend some time with you tomorrow. There is a great AA meeting on Sunday nights.

In the meantime, we, your family, won't leave you alone in this room, we won't leave Caleb in a room alone. There has been an attempt on both of your lives. We are all taking that very seriously. You're not going to be alone in this, we will sort it out, one step at a time. Any questions for me?"

James shook his head, no, and turned his head to fight the tears rolling down the corners of his closed eyes.

Char waited a few minutes, when James remained quiet, she said goodbye and without touching him, left his room, and went down the hall to a small family room. Ellen was lying on a leather couch, her head on Carmen's lap. She looked like she had been crying again. Her eyes were closed. Carmen was stroking her hair.

Ellen opened her eyes when she felt Char standing by her.

"What time is it?" Ellen mumbled, "You'd think I'd be too anxious to sleep but I'm nodding off again."

"I'm tired, too. It's almost noon but it feels later, doesn't it?" Char answered.

Tears filled Ellen's eyes again, she nodded. "Thank you for talking to him. How do you think he is doing?"

"I think he is sleeping again. Oh, he's full of piss and vinegar. I love that boy of yours, Ellen. I don't know what you two have talked about, but he admitted to me that he feels very responsible for what happened to Randall and Caleb. James has a lot of self-pity, too. He is being honest, I like that. I'm hoping he'll just go along with the flow for a while. We'll see. I'll go back and sit with him until Joe gets here. We shouldn't let them out of our sight right now."

Ellen was sitting up, "I'll spend the night in James' room again tonight. Now I've got to go home and get some sleep."

"I'll stay with Caleb tonight," Carmen said. "Who is with him now?"

"Willow."

Ellen dragged herself up to say 'goodbye' to James. His eyes were open, but he looked very tired.

"James, I'm just going to give you another hug and then I'm going home with Carmen. Last night I stayed here keeping semi-conscious vigil in this big too comfortable chair. I plan to do it again tonight." She hugged him and kissed his cheek. He leaned into her kiss and sighed. He was asleep again before she had left the room.

When Joe arrived, Char took the elevator down to ICU to see Caleb before she left the hospital. The elevator bumped and pinged and opened and closed on its way down from the fifth floor to second floor. Char closed her eyes thinking about how pale Caleb had been last night, the side of his face black and blue and puffy, beneath a tight, wide band. He'd been unconscious and on a respirator.

Char had talked to Caleb during the night as he lay unconscious. She told him all kinds of good things about their recent Thanksgiving together and about other times she remembered, when she gave him his eighteenth month sobriety medallion, stories he had told about his sister, and his mom and dad. She'd finally fallen asleep for a few hours, resting her head on the edge of the bed.

When Char arrived at Caleb's room, he was coming to with a murderous headache. A nurse was leaning over him, and Willow was standing a few feet away from him. He was blinking his eyes against the light of the room.

Char rushed up to him, "Caleb, do you know who I am?"

He shook his head slightly, indicating no, he didn't know who she was. He looked frightened, his eyes wildly shifting left and right.

Willow moved closer to the bed, "Caleb, do you know who I am?" she asked.

He nodded slightly yes and lifted his hand a little, she thought he wanted her to hold his hand. She moved closer to his side and took his hand. His restlessness subsided.

"Who am I, Caleb?" she asked. They had removed his breathing tube. His throat was raw and dry and he croaked when he tried to speak. Char spooned a few ice chips into his mouth. He swallowed, still trying to look at Willow.

"Who am I?" she asked again.

"You're my girlfriend," he croaked and closed his eyes again.

Char and Willow looked at each other and grinned.

"Wishful thinking," Char whispered to her granddaughter.

"I'll stay here until I'm relieved," Willow volunteered.

"Thanks," Char said, "I want a hot shower and a good nap. We'll have turkey and dressing sandwiches whenever you get home."

"I brought a good book to read, '*The History of Civilization,*' that should keep me going for a few years. Actually, I need to be done with it by next week."

"Good idea, move your chair closer to him, it doesn't hurt to hold his hand while you read. Where is the car?"

JOE SETTLED INTO JAMES' room and turned on a Wild hockey game keeping the sound low. James slept for over an hour, then woke up and propped himself up, feeling more alert.

"How's the body doing?" Joe asked conversationally.

"Oh, I'm going to live. I'm weaker than I thought I'd be after that last nap. But I'll be OK. What do you want from me?"

"You know we aren't leaving you until we get you someplace safe?"

"So, I've heard. I'm not much entertainment, I'm tired."

"That's OK. The Wild are playing the Blues. It's a good rivalry; OK with you?"

"Anything you want. Mom and I watched a lot of Wild games back when I lived at home. Actually, I'm starting to get hungry. I was out all night getting people killed."

"You bragging or complaining?"

"Just giving the facts, I guess."

"Stop it then. That's a line of self-pity I don't want to hear."

'Here it comes,' thought James.

"It's not like I haven't been there myself, lying in a bed like you, wishing I were dead. At least I had a single room." Joe motioned to the man behind the curtain, "That would be me, today, if someone hadn't taken the time to visit me in the hospital, fifteen years ago. I'd been beat up bad, but I deserved it. I'd done the same to my wife."

James looked at him in astonishment. "You beat up Char?"

"No, my first wife. She's a good woman, a beautiful woman. She was young, not as strong as Char, but I'm sure she has come into her own by now. No matter how strong she was, no one can fight back a drunk when the monster comes out in him. But no, I've never laid a hand on Char in anger. People can change, James. I changed."

James laid his head back on the pillow. "Who's in here to change?" He pointed to himself and said: "How do I change when I don't know who I am?"

"Sleep if you want, James. I'm not going anywhere," Joe looked at the hockey game again, James watched for a while then closed his eyes and slept again.

Willow casually held Caleb's hand while he slept. She read and watched him sleep, breathing in and out. She wanted to reach up and give him a soft kiss, he was so vulnerable in the narrow, white hospital bed. She had watched him on Thanksgiving. He was vital, alert, his dark eyes darting back and forth as he watched and enjoyed the warm family gathering. She was beginning to understand men, now, after dating James. She'd been awakened to men's sexual energy and was able to read the tell-tale signs of Caleb's interest in her. Gram really liked this man, Caleb, and Willow was drawn to him too.

Willow left after sitting with Caleb for nearly eight hours. He had slept and been rousted about and examined. She had fed him broth and a little ice cream. He held her hand as often as he could and looked so sad when she left.

When Carmen arrived, she talked to him about their Thanksgiving. He remembered her and had a smile for her, too. He cried out in the night several times. Carmen wiped his brow, smoothed his hair, fed him ice and held his hand.

IN THE MORNING, Ellen and James came to see Caleb.

James started crying when he saw how awful Caleb looked and tears over-flowed Caleb's eyes too.

James wiped his eyes on his fists and said smiling, "I didn't think you were as big a wuss as I am."

"I'm not, you be the baby," Caleb responded, pointing at James.

"You be the baby," James responded, pointing back at Caleb.

Then James strode over to Caleb and put both arms around him and tucked his head below Caleb's chin and squeezed his friend tight.

Caleb said, "Enough already." James stood back and grinned at his friend thinking, we've been close friends for over a year and we've never hugged each other.

"I guess I was making up for never hugging you," James said.

"What are you talking about?" asked Caleb.

"Man, I love you."

MANDEL EPSTEIN ARRIVED about noon on Sunday, Sandra was sitting with Caleb.

Sandra watched Caleb's father kiss his son over and over. Caleb cried in his father's arms. She appreciated Mandel's warmth and compassion. Sandra called Ralph and they agreed that Mandel would stay with them while he was in St. Paul.

Caleb remained in the hospital for nearly a week longer than

James. Willow, Char, and Carmen took turns with Mandel staying in Caleb's room. Willow was reading Caleb chapters of "The History of Civilization". Caleb was into the book and planned to buy his own copy when he got out of the hospital.

Sandra helped Mandel clean out Caleb's room and pack his things. Caleb would complete his semester online from New York and stay at his mother's place while he recuperated from his injuries and surgery. He wanted to go back to outpatient treatment, too. Char and Willow promised to take all his new plants and find homes for them.

Ralph was too angry to visit James but he was more than gracious to Mandel, chauffeuring Mandel to the hospital and talked to Caleb's surgeon with him and helped make connections for continued medical care in New York.

Chuck never went back to the hospital. Ralph was fearful that Chuck might be on the 'hit list' too and forbade Chuck from being seen with either James or Caleb. But Chuck and James talked on the phone often and they were fine with each other.

ON JAMES' discharge, Ellen and Carmen brought James over to Char and Joe's. Joe and Willow made brunch for everyone. James' appetite was returning and he piled his plate with eggs and bacon and pancakes.

Although Willow had visited James in the hospital, they hadn't really talked. After brunch, Willow invited him up to her room and they sat on her bed and hugged. Willow looked searchingly into his face and he cried yet again. They both laid down on her bed and snuggled together, Willow comforted him and held him tight, thinking she'd like to do the same with Caleb.

When Char came home early afternoon, she called up to Willow and James to come back downstairs. Then she dug out a notepad and pen and asked James to list his worries and brainstorm ideas about how to handle his worries. He asked if he could take a nap first. Char agreed that would be a good idea and walked him up to the guest bedroom. Willow packed up her books to visit Caleb in the hospital.

While James napped, Sandra arrived with a hot dish and unbaked yeast rolls from her freezer to pop in the oven. Char, Sandra, Carmen and Ellen sat in the dining room visiting while Joe sat in the sunroom watching hockey again. Carmen kept looking at the sunroom until Ellen said, "Join him Carmen, you don't have to sit with the women." Carmen gave her a grateful look and joined Joe in the sunroom.

"Before you fill me in, sisters," Sandra asked, "I'm filling you in about Ralph. He's rageful about James and Chuck's adventures and, rightfully, James and Caleb's drug use. He'll come around, but right now he's full of 'what if's'. I've been keeping an eye on him; he started hyperventilating and pulling at his shirt collar when we got home from the hospital Friday night. I was afraid he was having a heart attack. He assured me he wasn't."

Char and Ellen both grabbed Sandra's hands and Char quickly looked into the sun room to make sure Joe was OK.

Sandra pushed her friends' hand away, "Don't worry about Ralph, he'll be fine, he's watching TV. His Minnesota sports teams will give him a heart attack before Chuck and James do."

Ellen went next. "I sort of wish James would get out of town; Mandel suggested James stay with him in New York. James said he wanted nothing of New York. This is terrible to say, but at least James' dealer is out of the picture."

Char looked askance at Ellen, even Sandra gulped with surprise that Ellen would say that.

James came down from his nap, looking at the notes he had written. He stopped in his tracks seeing Char, Ellen, and Sandra sitting together around Char's oak table. The women had agreed not to all talk at once, to maintain decorum, but seeing James, Sandra jumped up and nearly smothered him in hugs.

"Come, sit with us," Char said, staring askance at Sandra. James hesitated, wondering who to sit by but decided to move a chair around so all the women faced him and weren't close enough to grab at him. He slid his list over to Char. "Here's the list of things that are worrying me."

Char quickly read the list, nodding her head:

1. Safety – where to live – Jerome's? Are they going to go after me?
2. Classes – finish the semester online?
3. My place – settle with the landlord, move things out.
4. Do I really need treatment? Can't I go to AA or NA instead?
5. What to do about the dealers who killed Randall? I heard the shots that killed Randall, I know the names of a couple of the dealers and probably one of the bosses. What should I do with that information? Randall before he died, on the phone, said 'don't go to the police!'

"I like this list, James," Char told him as she passed it onto the others.

"Have you called Jerome again?" Ellen asked.

"Jerome is ready for me to come to his place. He is excited in fact. I told him the truth, about the drugs and about almost getting killed. It fed right into his world of paranoia, and he is planning how I can get into his place without anyone seeing me and all that stuff. Do you think you should call his mother before we put this on him, Mom?"

Ellen, who had been Jerome's therapist when he was young had already thought about this. "His Asperger's doesn't classify him as a vulnerable adult, it's up to you two, but James, you have to be very sensitive to Jerome's particularities. Do you realize what that entails?"

"I think so, Jerome and I have a rhythm, he was excited about having me stay with him."

"Do you mind if I call Annie, his mom, and see what she thinks?" Ellen asked.

"Jerome told me he was going to talk to his mother today, so mother to mother is fine with me," James agreed and added, "I'll make it as safe as possible for Jerome. I'll follow his protocol for coming to his place, and we already agreed we wouldn't be seen together. His high rise has six floors and four entrances. It's huge. I'll be careful. How does that sound, everybody?"

"You're the psychologist, Ellen, if you're comfortable with it, so am I," Sandra said and looked to Char, who nodded her assent.

"Have you thought about leaving town James? Wouldn't that be better?" Ellen asked.

"I thought about it, Mom," James answered, "I thought about the lying I'd be doing, being on the run, looking over my shoulder, I'd be getting even more paranoid, I'd be lonely. No, I'd like to try it here, be careful here, does that make sense?"

They all looked at Char. Char nodded her assent. "Joe has already volunteered to help with the move out of the apartment. Elliot and Ron will help too, make sure it is safe to go in there. Maybe a couple of us could help with the move too. What do you think, gals?" Char asked.

"I'll volunteer Carmen and I," Ellen replied, "We have the day off tomorrow; we can put everything down the basement, most of it in James' room."

Sandra jumped in, "James, you better not come to any of our houses for a while. Are you OK with that?"

James squirmed, sitting at the table as three women decided his fate. "I agree," he said. "I don't want anyone else getting hurt because of me."

"Item 2," Char began, "This might entice you to go to CD treatment. You can explain to Augsburg that you're in treatment and not able to go to the last weeks of class and maybe work something out to finish your finals. You're almost done with this semester, aren't you?"

James stroked his chin, flecked off a few crumbs from the tablecloth, rubbed his ear. He didn't want to go to treatment, be brainwashed by quacks. Finally, he looked up at the three women's attentive faces, was there no way out?"

He shrugged his shoulders, looked downcast and nodded, "OK, I'll give treatment a try."

Char jumped in, "I loved treatment. It was hard, facing your demons is always hard, but it was so inspirational. If you're willing to go to treatment, Joe said you could have a kitchen job at the Cafe."

James rolled his eyes looking through the doorways at Joe roosting on his big chair watching a hockey game with Carmen. Ellen changed the subject, "You had better not be around when we clean out your apartment"

"OK, throw away the chairs if they're damaged. But I hope the table is OK, it's all in the family." James tried for a light note, but three serious faces stared back at him.

"I guess it isn't funny, huh?" he added looking down at his hands, blood on my hands, he thought.

"What about the last item, the dealers, any ideas?" James asked, steering away from the repugnant idea of treatment and sobriety.

"I've got some ideas," Sandra offered. "I'd like to do a little undercover work, stalk them."

Everyone wordlessly turned to Sandra, looking her up and down.

"We got to do something! These guys can't just get away with this. Our boys nearly died; Chuck put himself in danger, too." Sandra said sharply.

"Ladies and gentleman, 'Revenge is a life well lived.'" Char said with a snap of her fist into her palm. There was general agreement with that edict.

"I guess you got my life set out for me," James said with resignation.

41 / CHOOSE LOVE NOT FEAR

Two weeks after the overdoses, James had started work at Joe's Café. One snowy slow day at Joe's, James was cleaning up a table near the front entrance and took a minute to look out the big front window. Randall's top lieutenant D stood across the street, under the wide striped awning of the Wright Wing bicycle shop.

James closed his eyes hoping he was having a hallucination. The past weeks, he repeatedly thought he saw people from his traumatic past, then he'd look again, and find he was mistaken. He looked out the window again, this time it was D, the man was looking right at him. James had a full-blown panic attack. All his senses shut down, he couldn't see straight, he heard waves of sound, his heart raced, his esophagus closed, he choked trying to breath. He stumbled to a chair and almost fell off of it. Danielle rushed over to him and yelled for Joe.

They half carried him into the storage room, and sat him on a stool. Joe sent Danielle out and told her to close the door. Joe squatted in front of James, putting both sets of hands on James' knees. He breathed slowly with James, whispering to him "breathe in, breathe out, listen to me." When James was breathing evenly, Joe released his hands and patted his back.

"What happened James, can you talk to me?" Joe asked.

"Across the street, it's Randall's guy just standing there. I'm sure he was looking right at me. I got to run," James said and tried to stand up but he was woozy and sat back down on the stool.

"Are you able to sit here, by yourself? You need to gather your strength slowly. I got something to do, can you promise to stay here for a few minutes? Give yourself as long as you need, come out when you're ready."

James shrugged his shoulders and nodded, "OK, I'll be OK.",

In the already familiar storage room with shelves of red, gold, and black labeled cans and the bright freezer humming behind him, James felt safe enough to start thinking again. It was the eve of his twenty-first birthday. He wondered if this was the day that he died. He felt sorry for himself. He felt defenseless. Twenty minutes later he walked out of the storage room. The staff scurried around taking care of business and ignoring him.

Joe walked over to him and motioned for him to follow out the back door. They stood in the cold snowy air in their shirt sleeves, letting the wind bellow their shirts and sweeten their smell. James leaned against the brick. It felt good to be out of the overly warm kitchen. It felt good to shiver. Joe told James what he'd done.

"I had a conversation with your friend across the street. I told him you almost had a heart attack when you saw him. I told him that you said you owed his boss a lot of money. I just made that up, what do you think of that?"

James frowned, "I never said that, you lied to him, now he'll kill me." James balled his fists and shivered some more.

"Listen to me," Joe said and took James' fists and opened them. "I know this kind of guy. He wants to know what I know and I put him off track by telling him I thought it was about a debt. That's not so illegal, owing money, well sort of if you go to a loan shark, but it is acceptable to guys like me, much more acceptable than drugs are, it would make sense that he is watching you, making you be accountable."

"Then I said that I didn't want no trouble at my restaurant, that you were a good worker, quiet, but I'd get rid of you today if you were trouble for my business."

D said, "As long as he pays up there won't be any trouble from us."

Now James understood, "Oh, you lied for me. Do you think he believed you, Joe? I don't want trouble for the Cafe. I better quit." James half turned away from Joe.

Joe grabbed his arm and spun him around. "I talked to D like that so the drug dealers would think you and I aren't close, so they'll think I don't care what the hell is going on with you."

James watched Joe as he talked. He could have been talking about the weather, he didn't seem at all afraid of these guys. "Joe, am I a fool to be so scared of these guys?" he asked.

"No, they're scary. It's hard to know what they got going. They killed Randall and tried to kill Caleb and you. This guy sounded like they weren't going to hurt you if you 'took care of business.' I think he means keep quiet about what happened, these guys don't want to start killing randomly, now he knows I could identify him, is he going to kill me, too? Then what if I talked to someone? How many people can they kill?"

James' eyes teared, "You've been good to me and now you could be killed. Aren't you scared? Now how can I live with that?"

"Keep your nose clean, James. Work your program. Learn what you can change and what you can't. If you can't do that, move out of town for a few years. That's probably the safest option. But don't worry about me. I learned the hard way, James, but I learned it well. Choose love over fear, James. A life well lived is the best revenge."

James looked at Joe with amazement. He reached out to shake

Joe's hand and holding his hand said, "I'll keep my nose clean, Joe, I will."

James thought about it again, later. There were pluses and minuses to running. It was maybe the easy way, maybe the safest way, but somewhere inside he feared running, he feared he'd never stop running and never stop being afraid.

For several weeks Randall's men, D and Sammy, and some other guys James didn't recognize, blatantly sat in a running car several stores down from the restaurant. Then nothing, but James remained anxious whenever men of a certain age followed him too close or loitered in his vicinity, or when cars approached too slowly, or when men sat in cars along the curb with their engines running, but no one approached him and slowly his panic attacks subsided, but his paranoia remained.

PART 5
NEW BEGINNINGS

42 / OK, OK, I'LL GO

Four weeks out of the hospital, working at Joe's Café part-time and settled in Jerome's extra room, James started treatment. He'd stayed sober before treatment except for a few roaches he'd found in his clothes. He was tempted to take up smoking cigarettes or vape, just to suck smoke down his lungs, but he knew how that would work; he'd be hooked on tobacco in a flash.

Luckily for him, his withdrawal from heroin wasn't severe. Some of the guys he met in treatment walked around like zombies, trying to get past the craving for a rush of heroin.

James balked when Char and Joe recommended that he go to a private, expensive, inpatient treatment. His anxiety about being in any lock up kicked in, and he wouldn't agree to it. James didn't care who he was in treatment with. He wanted evening out-patient treatment, and he was more than willing to work at Joe's Café during the days.

He announced he'd rather take his chance with court than go to inpatient treatment. Char knew what the court would recommend, the county's ten-week outpatient treatment for drug offenders.

Although the program was housed in a new facility, the population they treated was mostly hardened offenders.

The outpatient treatment was ten weeks of monitored sobriety; four evenings a week of treatment, drug and alcohol testing weekly, and attendance of NA or AA weekly. The four nights of treatment consisted of an hour of lecture for nearly fifty clients and an additional two hours of small group process.

Walking into his first treatment, James felt superior to these suffering souls; he'd been a member of something like a cartel. He knew how to shoot dope, he'd had sex with a prostitute, and he was still a college honor student.

That first night, after the informational lecture for the full group of maybe forty people, James was ushered into a smaller group of ten men ranging in age from 17 to about 50.

James and two other guys were new to the small group. They jiggled their legs quietly together, a little apart from the rest of the group. The counselor, an ageless bearded guy, introduced himself as Howard. He asked the seasoned guys to introduce themselves to the new guys by telling a little about themselves.

As James sat jiggling with the newbies, he half listened to what they had to say, assigning them nicknames from the Seven Dwarfs.

Dave was the first to speak and the oldest in the group. He'd been a pharmacist. James labeled him 'Doc'. This was Dave's fourth treatment. His family had given up on him, and he'd given up on himself, too, but he ended by saying he still planned to give this treatment an honest try.

Next was Aiden, the youngest. James labeled him 'Bashful.' Aiden was a pretty boy, raised in and out of foster care and was living on the streets by the time he was fifteen. He had 'pro–pro–prostituted' himself for drugs. One of the new guys started chortling as Aiden began sputtering out his story. The old group members gave the new guy a wall of disapproval that sent chills down James' spine.

"Grumpy" was a perfect nickname for the explosively angry meth-head named Henry. Skinny, with long dark hair and blue jailhouse tattoos, he wore a short-sleeved shirt that exposed his needle marked inner arms. His dark eyes darted around the room, daring anyone to really look at him. He told his action story of falling asleep, stoned on uppers, while driving an oil tanker, spinning, and nearly blowing up suburban Bloomington. James kept his eyes down when Henry talked.

By the fourth or fifth guy, James had quit labeling and sat still, leaning forward to listen to their stories. They'd made drugs a way through life—most of them started using very young and had been in trouble with their addictions and the law before turning twenty. Some had more college than James had.

On the way back to Jerome's that first night after treatment, he stopped at a McDonald's and used the washroom. When he looked at his face in the mirror, he saw the same grim face as the rest of the guys he'd met at treatment.

What they had in common, and they had a lot in common, was the drudgery of daily or near daily use to intoxication and negative consequence after consequence from that use—neglect and harm to other people, as well as to themselves.

James thought about Randall, Angie, and Caleb—even the tears of his mother kept running through his head. He didn't pull the trigger, but his insane, selfish behavior had directly led to Randall's death, Angie's beating, and Caleb's awful ordeal.

But the consequences to him? Not even his semester at college was lost. He was allowed to quickly finish his classes online. These guys were train wrecks by comparison. What were the consequences to James?

At first, James embellished his story. He'd almost been killed, hadn't he? But as the weeks went by, he recognized his own bullshit, his lies and half-truths and his attempts to aggrandize and then demean himself. Lying had become a way of life for him.

After the first week, James recognized it was decision time. Go with the flow, pretend, make it through the classes, or walk the walk, take it seriously and learn. With the support of Caleb and their frequent communication, texting and calling each other, James decided to take treatment seriously. Caleb was back in treatment, full time; he'd been reluctantly into inpatient but due to his slow recovery from brain surgery, he wasn't given a choice.

One of James' treatment assignments was called 'The Life Line.' The first night of treatment, the new guys stayed after the group, and Howard explained the 'life line' to them.

Each of them was given a journal of blank pages with a line through the middle of each page. They put ages they were examining on the top of page (one-five, six-ten, junior high, etc. whatever worked for them) on the top half of the page they filled in the facts about those years of their lives: who they had lived with, where they lived, and what were their daily activities, just the facts. Below the line, they wrote significant events and memories from those years. Finally, at the bottom, was one question: What followed you from these years? The Life Line stayed at the treatment center; they had half an hour in group to work on it several times a week.

Howard read their Life Lines between groups, wrote some feedback, and lastly, gave them opportunities to share from their Life Lines during group.

The life line revealed so much about the all the group members. James listened with rapt attention; broken homes, broken bones, broken promises.

"I love you guys," slipped out of James' mouth one night. He got a nickname, 'lover boy'.

During a phone chat with Caleb, James explained the Life Line to him. Caleb thought it was a great idea and started doing a Life Line of his own. James, asked him how it was going a few weeks later. Caleb reminisced about spending time at the nursing home with his great-grandfather and grandfather when he was about five or six. His great-grandfather talked about the work camp he was in during WWII and then about the Holocaust that killed six million Jews.

Caleb deduced that this was when he started developing his apocalyptic fears for the future. Even in grade school, he read about the holocaust and was the fascinated and horrified. Caleb decided to do more reading about generational grief and trauma. Perhaps a few sessions with a Jewish therapist could help him and his family as well.

Caleb's insights motivated James to look harder into his early memories. The loss of his father, who he'd loved and who had another family now in California. Then moving next door to Sandra's family, becoming half Sandra's kid—all this this when he was pre-school.

The fights with his mother started when he didn't want to come home from Sandra's for dinner. He liked his anonymity in Sandra's family. He was just one of the kids, not the center of the universe like he was with his mother. Then, in his early teens, his early marijuana use coincided with his huge crush on Laurel. He remembered how anxious and secretive he'd been, sneaking out of the house and peeking in Laurel's bedroom window, lying to everyone about his feelings. Then, when he was 18, that one sexual experience with Laurel coincided with upping his marijuana use dramatically. Was it a coincidence that when he met Willow, he started using heroin? That was a connection he hadn't made before; his tangled feelings for women coinciding with his heaviest use of drugs.

HOWARD ENCOURAGED his clients to set up a family session during their ten weeks of treatment. James decided to set up a family meeting with just Ellen. He knew Sandra would want to be included, but he feared the two mothers would make it more about them than about James.

Ellen picked James up at Joe's Café, and she drove them to the treatment center. They were silent for the most part, Ellen paying rapt attention to driving in the rush hour traffic and James wondering if he had the guts to be honest with his mother.

Ellen head jerked back in shock when she saw the big sign outside the anonymous building, "Ramsey County Diversion Program" and in smaller print "All Are Welcome Here." James watched her. She seemed so small. He hadn't noticed her small size when he was growing up; she'd seemed big to him.

Howard came to the bullet proof front desk and welcomed them both. He offered tea or coffee or a soft drink. Ellen started to shake her head no but then acknowledged her throat was a little dry and asked for a Diet Coke. James wanted one, too.

While Howard got their drinks, Ellen lightly patted James' knee. "Thank you for asking me to meet with you and your counselor. He seems nice," she added.

James nodded, acknowledged that Howard was nice but then rolled his shoulders and cracked his neck. He felt defensive.

"I'm scared, Mom. I've lied to you so much—jeez, I don't know how to tell you the truth."

Howard was gentle. He'd heard James saying he scared to tell the truth and he started with that.

"If you did know how to tell the truth, what would you say to your mother?"

James scratched his hair and shook his head. He found it impossible to talk with the fear that had built up.

Howard encouraged him to take his time, relax, breath.

Finally James let it out, how he couldn't live up to her exacting measures, how small she could make him feel, how sharp her words could be.

Ellen wept. James squirmed, jiggled his knees.

Howard asked, "Do you genuinely care for each other?"

They looked at each and nodded.

"I'd do anything I can for you James," Ellen said.

James looked down when she said that, thinking that she'd do anything but accept him as he was. Then he wondered if he was being too critical of her. He remained silent.

"Can you tell me how you'd like me to do different?" she asked.

He gathered his thoughts and said, "Can you handle my truth? Can I stop lying, can you listen to me without being so judgmental?"

"I try to listen James. What do I do wrong?"

"You treat me like a client! You don't get involved in our conversations. It's like, like I'm a client. I want to be honest with you but I need you to talk about yourself too. It isn't a one way street, here and I need to know you won't quit loving me if I'm honest, tell you things you don't like hearing from me." He mumbled the last words.

"I get anxious James. I feel like I'm a better therapist." Then her words raced together…"I'mnotagoodmother."

"You are Mom, you are a good mother."

"I can try to not get all anxious, try to listen to you without judgement. I'll admit that sometimes I get bossy and act like a 'know it all.' That's my fear coming out. Maybe you could help me and comment when I get that way." Ellen listened to her own words and a quick smile passed over her lips. "You aren't the only one who has commented on how bossy I can get when I'm anxious."

The session went on for a while but the work was done. Ellen had heard him.

On their drive back, Ellen drove carefully with a smile on her face when she turned for quick glances at James.

James chuckled. Good for you, Carmen, he thought.

43 / FEBRUARY THAW

Anticipation of a winter thaw always grew to a fever pitch in Minnesota. This year the populous feared the thaw had skipped the region. Then on February 27, the temperature shot up from the middle teens to the mid-40s. College kids ran around in shorts and tee shirts, playing Frisbee in the street and on the crusty snow. Rivets of melted snow ran down the streets, forming wide puddles on the corners and giving fast, careless drivers the opportunity to spray old ladies waiting at the bus stops.

During the thaw, Sandra had called her sister half hysterical to report that Laurel had arrived at her house with bags packed. She had left Brian. She hadn't even called to say she was coming; she just walked into her parents' house with Roy in tow, fell into her father's arms, and cried.

"Damn it," Char swore looking down at her pant legs. She'd been sprayed waiting to transfer buses. She was riding the bus to leave a smaller 'footprint' on the earth and also because she had given Willow her car two weeks ago. Willow had accepted a grant to study dance in Chicago, and Char was letting Willow use her car to get the lay of the land in her new city. Willow was staying in a youth hostel and already practicing with the troupe.

Char was bussing to St. Louis Park for lunch with Sandra and Laurel. She had an idea for Laurel's housing in mind.

Laurel was waiting for Char in the living room and jumped up when the doorbell rang. After hugs and helping Char with her jacket, Laurel noticed Char's pant legs were wet and laughed, teasing her aunt. "What happened?"

"What do you think?" Char answered, rolling her eyes dramatically. "I'm taking the bus nowadays; Willow has my car in Chicago."

Laurel chuckled. "Have you lost your mass transit edge, Auntie Char? You have to anticipate the cars and leap out of the way when they splash by."

"I'm too old to play dodge ball. After this long bus ride, I think I'll look for another used car and let Willow keep mine. Laurel took her jacket and hung it with her tote bag on a hook in the foyer.

"Where's your mother, Laurel?"

"She's in the kitchen feeding Roy; we'll eat and talk about adult things while he takes his nap."

Char went into the kitchen to hug her sister and Roy; Laurel followed. Char turned back to Laurel and asked, "How do you like staying with your folks?"

Laurel and Sandra slid glances at each other. "I'd like my own place with Roy."

Char had an idea she couldn't wait to share. "Laurel you should ask Ellen if you can stay at her empty house right next door. Ellen lives at Carmen's house, although she is shy about it. But the house is empty and, as you probably know, James can't come home."

"Do you think Ellen would let me use her house?" Laurel asked her mother.

"Why not ask her? I'm almost sure she would love having you there."

"But doesn't James think he has rights over the house? He wouldn't want me there."

Sandra butted in. "What is it with you and James? He'd be OK having you two living there. You should know that."

"Mother, stop it. You don't know what James thinks. I just meant he has to give me his consent, too; he might be planning to move back."

"Laurel," Sandra said. "Believe me for once. Ellen and James will help you out. Dad and I would be so happy to have Roy and you next door. It would be so handy; you could drop Roy over here in the evening when you start classes or anytime."

Sandra's oven beeper went off. "We can eat lunch in about ten minutes. You two keep talking."

"James is nearly done with his outpatient treatment," Char said. "He goes to AA and NA meetings and has asked Joe to be his AA sponsor after his treatment is done. You probably know James works at Joe's Café. He does whatever is needed in the kitchen or dining room, no complaints. Joe says he's great. I think it's been great for Joe to have James around. With Willow in Chicago, we both miss having a kid around."

Laurel nodded her empathy about Willow leaving home. "I'm sure you miss Willow. I've only met her a few times, but we had a little chat at Thanksgiving and we are on the same page."

"Remember when we talked several months ago?" Laurel asked Char.

Char nodded that she remembered the conversation.

"I told you I wasn't happy in our vanilla McMansion and dreamed about living in a smaller, more intimate space."

"I remember that, Laurel."

Sandra spoke up, "Roy is ready to go down for his nap."

Char answered, "Just a minute—I forgot—I bought something for Roy."

Char swept up Roy, carried him to her tote bag, and searched for a little red plastic car. She showed him that the wheels spun and the doors opened. Roy climbed over her arm to grab his new car.

He happily took his new car into the bedroom with Laurel to take a nap.

Char went back into the kitchen to talk to Sandra. She picked up a stalk of celery to chew on, swallowed, and asked her sister, "Sandra, how are you holding up? You seem tired."

"I am. Tired of keeping my mouth shut around Laurel. She can be so irritating, so critical of me, but her father can do no wrong."

"Sandra, you're going to have to try a different approach with your daughter," Char said. "Do something about this impasse between the two of you."

Sandra looked darkly at her sister. "Why me? She's the one who is angry."

"Well, you are the one who is suffering, Sandra. Get some advice. Find another way to work this out with Laurel."

"I don't even know where to start. It's been going on since she was a teenager and is worse now that we are in such close proximity." Sandra answered before turning toward her sister and whispering, "I'm so afraid she will up and leave us and take Roy away from me. I love the little boy, Char. I'm scared.

"Maybe you could bring it up at your Al anon meeting," Char said casually.

Sandra was uncharacteristically quiet during the three women's lunch.

Before she left, Char issued orders to Laurel to call both Ellen and James about the house.

44 / JAMES MAKES AMENDS

Later that day, Ellen called James on his burner. "Hi James, how are you doing?" Ellen asked.

"Better every day, Mom—I guess. Are you calling about me finishing treatment and getting my three-month sobriety medallion? I'm finished with outpatient next Thursday. Sunday next, I receive my three-month sobriety medallion from Joe at our AA meeting. It is an open meeting, and I'd like it if you and Carmen would come to the meeting. Is it stupid of me to ask a bunch of people to come? I've already asked Char."

"It makes me happy to be included, James. We'll be there, with bells on. Thank you so much for asking us. I'm smiling big time, right now. It is up to you, of course, but Sandra would really like to come, too. Char already told her about it, and she asked me if I was going. I said I hadn't heard anything about it from you."

"Sure—Sandra should come. I'll contact her. This isn't just about me. It's about the people who have helped me make it this far. I love you guys. The dishes are piling up here at the Cafe. Is that what you called me about?"

"Oh, no. I wouldn't call and ask to be invited. No, this is about a call from Laurel. Do you know she is separated from Brian?" Ellen asked.

"Laurel?" James paused, "separated from Brian? No, who would tell me that? Why did Laurel call you?"

"She wants to stay in our house for a while. I'm just pretending that I still live there; I'll admit to you, James, I am living with Carmen, but I've got this sense of decorum, you know me."

"Does any other family use that word 'decorum' as much as our family does?" James said with a laugh.

"I'm not sure, James. Anyway, she is staying with her mother and dad. They love having her, but she and Sandra have their issues. Laurel would like her own place with Roy. She is facing many of the financial and emotional challenges I did when my marriage to your father failed. Laurel has already registered to start a graduate class. She wants to work with special needs children. Does that sound like anyone you know?"

James laughed. "You, Mom."

"Personally, I'd love to let her use our house," Ellen confided, "and I don't care if we let her live there free. But all that is up to you. I asked her to call you. I told her I had no idea if you planned to move back there anytime soon. I'd like you to decide if you want to charge her rent. As soon as I pay off the mortgage, and I've just got a few years left on it, the house becomes yours."

"Mom," James started, "I'm not letting you just give me the house."

"It'll be a few years, but that is my plan." Ellen said.

James remained silent; he didn't know what to say.

"Anyway," Ellen continued, "I wouldn't have even brought that up if Laurel wasn't asking to use the house. I thought you'd want a 'heads up' that she is going to call you. Tell her the truth—if you want to hold the house for yourself, tell her."

James laughed, "You don't have to stand on 'decorum' for me. I am not thinking of the house as mine. But if you want my approval about her moving in, you have it. I really have to go now, Mom. Talk to you later about the AA meeting, OK?"

As James went about putting the dishes through the dishwasher, his hands were shaky. He almost laughed at himself. It was scary to think of talking to Laurel. He took a few deep breaths. It's OK he told himself. It's OK to have feelings.

When he caught up on the dishes, he took a little break outside. Leaning against the brick wall, he listened to himself breathe for a minute and watched a little bare branched tree fighting to survive in the urban alley. Then he prayed: "God, grant me the serenity to accept the things I cannot change…"

Returning to the kitchen, he efficiently slammed things into place and kept busy until his shift was over.

On the bus ride to treatment, his cell buzzed. He picked it up and answered, "Yeah—this is James."

"Is this you or a recording?" the familiar voice asked him.

"It's me, Laurel. My mom called and said you were going to call."

"She didn't tell you what to say to me, did she?"

"Hell, no. You know Ellen, Ms. Honest. Hey, we haven't talked for years, but I know what you are calling about. I don't plan to leave Jerome's for months and even then, I'm not sure I want to go back to my mom's place. I'd love it if you and Roy stayed in the house." His knees bounced, and his shoulders hunched over the phone as he watched the bus go over the freeway. It was getting dark, and the cars were turning on their lights. In the half-minute he watched, the freeway began to glow. His stomach growled, waiting for her to answer him.

"Thanks, James. It means a lot. The last few months have been rough on all of us, Roy, me, and Brian, too. Anyway, Brian and I are going in different directions, and I like the idea of living in your lovely small house with Roy."

"Nothing lovely about the house but having you there would

change that. Oh, oh, I'm just teasing you. I've enjoyed watching him grow from a distance."

"We're all drawn to him. Brian loves him, too. He wants to be a good father. It'll be good if they can build a relationship separate from me."

She's talking to me, telling me about herself, Holy Shit! James thought. Calming himself, he stopped himself from jumping in with another wisecrack.

Laurel became silent. Had he been listening well? He wasn't sure.

"Thanks for sharing with me—I mean it," James said.

Again, there was a silence, and James' anxiety was building.

"Thanks, James." More silence.

"I'll try to get over there, maybe Monday and consolidate all my stuff to the basement room, OK?"

"I will be out that night; Mom and Dad will be watching Roy. I might be home late."

James responded, "That's good, I mean that's OK. I'll call Sandra, maybe drop over at your folks' place too, if it's OK with Ralph."

"Goodbye." Whew, James said to himself.

"Goodbye." Whew, Laurel said to herself.

When James was safely back at Jerome's after treatment, he warmed up some burritos from the Café for both of them, and, while they ate, he shared the news about Laurel moving into the house. Jerome was the only one who knew the whole story about James' history with Laurel. He hadn't been able to confide in any of the family when the sex thing happened three years ago."

Later, James went into his room and put in a call to Sandra's cell. Ralph answered.

"Hello—it's James." James hadn't talked to Ralph since the heroin overdoses. There was a pregnant pause. Here it comes, James thought. But still, Ralph didn't respond.

James finally said, "I meant to call Sandra. I didn't want to talk to you for the first time by phone, Ralph. I want to apologize to both of you in person. I'd like to stop by. I'll be very careful not to be followed. They aren't following me anymore, anyway, but I'm still very careful." He stopped himself from rambling on.

Ralph cleared his throat, "I'm in my study in the basement. Sandra left her phone here by accident. That would be fine, James. When were you thinking of coming over?"

"Would Monday evening work? Mom called and told me Laurel wants to use her house, and I want to get all my stuff consolidated into one room so she can move in. I am fine with Laurel and Roy living there." James omitted his conversation with Laurel.

"I'll check with Sandra." James was put on hold. It had been several minutes, and James was just about to hang up when Ralph came back on the line.

"Sorry about the hold, James. I had to wind around the house to find her. All the grandkids are visiting. Now James could hear little kids in the background.

"If you want to find a better time..." James started but was interrupted.

"No, let's get it over with. I've cooled off. You come over Monday evening; Sandra wants to feed you."

"She doesn't have to do that. I can't arrive until after treatment, so I won't get there until about 9 p.m." James thought he wouldn't have much appetite over at their house any more.

"OK, I'll explain to Sandra—Oh, here she is."

Sandra grabbed the phone. "You can't come for dinner?" She sounded disappointed.

"I'm just finishing my treatment; it goes until about 8, so I can't be there until 9. But I'd love to see you, Sandra, even if it is just for a few minutes. Then I'd like to go next door and put all my stuff into my old room downstairs so Laurel and Roy can have the whole house, except for that room."

"Sounds good," Sandra answered.

"Oh, by the way, I'm also calling to ask you if you would please come to my AA meeting a week from Sunday."

Monday evening, getting off of the bus in St. Louis Park after treatment, James walked the quiet parallel streets to Sandra and Ralph's house. He enjoyed walking in his old neighborhood. He was feeling better than he had for months, if not years. He was finishing primary treatment this week. His paranoia was decreasing and his urges to use lessening. He still had nostalgia for marijuana; he'd loved using it, but he hoped he'd outgrown it. He was amazed that he still thought about using it at all after all he'd been through.

The evening was crisp and clear. Snow was expected in the next few days, and the temperatures were back in the twenties. He walked quickly, winding up his arms now and then and letting out a few yips.

He remembered walking these blocks with his mother, how they'd enjoyed watching snatches of domestic scenes being played out in the evenings. Now, as he walked, he thought about the families living inside the well-lit homes. Kids were supposed to be studying but were probably using their media before getting ready for bed. The moms and maybe some dads were finishing the dishes and cleaning down the counters. He hoped the kids had a dad and a mom at home. If he had a family, he'd be helping his wife, his partner. He'd be helping the kids get to bed, putting things back in order, making lunches, getting ready to start a new day.

He walked by Petersons' house. He had gone to school with a couple of the nearly white-haired Peterson girls. Buffy, their yappy white-haired Terrier, was still alive and still tied to the front railing. He had wrapped his leash tight around the wrought iron railing and could barely squeak out a yip. James climbed the steps to the house and held Buffy as he untangled his leash.

Buffy licked James' hand. James felt a heavy-hearted twinge. He'd wanted to be a good kid; he'd wanted to help his neighbors.

James continued down the street. He noticed the skis and sleds leaning on the sides of garages. The neighborhood was turning over; younger families were replacing the older generation. These new young families would be the third generation of homeowners in his neighborhood. In a few years, he might fit in this neighborhood again.

His walk ended too soon. He stopped for a moment and looked at the little grey bungalow and then the substantial brick house next to it. The houses hadn't changed, but he was looking at them differently, seeing things more objectively, sans some of the negative feelings he'd carried for so many years.

Now, it's not all about me and my feelings, he thought. He hoped he'd remember that thought, that he could refine it for his treatment group. How he could look back at a few things and a few places now without the loaded emotions.

The drapes were open and Ralph waved to him as he walked up the sidewalk. James stood with his arm raised to knock and Ralph opened the door.

"Welcome, James. You don't have to knock. You can still walk right in." James nodded, stepped inside, and opened himself to a wide armed 'Ralph' hug. James hugged him back and accepted the forgiveness he was being offered.

"I'm so sorry for putting Chuck in jeopardy. I was out of my mind, stoned, crazy. I'm done with that." He wanted to say more, but Sandra was right behind Ralph, pushing herself forward to hug and kiss him. She hugged and kissed Ralph too, happy about his reaction to seeing James.

"I talked to Chuck today," Ralph said. "He thinks you might have saved Caleb's life by running into that dark building with no thought for yourself."

"Oh, I wish that were true. I wasn't thinking, really. Where are Laurel and Roy?" James asked.

"Roy's sleeping. Laurel is over at Brian's getting some more things and hopefully having a peaceful talk with him," Sandra answered.

Sandra intuited that James hadn't eaten dinner and made him sit down at the table. Ralph brought out two beers before remembering James was in treatment and not using drugs or alcohol. He opened both beers and took a swallow out of both.

"Thought I'd offer you a beer? Not on your life!"

James and Ralph both laughed too loudly. They all heard a little cry coming from the back bedroom.

"Can I get him?" James asked, jumping up and waiting for Sandra's permission.

"Sure, James. I think he knows you. Enter quietly, though."

"I know how to treat a baby," James said, although he really didn't.

He opened the door and went to Roy's crib. The light from the hall was bright enough to see Roy sitting up and looking around. James went over to him and squatted down, getting close to Roy's eye level height.

"Remember me, Roy?" he asked the little boy with blond curly hair. Roy gave him a serious nod.

"What's my name, then?" James asked him.

"James," Roy said shyly.

"Can I pick you up?"

Roy nodded and put his arms up for James, who grabbed him and swept him out of the crib.

"Can he come out of his room for a minute?" James felt the presence of Sandra right behind him.

"Do you want to sit on Uncle James' lap?" she asked Roy, and he nodded seriously.

James was beaming when he came back into the dining room

carrying Roy. Roy was smiling, too, and holding onto James' t-shirt. Ralph saw the two of them and cleared his throat. Roy was a little James with his blond curls and brown eyes.

Ralph and I are both so sentimental, James thought, as he watched Ralph's reaction. Tonight, he didn't care that he was sentimental; he liked being there, accepted by Ralph and Sandra, getting to hold their grandson.

James held Roy while he ate a sandwich and let Roy taste his dill pickle, and they all laughed at the face Roy made. Roy watched their reactions and then he laughed, too. James rubbed noses with Roy, but James didn't want to overstay his welcome. Too soon it was time for James to take leave, go next door and take care of his business. Sandra told Roy to say goodnight and carried him back to his bedroom.

Ralph asked James if he could drive him part way back after he did what he needed to do next door, but James shook his head. After goodbyes, James walked to his mother's house, unlocked the door, and took care of his business then quickly left to go back to Jerome's.

On leaving the gray house, James ran down the street as he had so many times. He felt good, right now, this very minute. Just as the program had promised. The program hadn't promised a state of constant happiness, but the good feelings would come and go and come back again.

James like the idea that feelings were like clouds in the sky. A cloud of feeling moved in, stayed over our heads for a time and then was replaced with another cloud of feeling. Of course, there were cloudy days, cloudy weeks maybe.

There he was half writing a lecture again. He surprised himself; he'd enjoyed treatment. He was learning a lot about himself, realizing, in the past, he reacted to life events with no real understanding of his motivations. Now, he was gaining some tools for recognizing emotions, for assessing what he wanted and needed, for measuring his behavior.

Tonight, when Sandra rushed, bullying past Ralph to hug and kiss him, her extreme behavior didn't upset him. She was anxious; he didn't have to react to her feelings and get anxious, too. What a relief. He didn't have to be angry at Ralph for being angry at him, either. And, surprise, he didn't even feel the harsh old feelings toward Laurel.

He half danced his way to the bus stop, and sure enough, there was a bus in the distance, coming to pick him up.

45 / SANDRA AND HER DAUGHTERS

After James left, Ralph looked in on Roy and went to bed. When Laurel came home from her talk with Brian, Sandra was in the kitchen with the tea kettle on. She asked Laurel if she wanted a cup of herbal tea and some freshly baked chocolate chip cookies.

"Chamomile sounds good but no cookies. What's up, Mom?" Laurel asked.

"If you're willing, I'd like to hear how it went with Brian," Sandra said as she chose mugs for both Laurel and herself and reached for her cache of teas.

"Are you sure you want to hear about it?" Laurel said.

"I really would."

Laurel looked at her with doubt.

Sandra asked, "You'd said something about wanting to talk to him about the time he is spending with Roy. Did that happen?"

Laurel opened up a little. "It was draining. He says he feels bad about having so little time with Roy but that he was overwhelmed when he had Roy alone for a weekend. I told him if he had helped me out more with the day to day childcare when we lived together, he wouldn't find it so hard to have Roy by himself now."

"That gave him something to think about," Sandra said. "Was there more?"

"He said we should have family time together with all three of us so Roy realizes we are still a family." Laurel looked at her mother quizzically. "Did I tell you or just Char how Brian suddenly started talking about 'being head of the family' right before the wedding. I knew he came from a conservative Lutheran family, but he hadn't been like that when we dated. He'd been head over heels in love with me, so his talking about 'family' time really upsets me. My 'family' time role was to do everything and let it go when he complained that Roy got too much of my attention. I probably should have called off the wedding, but you'd already spent thousands of dollars, and I didn't want to look like a fool, either. Anyway, that's why we were living in the McMansion and I was working as an administrative assistant. It was his 'head of the family's' agenda."

Then Laurel remembered a conversation she'd had with her mother shortly before she got married.

"Actually, I am sure we did talk about this before the wedding. I brought up my concerns about Brian telling me he'd be 'the head of the family.' You suggested I just play along with him until after we were married and then use my feminine wiles to get my way. I remember you actually saying that, Mom. Well, truth be told, I must be a feminist or something because I don't like playing games or kowtowing to men."

Sandra listened and nodded in near physical pain trying to kept her mouth shut.

Sandra had done some soul searching after Char had chided her to react differently to Laurel. She'd talked about her problems with the Al anon group. A couple of the women in the group had encouraged 'active listening,' really concentration on what her daughter was saying and encouraging her daughter to provide more information rather than responding to her daughter in a defensive way. This was her opportunity, and it was hard to do.

"It's your turn, Mom. What's on your mind?"

"Well, I'm all for you going back to college. I'm sorry I suggested you 'play along with him. That was stupid of me. Oh, by the way, James came over to consolidate his things into his bedroom downstairs. Your father finally listened to Chuck and believes James did his absolute best to save his friend Caleb's life."

Laurel shook her head. "Dad's such a pushover for those boys. Just like you are. No matter who says what, James is responsible for almost getting his friend killed."

"Anyway," Sandra said, "James and Ralph laughed too loudly and woke up Roy. James asked if he could go get him, and he did. Then James gave him a taste of his dill pickle; Roy's look was priceless."

Laurel shook her head again. "That was kind of mean, giving Roy a dill pickle."

"No," Sandra said, chuckling. "He was good with the boy."

They sat silently for a minute, sipping their hot tea. Finally, Sandra spoke up. "You know I've been going to Al anon meetings. I learned about having an "elephant in the room," something that everyone knows is there but no one wants to talk about it."

"I've heard the term, Mom. What 'elephant' do you think is in this room?" Laurel asked.

"Ok, I'll say it, but, please, don't bite my head off. I'd really like to know why you don't like James."

Laurel took a deep breath and looked at her mother. "I pushed him away because you told me to leave him alone. Do you remember that?"

"I never said that, Laurel."

"Mom, you told me to leave him alone. You told me that I was too old for him and you said that I was nasty, that I was coming on to him." Laurel's voice was rising. "That is the exact word you called me, 'nasty.'"

"I don't remember saying that."

"You shamed the hell out of me, Mom. You said that in front of Kimber—she remembers. I wasn't 'taking advantage of James.'" Laurel started to cry, angry, hurt sobs.

Sandra closed the kitchen door and stood by her daughter and tried hard not to cry herself. Laurel had her head on the high counter and her arms around her head and was trying to get a hold of herself, but the ragged sobs kept coming.

She sounds so young, Sandra thought. She wanted to put her arms around her daughter, but she held herself back. She wrapped her arms around her own chest, gasping for her breaths, too.

Finally, Laurel quieted and lifted her face from the counter. Sandra held out tissues for her, and she grabbed them, wiping her nose and face.

"I wasn't being nasty. I liked James, the way a girl likes a boy, and he liked me, too. You made it so ugly, and you made me so ashamed of myself. You said it was incest, too." Laurel started to get up, to get away from her mother and her shame.

Sandra grabbed her sleeve. "Don't go, Laurel. Please, don't turn away from me. Give me a chance to apologize to you. I'm sorry. I believe you. Oh, how I wish I could take back what I said to you, how I made you feel. I've made some terrible mistakes with you girls. But please don't leave us." Then Sandra cried and Laurel stayed quietly by her mother's side.

"I'm not going away," she said, patting her mother on the arm. It wasn't easy between them, but it was a start.

THE NEXT DAY, Sandra called Ellen and asked if they could get together. Ellen had a long lunch hour free and the two friends met at a quiet coffee shop with booths. Sandra told her friend what had happened with Laurel.

"We all make mistakes," Ellen said. "We do the best we know how to do—most of the time. Laurel came to you when her marriage was in trouble, and now, she took the huge risk—finally telling you why she's been so angry with you. Aren't you proud of her?"

Sandra listened and stopped sniffling. "I never thought of it that way. It must have been hard to tell me." Sandra looked around, grateful that no one nearby seemed to be watching them then she looked out the window next to their booth and said, "I've been trying to be a quieter, more thoughtful person. Have you noticed?"

"I thought you were quiet that afternoon at Char's after James got out of the hospital when we were all trying to help him come up with a plan. Until you brought up your idea to get the dealers."

Sandra chuckled in spite of herself.

"I was quiet," Sandra said. "I was so scared for James and Chuck and for Ralph with his heart problems. I was almost speechless."

"Getting back to Laurel and your conversation about James," Ellen said. "I've heard you ask her more than once why she doesn't like James. You've attempted to talk to her about it. She obviously couldn't talk about it until she was ready." Ellen thought for a moment about how deep she wanted to delve into this and decided to plunge ahead. "Why do you think you were so harsh with her when she had a crush on James? We all knew they had a crush on each other, but it sounds like you were quite harsh with her about it."

"I've been thinking about that, Ellen. I have a couple of ideas about what was going on with me. Is it OK to talk about this, now? Do you have the time in your work schedule?" Sandra looked around the half empty shop; obviously most worker bees were heading back to their offices.

"Go ahead, Sandra. I'll quickly call Amy at the office and remind her that I don't have any clients scheduled this afternoon. I don't have to go back at all." Then Ellen sat quietly, sipping another cup of tea and listening to her friend.

"This is hard to admit because it makes me sound like a regular sicko. Even though I was pregnant with Chuck, I wanted James to be the baby boy that I lost when I had the abortion. When James stayed overnight with me, as a newborn, I held him close nearly all night, counting his little toes and fingers and nuzzling his sweet face."

"Back when I had the abortion, I was sure the baby would be a boy. Then when you let me hold baby James, it was like my own son had come back to me. I loved him so much and still do. When Laurel started flirting with him, it was incest to me. He was a vulnerable boy. Boys mature slower than the girls, don't they?"

Sandra waited for Ellen's nod of consent and continued. "Laurel was his older sister in my eyes and the aggressor."

"Their flirting wasn't just play. I sensed something sexual between them, and it made me uncomfortable. When I finally confronted Laurel about flirting with James, she said nothing happened between them, and I was going to make sure nothing ever did. I watched them like a hawk. Oh, I don't know what's wrong with me."

"I think it was a misunderstanding," Ellen said. "Laurel probably felt uncomfortable with her feelings, too—if, in fact, she did feel sexual toward a younger boy being raised with her. I don't know how I would have handled it if I'd seen more of it like you did. I'd probably have kept my head in the sand and ignored it or grounded him for life. I know I would have reacted harshly, too. I wish I'd talked to him more about his feelings generally but specifically about sexual feelings. I talked out my fears and concerns about James with Elliot at work and Elliot encouraged me to talk with James, but I didn't. You were there for him much more than I was." Ellen wiped a tear from her eye. "I'm so sorry, Sandra. I didn't help you at all."

The women paused and looked around the room again. They both noticed a young couple, huddled in conspiracy. Ellen and Sandra looked up at each other, nodding and shaking their heads in mutual compassion for young people.

Ellen turned her thoughts to the positive. "You and Laurel have started being honest with each other. Some of the worst has been said, and it sounds like you still love each other."

Sandra nodded. "Laurel did say she still wants to move in next door and that she appreciates my help with Roy."

"Do you want to tell your daughters what you just told me about the abortion?" Ellen asked.

Sandra said she did.

Several days later, Sandra asked both her daughters to come for lunch. After lunch, the little boys went down for naps, and granddaughters built a train made of quilt-covered dining room chairs to take their dolls to Chicago. Sandra and her daughters sat down to talk in the kitchen.

Before the conversation started, settling their butts firmly in the chairs, first Laurel jumped up to get half and half for their tea, then Kimber jumped up to close the door to the kitchen, then Sandra started to rise, both girls said, "Mother, sit down!" And the three of them chuckled.

Sandra started by apologizing to both of her daughters for catering to the boys when they were growing up. She wasn't going to make that mistake with the granddaughters.

Then she told them about the abortion she had when she was twenty-three; how she had abandoned Terry, her wonderful boyfriend from her hometown, how Ellen had stood by her and finally, how she hadn't supported Ellen when Ellen invited a lesbian to their apartment. She was in tears several times.

Her daughters sat wide-eyed, hands to their faces at times.

Laurel put a foot up on her chair and bit at her cuticles. Kimber combed her bangs with her fingers and rolled her long hair into a bun. Listen to their mother being so vulnerable scared both of her daughters. But she plowed through what she had to say and before their eyes, Sandra became more human to her daughters.

Sandra told her daughters how happy she had been when James came into her life. He was her missing baby boy, and she loved him as much as she loved her own children.

Then Laurel told her sister about her talk with Sandra and how the past had come up. Kimber nodded; she was present when Sandra had called Laurel 'nasty.'

"Chuck and I knew Laurel and James were attracted to each other, and we made fun of them," Kimber said. She looked directly at her mother. "I think you made too much out of Laurel and James' attraction. It was like any attraction between a girl and a boy. It didn't mean something sexual was going to happen between them."

"Live and learn; it's impossible to be perfect," Sandra said, feeling the need to defend herself against their criticism. She tried to calm herself down.

Kimber continued, "Now that I'm a mother, and I think Laurel will agree, I realize we inevitably make mistakes along the way. It takes a lot of courage to be a good mother. All my life I had been afraid of making mistakes, and I've tried to be perfect. But now that I'm a mother, I can't afford to be perfect anymore. My kids need me to make bold, snap judgements sometimes, to say no to them, reprimand them or demand that they take a risk when they don't want to. Mom, you are a great role model; we had a lot of freedom growing up, but you set firm limits with a lot of love thrown in."

"I want that on my grave stone, Kimber," Sandra said.

Laurel agreed with her sister, and the relief on Sandra's face said it all. Laurel and Kimber looked at each other and snickered. "Group hug," Sandra called. She was amazed by her daughters.

46 / JAMES AND LAUREL

Several weeks later, Ralph called Laurel at her workplace. "See if you can leave early," he said. "The snow is falling harder, the roads are getting bad, and the freeways will be backed up at rush hour. Also, I'm a little worried about your mom. She was really congested when I left for work. If you could come home early and could check up on her, I'd stay at the hospital and help the emergency staff. There's been a ten-car pileup nearly at the door of the hospital. Some serious injuries, I'm told.

Laurel left work immediately and picked Roy up at daycare.

She called her mother's name as she entered their house but received no response. Sandra was in the darkened spare bedroom off of the kitchen, the room the family dubbed 'the sick room.' It was the only room in the house that hadn't been redecorated in the nearly thirty years Ralph and Sandra had owned the house. It's looming rose and gray wallpaper somehow comforted the sick, and it was right next to a seldom used bathroom. Sandra was sleeping; her raspy breathing sounded painful.

"Stay back, Roy, let Grandma sleep," Laurel said, closing the bedroom door. "We'll go down into the basement to look for the old humidifier Grandma brought out for us kids when we had colds." Laurel went down the basement steps ahead of Roy and turned to watch him take the steps one by one, holding tightly onto the railing.

"That's the way to do it," she complimented him. He raced around looking for mischief while she searched the basement storage room and found the humidifier under the stairs. In the same area, she found a box of her own school papers and mementoes she thought had been thrown out. She was surprised her mother had kept her junk.

The humidifier had a cloth cover and looked clean, ready to use. She and Roy brought it upstairs, and Laurel set it up for her mother. Laurel dug around in the small bathroom vanity for Vicks and placed vapor rub on Sandra's upper lip and chest. She watched her mom sleep for a few minutes before closing her door again. Roy peeked from the bedroom door.

"I'm the doctor, and you're the nurse, Roy. After we take care of our patient, we wash our hands." They both washed their hands and then went back down the basement stairs.

Laurel pulled out her box of mementos. Sets of report cards were neatly bundled along with a few art projects, loose pictures, and a complete set of diaries. Roy loved the paper-mâché horse Laurel made in grade school. She gave it to him to hold. He slapped it against the furniture, and she chided him to be careful. When he next slapped it against the wall, she grabbed it back from him and held the horse gently and rocked it in her arms.

"Mama loves her horse, Roy," she explained and gave it back to him. He held it gently and kissed it.

"That's my boy," she said. "We love our horse." He wandered away with the horse dragging in one hand.

She thumbed through her diaries. She'd dated them, one for each year of school, first through twelfth. She couldn't remember writing in them. She opened the second to last one.

James, James, James. She couldn't believe how many

references she'd made to that boy. This must have been the year she had a crush on him, when her mom had said the hurtful things to her.

She read the last entry: "I'm a bad person. We kissed but I hate him. He's the one who chased me, and I get blamed. Why doesn't she blame him, too? He's her golden boy. I'm not going to say what she thinks of me!"

She faintly remembered having warm feelings for him. She'd actively disliked him for years now; liking him seemed far, far in the past.

Then a memory came back to her. She had invited him to go canoeing with her when he was visiting at the lake place. She had languished in the bow, opposite him in shorts and halter top, making him do all the paddling. She sat watching him, making smart remarks, teasing him. He stopped paddling near some lily pads and pulled the paddle up, balancing it across the sides of the canoe. He leaned towards her and smiled. His right hand rippled in the water; his left arm rested on the canoe paddle. Their eyes locked, and they sat in a 'stare off'.

He awakened a passion in her. He was unabashedly moony-eyed. She finally couldn't hold his gaze. She giggled and dipped both hands into the water and sprayed it over his face. He smiled but he didn't wipe the water off of his face nor did he stop gazing into her eyes.

"I'm ready for you," he said to her in a throaty voice. She looked at him in disbelief. What had he meant?

The moment passed, but she had fallen a little in love with him, that skinny little kid she'd known most of her life who had grown much taller than she. For a short while, she had softened and loved that boy.

Brian never quite looked at her that way; in fact, once they were married, he never looked at her. Tears filled her eyes. Brian told her often that he loved her—he said the right words—but he never bared his vulnerable soul to her. She closed the box and headed upstairs with Roy in tow.

Ralph made it home after midnight. Laurel was asleep on the couch; Roy was in the crib that he was rapidly outgrowing. Laurel sat up and turned on the lamp by the couch. "Dad, come talk to me. You made it home; is it still awful out?" She motioned for him to sit down by her.

"It's snowing gently, and the wind has died down. I'll open the drapes so you can enjoy the beauty. That's what I like about snow storms. They rage and scare the bejesus out of us, and then they show their soft side, and all is forgiven. The snow plows have already cleared the main arteries. I made it to the driveway, but I'm not going to attempt the incline to the garage until I snowplow it. How is your mother?"

"I got out the old humidifier and filled it and put some menthol below her nose and onto her chest. Later, I made the three of us grilled cheese sandwiches and heated up tomato soup. Mom got up to eat then headed back to bed. But she thinks her fever has broken.

She told me that James called to say he's picking up his cross-country skis tomorrow early afternoon. Dad, if you'll watch Roy tomorrow afternoon, I'd like to ask James if I can ski with him. I'll settle Roy down for his long nap before I leave and won't be gone long. Mom thought it was a good idea."

"I'm surprised you'd even suggest doing something with James. Haven't you made it clear you don't like him?"

"It was a spontaneous thought, Dad. I'd been down in the basement for the humidifier and found some of my old journals. I read some passages about all of us cross-country skiing together; it was a big part of our fun growing up. People change, Dad. I don't want to be that mean person I've been to James and Mom anymore. Part of the reason I left Brian was that we were becoming so ugly to each other. We'd gotten into that habit and couldn't stop. And I'm sorry if I've acted that way with you too, Daddy."

Ralph reached over and wrapped an arm around Laurel. "You've never been mean to me, but you do have your mother's temper, and I've heard you be mean to her. It hurts me when the two of you talk that way to each other, but you've never been mean to me."

Laurel put her head on her father's shoulder for a minute. "Dad, you're the best part of me."

"Your Mom loves you, too. She's quick witted and says what's on her mind. She's my bird; I have to keep an open hand with her, not cage her in, but I wouldn't want her any other way. I'm so glad her fever seems to have broken. I'll take her temperature one more time before I go to bed. If she is better tomorrow morning, I'll be able to handle them both tomorrow afternoon. Go ahead—ski with James—not that it is any of my business. The spring snow will be great for skiing. Now let's get to bed, daughter."

Ralph looked in on Sandra. Her temperature was normal. She must have cleaned up a little after supper. She had fresh nightie on and smelled like Ivory soap, though he could still smell the residue of Vapor Rub in the room. He refilled the humidifier, added more Vapor Rub and fluffed up her covers before heading to bed.

James had just started driving his car again. His paranoia about being driven off the road or shot in his car had abated. Having his car available gave him a new sense of freedom. Today he was picking up his cross-country skis at his mom's house and heading out to his old favorite ski trails at Fort Snelling Park.

When he reached the gray house, he saw someone shoveling the front walk. His stomach lurched when he saw it was Laurel. He parked his car, got out, and kept his eyes down.

Laurel waved and started walking up to him.

"What are you doing here?" he said in a slur that sounded like he had been drinking.

She suppressed a grin and said, "What does it look like I'm doing?"

"I didn't know you did the shoveling. I would have come by and done it." His words were clipped, and he sounded like a robot to himself.

"When your mom wouldn't charge me rent, I compromised with her, and we agreed that I would pay the utilities and do the maintenance. Besides, I like the workout."

"I've come to pick up my cross-country skis. I only recently started using my car again, and I'm treating myself to a little adventure, skiing for the first time in a couple of years."

"Sounds fun, can I come along?" Laurel looked up at him, friendly, neutral. Some of James' tension eased.

"Where's Roy? He must be almost old enough to ski." James was kidding, but Laurel took him seriously.

"I found an old book online called *Toddler Skiing.* Definitely he'll be ready next winter."

"Well, sure," James said. "If we go skiing, can you make an hour or two without any critical remarks about me?"

That made Laurel sad and she nodded before excusing herself to gather her skis and poles. Then she turned to say, 'The door is open, James, go get your skis and I'll get mine." She had brought her ski boots and skis upstairs and went into the kitchen to grab them and to say goodbye. Ralph and Roy were getting ready to do some snow blowing before their naps. Sandra was dressed and fussing in the kitchen.

"Thanks for taking care of me yesterday afternoon," she shouted at Laurel from the refrigerator. "This cold has been lingering and yesterday it seems to have come to a head. I don't think I'm contagious; I've been feeling peaky for a week."

"Fine, Mom," Laurel said, giving kisses to Roy and a quick hug to her dad.

James walked in the front door. He was blown away. Laurel had already removed the old carpet and the hardwood floors underneath were decent. The walls were painted a misty blue/grey. He walked into the kitchen. Laurel was using the oak table. She'd taken the blue and yellow curtains James and Willow fitted for his old place and refit them to use in the bungalow kitchen. He shook his head thinking should he laugh or cry? Laurel!

Laurel and James drove quietly on the intermittently plowed side streets until James entered the freeway and started driving over the speed limit, looking over at Laurel, expecting criticism. She was facing the window. She could see his reflection, and he could see hers when he quickly glanced in her direction.

"I'm sorry," she started. "We used to get along so well."

"I was there," he said rather roughly. "For all of it."

She plowed on with her self-revelation. "Yesterday I found my old journals in my mom's basement storage, and I started reading about something that happened when we were younger. I don't mean that careless one time groping in the tree house, that groping before the wedding. No, I was thinking of a canoe ride years before that."

James remembered and nodded. "I was a dumb kid; I couldn't help myself. I didn't mean to fall for you—it just happened."

"What you don't know is that...Watch out," she yelled and he swerved to miss a snow plow.

"I'm sorry," he said. "I don't think we should be talking about those times now, while I'm driving on slippery streets."

"OK," she said, planning to let him take the lead on this if they talked about it later.

"Here we go," he said, bumping over the banks made by a snow plow and following the deep tracks to the park's skiing area. The shock of seeing her was wearing off. He was getting excited about skiing again.

"Here we are," James said, parking the car and getting out to take their skis off the roof rack on the car. Laurel got out of the car too.

"I'm going to call Mom and Dad, and see how things are going with Roy," she said, leaning on the passenger car door and trying her dad's cell. Sandra answered. She chatted about feeling much better and the naps the three of them were just about to take. Roy was still outside with his grandpa. Roy had a little red plastic shovel and his grandpa was snow blowing. James heard Sandra laughing and then Laurel started laughing, too.

When she got off of the phone, she explained the situation to James. "Dad accidently blew a pile of snow right onto Roy. Mom is getting a pic".

The phone beeped and they both looked at at Roy is just standing there, a perfect little snowman.

They both laughed. Laurel watched James, first his concerned look, and then his genuine laugh. He likes my boy, she thought. James truly likes Roy. He was family.

But he still didn't feel like a brother to her.

They took the beginner's trail. James told Laurel the history of his mother skiing there when she first moved to Minneapolis over thirty years ago and how she had taught him to ski in the same area.

Laurel said, "Well, I'll have to teach Roy right here, too."

The beginner's trail had been too easy for them. It only took them thirty minutes. They decided they had time for another trail. They took an intermediate trail with an unexpected hill following a turning a sharp turn. Laurel took a spectacular fall in front of James. To avoid Laurel, James rolled out and fell into the deep snow off the path. Then trying to help Laurel up, they both slipped back into the snow and they lay there in a heap, gasping, catching their breath, both feeling an electrical charge race through their bodies.

After taking their skis off and loading them onto the roof of the car, they hopped into the car, shivering with both exhaustion and invigoration and something else, too.

Laurel checked her phone and chuckled, passing the texted pic of Roy titled 'The Little Abominable Snowman.'

"He's the best kid, not crying, just standing there like a little lost soldier," James said as they looked at Roy.

Laurel leaned in and kissed the picture. "This kid is making a good mother out of me."

"Char, my mom, and your mom all bragged to me about what a good mother you are."

"Really? They don't think I'm a bitch?"

"No, just me," he said, still looking down at the pic.

"Today am I being a bitch?" she asked.

"This is just for today though, isn't it?" he asked, an old sadness rising up in him.

"Listen to me, James. I want, I will be different, especially to you." She opened her arms and turned her wrists, and smiled, trying to present another self to him.

"Thanks, well, we better get going. I want to run through a fast food and get some hot chocolate, maybe some cookies, too. How does that sound?"

"Can we eat at a real restaurant?" she asked quietly.

"I'd like that," he agreed.

THEY SAT in a booth at Perkins Restaurant, eating burgers, fries, and French Silk pie and drinking water and coffee.

Laurel said, "I like your mother. When I was little, I often wondered what it would be like to have your mother instead of mine. She took me seriously and actually listened to me when I had a chance to talk to her. She really wasn't around a lot. I think she liked girls better than my Mom did."

Laurel blushed. "I'm sorry I didn't mean that the way it sounded; I mean about her liking girls."

James laughed. "I know what you meant. I'm glad you like her. I like her better all the time. I think it's about growing up; I mean once you acknowledge you're making your own mistakes, too, it's harder and harder to blame your folks for their mistakes."

Laurel nodded. "Yeah, I feel like that about my mother now, too. I know she doted on you boys, and I didn't like that, but Kimber and I talked to her about that, and she promised that she wouldn't be that way with her grandkids. I was afraid that when I had a boy, she would try to take him over, like she did with you. You know my mom really took you in as a son, not a friend's son."

"I knew your mother loved me, and I loved her, too. That's good, isn't it?"

"Anyway, she's trying not to favor Roy over the girls," Laurel said. "Kimber and I are aware of the dynamics and plan to call her on it if she does it. Don't they have a name for that in treatment? Favored children becoming 'king babies?'"

"Was I a King baby, Laurel? Jeez, I guess maybe I was."

"I don't want to make too much of it. Chuck pounded you pretty good, and Mom didn't defend you against him. I don't know why I said that; we were all spoiled. I'm sorry I called you a king baby. Here I go, being mean again."

James leaned across the booth, wanting Laurel to hear what he had to say. "We're just talking, here, Laurel. I don't think you're being mean. I want you to say what you think, to be who you are. Does that make you a bad person? Not with me."

James continued, "I think you are a 'What you see, is what you get' kind of person. I think of you when I hear that phrase. You know what, Laurel? I still think about you a lot. I like who you are."

She laughed and almost cuffed him like her mother always had but stopped herself—she wasn't going to be her mother. She reached over and patted his cheek.

"I like you too, James," she said quietly, looking down.

James stopped the car at the brick house, and Laurel put her hand on the door handle. James reached over and stopped her motion.

"Before you hop out of the car, I'd like to ask you something."

"OK," she said without turning to look at him.

"Can I text you? Maybe plan a time to come visit you and Roy and take the two of you out somewhere?"

"OK," she said again.

"I know you're anxious to get back to Roy now, but remember back when we took that canoe ride together, when I was a kid and you were a less of a kid?"

She nodded.

"I'm ready for you," he said in a fake croaky voice, not unlike the voice fourteen-year old James had used back then.

Laurel turned to him, looked at him, and laughed and laughed. This was the laugh he remembered; this was the girl he remembered.

ONE MONTH LATER, Char, Sandra, and Ellen sat on bright yellow, green, and red Adirondack chairs on Sandra's deck, commenting on the advent of spring and cooling off after finishing Easter dinner clean up. Ralph, Chuck, Joe, James, Laurel, Carmen, and Roy watched the Twins get beat by the Yanks inside.

There were still patches of snow across the lawn, but pink rhubarb nubs pushed their way out of the ground, and daffodils and crocuses bloomed near the deck. Spring was roaring to Minnesota. It was a sunny, 50-degree April day.

James came bounding out of the patio doors with Roy perched on his arm, one little hand holding tightly to James' shirt.

"I pooped my pants," Roy said smugly, waving his other hand in front of his wrinkled nose to demonstrate how bad his pants smelled.

"Is James taking you home to change your pants?" Sandra asked.

Roy nodded.

"Roy, James stopped pooping his pants, maybe you should stop pooping your pants and start using the potty, we got him trained," Char said.

Roy looked quizzically at James. "James you pooped you' pants?" Roy asked.

James turned around to look at the three women with Roy on his arm. Together Roy and James looked at the women. All three of the women saw the similar curly hair, the similar brown eyes, and the identical half-opened mouths.

The women's collective unconscious awakened simultaneously. Sandra grabbed first Char's hand and then Ellen's hand. It was undeniable; they were staring at father and son.

Char was the only one to speak. "My God," she said. "You two look alike."

James continued looking astonished at Char.

Then he looked at Roy. "She is talking about my 'poopy behavior.' She is glad I'm 'trained now.'"

"Are we going to get you 'trained,' Roy?" James asked.

Roy shook his head empathically. "No."

The women laughed. James laughed and Roy laughed. Then James twirled Roy up in the air, grabbed him tight and off they went, James skipping his way to the grey bungalow, avoiding the last patches of snow.

"I wished you hadn't said that," Ellen said to Char.

"You have to be thick skinned to understand my Minnesota

nice," Char responded, looking over at Ellen with a friendly, albeit wicked, smile.

Ellen let go of Sandra's hand and shook her head. She was embarrassed for her son and for herself.

"Just what this family needs, another scandal," she whispered.

Sandra put her head down on her chest and closed her eyes still holding on to Char's hand.

James busied himself cleaning up Roy's messy butt, then rinsing the dirty cloth diaper in the toilet like Laurel did. After, he put the dirty diaper in the lidded diaper pail and went out to the living room in search of Roy. James didn't mind cleaning up after the little guy. He loved that Laurel had let him into their lives and into her bed.

He retrieved the bounding Roy and headed to the bedroom with him to put on a clean diaper.

It didn't really matter to James if Roy was or wasn't his son. That was out of his control. He kept reminding himself that love didn't mean ownership and life was only lived one day at a time.

He wished it was that simple, but it really wasn't, or was it?

He was sober, and he didn't plan to go back to dope, but sometimes when Char, the old Boomer, reminded him of his past, it pissed him off. Shit happened; boomers had to let it go. Then he softened—Char just wanted to keep him honest, help him to remember where he'd come from.

As James pulled up Roy's pants, he sang him part of an Elton John tune:

I'm not the man they think I am at home.

...I'm a rocket man.

Rocket man burning out his fuse up here alone.

—The End—

ABOUT THE AUTHOR

Leila Klasse is well acquainted with another era of drug addiction, the 1970's, when her own life segued from a career in psychology to the counter culture; where she swayed to the hedonistic adage: sex, drugs and rock and roll. Educator and realtor, formerly a drug counselor, the author resides in Duluth, Minnesota.